THE LOCKER

ADRIAN MAGSON

THE LOCKER

MIDNIGHT INK
WOODBURY, MINNESOTA

FIRST EDITION
First Printing, 2016

Book format by Teresa Pojar
Cover design by Lisa Novak
Cover art: istockphoto.com/7118998/© halbergman
Editing by Ed Day

Midnight Ink, an imprint of Llewellyn Worldwide Ltd.

Library of Congress Cataloging-in-Publication Data
Names: Magson, Adrian.
Title: The locker : a novel of suspense / Adrian Magson.
Description: Woodbury, Minnesota : Midnight Ink, [2016]
Identifiers: LCCN 2015037328 | ISBN 9780738746722 (softcover)
Subjects: LCSH: Kidnapping — Fiction. | Missing
    persons — Investigation — Fiction. | GSAFD: Suspense fiction. | Mystery
    fiction.
Classification: LCC PR6113.A3356 L63 2016 | DDC 823/.92—dc23 LC record
available at http://lccn.loc.gov/2015037328

Midnight Ink
Llewellyn Worldwide Ltd.
2143 Wooddale Drive
Woodbury, MN 55125-2989
www.midnightinkbooks.com
Printed in the United States of America

DEDICATION

To Ann, as always. Alpha reader, editor, timeline wizard, fan, supporter, and groupie. She makes me lucky.

ACKNOWLEDGMENTS

With thanks to David Headley of the DHH Literary Agency, who picked this up and ran with it, and the team at Midnight Ink, for turning the manuscript into the book.

ONE

The first thing Nancy Hardman saw when she opened the gym locker was a rectangle of white card on the bottom, stark against the dark interior.

She picked it up. It carried her name in heavy, black type.

And her heart went cold.

———

Hello, Nancy.

You're at your usual locker at Fitness Plus. The time is approx. 09.15. Your cell phone is dead, your home phone won't answer and your daughter, Beth, is alone with Tiggi, her cute Polish nanny.

It will take you 18 minutes to get home. If you drive fast.

Shame. You're already 18 minutes late …

1) Do NOT call the police. Beth's life depends on it.
2) DO tell your husband. Beth's life …

1

She stepped back as if stung.

Instinct told her it must be a sick joke, intended for some other Nancy; left by a friend with a dubious sense of humour. The clown face said it all. Didn't it?

But another Beth?

She glanced along the corridor, skimming over the banks of lockers and taking in irrelevant details; well-trodden carpet tiles, pale, clinical walls; the bank of identical steel boxes with bright orange key fobs hanging from the locks, waiting for the tumble of a token or a coin to release them. Only this one, her usual choice, had a large safety pin holding the key instead of a fob. It had stood out from the rest, quirky and different, and she'd used it for that reason ever since joining.

The building was quiet after the early rush, taking a deep breath in preparation for the next phase. It was still too early for the cross-trainer groupies rushing in after the school run, or the more intense spin freaks who drifted in quietly and made for their favourite bikes as if about to take part in a spiritual rite, or the older members who mounted the equipment with the care of those who knew that a fall might prove disastrous to fragile hips or knees.

Only a murmur of voices from the front desk and a peal of laughter indicated other signs of life.

Further away, music from a Zumba class leaked through the walls, carried on a muffled beat that seemed to echo in her brain and bounce off the ceiling tiles above her head. The instructors at Fitness Plus were young, trendy, and seemed determined to make the world go deaf in their pursuit of peak conditioning.

She scrabbled for her phone, cursing as the plastic slipped from her hand, slick with a sudden sheen of perspiration. She touched speed dial.

A joke, surely. Couldn't be anything else. Or a misunderstand—. *Your cell phone is dead.*

Nothing. The screen was blank. No light, no bars, no signal indicator. No screensaver of Beth grinning toothily over an ice cream sundae, taken on a rare day by the sea near Brighton.

She shook the phone as if it might stir the circuitry into life. A bad connection, that must be it. Nothing. She turned it over and tore off the back, surprised by the sudden strength in her fingers. Bloody thing was fiddly and usually took forever to get off. This time it fell away with ease, revealing the SIM card.

But no battery.

She fought back the desire to scream. *How could this be?* She'd used it last night to send a text to Michael, her husband. Just a few familiar words, tapped out with the point of a pen as she sat on the bed, followed by the press of a button. It was hardly a routine exactly, and no substitute for any kind of real contact, but it was all she had and she made sure it was regular enough to remind him, wherever he was in some God-forsaken back of nowhere, that she was here—*they* were here—her and little Beth.

She batted the locker door shut, turned and sprinted along the corridor towards the front desk, trainers silent on the carpet, her sports bag forgotten. There was a public phone out there in an alcove. Pray God none of the usual pensioners were on it, calling for a taxi or arranging their next round of bridge or coffee meetings.

It was free. She grabbed it, hands fumbling and sending the receiver falling to swing from the cord, the clatter attracting glances from two elderly customers in leisure suits and soft, old-lady shoes with Velcro straps. The duty receptionist, an alien being dressed like a beautician with an unlikely tan from the sun-bed upstairs and a vaguely see-through white top, threw her a painted scowl.

She dialled the number. It took forever to connect; first a series of quiet clicks followed by a louder one followed by the ring tone. The hand-piece felt sticky against her cheek and smelled of lipstick and dried sweat. Why couldn't people wash—

Still ringing.

Your home phone won't answer...

She waited through twenty rings, each one more painful than the last. A flicker of mental images told her with cool logic that Tiggi must be upstairs, in the bathroom, playing with Beth, teaching her Polish words, out in the garden, on her cell phone or sorting out the washing. There were a dozen other reasons for not answering, none of them helpful.

She cut the call and dialled the number of the phone she'd given Tiggi, with instructions to carry it always. Just in case.

No answer.

This can't be!

She felt her stomach heave and a sharp pain blossomed in her chest, threatening to burst out into the open. She had to get out of here before she threw up. She dropped the phone on the hook. It bounced and fell, but she left it and raced towards the exit, ignoring the receptionist's shrill call.

It will take you 18 minutes to get home.

She arrived at the car and reached for her keys. But they were in her sports bag. Back in the corridor.

She raced back inside, past the startled leisure suits and the receptionist, and jumped the revolving gate. Ran to the corner and turned left down the corridor, saw her bag lying on its side in front of the locker like a dead animal.

And a woman standing over it.

"What are you doing?"

The words snapped out before she could stop them, before she had time to take in the sports bag hanging awkwardly from one shoulder while the woman juggled with a purse.

The face was familiar. Karen? Or was it Clarisse? Nancy couldn't remember. Her mind had gone blank, clouded by the various thoughts tangled together like a jumbled mass of seaweed.

"I'm so sorry—"

The woman was dressed in dark Lycra and pink shoes, vaguely pretty and with the build of someone who benefitted more than most from a fitness regime. They hadn't talked much, hadn't even exchanged full names or backgrounds, but she'd been the only one who seemed willing to make an effort to break the ice.

"Hi." The greeting was bright, the smile fading to concern as Nancy ran up to the bag and stopped. "Are you all right?"

"Sorry." Nancy bent and scooped up her bag, hooking one strap and turning away, feeling her gut threatening to let go. "I don't feel well." Then she was running back along the corridor, praying nobody got in her way and hearing Karen's or Helen's voice floating after her, tinged with sympathy and concern and a faint hint of an accent.

If you drive fast.

She got in the car and turned the key, stamped on the gas and tore out of the car park, tyres squealing on the smooth surface. Out onto the main street and down to the end, where she turned left

5

under the nose of a cement truck, earning a blare of air horns and a hiss of brakes. She waved an apology, got an angry repeat of the horn and put her foot down, the car leaping forward and away.

Shame. You're already 18 minutes late…

She came to a corner, usually taken with care because of a tricky camber, but now cut short. A wheel hit the kerb and she heard the clatter of a plastic wheel trim spinning away behind her. A jolt made the steering jump and she wrestled with the wheel, sweaty hands glossing over the hard fabric until she regained control.

She swore long and loud, terrified at the thought of losing control. Wrapping herself around a lamppost wouldn't do anything to help Beth if she'd really been—

If what? If she'd been kidnapped? By who? And why? The idea was ridiculous, like something out of a Film 4 shocker with Liam Neeson playing the vengeful parent.

A glance at the dashboard clock. Pointless, as she had no idea how long it had been since leaving the gym. But anything familiar was a welcome distraction. Had it been three minutes? Five? More?

It felt like an eternity.

She slammed her foot down harder as the speed dropped, careening past a woman in a wallowing 4x4 with a phone clamped to her ear and unaware of other life forms around her. Oncoming vehicles flashed lights and sounded their horns, swerving to avoid her. A leathered motorcyclist eager to prove dominance failed the challenge at the last second, keeling over in a sideways skid and narrowly missing her charging bonnet, his face through the visor a brief glimpse of terror.

She arrived home a lifetime later, out of breath and feeling sick, subconsciously mumbling the only words that made any sense.

This was a joke. It had to be.

Had to be…

Had to be…

But who did she know who would joke like this? Nobody.

She jumped from the car and ran across the paved driveway and stopped dead.

The front door was wide open.

On the doormat lay a small bundle, arms and legs out wide, little button eyes staring unseeing into the sky.

Nancy buckled forward at the waist, a stab of pain piercing her stomach.

It was Homesick, Beth's favourite teddy.

Beth *never* went anywhere without it.

TWO

THE DOOR FLEW BACK under the palm of her hand and slammed against the inside wall, the glass panel rattling in the frame. She forced herself to breathe, the sound echoing hoarsely in the empty hallway.

"*Beth? Tiggi!*"

The words fell on empty air. There was nothing, save the flat, dull sound of a deserted building, devoid of human warmth, of movement, of the welcome vibration of living beings.

Her throat closed, tinder-dry, and she raced through to the kitchen.

Empty. Breakfast dishes in the sink, unwashed; a glass on the drainer with a residue of milk. Beth's morning drink, taken with fierce reluctance in what was a daily jousting match between them.

Next the living room, a sob bursting from her mouth at the familiar, the homely, the usually comforting.

But now empty and joyless, with toys scattered indiscriminately, the usual aftermath of Beth's decision-making on what to play with today.

The study.

Empty and cold, rarely used.

"Beth!"

No reply.

Up the stairs, feet drumming on hollow treads, her legs unsteady with imagined horror.

"*Beth!*"

Bathroom.

Empty. A smell of soap and Beth's bath-time Nemo lying stranded near the plughole, a bright flash of colour against cold white enamel.

Why the hell did toys, usually so cutely animated in play, suddenly seem so lifeless yet threatening?

Her and Michael's bedroom. Mostly hers.

Empty. Neat. As she had left it.

Beth's room next, a riot of untidiness left by the whirlwind squall of an active four-year-old. Blanket askew, clothes hanging half out of drawers, even more untidy than usual.

Empty.

Then the spare room Tiggi used whenever she stayed over, which was about once a week.

Empty.

She looked again. Something was wrong.

The wardrobe door was hanging open, revealing the bare interior. The few changes of clothing Tiggi kept there were gone, as were the trainers she favoured when walking Beth in the park. And the small alarm clock so she didn't oversleep. She took her duties seriously.

Gone.

But there was a small rectangle of metal lying by the bed. She bent closer, knowing immediately what it was.

The missing phone battery.

She snatched it up, trying not to think the obvious, and ran back to Beth's room. She went to the open drawers, fear escalating as she noted the empty spaces and the jumble of items tossed aside.

Some of Beth's clothes were gone.

With a sob she ran downstairs and out through the kitchen to the back door. It was open. She pushed it back and burst out into the small rear garden, with it's tiny patio and a meagre stretch of lawn with a plastic slide and a Wendy House. The rear windows of houses fifty yards away stared back at her, dark, blank and unhelpful.

Mocking.

She didn't need to see the back gate standing open to know the awful truth.

She fled back inside, her mind numbed, jumping as the front door slammed shut with the flow of air. The sound acted as a catalyst, bringing a sudden rush of tears down her cheeks, hot with fear and anger and impotence; of the agony of not knowing. She wiped them away but felt her heart was about to break.

Think. *Do* something.

Do **NOT** *call the police.*

DO *tell your husband.*

Call Michael? No, he was probably out of reach as usual. She couldn't even recall where he was this time. Somewhere remote and God-forsaken, that was a given. She could send a text message, as she did regularly, but it was debatable whether he ever received them all, since he so rarely replied until he was back near civilisation and reliable signals.

She ripped the back off her phone and replaced the battery. She would phone him; it was better to do something than sit here going mad. She dialled the number and waited. Nothing. As she stared at the small screen, it triggered a memory of something Michael had mentioned a long time ago. Something she should do if anything ever happened.

Something about calling a phone number here in London.

The study. She hurried through and opened the small filing cabinet housing the paperwork that was the governance of their everyday lives. Here lay insurance contracts, bank records, utility bills, her birth and marriage certificates, all the detritus required to prove they were who they were.

She pushed her hand to the back, skimming over the plastic tags. The last drop file held a single piece of paper. She snatched it out.

Cruxys Solutions Plc. The name was followed by a telephone number and an authorisation code: **HAR769M231** and the word **Red**.

Michael had told her that if she ever had reason to call this number, it would be an emergency, and to mention Code Red. It would light a fire under them and they would instigate an immediate response.

She had never asked what he'd meant by it or who "they" were, secure in the knowledge that it was something he had arranged for their own security, but that she would never have to use it.

She went through to the kitchen and picked up the landline phone. Her hands were shaking so much she had to take two stabs at dialling the number.

"Cruxys PLC. Your name and code reference, please." A man's voice, calm and assured. Like a newsreader, she thought, distant and automatic, unruffled by events in the outside world. Her world.

"It's my daughter," she muttered. "She's been taken—"

"Please give me your name and reference number." He was insistent, but his tone gentle. "We will help you but your number will give us all the information we have on file."

She gave her name and read out the number on the card, adding "Code Red."

"Thank you, Mrs. Hardman. Are you in any immediate danger?" The man's voice was still controlled but now carried a hint of urgency. She heard a keyboard clicking very fast, then a snapping of fingers in the background followed by a door slamming.

"No … They said I mustn't call the police."

"They?"

"A note."

"I understand. Can you tell me briefly what happened so we can set things in motion? Help is already on its way to you and will be there shortly."

"I was at the gym," she said, fighting for breath and wanting to scream with frustration at the sheer calm quality of the man's voice. "I found a card in the locker telling me my cell was dead and my daughter Beth has been taken and not to call the police. I came home and found the house open and empty. I don't know who could have done this—it's *crazy*! I don't have any enemies, I don't know anybody and Beth is just four years old, she's just an innocent little girl—!" Her throat closed with emotion and fear, chopping off the words in mid-stream.

"I understand, Mrs. Hardman. Did the note make any specific demands?"

"What? No, nothing. It said to wait—but that I should tell my husband they would be in touch."

"Very well. Try to remain calm. Stay where you are, lock yourself in and watch the front door. Help will be with you in a few minutes." The repeated assurance had become an annoying mantra, but she realised it was intended to help, to reassure, to calm.

She didn't feel calm. "How do you know?"

"Know what?"

"Know where I am? I don't understand—" She broke off. Of course he knew; the code number told him that. All she was doing was wasting time. "I'm sorry."

More tapping of keys. "There's no need to apologise, Mrs. Hardman. It's perfectly natural. Stay by the phone and our people will be there imminently. They're just a few blocks away. Their names are Gonzales and Vaslik and they will present ID. Let them in once you're satisfied but don't talk to anybody else and stay off the phone."

"What if the kidnappers call? They might call before Gonzales and—"

"Vaslik."

"—Vaslik get here."

"If they do, ask them what they want. Do you have a recording device in the house?"

"No. Yes, I—my cell phone." She was still holding it. "Why?"

"That's good. Turn on the loudspeaker on your landline and try to record the conversation. But don't hold the cell phone too close to the handset. Gonzales and Vaslik are on their way."

"Gonzales and Vaslik." She repeated the names automatically, stumbling over the second one. It sounded Russian. Why would a Russian and a Spaniard be working for these people? Don't they have any English—? Christ, what was she saying? Did it matter what their names sounded like? She clung to the phone and stared at the carpet,

13

numbed by the thoughts piling into the forefront of her brain in an insane jumble, most of them too horrible to contemplate.

"What will your people do? The note said not to tell the police—"

"We are not the police, Mrs. Hardman. Whoever left you the note doesn't know we exist. Now, check all the doors and windows are locked, make yourself a cup of tea but don't touch anything else in the house. Do you understand? Wait for them, don't talk to anyone else, touch nothing. Stay secure."

"I understand." She put down the phone and walked over to the kettle, flicking the button like an automaton. She didn't want tea, for God's sake; she wanted Beth. She checked the back door and all the windows, then walked through to the front room from where she could watch the drive and the street outside.

Outside, where everything looked so normal, so uneventful. People walking, driving, living life.

This wasn't real. This wasn't bloody *real!*

She walked back to the kitchen and picked up her phone, and thumbed a text message, the words spurred by anger and helplessness. Maybe, just maybe this would get through to Michael.

Somebody has taken Beth, our daughter. They've kidnapped her! Please tell me what to do! Please call me!!!. N. x

She hit SEND and walked back to the living room, and stood waiting.

———

She must have zoned out because when she looked next two figures were standing at the bottom of the drive. A slim man with pale skin and fair hair, and a woman with short-cropped dark hair and the build of a gymnast. Both were dressed in business suits, the woman holding a briefcase and the man clutching a clipboard to his chest.

Nancy felt a moment of hysteria building. They looked like insurance salespeople. Or Jehovah's Witnesses.

But she knew they were neither.

THREE

THE HOUSE LOOKED SMART enough to Ruth Gonzales, but nothing special, which surprised her. Typical of the area, which was north-west London, suburbia at its most normal and unthreatening.

Or, at least, it had been.

At the smaller end of the property design compared with some of the neighbours, it was a typical west London home for a young family; the kind where, given a few years and with regular promo-tions and increases in salary, they'd be on the move to somewhere bigger and better. Up-scaling their lives to the suburban dream.

"What's up?" The man behind her spoke with an American ac-cent. His name was Andrei Vaslik, although he'd asked to be called Andy. Third generation Russian, he'd explained briefly, his family long settled near New York.

"I was expecting more, somehow," Ruth replied. "Like the oth-ers." She nodded towards the houses further up. Bigger and neater, openly more opulent; smarter cars, too, mostly 4WDs gleaming and polished. Did the gloss indicate a higher standard of living or a greater level of debt? She checked her watch. 10:00 am. Some gone to work, others were still at home. Out of work or self-employed. Sometimes one and the same thing.

"Why more?"

"Because Cruxys clients have money—usually lots of it. This is not typical, believe me."

The houses she came to in response to calls were generally bigger, the locations more select. Even the problems were bigger, more acute in scale, even if sometimes imagined. Money always brought its own troubles, it seemed to her.

Still, you could never tell. The briefing notes on the client sent to her smart phone ten minutes ago had contained essential details but she hadn't bothered memorising them all. They would find out the really important stuff in the next few minutes. And house size or location wasn't the most crucial.

"How do you folks handle this?" Vaslik was new to Cruxys and still finding his feet in a strange city and a new environment. He'd been paired with Ruth as his mentor. Follow her lead, he'd been told; it was a kind of induction period. Then he'd be on his own unless teamed up with others for specific assignments.

For Ruth it was an unwelcome if temporary intrusion; she preferred working alone or with one of the other operatives, and had sensed that Vaslik wasn't overjoyed, either.

"We go in, we pull Nancy Hardman down off the ceiling and calm her down. We try to figure out who took her daughter … if that's what really happened."

"You doubt it?"

"I've seen it before: domestic stuff. Just because our clients have money doesn't stop them falling out and doing something stupid."

She looked at him. "But I suppose you wouldn't have seen much of that in the DHS."

He shrugged, not responding to the implied query. She'd been told that he'd been headhunted from the Department of Homeland Security, the huge standalone US federal agency set up in the wake of 9/11, and before that he'd been a New York City cop. His name had come on recommendation of contacts in the US, and he'd been recruited to add to the company's footprint with US corporations, which was a fast-growing market for a hungry company.

In the private security industry, she was learning, presentation and identity were every bit as important as they were in banking.

"We should get in there." He gestured at the house with his clipboard.

"We will, Slik. Let's allow her a good look at us first. We don't want her thinking we're part of whoever snatched her daughter."

"Call me Andy."

"Whatever." Slik suited him better; Andy was too boyish, too … everyday. Slik fitted his look, which was slim, clean and contained, like a ballet dancer she had once known. He even had the face, with cool eyes, high cheekbones and hungry features, undoubtedly part of his Slavic ancestry. Probably couldn't dance worth a toss, though.

She walked up the paved drive. A Nissan was parked at an angle with the driver's door hanging open, abandoned in a rush of panic. She nudged it shut with her hip. No point adding to the woman's problems by having her car nicked.

She knocked on the door and stepped back, saw a ghost of movement behind the front room curtains. She waited for a shadow to appear behind the frosted glass door panel. At her feet lay a small teddy. It looked forlorn, abandoned. She picked it up.

A metallic clunk sounded as the door opened and was stopped dead by the security chain. Good girl. She'd listened to instructions.

"Mrs. Nancy Hardman?"

"Your names?" The voice seemed to be squeezed with difficulty through the gap, like old toothpaste from a tube. The tone was hovering on the edge of breaking.

"I'm Ruth Gonzales," she replied calmly, and took out her ID wallet. She held it against the gap and let it go when it was taken. "My colleague is Andy Vaslik." She signalled to Slik to hand over his ID, which he did.

"You were quick."

"We were in the area." After the call had reached the Cruxys control room and the operator had punched in the code red indicator, the system had automatically picked up the nearest team available. She and Vaslik, on the first full day of being paired up for a show-around of his new work territory, had been it.

"Wait." The door closed and the chain rattled. When it swung open again it revealed a woman in her late thirties dressed in gym gear. Trainers, leggings and a top, all clean but worn. A reflection of the woman herself, thought Ruth. Fit but no fashion-conscious gym bunny. And by the haunted expression in her eyes, stressed to hell.

As they stepped inside, Nancy Hardman leaned out and scanned the street.

"Don't do that," Ruth said. "We don't want to go public. If anybody asks, we're from the water company." She took back their ID in exchange for the teddy and waited while Nancy looked guilty then mortified for not having picked it up, before turning and leading the way into the living room.

The furniture was neat, clean and reasonably modern, but not top of any range. It pointed to a restricted budget—or careful spending, depending on your point of view. She took a seat on the settee while Vaslik wandered away to check the front and rear windows. He was careful not to touch the curtains, before walking back into the hallway.

"What's he doing? Nancy queried, her voice brittle. "Where's he going?"

"He's doing his job," Ruth replied softly. "He's going to help find Beth. To do that we need to see if anything has been left behind that might help us."

"What sort of thing?"

"We won't know ... until we find it."

She waited for Nancy to settle, then said, "Right, Mrs. Hardman—can I call you Nancy?" At a nod she continued, "As I said, we're here to help you find Beth. That's our sole priority. First I need you to tell me what happened. I know you told John, our controller—the man on the phone—but I'd like you to go over it again for me." She opened her briefcase and produced a small digital recorder, which she placed on the coffee table between them. "Don't worry about speaking up—this will pick up your voice quite easily. Take your time."

Nancy nodded and cleared her throat, then spoke about everything she could remember after arriving at the gym, from opening the locker, finding the card, and leaving. Her words faltered several times, her head dropping as she fought with memory, but she pressed on until she was finished.

Ruth picked up on the missing phone battery. It was the first oddity. "You've no idea how it could have got into the nanny's bedroom?"

"No. I used it last night, so I know it was fine then. And I haven't been in her room—she has a right to privacy."

"Maybe you dropped it by accident this morning and she picked it up to give it back to you later." Ruth didn't believe it but it helped to get the woman involved and thinking, rather than sliding down into a helpless mess. The only alternative was that the four-year-old daughter had managed to take the battery out of the cell phone, but that seemed unlikely. She suggested it, anyway.

"She couldn't have done. It was a very tight fit. Anyway, I put it in my sports bag when I was getting dressed, the same as always."

"Always?"

"I use the alarm on the phone every morning. When I switch it off, I put it in the sports bag or on the side table alongside my purse, depending on what I'm going to do."

"Did you see anybody in the street when you left home this morning or when you got back from the gym?"

"No. I mean, I don't remember. I wasn't expecting to have to look."

"Fair enough. Have you had any unexpected visitors recently—or received any odd phone calls? Any silent calls where the caller hung up, any visitors who'd got the wrong house, stuff like that?"

"No. Nothing. It's been absolutely normal. Until now."

Ruth consulted a notebook. "You live here with your husband Michael and daughter Beth, correct?"

"Yes. And the nanny if I need her to stay over." She flapped a hand and explained, "I work part-time as a bookkeeper; I occasionally have to work late."

"The nanny's name?"

"Tiggi Sgornik. She's Polish, from Warsaw."

"So many of them are. You trust her?"

"Of course. At least, I have no reason not to."

"Where's your husband?"

"I don't know."

Ruth looked up, her head to one side. "Pardon?"

"He's somewhere in Africa … I think." Nancy's face coloured. "I didn't mean that to sound the way it did. He's a charity field worker; he moves around to wherever he's needed most. Last week it was Nigeria, the week before, Congo. Today, I don't know." She flapped her hand again, chopping the air. "The phone coverage isn't great."

"Tell me about it," Ruth agreed easily. She knew Africa. "I've been there a few times. Some places it's quicker to send a man on a bike." It was true enough, she had been there, but it helped build a rapport with the woman, to establish a common experience. Lower barriers. "Isn't there any way of getting in touch with him through the charity's head office?"

Nancy looked surprised, then sheepish. "God, I didn't think—" She started to rise but Ruth stopped her.

"It's fine. We'll do it. If you have a contact number we'll call them. But he's definitely out of the country?"

"Yes."

"When was he here last?"

"Why is that important? I want you to find Beth. Please." The word came out low, full of pleading.

"We will. It's just background information, that's all. Anything and everything helps us build a picture."

22

"Oh. Sorry." She looked at the ceiling in thought, her eyes moist. "It was ten days ago. He's due back in the next couple of weeks, I think."

"Do you have family or a close friend you can call on? It helps, sometimes to have somebody to talk to while we get things moving."

"Not really." Nancy looked embarrassed. "Michael and Beth are my family. We haven't been here long and I don't socialise much. The gym, work, shopping—and Beth's pre-school group. The neighbours seem to be out all day. Or busy." Her face gave a briefly sour twist.

Ruth nodded. "Yeah, I saw the cars. I've got neighbours like that. Don't know the first thing about most of them and prefer to keep it that way. Seems to work for all of us." She looked up. "The card you found in the locker—did you keep it?"

"Yes." Nancy reached inside her leggings and tugged at a pocket. She brought out a crumpled piece of white card. "Sorry—I'm afraid I've probably destroyed any fingerprints. I wasn't thinking clearly."

"Don't worry about it." Ruth took the card and flattened it out using the back of her hand. "If there's anything to lift, our people will find it." She read the message and was surprised; whoever had written this was clearly intelligent. The layout carried the right amount of shock, instruction and threat, guaranteed to knock any certainties about the woman's world from underneath her one by one. The evident close knowledge about her family and her life, and even describing the Polish nanny, who she bet really was cute, was another stage in the process.

She placed the card in a plastic bag in her briefcase. "Is it true what they say?" Nancy murmured faintly. "About the first few hours of a child kidnap?"

"What's that?"

"That there's a very narrow window before something … bad happens." Her eyes went wide as she said it, and a tear rolled down her face and dropped onto her arm, reality finally given voice.

"Don't think like that, Nancy. It's bullshit." Ruth was matter-of-fact, the absence of polish a deliberate ploy. Some things were best said blunt and harsh, no messing. It cut through the anodyne platitudes used by so many agencies when dealing with victims. She pointed towards the card, which had given the affair an entirely different spin. "Anyway, this isn't a child abduction—at least, not the kind you're thinking about." She didn't know if it would help or whether Nancy would believe her, but anything that stopped her thinking the worst would help keep things simple.

"It's not?"

"No. Whoever did this wants something." Like your husband, she thought. If it was a paedophile who'd snatched Beth, Nancy wouldn't have heard a thing. A paedophile wouldn't have gone to these lengths to taunt her. A paedophile would be solely interested in the child, not the family. It was too focused, too deliberate for some grubby little toe-rag of a man with the personality of a germ. "Does your husband have any enemies?"

"No. I told you, he's a charity worker." The response was automatically defensive but Ruth ignored it. Defensive was expected; it helped let out the tension like a steam release valve.

"Yes, I remember."

Vaslik came back in the room, hovered for a moment, then went out again. Ruth ignored him. The man was like a wraith. She hadn't known him long enough to judge what made him tick, and what little about himself that he'd let out had been fairly monosyllabic. He hadn't liked her calling him Slik but she didn't care. As far as she was concerned he could call her whatever he liked in return, as long as they communicated and got the job done.

Ruth's path to the private sector had not been widely different. She had served in the Ministry of Defence police before transferring for five years to the Met, then leaving to join Cruxys when they had shown an interest. They needed more women investigators, they had told her during the interview; especially with MOD and police experience. And firearms training. She had confirmed yes, yes and yes, a flutter of reluctant excitement in the pit of her stomach at the mention of guns. The offer had landed on the table seconds later.

Nancy nodded after Vaslik's departing back. "Does he ever speak?"

"Not much. He's American—his family's Russian. Ex-cop. I call him Slik because it's easier to remember."

"He moves like a ballet dancer."

"You think?" Ruth pretended to consider the idea as new, another move to build rapport. "You're right. Maybe he's an escapee from the Bolshoi. I should ask him. Not that I care. He knows what he's doing, that's all I need to know."

FOUR

A CURSORY TOUR OF the house was sufficient to tell Andy Vaslik that nothing had been left behind. A pity, but not unexpected. Not every crime scene dripped with clues like a television drama. Some were almost clinical in their absence of evidence, with no more signs than were left by a passing breeze.

He'd seen it many times before.

As a member of a specialist police unit in New York, he'd been to more scenes of crime—especially kidnappings—than he cared to remember. Many of the houses and apartments had been trashed by ignorant and drugs-fuelled invaders looking for an easy score. In his experience, while these criminals—mostly from eastern European or Latin American gangs—were overly ambitious in scale and reach, they were rarely the hottest cards in the deck. They never imagined getting caught, so did little to bother hiding their tracks.

Which was both good and bad.

Good meant they usually got caught. Bad meant they didn't really care.

It was a measure of how they saw the miserable trajectory of their lives and most did nothing to break the pattern. They'd go in hard and brutal, prepared to kill regardless of consequences because to do it any other way simply never occurred to them. If the authorities were lucky, the perpetrators left enough forensic matter and sometimes personal crap that linked them as tight to a crime as a full reel of studio-quality photographic evidence.

This, though, was different.

No clues, no crap, no handy little personal belongings dropped in their haste. Whoever had snatched the little girl had come in clean and left the same way. In, lifted and out again, no damage, no fuss.

Unless they had performed the lift on the outside and the house left open was to confuse the investigation. It wasn't uncommon and the pick-up wouldn't have needed much; a van or large car stopping on a quiet street, the driver smiling to ask directions of an unsuspecting woman and child.

Then wham—all gone.

Professional.

There was always the other possibility: that the woman, Tiggi whatever her name was, had not been so unsuspecting; had in fact been complicit in the abduction.

He sniffed at the pillow on her bed, picking up a trace of perfume to get a feel for her. It wasn't a sexual thing; he was simply rolling through a database of smells and matching them to other women he had come across in years of criminal investigations. Sometimes the perfume a woman wore told you a whole lot more about her character and the people she mixed with than any other details.

This one told him cheap but with some taste. A boyfriend, undoubtedly, but not over-generous or rich.

Her room had been cleared. There should have been something left behind: underwear, wash gear, a change of clothes, lipstick, face-wipes—even something accidental like a bus ticket or a shop receipt. But the place had been sanitised, as devoid of character as a motel room.

Strike one against the nanny.

He moved into the main bedroom. Although shared by a man it was mostly a woman's space, personal, soft and colourful with cushions and the light touches no man would ever consider. Well, most men. He'd known a cop in New York with ambitions as an interior designer whose apartment was like a repro of the Ziegfeld Follies. But he'd been a one-off.

He listened to make sure the Hardman woman wasn't going to come up after him, but all he could hear was Ruth's voice, probing for information and clues. He hadn't got the measure of her yet, only that she didn't seem too keen to have been selected to show him around. Maybe it was the result of a previous pairing. There were partners he'd be pleased never to see again; it was always a danger in their line of work, being in close proximity to an opposite for several hours a day or night. Most of the time you got on and did the job because that's what you had to do. Sometimes, though, it was easier to hope for a transfer out.

He moved around the room, checking the dressing table, bedside cabinets and wardrobe, quickly flicking aside the corners of the carpets. He wasn't sure why he did this here, only that in the past it had yielded results out of proportion to expectations. Some had revealed letters, recreational drugs, bank documents, even large amounts of cash where there should have been none.

He'd even found a body once. That had been something none of them had expected—least of all the householder who'd claimed his wife had been kidnapped.

The fact was, everybody lied about something. Some were light and white, concealing embarrassment or personal failings; some carried darker lies in the way of stored secrets they preferred to hide close by where they could touch them or take them out occasionally to pore over them in the dark hours.

This room didn't tell much of a story and yielded no useful clues. The man had little in the way of clothing, most of it casual and functional in muted colours of green and brown. Perhaps he was a closet camouflage nut. In fact there was so little, he probably carried more with him than was left behind.

The woman had more, but much of it was not new although of good quality. Not a shoe freak, which was refreshing, but she seemed to favour lacy underwear. He wondered if she kept it for the husband's rare visits home or if she had a friend with benefits on the side.

Not relevant? Maybe.

There was a phone extension by the bed. He unplugged it as he passed by and took it with him. From here on in they would control all calls in and out. He'd deal with the inevitable fall-out later. Some people were OK with it, others saw it as an infringement of their personal liberty, apparently oblivious of the fact that having a relative snatched was pretty much the biggest infringement you could get.

The little girl's room was a wreck—but the wreckage of all little girls who haven't got someone clearing up after them. Toys, fluffy and plastic, games, picture books, posters and clothing, scattered indiscriminately yet possessing an order he recognised. Ask this child where anything was, and she'd know instantly. Take something away and she'd probably scream the place down until it got put back.

The teddy on the mat downstairs told its own story.

He lingered over the open drawers but didn't touch. They told their own story. Someone had selected a change of clothes—maybe more than one—for the little girl.

Strike two against the nanny.

He used a chair on the landing to flip the roof hatch and check inside the loft space. It was small and cramped, the roof pitch angled down sharply, with no boards across the joists. It left little room to do much more than store a few lightweight items. It, in this case, a single empty suitcase sitting on a thin layer of insulating material that tickled his nose when disturbed, and some faded Christmas decorations in a cardboard box which he guessed had been left by a previous resident.

He closed the trapdoor and replaced the chair, then went back downstairs and joined the women. When Ruth looked up he gave a minute shake of his head.

Then he headed for the other rooms.

The study felt underused, cool and dark. It reminded him of his parents' front room, kept for best and cold as a morgue; the last place anyone would choose to sit in comfort. This one held a desk and a filing cabinet, two armchairs and a small sideboard which was empty.

He flicked through the drop files in the cabinet, walking his fingers across the title cards for insurance, banking, car details, legal and a host of other tags that make up the average family life story. No surprises except that all the correspondence was in the wife's name, as were the bank account and credit cards.

Now there was a thing.

There was nothing for or about the husband.

FIVE

VASLIK WENT AND STOOD by the front door, eyeing the street but being careful to remain out of sight. Previous experience had taught him that kidnappers weren't always far from the victim's family in the first few hours. The pros usually wanted to keep an eyes-on to the situation to monitor any police response and gauge the right time to make their initial contact. If they were in a hurry, the demand would be made fairly early on. If not, they would bide their time and ratchet up the tension for those left behind.

The bad ones were more difficult to assess. By their nature, they were unpredictable, usually less controlled and far more likely to panic at the first signs of trouble. They were also prone to impatience, and not waiting long before going for the prize ... or cutting their losses.

And that was never good news for the hostage.

He walked through to the back door and down the rear, where a gate opened into a narrow service lane. It was lined each side with hedge growth, and not overlooked. A blank spot and easy meat for anyone with evil intentions.

A bad sign.

He stood for a moment, his antennae twitching. Was this the kind of thing he was supposed to be looking for? But how could it be? It didn't involve any threat to the US.

Although no longer in Homeland Security, like many former employees he was on a reserve list which carried certain obligations. One of those was the expectation that he would be ready to assist in helping protect his country's security in any way he could. Shortly after arriving in London, he'd received a call from a middle-ranking member of DHS gently reminding him of his duty and asking that he be on hand to assist if required.

"We appreciate that you're now in the private sector," the woman had said carefully. "But we may need your help on the ground. You have experience that's valuable to us."

"Sure," he'd agreed. "How can I help?"

"I'm afraid I can't comment in detail, only that it might involve the abduction of an important American citizen. I've merely been asked to contact you so that you know the situation and can be prepared. This is not unusual and many other former special agents receive requests like this when we feel it's necessary. I'm sure you're aware of the heightened state of alertness we're all under at this present time."

She had rung off without going into further detail.

Vaslik had put it out of his mind, hoping it wouldn't come to anything. He'd known plenty of reserve list officers who had never heard a word until they hit retirement age or beyond, when their service ended with a polite letter of gratitude from whichever government department had been keeping them on a string. End of duty. Sorry we never called. You're off the hook. Goodbye and have a quiet life.

He dismissed it from his mind; Beth Hardman was neither American nor important, except to her family.

He stepped out into the service lane and walked to the end. He turned right, then right again until he was back in the road leading past the Hardmans' front door. He could see the Toyota further down, and walked towards it, his cell phone clamped to one ear and juggling a notebook in his other hand. He was looking for something intangible; it could be a vehicle parked nearby with someone on board; it might be a building that had a feel about it. He wouldn't know until he saw it.

The cars were all empty and the houses normal and devoid of suspicious signs. By now most people who were going out had gone, so most of the houses had that empty look that burglars search for, coupled in a way that won't attract the attention of neighbours. He saw nothing that stood out; just people going about their business, washing windows, taking in shopping or doing the mundane have-to-do things people attend to every day.

A little way up the street on the opposite side from the Hardman house Vaslik spotted a man with a camera. He was taking shots of a property from various angles, sinking to one knee then checking the screen for the results before trying again. Real estate agent, Vaslik guessed. The man moved back and snapped a few more photos before walking down the side of the house and disappearing.

The house looked empty and sad and Vaslik didn't envy him his job. It would be a tough sell.

When he returned to the house through the rear gate and stepped into the living room, Ruth was standing by a shelf where an electronic frame showed a series of photos flicking past in sequence. Family shots, clearly; some grouped, some single, smiling faces against a variety of backgrounds, in living colour. Happy times. Nancy, a small girl and a man, although his face never quite spoke to the camera.

"Is that your husband?" she queried, pointing at one shot. The man was slim and tanned, with a fading smile as if he had just been dropping a pose a shade too early. Or was turning away.

"Michael, yes." She gave a ghost of a smile. "He hates having his photo taken. His parents were always shoving a camera in his face and he says it put him off for life."

"It would be good to have some shots of him and Beth. If you don't have any handy I could take the disc out of there and have some printed." She opened her briefcase and took out a slim notebook computer. "I wouldn't have to take it away—I can download what we need right here."

Nancy frowned. "Why do you need a photo of Michael?"

"It helps," Ruth explained, "especially if we need to circulate pictures of Beth. Photos jog memories and a family group carries more weight than a single shot. Makes it more urgent, more real. People are prepared to make more effort with a family shot because they can relate to it."

Nancy nodded. "I see. Of course. Help yourself."

Ruth took the frame down and extracted the disc from the back. It was the size of a postage stamp. She opened her computer and took a card reader from her briefcase, sliding the disc into the smallest slot and plugging the reader into one of the USB ports.

"What's that?" Nancy looked worried. "You won't lose them, will you?"

"No, this opens the files so I can see which one to copy. I won't be a second." She glanced past the woman's shoulder at Vaslik and gave a minute tilt of her head.

He got the message.

"Is he secretive, your husband?" It was the first time he had spoken in the house. He had a pleasant accent without the throatiness of many American men.

"I don't think so. No more than most. Why?" She looked down at the extension phone in his hand, the wire coiled around it. "That's from my bedroom. What are you doing with it?"

He dropped it on the settee. "We don't want you taking calls while you're alone."

"You can't do that!" She snatched up the phone and clutched it to her. "You have no right."

Ruth moved across and sat next to her, and gently but firmly took the phone from her. "It's OK, Nancy. He's right, I'm afraid; that's what we're here for. You can take any calls that come in, but if it's the people who took Beth, we have to be here to advise you." She placed the phone to one side. "We're used to this kind of thing. Where is your cell phone?"

"You can't take that, too."

"We're not going to. But you should leave it down here whenever you go to bed." She had no way of explaining how traumatic it would be waking up suddenly in the middle of the night to a call from her daughter's kidnappers.

Nancy relented. "It's in the kitchen."

Ruth nodded at Vaslik, who stepped through the door and retrieved it, placing it on the arm of the settee. He stepped towards the window, drawing Nancy's attention away from what Ruth was doing. "Your daughter must miss him, being away so much."

"Yes, she does." She shivered and moved towards him, glancing back at Ruth. "In fact there are times when I think she can't really remember him. She's so young." A tear erupted and trickled down her cheek. She brushed it away and looked down at her feet. "I hate it when he's away."

"Do you trust him?"

She looked at him. "What do you mean?"

"Slik." A soft warning from Ruth, crouched over her machine.

"Could he be having an affair with your nanny?"

Nancy's reaction was instinctive; her arm swung up and round, the slap echoing sharply in the room. Vaslik barely moved, turning enough to take the sting out of the blow as if he were used to being hit. His only response was a hint of a smile.

Nancy went to hit him again but Ruth stood up quickly and clamped her arms close to her side.

"You do that again," she said softly, "and we're out of here." She threw Vaslik a furious look, and he shrugged and walked away.

"I'm sorry." Nancy's voice was dull and flat as if all the tone had drained out through her feet. "He shouldn't have said that."

"I know. What can I say? He was being a dick. Sit down—I'll be right back."

SIX

Tea: the panacea for all ills. Ruth went into the kitchen. It was tidy and methodically laid out, more hotel room than a home, everything easy to find with no clutter. While the water boiled she slid open a couple of drawers, one close to a wall phone. Most houses would have had a notepad or whiteboard nearby for phone numbers or names; but not this one. There was nothing; no unnecessary paperwork, no jottings, letters or bills.

Spooky.

She took the tea into the living room. Nancy had been crying, the telltale tracks of tears down her cheeks. Vaslik was making no effort at conversation, but staring through the front window with a blank expression. A monolith in a smart suit. She was angry with him, wanted to rip off a stretch of skin for what he'd said. But she recognised the tactic. If there was something else going on here, something from deep in the private fabric of the Hardmans' lives, they had to get to it fast and not waste time. It wasn't out of the question that Hardman *had* been screwing the nanny, and had decided to take off with her and his daughter and stage the thing as a kidnap. If so, it was stupid and elaborate and extremely cruel.

Men being led by their dicks did stupid things. But so elaborate and cruel? Unlikely.

She glanced at her computer. It had finished downloading the photos from the disc, including a couple of Tiggi. Long legged and striking rather than pretty, she had the cool look of a catwalk model. Ruth revised the likelihood of a husband-nanny fumble under the stairs having turned into something more serious. Having someone like her around the house would be a temptation for any man. She tried to recall who the young woman reminded her of but it wouldn't come.

With a faint touch of guilt, she found herself thinking the same thoughts as Vaslik. Had Hardman jumped her in the bathroom one day while wifey was out? Told her it could all be so different if only they could be together? Or had Tiggi been the instigator, a sexy chick looking for a new life in the UK and a man to latch on to?

Nancy jumped to her feet, reacting to Ruth's return as if she had just arrived. It was a strange leap in timing but probably triggered by a delayed reaction.

"Who are you people? I mean, what are you?" She was gabbling as if trying to make sense of their presence, her body vibrating like a tuning fork. She brushed angrily at her eyes and threw a cold glance at Vaslik, the clear enemy. "What are you doing here? I don't understand what the number and code were about or why I had to call you."

"We're your case officers." Ruth handed her a mug of tea. She had added two sugars to help in the calming process. "Think of us as investigators."

"Like police."

"No. Not police. The number you called is to a company called Cruxys Solutions. It's like an insurance company and we're like claims investigators—only we sort out situations, we don't pay out claims."

"Is this all this is to you—a situation?" The retort was immediate and confrontational, the air around them sizzling with anger as if she had just found a new voice and was able to give vent to her emotions.

Ruth ignored it; it was something she was used to. She wasn't absolutely sure how she'd react if anyone close to her was kidnapped, but it wouldn't be calm, she knew that.

"That's not what I meant." She took the smart disc from the reader and replaced it in the photo frame, making sure Nancy saw her do it. The woman needed to hold on to whatever was familiar, whatever was close to her, to get her through this nightmare. "I've got the photos I need. I'll get them printed and ready for circulation if we need them." She pressed a button on the side of the frame and the images began scrolling through once again, distracting Nancy's attention. A quick glance showed she had visibly relaxed, although she was clearly affected by seeing the familiar pictures again.

"Why later?" She sounded bewildered. "You could do it now, couldn't you? Somebody may have seen her."

"We can't put them out there yet—not until we know more. If the people who left the note know we're here, they'll assume we're police." Using the softer reference of those who had left the note, rather than who had taken Beth, was deliberate; avoiding triggers and buzz words was a key approach to alleviating surges of stress in the ones left behind.

It seemed to work. When Nancy next spoke, she sounded calmer. "I still don't get it. Why did I have to call you at all?"

"Didn't your husband say?"

"Not really. He mentioned it once, and said if there was ever a problem … like anything happened to him and I needed help, I had to call that number. To be honest I didn't go into it further because it was something I didn't want to think about. It's bad enough knowing the kind of areas he must work in without considering him never coming home again."

"You're not alone in that. As to why, your husband was merely looking after you; the contract would do that. We call it Safeguard."

"Like an insurance policy?"

"Like that." She explained that Safeguard had originally been conceived for executives posted to Latin America, where kidnappings were once big business. Now, however, they were global and often used to cover oil workers or mining engineers in Africa and the Middle East. What she didn't say was that it didn't guarantee a safe return, but knowing a team of specialists—mostly ex-military—would be despatched to conduct a search was worth its psychological weight to victim and family. "The contract means that if there's a problem, we step in and do whatever's necessary."

"Like what?" The woman's eyes were dull liquid, the head not listening, only hearing.

"We arrange alternative safe accommodation if required; funds to tide the family over if there's a shortfall; a channel of communication if that's possible, to keep everyone informed; even alternative schooling for children if they have to be moved temporarily." She didn't say why that was ever necessary. Telling this woman right now that some families were under direct threat, not just the person kidnapped, would in all likelihood kick her over the edge. "Our clients are global. They're companies, governments, individuals."

"What kind individuals?"

"All sorts."

"Rich people?"

"Yes. Is your husband rich?"

"No!" The word gusted out on an explosion of bitter laughter. "God, I wish. He's a charity worker. We get by, that's all ... most of the time."

"But you employ a nanny. That's not cheap."

"I pay that out of my part-time work. I'd go mad stuck in here all day every day." She gave a harsh laugh. "I know that makes me sound selfish, but I can't help it. Have you ever tried holding a conversation with a four-year-old? It probably makes me a bad mother, too, but that's tough. Anyway, as for money, Tiggi charges very reasonable rates. At least, she did."

"Don't dwell on it." She allowed the silence to increase while Nancy calmed down, and checked her phone to bring up the summary of the Hardmans' contract with Cruxys. Nancy was clearly feeling volatile—who wouldn't be?—but that was good in its own way; she was beginning to let out more about herself and her family. Ruth wasn't about to assume the worst about this woman, but something was off about this whole deal and she couldn't put her finger on it. It was about time to add a little pressure of her own to the mix. "Mmm. Interesting."

"What? What have you found?"

"Nothing. I was puzzled, that's all. Why do you move so often?"

"How do you know we do?"

"Your record shows several previous addresses." It also showed that Michael Hardman had taken out the Safeguard contract with Cruxys just over two years ago, but she didn't say it. Some couples were like that: one half preferring not to know about the mundane stuff, the other seeing no need to talk about it. For whatever reason, the Hardmans had moved house five times in twenty months and Michael Hardman had taken measures in case something happened to him. Neither was a crime, and people moved all the time. But five different addresses?

"We're not rent jumpers, if that's what you're thinking." The tone was sharply defensive. "Michael doesn't like being tied to one place, that's all. He's got itchy feet. And he's always off somewhere new. He says it's not worth buying property until we're settled."

"And you? What do you think?"

Nancy shrugged. "I go where my husband goes, of course. Are you married?"

Ruth shook her head but said nothing, allowing the atmosphere to cool. She watched as Nancy tasted her tea. If it was too sweet she didn't seem to notice. She said, "You asked what we do, Nancy. Slik and I have been assigned to you until this matter has been resolved. We're here to help you."

"*Resolved*?" Nancy's voice flared instantly, a shade away from hysteria. "You think this is a crossword puzzle ... that it will be all tidied up by tea-time? For fuck's sake, this is my daughter you're talking about, not a case of dry rot! She's been kidnapped!"

"Sorry. Bad choice of words." Ruth was unmoved. "Until we get her back, I meant. And we will. But you have to help us."

"How? Christ, *I don't know anything*."

"You might think that. We'll see. First, though, we need to bring in our experts to check the house. Room by room, starting with Beth's."

"Why?"

"It's what we do, in case anything was left that we can't see. How often did your daughter's nanny stay over?"

"Not often. Only when I needed to be out late. She lived not far away but I didn't want her getting back late at night. She shares a house with several others."

"Others?"

"Other Poles, I suppose. They come and go, looking for work."

"How long had she worked for you?"

"Six—no, eight weeks."

"You've no idea why she would have taken her things away? You didn't fall out with her, give her reason to leave?"

"No, nothing like that. She was fine yesterday."

Ruth produced a lined A4 notepad from her briefcase. "I'm going to have a chat with my colleague and ring the office to arrange for the inspection team. Do you have a rear access to the garden? We don't want to make their presence obvious."

"Yes. There's a gate to a service lane at the back. It's not locked."

Ruth exchanged a look with Vaslik, who lifted an eyebrow at the implications and went outside. Then she said, "While we're doing this I want you to write down everything you know about Tiggi; full names, description, age, contact details, friends, family, home address, clubs, pubs, hobbies—anything you can think of. And I mean anything. Doesn't matter how trivial or salacious it might seem. This is about Beth, not her."

Nancy stared. "Surely you don't think *she* took Beth? That's crazy—why would she? She doted on her."

"I'm sure she did." Ruth handed over the notepad. "Anything that comes to mind. Also about your husband's work, names of colleagues, friends, places he's been. It doesn't have to be in any kind of order.

Stream of consciousness will do." Her face softened. "It usually helps to just let it all out."

"Usually? My God, how often do you have to do this kind of thing?"

Ruth didn't reply. She waited for her to start writing, then left the room and went in search of Vaslik.

SEVEN

"SHE'S LYING." VASLIK WAS standing by the rear gate. He spoke without any hint of surprise, as if the human condition was an open book.

"Of course she's lying. Everyone does about something. But why—and what about?"

"I don't know." He told her about all the documents being in the wife's name. "Hardman's name doesn't appear on anything as far as I could see."

"I'm not surprised. He's never here, is he? She's the one left running things. It makes sense that she has to sign off everything. Hell, you tangle with our Data Protection Act and you'll see what I mean."

"She's too calm, though."

"You call that calm? That was some slap; you're lucky she didn't rip your face off."

"It didn't hurt."

"Only because you anticipated and rode the blow. Are you in the habit of getting knocked about by women?" When he looked surprised she snorted and said, "What—you think women don't know about rough-house techniques? My dad was a cop and a part-time boxing coach; he taught me to defend myself."

Vaslik said, "You know the sign of a male chauvinist?"

She gave him a wary look. "You mean other than a small dick and an IQ to match? Let's pretend I'm dumb, shall we?"

He waved a dismissive hand. "Don't worry your pretty little head about it—you're just a girl." As he turned away she swore she heard him chuckle, and smiled in spite of herself.

She said, "Can we get back to the matter in hand?"

"Sure, why not. What's bothering you?" When he turned back, his face was serious.

Ruth gestured at the house. "You're right. She's too calm. She should be climbing the walls, screaming at us and all the rest, demanding to know what the cops are doing about her daughter. Any mother gets her child snatched should be incandescent with anger and fear. But not her. Not on the same scale, anyway. I can't figure out why."

Vaslik tilted his head in agreement. "She's scared, but controlled. It's unusual, but I've seen it before. With some people the full emotion takes time to kick in."

"Seen it before how?"

"I should have mentioned it. I was in a child abduction unit in New York City before joining the DHS. We had to deal with a lot of family situations; fathers or mothers taking the kids to make a point or protect them from harm. Once we knew what we were dealing with it made the picture much clearer."

"Is that why you made that dig about the nanny—to get under her skin?"

"Yes."

She almost smiled. "You must have got slapped a lot."

"Not true." His mouth twitched. "Although one pulled a gun on me. That was a surprise; she was an eighty-one-year-old grandma. She didn't like cops."

She was silent for a few moments, then said, "OK, so you know what you're doing. That's good; we can use that. What else did you find in the house?"

"Other than the nanny's room having been sanitised and changes of clothes for the kid taken, nothing."

"You think she's involved?"

"Could be. She would know which clothes to take and where to get them, and the fact that all trace of her is gone, too … now that's unusual."

"Why?"

"Whoever did this made sure there's nothing we can use. That means it wasn't a spur-of-the-moment or emotional thing, but planned."

"So it could be the husband."

"Maybe." He indicated the open gate and the rear access lane, which was thinly layered in tarmac and just wide enough to bring a car or small van for residents to move bins and garden rubbish. Both sides were lined with hedging that had been left to grow wild. "If it wasn't him, they'd have come in this way. There's excellent cover all the way. Anybody coming through here would be screened by these hedges. It's how I'd do it, anyway."

Ruth agreed. Entering through the front door risked being seen along a street that probably lived on gossip and curtain twitching. Leaving the front door open as if in the aftermath of a snatch had merely been a psychological trigger to put a final scare into Nancy.

After the card with its initial trigger points—the dead phone, the unanswered calls—seeing her home wide open and with the abandoned teddy on the doormat would have been the final piece to convince her it wasn't a hoax.

"But why would they do this? Hardman's a charity worker."

"That's what she says." Vaslik was looking up in the sky. "Doesn't mean it's so."

"All right, brains, out with it. What do you know?"

"About this? As much as you do. There are several reasons for child abduction: there's family stuff, like I mentioned, usually involving an absent parent. Then there's outside motivation. The main reasons are sex, money and leverage. This could be sex but I'm betting on money or leverage."

"Agreed. But who?"

"Good question. Off the top of my head I'd say the nanny's part of it, and one of the workers at the gym, which means these people have some reach." He shrugged. "More than that, until we find out who could want something from these very ordinary suburban people, I'm just guessing." The way he placed emphasis on the word "suburban" indicated a strong degree of cynicism.

She took out her cell phone and dialled the office. It was time to get a team in. She gave directions on how to reach the rear gate, listened for a few seconds, then said to Vaslik, "Come on, let's go ask more questions. This time, try to be nice."

———

They found Nancy in the same position, as if welded to the spot. Her face looked drawn, but there were no more signs of tears. Cried out for now, Ruth guessed, the well gone dry.

The notepad was on the coffee table, covered in neat handwriting. "Done?"

"Yes. I'm not sure it will help much." Her voice was flat with defeat, as if writing down the details had added another layer of doubt about the people close to her.

Ruth ignored the pad. Making sense of it would come later. For now the questions were the priority.

"The team is on its way. They're also sending someone to stay with you—a woman named Gina Fraser. If you're agreeable, she'll use Tiggi's room."

She'd been surprised by the selection of Gina Fraser for this job. A former member of the Diplomatic Protection Group responsible for guarding government ministers and foreign embassies, she had only recently returned to work. After joining Cruxys she had been assigned to support a wealthy Qatari family who had incurred the wrath of a rival family by denying the marriage of their daughter to the other family's son. The marriage had been aimed at healing a historical tribal rift. What had at first seemed an inter-family spat had quickly turned violent. Two of the spurned son's uncles had arrived from Qatar, threatening consequences for the perceived insult. Gina Fraser, seen as the outward "face" of the family, had been targeted and shot twice as a warning.

She had nearly died. After two operations and months of therapy, she had come back, but Ruth wondered if she was back to full form. If anything blew up here, the consequences could be awkward.

But she bit her tongue; it wasn't her job to second-guess the Cruxys selection process.

"Why send someone else?" Nancy looked worried. "I thought you'd be staying here." She didn't include Vaslik, his presence clearly discounted.

"We can't, not all the time; we need to be out there looking for Beth, following up any leads."

"Like what? What have you found?" She leaned forward, instantly alert.

"Nothing yet. There are a number of things we have to do, such as checking Tiggi's background, talking to the people at the gym … and to the charity Michael's working for. For that we'll need a contact number and name."

"Oh." Nancy's shoulders slumped at the mundane sound to the list.

"You have to realise that the kidnappers might wait a couple of days before contacting you again. It's better if Gina's here full-time to support you. You can trust her—she's very good at what she does. She and the team will come in through the back gate. They know what to do, so you don't need to do anything. Right now I need to go over a few things with you about your husband."

"Why?" She seemed disconcerted by the sudden change in tactics, and Ruth put it down to stress. It was something she was going to have to get used to.

"Simply because he was mentioned specifically. They want him to know what happened. Why? Like I said before, this is not about you and not even Beth. It's about something else … maybe something your husband knows or did. But until the kidnappers come back and tell you what they want, we're in the dark."

"You think they will contact us?"

"For sure." Vaslik spoke from by the front window, his voice was soft. "Kidnappers work for profit—for an outcome. The note they left tells us that. We have to find out what that outcome might be, what they're willing to risk being caught for. Maybe they'll tell us soon. If we can make a connection, it gives us a lead on who could have planned this. Who stands to gain by it." He spoke fluidly, clearly experienced with such events, then added carefully, "I want to apologise for what I said earlier. It was rude of me."

Both women looked at him in surprise, Ruth especially.

Nancy shrugged, said nothing.

"Right," Ruth said, to puncture the silence, and took out the recorder and placed it on the table. "Let's do this. Have you tried contacting your husband again?"

"Yes. Just now." She indicated the cordless phone on the seat beside her.

"And?"

"It went to voicemail. He's probably out on a field trip. The local coverage could be patchy or nonexistent. I left a message."

"May I?" Ruth picked up the phone and touched redial. A standard voicemail robot, sexless and bland. She put the phone down. "Where can we find his employers?"

"I tried the only number I've got. There's no answer."

"Is that normal?"

"I don't know—I don't often have to tell them my daughter's been kidnapped." She shook her head in irritation. "Sorry. I didn't mean that. The charities he works for ... they're not mainline; they often work from temporary offices with minimum staff, putting all the money into field operations and resources."

"We'll need the address details."

"I'll look." Nancy stood up and left the room. Ruth and Vaslik exchanged looks but said nothing. When Nancy came back she was carrying a ring binder. She flipped it open, frowned when she found what she was looking for, then scribbled on a post-it note.

She handed it over. "Sorry—that's all I've got."

Ruth checked it. It was a phone number. "Does this charity have a name?"

"Probably, but I don't know what it is. I told you—he works for more than one. I forget which one this is."

Ruth handed the note to Vaslik, who took out his cell phone and walked into the hallway.

To get her back to talking, Ruth asked, "What did your husband do before the charity thing?"

Nancy frowned. "All sorts. I think he worked in the city for a while, then he got tired of it and decided to do something worthwhile."

"Did he make any money?"

"No. It wasn't that kind of job. I think it was more admin than anything. He never spoke about previous jobs—I don't think he considered them of value compared to what he does now."

"So he's an idealist?"

"Is that wrong?"

"Not at all. How did you meet him?"

For the first time there was the ghost of a smile. "I was in Paris, helping at a business conference. I used to work in marketing. I was walking past Sacré Coeur during a break and snapped the heel of my shoe on a cobblestone. God, I was so embarrassed. But suddenly, there he was. He came to my rescue and got me a cab to my hotel. We started dating when I got back to London."

"How romantic. And he was a charity worker then?"

"Yes. I believe he was with Oxfam at the time. But he left them not long afterwards to go freelance. He said there were lots of smaller organisations who needed all the help they could get without paying big bucks to their staff." She lifted her shoulders. "If that makes him something of an idealist, then I guess he is."

"What places did he work?" Vaslik had re-entered the room. He was juggling his phone in one hand.

"Mostly in Africa. He was a field coordinator and travelled all over."

"Name some names," said Ruth.

She hesitated, blinking, as if her mind was mired in glue. Then she said, "Rwanda, Mali, Somalia … countries where they've had the guts ripped out by war, famine, disease—you name it. I can't remember where else—he goes wherever he's needed."

Ruth glanced at Vaslik. "None of them gel for me." When she received a nod of agreement she added, "Where else—away from Africa?"

"I don't know. Places—I forget where."

"Did you ever go to any of these 'places?'"

"No. He never invited me. It was hardly likely to be a holiday, was it? Anyway, I'd have been in the way, excess baggage." The words were tinged with a trace of sadness, and she added, "Sorry—I didn't mean that."

"Fair enough." Ruth stood up and Vaslik moved towards the door.

"You're going already?" Nancy sounded alarmed.

"We have to. We've got things to do if we want to get on top of this. Gina Fraser's on her way and should be here in a few minutes. She'll stay here with you. We'll be back, though, soon enough." She had a thought. "The gym you go to. Are you a card-carrying member?"

"Yes. It's called Fitness Plus."

"How do you check in?"

"Members have a swipe-card to open the gate through to the inside."

"Do you ever speak to the receptionists?"

"Not really. They're usually busy with other people. It's the way I prefer it; I can come and go as I please."

"How often do you go and at what times?"

"Three times a week, sometimes more—always in the morning. I get there just after nine. It's quieter then, after the early office workers have left. Why all these questions?"

"Because somebody knew which locker you used and the time you'd be there."

Nancy's eyes went wide at the implication. "You think a member of staff put the card there?"

Ruth resisted the temptation to go "Duh." Instead she said, "Possibly. It's too early to say. Question is, who else would know your routine? Your check-in time would be on the computer, and it's not difficult to keep an eye on a regular visitor without them noticing. Do you always use the same locker?"

"Yes. It's nearest the door and handy. No. 2. It's got a safety pin holding the key. I know—stupid."

"Don't beat yourself up," murmured Vaslik. "We're creatures of habit; even cops and emergency workers. We all like to use the same locker; it's like a talisman, unchanging and familiar." His tone suggested that it was a habit he didn't actually share.

"I can't believe this," Nancy replied, looking uneasy. "I mean, I hardly know anyone here in the street, and even less so at the gym. I'm sure I'd have noticed if anyone was watching me."

"Did you ever see any of the workers hanging around while you were there?"

"No. The reception area is out of sight and the staff members are always on the go."

"Exactly. They walk by and you don't notice; they wipe down a piece of equipment but you don't see them. They are workers, not people."

Nancy didn't reply, but blinked, her eyes distraught.

EIGHT

NANCY WATCHED THEM THROUGH the front window, and felt a bubble of panic rise in her chest. She had hated them being here, the woman almost as much as the man, her sex meaningless in the question of strangers probing her life and her home, silent invaders asking questions that surely had nothing whatsoever to do with finding Beth. Box-ticking, that was all it had been; going through the motions like a real insurance company claim about a damaged car or a ruined carpet. No real emotion involved but a remoteness that was intended to get the job done, nothing more. She'd been glad to see them go.

But now they were leaving she wanted to rush outside and beg them to stay, to give the house a least some semblance of normality. Of warmth.

She felt sick at the realisation that they were the only human contacts she currently had. Not work, not the gym, not Beth's pre-school. Not Tiggi.

What did that say about her life?

Her face was wet again. She brushed at her cheeks, feeling the sting of salt on her skin. Michael would be cross if he saw her now. He always talked about being strong, about not letting anything get to you, about relying on oneself and pushing away doubt. When she'd first thought about it, it had seemed such a strange thing for a charity worker to say, about never relying on others. But that was so much a part of who he was, who he had been ever since she'd first met him. And over time she had come to understand him and his philosophy, and it now didn't seem odd.

She turned and walked through the house, trying to pick up a sense of him, a feeling that at least a part of him was here with her when she needed it. But all she got was Beth and Tiggi, the perfume of one and the child-smell of the other.

She sat on the double bed in her bedroom, then stood and went through to Beth's room, anxious and agitated. Sight of the empty bed made her start crying again, and she finally gave in and allowed herself to erupt in sobs, throwing herself down on the duvet cover with a pink princess motif that was her daughter's favourite; Beth didn't even like it being taken away to wash, and would stand by the tumble dryer waiting for the cycle to end before snatching it out and rushing upstairs to place it back on her bed, beaming with pleasure as her world was put right again.

Nancy took a deep breath. Sat up and wiped her face. What if Beth came back right now? What if those two investigators appeared at the front door with her in tow? How would it look if Beth saw her own mother, red-faced and puffy-eyed, standing there?

She went through to the bathroom and splashed water on her eyes, patting away the droplets with a towel before forcing her breathing to settle. Control. She had to remain in control. Michael would expect nothing less of her.

Except that Michael wasn't here, dealing with this problem. She was.

She caught sight of herself in the mirror. God, she looked like a disaster victim, her hair stringy and wild, her normally clear skin blotchy and red.

She got changed out of her gym clothes, dumping them in the wash basket even though they were clean. Washing them would take away the association she wanted to avoid: the gym and the note. She put on jeans and a jumper. Back to normal. At least, in part.

She walked back downstairs and stood in the kitchen, staring at the phone. Why didn't Michael call? She was accustomed to his silences, to his long absences. It was something she had been forced to accept about him, the side of his life that put duty and others above himself and his family, that allowed him to deliberately distance himself. But right now, at this moment, she needed him to forget about duty and calling and be here for her and Beth—even if only at the end of a line.

Bloody duty. She suddenly hated the very notion, and felt not a trace of guilt.

She switched on the television in an effort to fill the living room with noise and colour, to push away the dread thoughts about where Beth might be; what she might be feeling; how she was being treated.

DO tell your husband. Beth's life…

Unable to hold back, the tears began to flow.

NINE

"Fraser? I heard about her." Vaslik barely waited to step away from the front door before making the comment Ruth knew was coming.

"Not my call," she said neutrally, surprised that office gossip had got to him already. "The bosses must think she's up to it."

He looked doubtful and she couldn't blame him. It was a harsh judgement but they worked in an environment where a client's life—and possibly that of a colleague—might depend on a person's ability to react instinctively. She knew others who had been shot and never fully recovered, their previous edge lost in one stroke. It was a hard truth for any professional to stomach.

Vaslik shrugged and walked away across the street, where he began scribbling on his clipboard, bending to check out numbers on water meter panels. Ruth did the same on her side, occasionally stopping to go to a front door and knock. There weren't many takers, each time receiving a smile if she was lucky and an assurance that their water pressure was fine.

"Just checking," she told each one. "We've had a complaint about a drop in pressure. It could have been a temporary blockage."

"If it was her up at thirty seven," said one woman, pointing to the far end of the street, "you shouldn't take any notice. She's always bitching about something."

Ruth smiled knowingly and thanked her without comment, happy to allow the woman to get the wrong impression. Natural gossip would soon divert attention away from them being seen at the Hardman house.

"Do you have to frighten people?" she said when she caught up with Vaslik, who had been conducting the same exercise.

"I don't know what you mean."

"Have you seen the film *I, Robot*?"

"I don't watch films. They lack integrity."

"Yeah, right. *Jungle Book* has all the integrity anyone needs. And it's got singing. You should see *I, Robot*. You could double for the lead—and I'm not talking about Will Smith. You're a spit for Sonny. He's the robot by the way. He scares the crap out of people. Did nobody ever tell you?"

He shrugged. "People tend not to criticise me."

"Exactly. Proves my point."

He blinked. "Are you trying to be rude?"

She leaned towards him. "Don't try that spooky, third-generation Slavic shit on me, Slik. I don't know you at all but I know you that much."

A flicker of movement touched his mouth. It might have been a smile. "If you say so. Where do we go from here?"

60

"I took a look at what she wrote down; there's nothing useful. It's stuff we've already got or historic details about where they've lived, where they've been. Nothing rings any bells."

"It's on the husband, then."

"Looks like it. First we need a briefing at the office to get all the balls rolling. After that, we find Michael. This day and age, how can anybody be out of touch for longer than ten seconds? Haven't they heard of sat phones?"

"We should talk to his employers. I rang the office, too, and got the researchers checking out the phone number for an address."

"Good. I'll leave it to you to handle that."

"What are you going to do?"

"Check out at the gym. Whoever left the card in the locker knew her routine, what she did and when. It had to be somebody who could watch her without appearing to. Ergo, inside job."

"*Ergo*. Latin for 'therefore.' Tell me, why do the English hold onto other languages so much?"

"Because it makes us sound almost as smart as you Russians."

"I'm American, I told you."

"No, you're not. Not really."

———

Thirty minutes later they were stepping through a security screen at the company offices in London's Upper Grosvenor Street. The building was a stone's throw from Park Lane and was immaculate and richly decorated, courtesy of a previous tenant who had gone bust. The expensive mouldings, discreet lighting and a quiet air of organised activity was a sharp contrast to the solid, even bland exterior and the uninformative steel plate next to the front step. Even the hum of the electronics which formed the core of the company's world-wide communications network came and went as doors opened and closed and was no different to a hundred other organisations.

Only the controlled intensity of some of the staff hurrying along corridors and the palpable air of tension in the air was an indication that all was not well.

"What's up?" said Ruth, as they made their way down to the Safe-guard Incident Room. She nodded at two familiar figures hurrying up the stairs. Both carried heavy nylon grab-bags, and were members of Cruxys's international response team. She guessed they were on their way out of the country, probably by jet from Northolt air-field. Both were former special forces and used in extreme situations. She didn't envy them their jobs.

They both pulled up chairs and sat down. In the background, two researchers were pulling together whiteboards ready to construct a time- and storyline, to which they would add from all available information as it came in, including the reports which Ruth and Vaslik were about to make.

"We've lost two contract security guards and two more have gone missing at an oil installation attacked by extremists in Nigeria." The speaker was Richard Aston, a lanky, skeletal figure in a pinstripe suit and regimental tie. He was Cruxys's Operations Commander. A former Parachute Regiment colonel and one of the co-founders of the company, he was responsible for research, staffing and day-to-day assignments related to the company's clients. He possessed a mind like a steel trap and hated inaction. Now, it seemed, he might have wished for a surfeit of the latter.

"There's been a lot of internet chatter about bombing threats," he continued. "Most of it from groups thought to be on shoestring budgets and with little serious capability beyond lurid threats. But we shouldn't ignore it. Something or someone has stirred them up and it could be linked to Boko Haram. If they're involved, it's not good news."

It certainly wasn't. Boko Haram, as Ruth knew from official briefings and news reports, was an extremist organisation intent on building an Islamic state in northern Nigeria. They had long been suspected of having strong links with other groups in the area, such as Ansaru in Nigeria, al-Shabaab in Somalia, and even with al Qaeda. If a smaller, previously little-known organisation was suddenly in a position to carry out such attacks, it didn't bode well for the region; other like-minded cells might be fired up and join in.

"Are we exposed?" Strictly speaking it was nothing to do with her, but Aston seemed inclined to want to talk about it.

"Potentially, yes. Everybody is focussed on known al Qaeda affiliates, but there are many more out there with similar intentions. Initially, it's more work for us, but there comes a point where the big corporations will cut their losses and pull out."

"Initial reactions?" He looked at them in turn. "I know you've only come together for this assignment, but first thoughts will do for now."

"It looks real enough," said Ruth. "Nancy Hardman's distraught but hanging on. The husband sounds like a selfish do-gooder, off doing his righteous thing and leaving her to bring up the daughter. But until we know more about him, and until we hear what the kidnappers want, we can't judge."

"Quite right—we can't."

The voice came from the doorway. They all turned. The new arrival was a slim, almost ascetic looking figure in an immaculate grey suit and white shirt. Martyn Claas was a new board member. He had joined Cruxys from his base in Amsterdam, bringing with him the power and global financial reach of a conglomerate with its headquarters in the US. He had made it clear from the start that he intended to have a hands-on involvement with the company's operations and his aim was unambiguous: to make Cruxys Solutions a world leader in the security and risk assessment field, and to increase profitability.

Aston retained a neutral expression. He didn't ask Claas to elaborate, but nodded towards a vacant chair and said, "You all know of each other? Good." He glanced at Ruth and Vaslik. "Where were we?"

Vaslik took up the baton. "I think the nanny's part of it. Or dead." He nodded at one of the whiteboards, where Tiggi Sgornik's name had been added to the rapidly growing information on the Hardman family. There were no photos yet but they would come once Ruth downloaded the files from her computer.

"May I ask why?" Claas again.

Vaslik spread his hands on the table surface. "She's the perfect insider. Her belongings have gone from the house, we believe the kidnapper or kidnappers knew how to get in from the back without being seen, and the Hardman woman's missing cell phone battery was found in the nanny's bedroom. She would also be familiar with Hardman's timing at the gym, which seems to have been crucial for her finding the kidnap note."

"Why do you say dead?" Claas's Dutch accent was noticeable but slight, with a faint American intonation.

"Because in my experience, people like her don't survive long. Insiders are bought or coerced, which means they never really fit in.

64

This makes them weak links. Liabilities. If they can be turned once, they can be turned again. Here or New York, it makes no difference." He spoke with conviction, his background one of the reasons he had been taken on by Cruxys.

Claas looked faintly doubtful but said nothing. Aston kept his thoughts to himself, experienced enough to know that things rarely if ever turned out quite the way they first seemed.

"What bothers me," Ruth put in, "is the why and how. Why did Hardman take out a contract with Cruxys? He's a freelance charity worker; you don't get a more unlikely target for kidnapping than that—so the snatch can't have been for ransom."

Aston nodded. "Agreed. And the how?"

"How could he afford it? We're not exactly cheap and the last time I looked we weren't doing discounts. His wife says they don't have private money, so we're currently trying to find out what makes them a target."

Claas waved a hand, cutting in on his fellow board member. "Surely, how our clients fund their contracts with us is hardly your concern, Miss Gonzales." He spoke reasonably but fixed Ruth with a dead-eyed stare that challenged any argument. "As long as they pay, that is all we need to know, don't you think?"

Ruth ignored the look; she was accustomed to having her say and throwing questions into the air like this was a way of getting the thinking process going. All the same, she was puzzled by his apparent opposition. Was profit his sole motive here?

"It's of concern," she said, "if it has some bearing on the kidnap of his daughter. And that's our main consideration at the moment, surely." At his blank expression and the faint flush that came to his cheeks, she added quickly, "I should explain: if he's got dirty money

65

we could be looking at a nest of trouble. And Slik and I could be right in the middle of it. As could Gina Fraser—again."

"Fraser is fine," Claas responded. "I reviewed her file when I arrived here. What happened to her was unforeseeable, and I approved her return to duties. Do you have a problem with that?" The challenge was more obvious this time, his stare unyielding, and Ruth realised she was facing a boardroom bully who didn't like giving way.

She kept her reply calm but firm. "Actually, she's not fully recovered—everybody knows that. What concerns me is that if there's a problem she could be vulnerable." As might the rest of us, she wanted to add, but didn't. If Claas didn't understand that, telling him here and now wasn't going to make him any friendlier towards her.

There was a lengthy silence, and she wondered if she'd overstepped the mark. But Aston intervened by flicking open a folder in front of him. "I asked for a payments summary of the Hardman file. He opened the contract and paid for three years up front, with future premiums to be paid by direct debit through a London bank. All pretty standard stuff."

"So nothing unusual, then," said Claas. He was staring at Ruth like a dog studying a bone he desperately wanted to bite.

"Indeed. Beyond that we don't know where his money comes from." He looked at Ruth. "You might want to check with accounts for a copy of the original contract, see if there's anything in the margins." He was referring to jotting and notations sometimes made by clients when signing up, including phone numbers, bank accounts, solicitors' details and so on. He glanced at Claas, who seemed about to interrupt, and continued firmly, "He also lodged separate funds with us to cover any contingencies, as we ask all our clients to do."

Contingencies. It was Cruxys terminology for the main party of the contract being incapacitated or killed, the lodged funds being sufficient to cover the following year's contract or to be refunded to the contractor's family if not required.

And, *in extremis*, to bury whoever was left.

"We'll have to dig," he continued. "Unless and until she hears from the kidnappers, all we can do is find him, locate people who know the family. If there's anything relevant in his past, it will be there somewhere." He took a slip of paper from the folder and passed it to Vaslik. It held a street address in west London. "The address linked to the charity's phone number."

Vaslik nodded and tucked it away. "I might not have very long to do this."

Claas looked at him. "Please explain?"

"The snatch occurred just over six hours ago. Abductions-for-ransom mostly follow a pattern, from the taking of a valued asset followed by the first contact and demand, to negotiation."

"But you don't know if there is a ransom."

"True. But the note, as vague as it is, points towards some kind of negotiating position: tell your husband. It implies that he will be faced with a demand."

"I see. How quickly then, overall?"

"It could be from a few hours to several days depending on how secure the kidnappers feel about themselves to the strength of their desire to achieve their aims. Beyond that, we're in unknown territory." They all knew what he meant: that not all kidnappings came to a satisfactory conclusion, either through precipitate action on the part of the authorities or panic on the part of the criminals. Both often led to the death of the victim, as did a delayed response to their demands.

And this one was already entering a dangerous phase.

"Well," muttered Claas, "let's hope it does not go on too long." He stood up and walked from the room, leaving behind a leaden silence.

"As quickly as you can, I think," Aston suggested softly, and nodded towards the two researchers, who were waiting for information. "But do it right. Let's get as much background detail as we can and start digging for anything new."

———

Ruth handed her laptop to one of the researchers, to download the contents of the photo frame for the storyboards, then walked up to the admin and accounts department where all the client records were lodged. They had been forewarned by Aston and a folder was sitting on the department supervisor's desk.

"It's a bit thin." The supervisor's name was Margie, who spoke with the gravelly voice of a confirmed smoker. She opened the folder and showed Ruth the original contract, signed by Michael Hardman and countersigned by the then contracts manager, who had since left. The initial payment was by cheque drawn on a bank in Kensington, with the client's address shown as Finchley. The contract agreement was for three years, renewable automatically every twelve months thereafter unless cancelled by the client.

"He believed in thinking ahead," Ruth murmured. "What's the usual sign-up period?"

"Twenty-four months, but it's flexible. If the client wants to make it several years and pays up front, we don't argue. Some of them get posted for long periods to the back of beyond. If they cancel the contract because they no longer need it we make a pro-rata refund."

"Is this complete?" Ruth was looking at a list of five alpha-numerics, all in Greater London. They were the previous postcodes for the Hardmans' addresses.

But Margie dashed her hopes. "It would be if we had anything more to enter. As you can see, they've moved about a bit since the initial contract. That's all we've got." She turned to her monitor and entered the client contract reference. It brought up a record of the Finchley address, with a phone contact number followed by the postcodes on a series of change-of-address panels. The last full address listed was at the house now occupied by Nancy. "The contract began in Finchley, as you can see, but they moved and notified us each time of their new postcode, to keep the records active." She sniffed. "Waste of time if you ask me. No good taking out a Safeguard contract if we don't know where to find the client."

"Well, we knew this time," Ruth said. "Perhaps they didn't get on with their neighbours. You don't keep the addresses, I suppose?"

"Not beyond the first one, which we need for legal purposes. We try to delete old information as a matter of course, but we must have missed these postcodes. Not that they'll be much use; they won't show which house or flat they lived in."

Ruth took out her cell phone and dialled the phone number listed. Out of service.

"We run regular data checks to update the client profile and contact details," Margie added. "But if the client moves away and doesn't tell us, there's not much we can do. This one must have told us about the new addresses but not the contact number. I guess we didn't need it until today."

Ruth decided to have Vaslik check the Finchley address. It was a long shot but maybe they'd get lucky and find somebody who had known the family and could give them some information on Michael Hardman.

TEN

FITNESS PLUS TURNED OUT to be an upgraded, upbeat leisure centre and gym run by a private management company on behalf of the local authority. Constructed of red brick with a Scandinavian-style low pitch roof, it had a car park at the front and side with perhaps a dozen vehicles, and a large banner over the front entrance offering monthly and annual deals on fitness programmes for senior citizens and "early birds."

The aroma of scented air freshener hit Ruth the moment she walked through the entrance, accompanied by the throb of Latin dance music coming through the walls. Zumba, she guessed; she'd tried it once and hated every second.

She walked past a water feature and a booth advertising fitness clothing, and approached the desk alongside a steel security gate equipped with a swipe-card reader.

A young woman receptionist in a white coat was deep in conversation with a muscled youth in a uniform vest and stretch pants. She was leaning back so that he might appreciate her full chest, tantalisingly near-visible through the thin material, but he seemed unimpressed by what was on offer, and more concerned with plucking at a new tattoo on his forearm. It looked like a Smurf but it was hard to tell.

"Can I help?" She flicked a reluctant inner switch and the young hunk moved away gracefully with a vague smile and disappeared down a short corridor, flexing his triceps as he passed another trainer coming out of an office.

"I'd like to take a look around," said Ruth. "I'm thinking of taking out membership."

"No problem. We have inductions twice a week, and the next one is tomorrow. Nine o'clock?" She reached for a pen, then paused as a phone rang in an alcove behind her. "Sorry—excuse me just one second." She turned and disappeared, and Ruth heard her talking to someone about a cancelled booking.

She looked longingly at the security gate. A quick jump and she could be over and gone in a split second. The Barbie doll in the white coat wouldn't even notice.

She came back. "Right, where was I? Oh, yes, all the facilities will be explained then and—"

"I'd rather do it now. Just let me wander. I'll find my way and I won't steal anything, I promise." She held up her Cruxys ID card. It looked sufficiently authoritative at a quick glance to convey the possibility that she could be official and therefore not to be messed with. It worked. The girl straightened up and pressed a button below the desk, and the steel gate swung back with an efficient click.

"Help yourself. I can't leave the desk, otherwise . . ." She shrugged, already looking beyond Ruth to a new arrival.

Ruth thanked her and walked through, taking out her phone as she went. She called up the camera and began taking discreet shots, eyeing the cold lenses of CCTV cameras on the ceiling. She made a mental note to get Aston on the case; gaining access to any footage would take a bit more muscle than she possessed, and the Cruxys operations commander was known to have friends in high places.

She reached a junction in the corridor and looked right. A strong tang of chlorine hung in the air and the sound of running water echoed along the walls. She turned left and walked along another corridor, this one lined down the right-hand side with steel lockers three high and a bank of vending machines stacked with cold drinks and snacks.

She walked straight past, checking out the glass panels in doors on the left. One was to a small interview room, another to a room with a treatment table, and another to the main fitness studio complete with equipment, mats and weights.

The end of the corridor ended in a fire door, so she turned and retraced her steps, stopping level with the last line of lockers and holding her phone to her ear. A camera stared blankly down at her from the junction leading to the front desk or the pool.

Miming a conversation, she studied the bank of lockers. Just as Nancy had described, the key to No 2 was held by a large safety pin, unlike its neighbours which all had orange fobs.

Still talking to an imaginary person, she reached out idly and flipped the door open. Just a locker, empty of cards, threatening or otherwise. And from here, there was no way anybody loitering near the front desk could see who was using them.

But the camera could. She felt a tingle of hope.

She closed the locker and turned to check the doors on the other side. The glass viewing panels revealed little. It was possible, at a stretch, that somebody inside the rooms or the fitness studio could see the lockers. But which one?

She had seen enough.

She dropped the mime act and dialled the office number, asking to be put through to Aston. She walked back past the reception desk, waving at the girl in the white coat, and noting the name of the management company from an information brochure in a rack by the door.

"Aston."

"I need access to some CCTV footage." She explained where it was and the possible significance, and gave him the name of the management company.

"I don't know them personally," he murmured. "But I'm sure I can find somebody who does. Leave it with me."

"Thank you."

"What are your thoughts?" It was one of his more common questions; he liked his investigators to voice their initial reactions to a situation and get them out there for discussion.

"About this place? Could be a member of staff with access to the security footage. All they'd need to do is watch on the days she was in here and they'd soon build up a pattern. But the building is wide open in other ways. If we can see who placed the card in the locker, we've got it nailed."

He grunted, carefully non-committal. Luck like that rarely came along, and they both knew it. He added, "One thing, Ruth; you might be careful of our latest addition to the board. He comes with a lot of investment capital and likes to give the impression of wagging the dog. But in the final analysis he's also following orders. That makes him anxious to achieve results as quickly and as cost-effectively as possible." He was warning her about Martyn Claas.

"You mean not cutting in too heavily to the Safeguard premiums, even though that's the reason they were paid to us?"

"Precisely. Go to any insurance company and you'll find the same argument."

"Who gives him those orders?" Apart from office gossip, she knew next to nothing about most board members, and even less about this latest addition.

"Claas is Dutch, along with nearly half the European board in Amsterdam. But the bigger piece of the cake is American, from a group called Greenville Inc. Between them they pretty much dominate salvage and IT on the Dutch side, and Security, venture capital and Risk Management on the US side. Claas is believed to be building strong links with the US State Department, and is pushing hard for a slice of their market. It was he who approved bringing in American personnel like Vaslik and James Ellworthy, to show that we had the right employment credentials."

Ellworthy, she recalled, was an IT specialist who lived somewhere in the basement surrounded by electronic toys, but she had never met him. It worried her slightly that Slik had any kind of connection with Claas, and she wondered how close it was. She only realised that she'd spoken her thoughts aloud when Aston responded.

"Vaslik doesn't know him. He was recommended along with several other names, but he had to pass an interview panel the same as all employees. He did so on his own merits. Does it bother you?"

"No. I just like to know I can trust whoever's got my back."

"Fair comment. But remember Vaslik's the fish out of water here; he probably feels the same about you."

She switched off the phone and walked back to her car deep in thought about Claas and the people above him. Bloody venture capitalists; modern-day alchemists with their fingers in all the pies.

———

Andy Vaslik liked using London's underground. It bore little comparison to the marble, stained glass and chandeliers of Moscow's famed metro, which he'd experienced, or even the New York subway, which he'd lived and breathed for most of his life. But it was anonymous enough for him to move among people while remaining faceless; one of the crowd, in the background. Most of his fellow travellers, whatever their nationality, were happy to keep to their own space, unthreatening and reserved. He liked that. He felt more in control here than in a car, where eyes on the sidewalks and in other vehicles were drawn towards those fortunate enough to be insulated from the masses and the relentless push and shove of pedestrians.

He emerged onto the street at Lancaster Gate into the grey light of threatening rain, and followed his nose to Queensway. He turned up the bustling shopping area and stopped at a side street containing a handful of smaller shops. He checked the numbers and found the one found by the researchers matching the telephone number given by Nancy Hardman. The property was vacant and sandwiched between a record shop and a travel agency. The front window was heavy with grime and a look of desolation, and plastered on the outside with posters of music events, clubs and missing persons.

He tried the door on the off-chance. Locked tight. The fascia overhead bore the remains of lettering suggesting the premises could have been anything from a topless bar to a laundromat. All he could make out through the glass between the posters and dirt was an empty space with electric cables hanging from curling ceiling tiles and a pile of junk mail and old newspapers growing brown and sun-faded behind the door. Somebody had taped up the letterbox to stop a further accumulation of paper and other detritus.

He went to the record shop next door. It looked as if it had been there since Cole Porter was a boy. A bell pinged as he entered and a youth with an unreasonably long and plaited goatee beard looked up and smiled a greeting.

"How ya doin'? The accent was Australian, friendly.

"The place next door," said Vaslik. "Anybody been there recently?"

"You from the council?"

"No. Just asking." He looked round and saw a box of classical music CDs. Reached across and plucked out one by the Ossipov Balalaika Orchestra. It wasn't a personal favourite but it would serve a purpose. "I'll take this." He placed a twenty on the counter but kept his fingers firmly on the end.

The youth got the message. "No worries. I've been here eighteen months and nobody's used it all that time. What I hear is the owner died and it's in the hands of blood-sucking scumbags in smart suits."

Lawyers, Vaslik figured; the same in any language. "Not even a pop-up?" Vacant stores were sometimes used as a temporary home to charities unable to afford high street rents. They'd come in, do their work, then move on.

"Never a pop-up anything 'cept for rats ... and a piss-hole for drunks."

Vaslik let the note go, took the CD, and left.

ELEVEN

NANCY OBSERVED THE ARRIVAL of the forensics team with feelings of resentment. Two men and a woman in casual street clothes, each carrying a large aluminium briefcase. They filed through the back gate and into the kitchen with courteous nods, but she could see the thoughts behind the eyes, knowing that they were judging her. What mother, they were thinking, goes to a gym and leaves her young daughter in the dubious care of a nanny, while her husband is off somewhere where she can't even get hold of him?

Screw them, she thought; they don't know anything about me or my family. And neither, she decided, does the tall, rod-thin woman with the coffee-coloured skin who followed them minutes later, and proceeded to prowl the house like a tiger. She introduced herself as Gina Fraser and announced that she would stay with Nancy until her daughter was returned. For now she wanted to get a feel for the layout of the house and its surroundings.

"Why?" Nancy didn't want her here any more than the others, and she definitely didn't care for the cool manner with which she was being studied, like a laboratory specimen on a glass plate.

"Because it's my job. It's what I do." Fraser's attitude was short on social skills, with a take-it-or-leave-it tone that precluded idle chat. "I'm here to look after you, to make sure you're safe. To do that I have to know my way around." Her manner softened momentarily as she added, "You need to be here for when Beth gets back. It's my job to see that you are."

"You're a bodyguard?"

"Yes."

"Are you armed?"

"Would that bother you?"

"Yes, of course. Why would you need a gun in my house?"

Fraser shrugged. "To shoot anyone who tries to harm you."

Nancy wasn't sure if she was joking, but felt herself repelled by the idea. "Just like that?"

"No. I'd probably warn them first. Or not." A lift of an eyebrow was the only hint she gave that she might not be serious.

Nancy followed her around the house, watching as she tested windows, checked locks and viewed every aspect from the house of the road, garden and neighbouring properties. It looked casual, but she was certain the woman didn't miss a thing, and began to feel that Fraser, at least, had her best interests at heart, unlike the other people currently burrowing into every aspect of the house, scooping up material, vacuuming the carpets with small, hand-held machines and placing debris she mostly couldn't see in neat plastic bags.

After a while she broke away from Fraser and watched the team, led by a man who had introduced himself as Jakers. A robust looking individual in his fifties, with steel-grey hair and rimless spectacles, he seemed to look right through her. It made her feel uncomfortable and she broke away after a while and watched from a distance.

"Do you have to go through my things?" she demanded more than once, when drawers were opened and cupboards inspected. "Nothing in there has been touched, I can tell you now."

"Won't be long," Jakers responded each time. "We'll be out from under your feet in no time." He might as well have added the words, "if you leave us alone to get on with it." But he didn't.

She stopped in the living room in front of a photo of Beth, all smiles and pink-faced. She felt instantly the eruption of tears coming on and rubbed her eyes before they could spill. Breaking down wouldn't do, not here and now. She had to remain in control and wait for Michael to get here. Then Beth would be returned and everything would go back to normal.

She looked round for her phone, then remembered the American, Vaslik, taking it from the kitchen. She waited until the searchers had moved into the living room, then went through to the kitchen and opened drawers until she found it, lying on top of some tea towels. She had to try Michael's number again, to tell him what was going on. Not having some kind of contact was driving her out of her mind.

A shadow moved and Fraser appeared behind her like a ghost. "What's up?"

"I want to try Michael's phone again."

"It's best you don't," Fraser replied, and eased the phone out of her hands. "You need to stay off the lines in case they call."

"They?" She thought Fraser was talking about her two colleagues.

"The people who took Beth."

Her throat closed tight at the reminder and she felt a momentary panic at not being able to breathe. She swallowed hard to regain control, then said, "How would they? They don't know the numbers."

"You think?" Fraser cocked her head to one side. "They got close enough to take the battery out of your phone. I think they'll have the number of your landline, too."

Nancy backed off, suddenly reminded that whoever had taken Beth had somehow managed to worm their way into every aspect of her life and routine. Fraser was right: they had controlled her phone, so what else had they managed to take over?

She went into her bedroom where the team had just finished searching. Everything had been put back neatly enough, but there were the inevitable signs that nothing was as it had been before, the subtle differences in layout showing that somebody other than herself had been here.

It was a further reminder that her life had changed, and there was nothing she could do about it but wait and put her trust in divine providence.

Not like the woman, Gonzales; a strong woman, assured and forthright, who probably never experienced a moment of doubt. She wouldn't baulk at such events, but would know precisely what to do to fight back.

She found herself almost envying her that strength. But she countered it by thinking that Gonzales didn't have somebody like Michael in her life. Or Beth.

She sat on the bed, feeling utterly alone, wondering what was going to happen … and what kind of catalyst had brought this nightmare onto her and her family.

TWELVE

"What's this for?" Ruth was holding the CD. Vaslik had dropped it in her lap without comment. His clothes were damp with rain and his face gleaming in spite of the car's heater. He appeared not to notice.

They were sitting in Ruth's car a block away from the rear entrance to the Hardman house. The rain was steady, one of those relentless London showers that takes no prisoners and obscures the surrounding scenery like a veil.

"Call it a visitor's gift. It's good for the nerves."

"I don't need my nerves soothed, and if I did I'd play whale music, not the Balalaika." She turned it over and read the blurb. "Still, might make me less suicidal than bloody Snow Patrol. Thank you. Did you come up with anything?"

He described the empty shop. "I think our Mrs. Hardman is hiding something."

"Or she's gullible and believes everything her husband tells her. It happens; people believe what they're happy to hear."

"Wives, you mean?" Vaslik smiled. "I didn't know you were a feminist."

"I'm not. But look at the facts: most husbands have more control in one way or another, and most wives let them. I'm not saying it's the fault of the men or the weakness of the women, it's simply the way it is."

"You think that's the case here?"

"Sort of. But I think Nancy Hardman is an extreme example; she believes utterly in her husband, accepting his absences without question. She's adopted the position of never asking where he goes or what he does: she just accepts it as part of the job he's chosen in life. I don't understand that kind of relationship, but I know it's not uncommon."

"So her part of the bargain is to run the family life, bring up the daughter and act like it's normal? I don't get that."

"It's normal to her. It probably wasn't once, but she's hardly a firebrand; she knows next to nothing about his life before they met and seems happy to go along with what he wants. That's a little weird but I bet she's not the only one."

"Do you want to confront her about it?"

Ruth shrugged. "And say what—that she's a submissive drip who allowed her husband to impose his life on her without question?" She shook her head. "Let me think about it."

"What about the nonexistent charity shop?"

"She might not know about that. It was just an address somebody gave out to get the phone. Doesn't mean they ever went there."

"Or it was cloned."

"Or that. Either way, if the whole thing is a fake, telling her could do more harm than good."

She told him about Fitness Plus and how it wouldn't have taken much to bone up on Nancy Hardman's every movement. "I could get past the desk without trying, but my money's still on the CCTV. If there's anything to see, Aston will get it."

"And in the meantime?"

"We'll go in and check on Fraser and have another swing at the wife. I just don't believe Hardman could go this long without getting in touch with her. Something about this doesn't feel *kushti*."

He lifted his eyebrows. "You speak Romanian?"

"I speak street. Come on."

They left the car and made their way through the rain to the rear gate. They were halfway down the garden path when a figure stepped out from the side of the house near the kitchen door. It was a woman. She had one hand behind her back. The other held a rolled-up newspaper.

Ruth put out her hand to stop Vaslik, who was already moving away to the side, his stance stiff with tension. "Steady—it's Gina."

Fraser looked calm and controlled. She was dressed in boots, jeans and an all-weather top, as if she had just popped out between errands to take in the washing. But Ruth wasn't fooled. The newspaper was a blind; make a wrong move and Gina would toss it in the air to draw the eye while bringing out her other hand from behind her back. The rest would be textbook—and deadly.

Gina saw Ruth and relaxed. "Hi, Ruthie. How are you doing, girl?"

"I'm good, thanks. Have you met Slik?"

Gina nodded and brought her hand to the front. She was holding a small semi-automatic pistol. She flicked her jacket aside and slipped the gun into a holster high on her hip. "No, but I heard about him. You OK, Andrei?"

"Always." Vaslik walked past her without smiling and entered the house.

"Friendly. What's his problem?" Gina commented wryly.

"Hormones, I think." Ruth couldn't do much about Slik's attitude; he'd probably heard about Gina getting shot and was doubting her capabilities to carry out her job effectively. She found herself sharing as little of those doubts. The former bodyguard looked good at a distance, but up close she looked wasted, with dark rings round her eyes and an unnatural gauntness to her cheeks. Given what she had been through, she had good reason.

The gun was something else.

"Are you supposed to be carrying?" Ruth asked her. Cruxys employees were not officially authorised to carry weapons, although in extreme situations where life and limb was threatened, some were known to bend the rules. She wondered what Vaslik felt about that, having come from a gun culture where going armed was a factor of daily life for those involved in law enforcement and security.

"They said it was OK, considering."

Ruth didn't believe her, but let it pass. In Gina's place she'd have been carrying a Heckler & Koch MP5 switched to full auto. "How's the lady of the house?"

"Not great. She doesn't like me being here and doesn't hide it. I can't make out whether she's a latent racist or if it's a territorial thing."

"She's hard work, I agree. But give her the benefit of the doubt; she's just had her kid snatched and her life's gone belly up. Any calls or visitors?"

"None. The team did their bit and left. I don't think they found much. Jakers was getting truly pissed because she wouldn't leave them alone for two minutes, always hovering and asking what they were doing."

Bill Jakers was a former Met Police Scene of Crime officer in charge of the support team who ran forensics and provided equipment and logistics for case officers like her and Vaslik. He normally had the patience of a saint but clearly Nancy hovering over his shoulder had tested it to the full.

"I think he was hoping I'd put her in cuffs and lock her in the bathroom. It was tempting, but I resisted." She hesitated, then said, "Jakers found a small spot of blood in the nanny's room, on the doorframe. He said to mention it."

"Significant?" In other words, was it fresh.

"Fairly. Just a spot. Could have been nothing."

Ruth absorbed the information. It might prove that the snatch had happened here, rather than on the street. If there had been a struggle, such as the nanny protecting her charge, then she'd have been the first obstacle down. Or it could have been coincidence.

"Thanks, Gina." She was no further forward, save that it might knock on the head any idea of the nanny being involved. But if she wasn't, where was she? Would they have bothered taking an adult with them? It increased the risk of exposure considerably, having a hostile along who could kick off at any moment.

She'd been studying Gina while she was talking, her eyes in particular. It wasn't her job to run field assessments of other staff members, least of all one who'd been injured in the line of duty; but she was trying to figure out how much Gina had changed since the last time they had met. Self-confidence was a must for her job, but it could easily vanish after the kind of hot contact she had experienced. She could only judge by appearances, but in spite of her colour and thinness, she had to admit that Gina looked good and ready to go. She'd certainly come out here double-quick and ready to intercept them, so she had lost none of her alertness.

"Where's the camera?" She meant the one that had spotted their approach.

Gina nodded towards the rear gate. "There's a minicam covering the lane and others on the sides and front. I saw you coming but the rain killed some of the detail." She brushed moisture off her face. "Which reminds me, can we get inside? I don't want to push my luck and catch pneumonia."

They walked inside, Gina turning to scan the rear garden before following and closing the door. It was done smoothly and Ruth decided to try and get Vaslik on-side about her. Just because he had high standards and some women didn't seem to figure, it wasn't fair riding her because she'd got herself shot.

The kitchen had been turned into an observation room. Two monitors sat on the work surface, each with a split screen linked to separate cameras. The pictures were good apart from the rain, but clear enough to give adequate warning of an intruder.

Nancy was waiting for them in the living room, body as tight as a bow-string. She stepped forward to greet Ruth, face open to receive news. She looked fragile, as if the intervening hours since they had last spoken were draining her of vitality.

"Have you found anything?"

"Not yet." Ruth glanced at Vaslik but he gave a minute shake of his head. She still hadn't decided whether to tell her about the deserted shop in Queensway; finding out that her husband's supposed charity base was empty might be enough to undermine her world even further. At worst it would prove nothing except that the charity was a fake.

And that her husband had lied to her.

THIRTEEN

"I'm sorry to do this. It must seem pointless but I want to go over a few things with you." Ruth took the armchair while Vaslik stood by the front window. Gina was watching the CCTV monitors in between patrolling the house, automatically trying door and window handles and noting any movement outside.

"What sort of things?" Nancy was on the settee clutching Beth's teddy, Homesick, against her tummy. Ruth was shocked by how fragile she looked, and asked if she should call a doctor. But Nancy wouldn't hear of it.

"I'm fine. Just tired, that's all. What do you want to know?"

"I'm trying to understand what the link is between your husband and why Beth would have been taken. There's clearly a connection and we need to isolate that if we stand any chance of finding out who took her and why."

Nancy shook her head, her eyes strained with exhaustion, and Ruth wondered if some sleeping tablets would work. She might speak to the tame doctor Cruxys kept on call. "But why should it involve Michael? It could be anything or nothing. These things are so random, aren't they?"

Ruth went over the words on the card again. "I've seen kidnap notes before, Nancy. Some in live situations, lots of real examples used in training. They all follow a similar format and carry the same message: it's usually *We've taken someone of value to you* and *Don't tell the authorities.* If not immediately, there's usually a follow-on shortly afterwards saying what they want in return."

"Isn't that what this one says—not to tell the police?"

"Yes. But that's not all. It tells you that they've taken your daughter, but there's no demand. No phone calls, no follow-on communication, nothing. However, there is one difference: they tell you to tell your husband. Believe me, that's significant." She paused to let that sink in, although by the way Nancy's eyes were fluttering, she wasn't certain it was making much headway.

"The punctuation is very specific," she continued. "It says *Do NOT call the police. DO tell your husband.* Two seemingly separate statements but meaning one thing: they want Michael to know what's happened. That's so pointed it has to be for a reason, don't you think?"

There was no response, merely a drained look of utter incomprehension.

Vaslik came and sat down alongside Nancy. She flinched but didn't move.

"Whoever wrote that note," he said softly, "wants your husband to know. But why? He's hardly ever here and you handle all the household finances and stuff, don't you?"

She nodded, apparently beyond being curious about how he would know that.

"So if it's not money they're after, what could Michael give them that you couldn't?"

"He's right," Ruth added. "The lack of explanation or demand means they're giving you time to contact him. But why?"

"I don't know!" The words were squeezed out with a high keening sound, and Ruth felt the hairs on the back of her neck bristle. She leaned forward and took Nancy's hands in hers. It was like holding onto two steel rods. She looked into her eyes with as much intensity as she could muster, waiting for her to calm down. The last thing they needed right now was for this woman to suffer a breakdown.

"It's all right, Nancy," she said firmly. "We're going to find Beth. But to do that we need to understand what could have brought this thing on. Why they took her."

Nancy relaxed by degrees, demonstrated by a slow softening of her bodyline. Her eyes became more focussed and her shoulders lost their tension. Instead, silent tears flowed down her face. "I'm sorry ... I just want Michael and Beth to come home." She found a handkerchief and wiped her eyes, slowly regaining control before saying, "Tell me what you want to know."

"I want you to try and remember which agencies your husband has worked for—and where. It doesn't have to be the last one; we checked the number you gave me but there's no reply. They could be out in the field somewhere. We'll keep trying. In the meantime it would help if you could recall any other names or details."

For a moment Nancy didn't reply, and Ruth wondered if she had pushed her too far. Then the woman stood up and walked out of the room towards the front of the house.

Ruth looked at Vaslik, who shrugged and made a motion for her to wait. Gina was out in the hallway and would keep an eye on her.

Five minutes later, Nancy returned. She was carrying a small address book. She dropped it on the coffee table. "I'd almost forgotten about this," she murmured. "It's Michael's. He didn't use it much. One day he sat down and said he wanted to make a list of the agencies he might work for and the places he wanted to go. He said it was a kind of wish list."

"Did you help him?"

Nancy nodded and gave a wan smile. "He didn't want me to, but I needed to be involved, to be a part of his work. It was important to me that we share it. In the end he let me help."

Ruth opened the address book. It was leather-backed, with pages for the recording of basic information such as phone, address and email, and a short space after each contact for brief notes.

It was like looking at a UN list of aid organisations, with the big names first, such as Oxfam, Médecins Sans Frontières, and Save the Children, followed by many names Ruth had either only vaguely or never heard of before.

"I wasn't much help, really," Nancy confessed. "I could only think of the obvious names like the ones you hear about in the news."

"I'd be the same," Ruth agreed, flicking through the pages. "I've never heard of most of these. How did you find them?"

"Michael researched them at the library, although I think he already knew about a lot of them." She looked sheepish. "I'm afraid you'll think we're Luddites—we don't have a computer. I guess that makes us really unusual, doesn't it?"

Ruth didn't say anything. Checking the household computer had been on her list of things to do, but that was clearly not an option. She wanted to ask why, but Vaslik beat her to it.

"You don't like technology?" he said. He sounded shocked.

"Michael doesn't trust it," Nancy explained. "He prefers to use the library if he needs to access the Internet." She shrugged. "We get by. I don't need one apart from at work so it's never been a problem, but I suppose Beth will want one someday—" She stopped suddenly, realising what she was saying, and looked down at the teddy.

"She will," said Ruth firmly. She pointed at the book where some of the names listed had ticks against them. "What do the ticks mean?"

"I put them there. I got into the habit whenever Michael went away of ticking off the name of the agency he was working for." She looked a little wistful and even guilty. It became clear why. "He would rarely remember to tell me who the latest assignment was for, so I decided to keep track myself. But after a while I realised it was pointless."

"Why?"

"Because Michael does his own thing. He changes his mind at the last minute. He says it's because he feels different priorities— places where he's needed more and where he can do the most good."

Sounds a regular saint, Ruth thought drily. "Didn't he realise that was hard for you, disappearing like that without a word?"

"Sort of. But it made no difference. He's so committed … it took over his life. Our lives." She twisted her fingers together. "I rang a couple of agencies once when I needed to get in touch with him. Beth was really unwell and I was panicking because nothing I did seemed to do any good."

"What happened?"

"I was told he wasn't working for them. At first I was sure I'd got the numbers wrong. Then one of them said he'd failed to turn up as planned, and called to let them know. I found out when he came back that he'd switched agencies to help someone out." She shrugged at the memory, pushing it into a deep recess.

"What did he say?"

"He wasn't very pleased. He accused me of checking up on him. So I stopped." She looked like a little lost girl who'd been caught out with her hand in the biscuit box.

Ruth slipped the address book in her pocket, wondering if there was any significance in what Nancy had told her. Probably not. The man was an idealist and, by the sounds of it, as selfish as hell. But the list of agencies might bear studying later. Whether it would turn up any ideas was doubtful but right now it was all they had.

"There's one other thing," she said. "Back at the beginning, you didn't seem to know much about the Safeguard contract, other than having to ring a number and give a reference code if something bad happened."

"Code Red, yes. You must think I'm a helpless woman." She looked Ruth in the eye and said, "You're probably right. All I knew was what Michael told me: if anything happened, ring the number."

And that was good enough for you?"

"Of course. Why wouldn't it be?"

Ruth felt like telling her she wasn't a doormat, that was why. Instead she changed tack. "Earlier you agreed that all the household finances and official dealings are in your name."

"Because Michael's away so much, yes. So?"

"Where is your bank account held?"

"In Edgware. I've had one there for years and never got round to changing it."

"And Michael?"

"We use my account for everything."

"So he doesn't have one?"

"I—That's right." She paused as if realising for the first time how odd that might seem. "It's a little unusual, I suppose, but that's the way we do things."

"How does he support himself while he's away? Do you send him money?"

Nancy's face went stiff at Ruth's tone and the intimate line of questions. She blinked repeatedly. "Why are you so interested in bank accounts? What does it have to do with my daughter's disappearance? How will it help Beth?"

"That's what we need to find out, Nancy. If your husband has money—even if it's money you don't know about but somebody else does—that could be what these people are after. Ransom, pure and simple."

Nancy swallowed. When she spoke, her voice was hesitant. "Michael never says much about when he's out in the field. And I've never asked. I know that might seem strange to you, but he takes care of all that—it's how we are. I think it can sometimes get too much for him, all the misery and tragedy, so I let him deal with it in his own way. What makes you think he has an account I don't know about?"

"Because we know you didn't pay for the Safeguard contract."

No reaction.

"There's really only one other person who could have done, isn't there?"

There was a lengthy silence as Nancy absorbed the implication of what Ruth was saying. The only sounds were the ticking of the immersion heater, the drone of a car moving along the road outside and the shrill squeak of a child laughing in a neighbouring garden. "I don't follow," Nancy said. She had jumped at the child's laughter, no doubt sharply reminded of Beth, and was looking alarmed, her eye-blink rate increasing rapidly.

"You never wondered about it? Where the money came from? The policy isn't cheap."

"No, I-I never thought about it until now. Michael must have mentioned it before, I guess, but…' She shook her head as if it might help process the information. "How did he pay for it?"

"By cheque through a bank account in Kensington. The renewals will be paid out of the same account."

"Kensington?" She blinked rapidly. "But how can that be? There must be a mistake. We don't have an account there. It's in Edgware— I told you."

"Did he have an account when you first met?" Vaslik asked.

"I don't know. I suppose so, for getting paid and stuff. It wasn't something we talked about."

Ruth felt a brush of impatience. Nancy was, intentionally or not, giving them the run-around. One minute angry and defensive, the next playing the helpless woman. Yet the latter role didn't equate with her handling all the household finances and paperwork, or even her accounts job. If she was organised to cope with officialdom in all its forms, keeping track of another bank account should have been a piece of cake.

Or was it another pointer to her husband not telling her everything?

FOURTEEN

"I NEED AN HOUR of down-time," Ruth told Vaslik. After the session with Nancy she was feeling drained. Life was a lot easier dealing with suspects; at least you could get heavy with them with some justification. But grieving mothers with daughters who'd gone missing and whose husbands turned out to be something of a mystery were altogether different.

In spite of them trying different lines of questioning, Nancy had continued to maintain that she knew nothing about any Kensington bank account, even agreeing that it was probably a remnant of Michael's previous life. But Ruth sensed that she was being deliberately vague. If so it could be simply out of embarrassment at not knowing something key about her husband's financial affairs, or that she was in denial. In the end she decided not to push it. There had to be another way of getting some answers.

While talking to Nancy a question had occurred to her; something that needed to be dealt with by her alone. She handed Vaslik the note she'd made of Hardman's Finchley address. "Could you check on this place while I'm out? See if anybody remembers them. They left a while back but there might still be somebody around who remembers them."

She was relieved that they were able to split the tasks between them; trying to check out all the details together would take too long. At least this way they could spread the load.

"No problem," he said easily. "Call if you need me."

———

Ruth's parents lived in a neat maisonette near Gerrard's Cross. It was actually Denham but they liked to think that they rubbed shoulders with the wealthier neighbours up the road. You could still hear the twin traffic flows on the M40 and M25, Ruth always reminded them, but they claimed she was deluded. It was a harmless pretence on their part, and she played along with it willingly.

She visited them whenever she could, which was less than they wanted. Her father had retired after twenty-five years with the Met Police and a further ten years as a corporate security advisor. He now played regular golf—badly—and the two of them danced more than adequately with a local ballroom class.

On the way, she picked up the CD Vaslik had given her and slipped it into the player. The music was cheerful, upbeat and different, and she switched it off after ten minutes. Maybe she'd get him some English folk music in retaliation.

"Nail down the silver," her father said as she stepped through the front door. It was his usual greeting followed by a hug. He still had the build of the rugby player he had once been but was showing signs, she noted, of thinning hair and liver spots.

Ruth's mother, ten years younger and slim, rolled her eyes at him and gave Ruth a kiss and a long squeeze, then went to make tea.

"What's up?" her father queried, walking through to the living room.

"Does there have to be anything up?" she replied, then gave in when he looked at her with raised eyebrows. He could read her and most other people like a book. "Sorry, dad, but I need to run something by you. Do you have time?"

He smiled and sat back. "Always got time for you, Ruthie. You still with that bunch of corporate mercenaries?" It was the one piece of grit between them, partly professional disapproval on his part, the other part concern for her safety. It had been just the same when she joined the MOD Police, although the differences between their two policing jobs were less marked. The question also signalled his continued interest in what went on in the world, especially where crimes and trouble were concerned. And he looked on Cruxys as a connection to both.

She told him about the kidnap and the events that had followed, and the brick wall they had encountered with Michael Hardman's whereabouts. While she was talking, her mother joined them, pouring tea and offering biscuits.

"Sounds a bit rum," her father agreed mildly. "You'd think he'd have left some better contact details for his wife at least. Mind you, anybody takes out a Safeguard contract with your lot has got to be a bit shy of a good, normal life, haven't they?"

"Jim," his wife cautioned gently. They both knew from Ruth that Safeguard contracts were taken out by executives and others working in "difficult" regions of the world. "He was doing the right thing, in case he got ... you know."

He pulled a face but didn't argue. Instead he reached over to a side table and picked up a small black diary. He riffled through the pages, then stood up. "Be back in a minute."

"He's still got the little black book, then," said Ruth. It was something she'd been counting on. Her father's list of useful contacts had been as legendary in the family as it was among his police colleagues, and was a habit he'd obviously found impossible to break. Many of the names listed were probably long gone by now, but she knew he tried to keep them up to date. It was his way of keeping in touch with his past.

Ruth's mother nodded. "It's got more names in more businesses than 192," she murmured. "I bet you he comes back with someone to talk to."

Five minutes later she was proved right. They heard the ting of the phone being replaced in the hall, and her husband walked back in and handed Ruth a slip of paper.

"George Paperas," he said. "He knows more about charity organisations than any man walking. He's worked with the best, including the UN, and still gets called in for advice on disaster response. He knows everybody in the field of aid relief. If anybody can help it'll be him. Buy him a pint and he'll write you a book on it." He looked at her with a proud smile. "With a kiddie out there missing, I'm guessing you'll want to see him straight away. He's waiting to hear from you. He's a hop and spit from your offices, so he'll be easy to call in if needed."

Ruth stood up and gave him a squeeze, then did the same with her mother. "Sorry about this, mum. Dad's right—it's already been several hours and we need to keep on top of it."

Her father stopped her as she opened the front door. He looked serious. "I know they said no police, Ruthie, but you know they'll have to be brought on board sooner or later. You can't not tell them; when it gets out, they, the Home Office and the media will crucify the lot of you for keeping it quiet. Especially if it turns bad."

She nodded, the reminder giving her a sick feeling in her stomach. "I know, dad. But it's not my call."

She left them standing at the door and drove back into London, calling Paperas on the way and setting up a meeting at a pub near where he worked as a charities consultant. Then she tried Vaslik's number. The signal kept dropping out. She called Gina for an update.

"All quiet," Gina replied softly. "No calls, no visitors. Nancy's upstairs." She hesitated then said, "I gave her one of my sleeping pills."

"What?"

"I know—I shouldn't have. But she was pretty pissed about all the questions. I told her it was standard procedure, but she looked like she was about to freak out with exhaustion. I figured it might help if she got her head down for a bit."

"All right." Ruth saw the sense in what Gina had done. But it wasn't a clever move if anything went wrong and it turned out the person protecting her had shared prescription drugs with her, no matter what the reason. "But no more pills, right? We'll call in professional help if we have to."

"Right. Sorry."

"What about you—how are you feeling?" The idea that Gina was carrying sleeping pills and might be relying on them to combat the trauma of the shooting kicking back in was a worry. It was another sign that she still wasn't fully fit and therefore in no real state to be looking after the mother of a kidnap victim, let alone carrying a weapon.

"I'm fine. I'm not using the pills, if that's what's worrying you. I just had some with me."

"Fair enough." She checked her watch. Time was trickling by. "Could you call Slik for me?" She gave Gina the name of the pub where she was meeting Paperas and said, "Get him to meet me there."

———

Andy Vaslik exited East Finchley underground and turned north, pausing to check the map on his phone for the location of the Hardman's original address. He walked the length of the street, his target number 24. But instead of a house he found a flower shop nestling alongside a restaurant, a pizza shop and a drug store, all with apartments overhead. The buildings were of red brick, with dormer windows looking out over the road, and the surroundings were neat, unassuming and suburban. The people here were not overtly rich, he guessed, but prosperous enough and proud of their homes. A good sign, since they would notice and remember more about their neighbours than most. Anybody unusual would stand out.

He walked round the block, checking for rear access behind the shops. There were doors, but none that looked like openings onto individual apartments. He returned to the front and entered the florist. A woman in a nylon coat and gloves was trimming the stems of some red roses, and turned to greet him, brushing away a fringe above her eyes.

"Hi. Can I help you?"

"I hope so, but I may have the wrong address." He showed her the slip of paper with the Hardman's address and phone number, and explained that he was trying to trace the family for a firm of solicitors. "It's a bequest situation," he added.

The woman looked puzzled. "I think your information's incorrect," she said. "All the flats upstairs belong to the shops. I've been here five years and there's never been anyone else here. What was the name again?"

"Hardman. Nancy and Michael. They had a small daughter, Beth."

The woman looked apologetically blank. "Like I said, there must be a mistake. The newest tenants here are the family running the Mahal restaurant next door—and they've been here three years." She went on to explain that the turnover in the area was low, which made the movement of neighbours easy to track. "We get to know each other quite well around here; it's like a small village. The name doesn't ring a bell, I'm afraid."

Vaslik thanked her and stepped outside. His phone was buzzing. It was Gina, with directions to a pub close to Piccadilly where Ruth was meeting a contact.

"On my way," he said, and disconnected.

FIFTEEN

GEORGE PAPERAS WAS IN his late sixties, deeply tanned and full of vigour, one of life's doers. He bustled into the pub from the direction of upper Mayfair, greeted the barman like an old friend and ordered drinks as he made his way over to join Ruth at a corner table.

"It has to be you," he said cheerfully. "I can see the likeness to your parents." He tactfully refrained, Ruth noted, from saying which of her parents she resembled most. "I've ordered gin and tonics—I hope you don't mind. It's nearly that time of day and I'm sure we both deserve it. How can I help?"

She thanked him for coming and they talked small talk until the drinks arrived, then clinked glasses. Ruth was hoping Slik would be here but she decided to go ahead and find out what she could from this man. She wanted to get the blunt question out of the way first. If the answer was a yes, it would save a lot of talk.

"Have you ever heard of a charity field worker named Michael Hardman?"

Paperas thought about it, then shook his head. "He doesn't sound familiar. Why?"

"We're trying to contact him. His daughter's gone missing."

He lifted an eyebrow and asked the obvious question. "Has he gone missing with her?"

"We thought of that, but there are ... circumstances that indicate it's unlikely. He's somewhere in Africa, his wife thinks, and has been for a while, working for a small group thought to have had a temporary base in west London. We can't confirm that and we don't know the name of the agency ... and his cell phone is out of range."

"Lord. You've got yourselves a problem, then. There are vast areas in Africa where you can't get a signal unless you have the latest in satellite technology. And there aren't many charities who can run to those, especially the very small groups."

She laid out the leather-bound book Nancy had given her containing the list of charities the couple had compiled, and explained what it was, including the ticks against some of the names. Paperas jumped on it immediately.

"I've seen lists like this before," he said. "It's a wish list for people wanting to get into aid agency work. They usually begin with the big ones—Oxfam and so on—then work their way down until they find someone prepared to give them a chance."

"Surely all agencies are crying out for help, even the big ones."

"It depends what the volunteers are after. There are lots of young people with ideals—and some of them with money—who see the only valid charity work as out in the field, roughing it, to be brutally honest. But most agencies like them to put in some basic grunt jobs and training first before committing them to field work."

"Why? Help is help, surely?"

"It is if it doesn't slow down the aid effort. Even enthusiastic idealists need to know how to go about it. They have to be trained in procedure, local culture, logistics, health and safety—all manner of things you wouldn't believe. Interacting with local officials is hugely important, as is understanding who you're trying to help and what their sensitivities are. A lot of aid effort portrayed in the media looks as though it's on the hoof and consists of little more than dolling out food, water and ground sheets to starving victims of famine, floods, disease and warfare. People who rush in and don't observe the rules are of no use if they fall victim to disease themselves. It happens, of course, but among the reputable organisations there's a logistical network to ensure that it's rare. Unless aid workers understand what the particular charity wants to accomplish, they're little more than an additional burden. Who did he work with?"

"That's the problem—we don't know." Ruth explained about his wife's blank spot regarding her husband's work and movements. "I think he's tried numerous agencies, more on the hoof than anything organised."

"Really?" He looked surprised. "He sounds like a pain in the arse to me. You can't have people turning up in the field unannounced; the local governors and officials don't like it." He flicked through the pages of the book, then dropped it on the table. "I know many of these, but there are names I've never heard of—and I know more than most people. Some of them are probably two-man bands with high hopes and a bit of money from charitable collections, who think they can simply go out to wherever they like and all will be well. I'm afraid it's not that easy. A lot of them get into trouble and are forced to come back with their tails between their legs. And that doesn't help anybody." He took a gulp of his drink. "Does he have private money?"

Ruth was cautious answering. "Not as far as we know. Why do you ask?"

"I'm wondering why he moved around so much. Most aid workers like to find a niche and stick with it. Chopping and changing really doesn't happen that much. Charity workers like to change direction and face new challenges like anyone else, but too much movement can indicate a lack of staying power. Some of the people I know have been in the same organisations for years. They do it because they feel a passion for the work and the people they help. But there are a few cruisers."

"Cruisers?"

"The ones who don't stick. They do a bit then move on. They're not exactly unreliable, but they can signal a break in continuity. Charities are like commercial organisations; they like to know the workforce is going to be there in the morning when needed." He nodded at the book. "And the names I know on that list with a tick against them are all very small. One person dropping out midway would floor them completely; they can't function if that happens."

"I see." She went to put the book away but he stopped her. "Tell you what I can do. "Let me contact the ones I know and see what I can find out. It's a long shot, but the best I can do. I'll ring you if I find anything."

She nodded gratefully. "Thanks, George." She waited while he made notes of the names he knew, then took back the book. Paperas stood up and, glancing at his watch, said goodbye and that he'd be in touch.

———

When there was still no sign of Vaslik after ten minutes, she tried his phone. It was engaged. She decided to make her way back to the Hardman house. When she emerged from the pub she was surprised to see Vaslik waiting for her across the street. He made no move to join her but gave a subtle signal for her to follow but stay back, before setting off along the pavement towards Piccadilly.

She did so, wondering what he was doing. A few minutes later she caught up with him in the Burlington Arcade, where he was waiting by a men's shoe shop.

"What's going on, Slik? Why didn't you come in?"

He ignored the question. "The guy you were with; was he old-ish, tanned, walks like his feet are on fire?"

"Yes. His name's George Paperas. He's a charity consultant. Why?"

"As I came down the street, two guys were waiting, one on each side. When your man came out they immediately latched onto him—one in front, the other further back. I wouldn't have thought much of it, except I recognised one of the tails."

Ruth felt a flutter of disquiet. "Who was he?"

"The last time I saw him was at the DHS Glynco training facility in Georgia. A guy who knew him from law school pointed him out. He said he must have left law and moved up in the world."

"Good for him. Why would Homeland Security be interested in George Paperas?"

He shrugged. "That's just it: he's not Homeland."

"So what is he?"

"He's CIA."

SIXTEEN

"THERE'S SOMETHING NOT RIGHT about the Hardmans story," said Vaslik, as they walked towards where Ruth had left her car. First they'd checked to make sure they weren't being followed. It had entailed splitting up and circling the block, but once they were certain they were clean, they met up again.

He told her what he'd found at the flower shop in Finchley. "The owner seemed pretty certain of her facts. If she's right, it means Hardman was never anywhere near the place."

"Damn," Ruth muttered. "I'm getting more and more confused." She was also getting tired of Nancy Hardman's economy with facts. It surely wasn't that difficult to remember where you had lived ... unless you were being deliberately evasive. But why would she be? And why would the Central Intelligence Agency be following George Paperas?

"Is there any way we can check," she asked, "about your CIA man?"

He gave her a sideways look. "You can't just ring them and ask. It could be a coincidence—they might have had him in their sights for unrelated reasons. And they never explain. What line of work is he in?"

She told him what she knew about George's background, and he nodded. "That's it, then. Guys like him have a lot of expertise and the CIA isn't ashamed to ask for their help when they need it. If he knows people and he's got the ear of the UN, he'll have access to a lot of information the CIA doesn't have." He frowned. "Not that I think anybody in the charity field would want to be seen dead talking to them."

As soon as they arrived back at the Hardman house, Ruth pulled Nancy to one side and said, "Tell me about Finchley."

"Tell you what?" Nancy looked puzzled.

"It was a previous address. We got it off the Safeguard contract file."

"I never said *I* lived there," Nancy protested. "It was where Michael was living when we first met. I was in Edgware. He shared a flat with a friend and didn't want us to move in together." She smiled. "He felt it wasn't right to start off our life together that way. He's old-fashioned like that, which was another thing I liked about him."

"Did you ever see this place?"

A slight hesitation. "Well, no. I mean, he said it wouldn't be right, so I went along with it. We used to meet at my place. But after a few months we decided to share an apartment he'd found in Harrow."

"Wow," Ruth murmured in admiration. "A few months? You must have taken a lot of cold showers."

Nancy blushed at the comment and plucked at a piece of stray cotton on her sleeve. "Yes, it was tough—especially the not ... *being* together, if you know what I mean."

"No sex. I get it."

"When we did move in together, he said something which I thought was really sweet. He said us being a couple finally made him feel whole—and gave him a sense of history. Then Beth came along and we were three." Her eyes glistened at the memory and she grabbed for a handkerchief.

Ruth stared at her and wondered with a tinge of guilt whether Nancy was cosmically dumb or genuinely sweet. Then she realised that there was something she'd just said that plucked at the corner of her mind, but it wouldn't become clear.

"So what happened with Finchley?"

"I think he continued paying some rent on that for a while so as not to let his friend down."

"Do you know the name of this friend?"

"No. Sorry. I never met him. Michael said they were at college together. I gather he was having a hard time."

"I don't suppose you know which college?" She already knew the answer to that one, but had to ask.

Nancy looked sheepish. "No. If he told me I forgot. Why—what's the problem?"

"Nothing. Crossed wires, that's all." Damn, she thought. Another puzzle. Why would Hardman tell his wife he'd kept up an address in Finchley when there wasn't one? Even if he'd had a genuine place in the area, why lie about it? One thing was certain: wherever the apartment was, it certainly hadn't been above any flower shop.

Unless the "friend" had been a woman.

Nancy was still in sugar-sweet memory mode. "It was when we were in Harrow that Michael began, as he said, to build his life," she said quietly, adding, "*our*" life. He'd given up working in the city shortly before we met and had begun working with charities. Once we were together he started with the list and went on from there. It was like a door had opened into the real world, he said. The start of a whole new life."

"Lovely," Ruth said, and wondered if the holes in that story were genuine, or a product of her own suspicious mind. Was the man for real? Nancy was no slouch in the looks department, yet Michael had resisted moving in with her for months. Then he'd started doing charity work. By any standards, sainthood was just a matter of time.

She went in search of Slik, who was out checking the rear lane, and gave him a run-through of the conversation. It gave her a chance to vent in safety.

He seemed amused by her scepticism. "You should visit the States; there are lots of guys who don't believe in cohabiting before marriage. What's wrong with that?"

She gave him an icy look, suspecting that he was winding her up. "What's wrong? I'll tell you what's wrong, Slik: this is London, not some small-college town along the bible belt where touching below the chin is a mortal sin. Sex before marriage here is a way of life and I don't believe for a second the crap about him paying rent just to help out a friend—unless the he was a she. As for starting their life together and making him feel whole—Yuk! Give me strength."

Vaslik nodded. "I agree. But sugar-sweet is not a criminal offence."

"You agree with me?" It surprised her. "Since when?"

"Since a while back. As I said earlier, there's something a bit screwy about this whole set-up. Trouble is, I doubt we'll ever find out where he was living when he met her. In fact I can't help thinking it was almost deliberate—as if he chose her because of the kind of person she is."

"Really? I think she comes across as gullible, but she's no kid; we're not talking about a grown man taking advantage of a school girl."

"Maybe not. Anyway, I don't think the Finchley place matters any more. Everything he did was from there onwards. The rest is a blank."

They toured the block, checking cars and faces, talking out the kinks in what they knew so far. A lot of it made no real sense, but there wasn't much they could do until the reasons for Beth's kidnap and the kidnappers' interest in Michael Hardman became clear.

"Do you have family?" Vaslik asked, as they turned a corner.

"Sure. Two parents, five aunts, three uncles and a few cousins."

"I didn't mean that kind."

"I know." She smiled. "You meant husbands, boyfriends or significant others."

"Yes."

"I'm not married and my last significant other bailed out three months ago. That do you?"

"Sorry. I didn't mean to pry. Did he get promotion?"

"She."

He didn't miss a beat. "Same question, switch gender." He was smiling now, but she wasn't sure whether he was teasing her or simply pleased with himself at having wormed out an answer.

"She went to Australia on a police exchange program. I'm not sure if she's coming back, though."

She and Lisa had begun drifting apart, their lives on divergent courses until a row had propelled Lisa into applying for the exchange post. It had suited them both at the time, providing a seamless and easy cut-off to their three year relationship. Ruth had missed her almost immediately, and was still unsettled by the constant reminders of her and the distance between them.

She wasn't sure if Lisa felt the same way; only time would tell or until one of them made the first move.

Vaslik nodded but didn't say anything.

She stopped walking. "Is that it? You ask but don't give?"

He turned and waited for her to catch up, staring at the sky. "I'm divorced, no kids, no pets. Cops and marriage don't always go together, DHS even less so. Since we split I've been too busy moving around and haven't had time to develop a significant anything."

"You should," she advised him, detecting a glimmer of something softer in his outer demeanour. It made him seem suddenly less faceless. "The ice-man image really doesn't suit you."

They arrived back at the rear of the house and found Gina waiting at the back door.

Vaslik nodded and walked past to check the front of the house and the street.

"Anything?" said Ruth. There was no sign of Nancy and the building was silent. She thought Gina looked brighter, as if she'd got a second wind. Or maybe she'd taken some of her happy pills.

"Nothing. No mail, just a charity bag drop. I thought that was ironic, considering. You?"

"Lots of questions, not many answers."

"It's still day one." The kitchen clock showed 6:30 and Ruth wondered where the time had gone. She was beginning to feel drained. But Gina was right; they were still at the beginning. The kidnappers were probably waiting to see who showed up first—the cops or Michael Hardman.

She asked Gina if she had slept.

"Cat-napped." She blinked as she said it, instantly conscious of the similarity in wording and their reasons for being here. "Sorry."

Ruth waved it away. It was too easy to get paranoid about what was said in these situations in a rush of over-sensitivity for those left behind. "Don't worry. I once baby-sat a senior banker who'd received death threats; a note said he was going to be chopped into minced-meat for refusing a loan. I mentioned at one point without thinking that I could kill for a burger; he wasn't impressed."

Gina turned her head towards the front of the house. "How's the all-American boy? Has he come onto you yet?"

"I'm not his type. You?"

"I don't think he trusts me enough for that. The feeling's mutual, come to that."

"Why?" She felt disloyal talking about a colleague like this, but her interest was piqued. Damaged or not, Gina Fraser was still a cop by instinct and training. Her job entailed studying people and making assessments based on behaviour, attitude and her own instincts.

"Not sure. There's something about him. I've met a lot of American cops and quite a few of their Secret Service people. Vaslik feels more spook than cop." She checked the camera monitors then said, "Or maybe it's post-traumatic shock kicking in and making me suspicious of everybody around me—even the friendlies."

Ruth admired her honesty. "A spook? How's that, then?"

"I don't know … he's very self-contained, as if he doesn't really fit—or maybe doesn't want to. Like he's rising above everything and playing a part. Their Secret Service agents are like that: totally focussed on the Main Man and disconnected from the rest of humanity unless they pose a threat."

"He's a kidnap specialist and a former Homeland Security agent. Not so different, I guess."

Just then Vaslik stepped back into the kitchen. "All quiet. We staying here?"

"Yes." Ruth felt tired. She needed something to eat, then sleep. She would have preferred her own flat and bed, but the likelihood was that if the kidnappers made contact, it would be sooner rather than later. And Gina needed to be spelled, too; she couldn't keep going even if she pretended otherwise. Being high on adrenalin was no substitute for rest, and they would need her at her best if this thing went off.

"You don't have to," said Gina, reading her mind. "I'll call if anything happens."

"We're staying." Ruth gestured at the sofa. "We'll take turns to kip; four hours on, four off. You go to bed and I'll take the first stag."

Gina shrugged and wandered off towards the stairs, yawning, while Vaslik looked unmoved. It was nothing he wasn't used to. He made a show of checking the sofa for firmness and went to do another scan of the building.

SEVENTEEN

Nancy Hardman lay in bed, staring into the dark and listening to the sounds of the house; the ticking pipes, the settling brickwork, the soft fluttering of a bird in the eaves above her window. Further away was the familiar low buzz of traffic or an occasional emergency siren, a melancholy wail in the night. The after-hours tunes of any big city, at times both comforting and disturbing.

Only now there was another sound she was trying to cope with, this one inside the house: the movement from the three strangers sent to look after her. Endlessly prowling as they checked windows and doors and the camera monitors, they seemed to operate on some hidden reserves of calm certainty, yet were clearly keyed up to counter any threat that might present itself.

She listened as Gina moved into the spare room and lay down on the bed, followed by the click of the light switch. It reminded her body that she was tired herself, but she knew sleep wouldn't come that easily now the effects of the pill she had taken were wearing off.

She turned on her side. Her skin was itching with restless energy and her brain moving at a lightning pace, a stuttering gallery of thoughts and images like a newsreel in fast-forward. Fear and anxiety for Beth were uppermost, but closely followed by questions about Michael. Where was he right now? What he was doing?

She pulled the duvet around her and wondered what he would say if she told him about the sleeping pill. *If?* The notion that she might not tell him almost frightened her, filling her with a strange feeling of rebellion. She couldn't *not* tell him; theirs was a relationship built on absolute trust, a faith in each other stronger than anything she'd ever seen between other couples. Not confiding everything that was important would be like a betrayal.

If only she could speak to him.

She flung aside the duvet, suddenly too hot, too agitated, her chest beaded with perspiration. The message; she had to send him the usual message. He had always insisted that she text him at least every two or three days, to let him know all was well. Even if the messages failed to arrive, it was a habit he had insisted she followed to let him know everything was good. And she had done so ever since. The idea that she might need that contact just as much as he had never been voiced, but she had welcomed at least the chance that he might see one of her messages and respond from whatever far-flung corner of the world he was in.

She slid from her bed and put on her dressing gown, then padded to the bedroom door. Stood and listened. No sounds, no creaks from up here. Nothing from downstairs, either, but she knew they were there.

She moved to the stairs and walked down, nerves making her jumpy at the thought of a confrontation. She reached the bottom step and paused. Still no noise; just the soft, flickering light from the camera monitors bouncing off the walls and ceilings. She moved in line with the living room door and stopped, her heart jumping.

Gonzales was watching her from an armchair in the darkened room. She was unmoving, her face a pale blob.

"Problem?" Her voice was soft, probing. She sounded fully alert and Nancy wondered how any of them did this work, constantly ready for anything.

"I couldn't sleep. I need some soda." There was a bottle in the fridge, the household beverage of choice and Michael's favourite. Beth's too, only she liked hers flat.

Gonzales didn't move to stop her so Nancy stepped into the kitchen. Vaslik was standing by the back door. He gave a nod and walked out holding a flashlight, and she heard him going upstairs.

She opened the fridge. The door shielded her from Gonzales's view. She slid open the drawer next to the fridge and saw her cell phone lying there. She found a glass and poured a drink, taking a long pull before putting the glass down to refill it. As she replaced the bottle in the fridge door she reached out with her other hand and took out the phone, dropping it into her dressing gown pocket.

She was surprised how easy she found it, slipping into the role of ... what was she—a conspirator? Was it really this simple, a case of them and us? She swallowed hard and closed the fridge door. Moved back towards the stairs.

"Aren't you forgetting something?" Gonzales's voice floated through the dark.

"I don't think so." Nancy felt another skip of her heart. *She'd been seen.*

"Your soda. Might as well take it with you, don't you think?"

She went back for the glass, cursing under her breath. The bloody woman didn't miss a thing. Had she seen her pocket the phone? Was that the next thing to bring her up on?

She walked back upstairs, shoulders straight, feeling faint with an overwhelming rush of … was it adrenaline? Fear? Excitement? Whatever it was, she found it quietly exhilarating. She went into her bedroom and half-closed the door, waiting a moment to see if Vaslik would appear, alerted by her approach.

No movement. She had to move quickly, in case Gonzales had realised what she was doing. She closed the door and switched off the light, then put down the glass and powered up the phone. The message wouldn't take long; she had perfected the sentence over the months and could do it in the dark.

We're here. We're well. We're missing you.

It wasn't romantic, as far as messages between husband and wife went; nor was it accurate. But Michael would know that it meant she and Beth were with him, body and spirit. She deliberately hadn't mentioned Beth again; she had done that already. Reminding Michael that their daughter was missing was enough. He would respond if he could, she was certain.

She pressed SEND and silently wished the words on their way, hoping that somewhere, in some dark corner of the world, Michael would see them and respond. Once done, she deleted the message.

Moments later she was back downstairs, placing the glass in the sink and slipping the phone back in the drawer.

She was aware of Gonzales watching her walk past the doorway, but nothing was said.

———

Ruth debated going after Nancy, but put her inability to sleep down to trauma. The walk down the stairs and back up again probably helped calm her down. She did a tour of the ground floor instead, checking windows and doors, standing for a while to watch the road outside.

A fox trotted out from a driveway fifty yards away and stopped, oblivious to the pool of street light overhead, confident in its urban surroundings. It sniffed the air, head switching from left to right, then turned and ran up the centre of the road, unhurried and graceful, before disappearing into deep shadow.

She went into the kitchen and stood for a while checking the monitors. The images were sharp and clear, the only movement coming from a neighbourhood cat grooming itself in the back garden, and a hedgehog trundling past just a couple of feet away. The animals ignored each other, night-time regulars secure in their routine and unthreatened.

She went out into the hallway and heard a faint rasp of breathing coming from the study. Vaslik, showing his independence by eschewing the sofa over the more Spartan leather club chair.

She returned to the living room and sat down. Closed her eyes.

And was jerked instantly awake by the jangle of a telephone.

It was the landline on the table at her elbow.

She snatched it up and remembered to hold the mouthpiece away from her lips before answering.

"Yes?" She uttered the single word in a rush as if dragged from reluctant sleep, the sound not long enough for anyone to determine who was speaking, only that it was a woman and hopefully, Nancy.

"Tell your husband." The voice was male, harsh and clearly disguised, with no clue to accent or inflection.

It was uttering the last line from the kidnap note:

It was them.

"I don't understand." She allowed her voice to break and rise in pitch as they would expect. *'Who are you? Why are you doing this?'* She watched the doorway to the hall, hoping Nancy hadn't heard. If whoever was doing this was to be convinced that the police weren't involved, she had to come across like a terrorised, frantic mother.

It worked.

"Tell your husband. Tell him." The voice was insistent but showed no signs of suspicion.

"Where's my daughter?"

The caller rang off.

"Them?" Vaslik was in the doorway, speaking softly, fully alert. He checked the curtains were pulled tight before switching on the light. If the kidnappers were close enough, it would be the expected reaction; a need to see familiar things, to come out of the dark.

"One of them."

Behind Vaslik, Gina was a darker shadow, moving quickly down the stairs in her bare feet.

Ruth waited until Gina joined them before repeating what the man had said. "That seems to be their main message, don't you think? They want the husband."

EIGHTEEN

GINA WAS UP AND patrolling the house when Ruth got in from a short walk at eight the next morning. The former bodyguard met her at the back door, glancing hungrily at a bag of croissants Ruth had bought at the supermarket bakery.

"Yum. I could eat that lot myself."

"Anything doing?" Ruth put the croissants in the microwave for a quick zap while Vaslik stirred and went off to do a visual check of the perimeter. Somehow instinct had allowed them all to snatch a few minutes with their heads down when they needed it, but none had had a full four hours.

"Not a peep. A few cars have come and gone but none that shouldn't be here as far as I can tell."

"Did Nancy wake up?" Ruth dusted off her hands and sniffed the air appreciatively. "Can I smell coffee?"

"Yes, you can and yes, she did. She's in the shower. She was up and about in her room a couple of times, but in between I checked on her and she was spark-out."

Ruth nodded. "I tried talking to her when she was up but she didn't seem too interested. In the end I left her to it. Did she say anything to you about our talk last night?"

"Only that you'd got a bit personal. I told her we had to talk about this stuff because it might help find out who had an interest in Michael. Find who that is and we find Beth. She seemed OK after that." Gina poured coffee all round and helped herself to a croissant, wolfing it down. "I've seen this up-down reaction before, though: I think she's a little stir-crazy. Not surprising with her daughter missing, but she asked me for more pills. I said no and she called me a mean bitch."

Ruth wasn't surprised. Nancy had looked fragile enough yesterday; now Gina was withholding the sweeties she'd introduced her to, she was feeling resentful towards her.

"I'm going to call the company medic to check her over." Cruxys had a consultant on tap for emergencies, and he would make sure she was holding up and prescribe pills if necessary. Whether Nancy would go along with it was something else, but they couldn't allow her to fall apart without trying to do something to prevent it.

"Take her shopping." Vaslik had returned without them hearing him. He picked up a croissant and sipped his coffee. When he saw them staring at him he explained, "The ones left behind are the most stressed in these situations. Looking at four walls while waiting for news is almost the worst thing they can do; it's like their brains go into free-fall. We need to break the spell, allow her to breathe." He gestured with his croissant at the large fridge in the corner. "She won't agree to go, but I'm pretty sure there's stuff she needs, anyway. It'll do her good."

Ruth agreed. "Good idea—if we can get her out. She won't go willingly; she'll be frightened of missing a call. Frightened of being a target herself, too."

"Quite possibly." He looked at her. "That's why Gina should go with her and you should stay here. She trusts you more than us and to anybody watching, Gina looks more like a friend than a cop."

"Gee, thanks. What will you be doing, hot shot?"

He gave a smile and swallowed the last of his croissant. "Me? I'll be ghosting along in the background, watching for anybody taking too close an interest."

Gina looked intrigued. "You think that's likely?"

"I'd bet on it. Kidnappers never fail to watch for a reaction after the event. It's part of what they do. No reaction and they've already lost the initiative. It means they've got to come out from cover to stir things up. They don't like doing that."

"Does that ever happen—where people don't react?"

"I've seen it two or three times. A family isn't that close or the victim's colleagues don't care enough to do anything—end of game. Admittedly, the people involved aren't exactly normal, you understand, so that explains a lot."

"And here?"

"They're watching." He nodded towards the front of the house. "Every time I go near the windows I get the feeling we're under observation."

"Have you seen anything?" Gina looked sceptical.

"No. But I've experienced it too many times to be imagining things. I can't prove it but I'd like to give it a try."

"You want to bring them out?" Ruth looked intrigued.

"Why not? It's better than sitting here waiting for them to pull the strings, don't you think? Stay local, though."

Neither of them argued with that.

———

Ruth watched as Gina and Nancy left the house. It was just after eight. They had had a hard time convincing Nancy that it was OK to go out and that the fresh air would do her good. Most of all they had stressed that it was safe for her to be away from the house and leave Ruth behind to watch over things. They would only be a short distance and a phone call away if anything happened.

She finally gave in and put on her coat and shoes. The plan was simple: to go to the nearest supermarket, a large building where they could walk around without attracting attention but where Vaslik could keep an eye on them from a distance. If anybody did latch onto them, he would soon know it.

Ruth felt an instant loss of control as the two women walked away down the street and Vaslik exited via the rear gate. It was a familiar feeling from previous assignments, signalling a disconnection from the main players of an event while the pieces on the chessboard were moving into position. Gina was at the end of a phone, but it still meant the two women could be dangerously exposed and beyond her immediate reach. It was a feeling she would have to get used to.

She opened her laptop and called up a map of the area, then switched to Street Map so she could see the same picture that they would see. It wasn't very up to date and the traffic and weather conditions wouldn't be the same, but it gave her something on which to focus, as if she was moving along with them and sharing the route.

With the house empty, time seemed to pass grindingly slowly. She made coffee, resisted another croissant, did a tour of the rooms and constantly eyeballed the monitors. She resisted the temptation to call Slik for an update. If he had something, he'd call, she knew it.

There was a knock at the door.

She went to the front window, which gave a narrow view of visitors. It was a woman, dressed in jeans and a baggy jumper, hair scrunched out of sight beneath a gaudy yellow-and-mauve beanie cap. She wore heavy glasses balanced on her nose and she kept touching them with her forefinger and brushing her face. She was holding a couple of magazines in her other hand.

Neighbour, thought Ruth. Coffee and chat call? Somehow she couldn't see Nancy in the chat or sugar-lending category.

She shrugged off her jacket and stepped into the kitchen, picking up a tea towel and a mug as props, then went to the front door and opened it.

"Hi, Nancy—" the woman began with a bright smile. Then her face changed when she saw Ruth. "Oh, sorry. I was expecting … Is Nancy in?" She had the faintest American intonation, Ruth noted, overlaid with something she couldn't quite place. A displaced foreigner too long away from home, she guessed.

"Not right now. She's just gone to the supermarket to get some cakes. I told her she shouldn't bother but she said she needed some fresh air, too. Can I help?" She peered at the cup and rubbed it with the tea towel, then shrugged. "How do you get tea stains out? I hate yellow patches on crockery—it's like nicotine fingers."

"I don't know." The woman looked slightly perplexed. "Umm … I'm a neighbour—Clarisse—from up the street. No. 38. I haven't seen Nancy for a couple of days so I thought it was time we caught up and did some girlie things. Are you local, too, uh …?"

"Ruth. No. I'm a friend from school. I finally decided it was time to come and say hello again. I think I might have interrupted her gym visits today. Not that she needs it, the slim-line bitch." She waved a hand at the woman's frown. "It's OK—we talk about each other like that all the time; we've been friends too long to take offence."

"Of course." Clarisse gave a weak smile and moved away. "I'd better get back. Let her know I called, will you, and I'll come round another day. We can do lunch, maybe."

"I'll do that."

Ruth moved back into the front room and watched the woman walk along the street and turn into a house several doors up. She had the springy walk of an athlete, proving that gym visits worked for some people. But hell, Ruth thought sourly, don't they have better things to do?

Moments later Clarisse appeared again, this time pulling on a coat. She walked along the street, head down and collar up, and turned the corner out of sight. She looked as if she was in a hurry to get somewhere, and Ruth wondered why.

NINETEEN

LESS THAN HALF A mile away, Andy Vaslik watched as Gina and Nancy walked arm-in-arm past a parade of shops, stopping occasionally—mostly at Gina's suggestion, he figured—to study something in a window display. His opinion of the former bodyguard was improving steadily; she had Nancy fully covered and was giving Vaslik every chance to keep up with them and study their back-trail for watchers. She had clearly done this before and would be familiar with the problem of trying to run surveillance on a person of interest without blowing everyone's cover.

The sidewalks were busy with workers on their commute and early shoppers, he noted. He had no problem keeping them in sight with Gina's tall figure, but casing all the other people around them while remaining unseen would get tougher as time went by. He took out his cell phone and snapped a couple of covert pictures to check the quality.

Pretty much perfect.

After inspecting all the smaller stores, the two women approached a large supermarket car park situated on the left-hand side of the road. Vaslik crossed over at an angle slightly away from them and waited at a nearby bus stop, blending in with the line and nodding genially at a couple of elderly women. He checked both ways, noting everything that moved. Nothing obvious near the two women yet, mostly other shoppers, a few kids and some older people.

Then his antennae gave a twitch. Something was different. Or someone.

There. A young guy was cruising along in their wake. He'd come right out of nowhere. Tall, bulky but moving easily, eyes definitely locked on Gina and Nancy. Dark coat and pants, could be an office worker who worked out.

Vaslik tensed. A grey van was approaching slowly on the same side. Maybe a coincidence but it was moving just a little too slow. It drifted into the side of the road and stopped thirty yards behind the women, the driver flicking a hand to allow a couple of pedestrians across. Now why would he do that with a crossing just yards away? The near-side wheels were almost touching the kerb on double-yellow lines, which was bad positioning for any vehicle on a busy road. Was he stopping or not?

The two women moved out, ready to cross the road to the supermarket, unaware of the potential threat. Vaslik went to full alert. This didn't look good.

He took covert snaps of the tall man and the van, but couldn't get a facial of the driver or see how many others were inside. Then he turned away and pretended to take a call, in case any of the watchers picked up on his presence. When he turned back again the women were on the edge of the kerb, still checking traffic.

But wait; Gina must have sensed something. She was tugging Nancy away from the kerb, her shoulders tensed. They walked further along to the crossing. It was busier there and there was safety in numbers.

He forced himself to relax. Fraser knew what she was doing.

He moved away from the bus line and snapped away, catching faces going in the same direction as the women; another man, young and fit looking, dark skin; two women in gym clothing beneath fashionable tops; another woman hurrying along and nearly getting clipped by a taxi cutting the turn into the car park.

The van had disappeared and the tall, bulky guy was continuing on down the street, paying no attention as Gina and Nancy crossed and disappeared into the supermarket.

Vaslik followed, long strides eating up the ground until he was inside and on their tails. He felt a rush of relief as he spotted the two familiar backs down the first aisle, with Nancy pushing a trolley.

Gina turned and looked back, no doubt sensing his presence, and made a subtle A-OK sign with her thumb and forefinger. She had it covered.

He stayed around, anyway. He'd seen enough to know they were being watched. And it wasn't by one person, either; it was a team.

———

Ruth was waiting when the two women returned. It was nine-thirty and Nancy was walking fast, she noted, impatient to be back in familiar surroundings, her brief taste of normal fast dying on its feet. As they walked in the front door, Ruth checked the monitor and saw movement at the back gate.

Vaslik.

When they were all gathered in the living room, Ruth addressed Nancy. "You had a visitor."

The tone of her voice was enough. Everybody stopped moving. Gina glanced towards the windows, Vaslik looked interested and Nancy turned to stone.

"Who?" Her face was ashen, expecting the worst.

"A woman named Clarisse—from No. 38. Young, heavy specs, a bit grungy, slight American accent?"

"Clarisse? I don't know—" Nancy walked to the window and looked through the net curtain, her mouth moving as she counted off the numbers. When she tuned back, she looked sick.

"No. 38?"

"That's what she said. Problem?"

"It's wrong. It's impossible." She wobbled and looked very pale.

"Why?" Ruth hurried across to her, offering her arm. Gina moved, too, ready to step in. "Why, Nancy?"

"Because I don't know anyone called Clarisse. And that house has been empty since before we moved in. The owner's in a care home."

———

Gina accompanied Nancy up to her bedroom while Ruth called Cruxys with an update report on events and asked for their medical consultant to come round urgently. From almost breezy while at the supermarket, according to Gina, she'd gone to near-collapse on hearing about the woman visitor.

"So what's going on?" Ruth demanded, as they gathered in the kitchen. She'd been tempted to dismiss Nancy's claim about the empty house, but her instant reaction to news of the caller had been too compelling. Now with this latest turn of events the situation seemed to have accelerated.

Vaslik filled them in on what he'd observed, keeping it brief. Too much detail sometimes led to over-elaboration which could cloud the real issue. "I'm guessing there's more than one person on this. And whoever they are, they're good."

"A team? Are you sure?"

"Has to be. I made at least three, maybe more if the van was involved."

Ruth chewed it over. In spite of her earlier reservations about Vaslik, so much had happened since first being paired up with him that she realised she trusted him implicitly. If his gut feeling told him something, it was good enough for her. "Let's go over this in order. Gina, what did you see when you were out?"

Gina described noticing the same van as Vaslik, and a tall man, well-built and heavy across the upper body, like a weightlifter. Both had seemed out of place, yet neither had appeared directly threatening towards Nancy. "You see people and vehicles that stand out all the time; it doesn't mean they're a danger. But we're on the lookout for possible threats, so we'd notice anything out of the ordinary. Other than that, I have to say I didn't *see* anyone. But I agree with Andy: something was going on. It had that feel, you know?"

She knew. "Anything else, either of you?"

Vaslik nodded. "Don't forget I could see from an angle Gina couldn't. The tall guy was focussed on them, I'm certain. But you'd have to have been in my position to see it."

"And the van? Could it have been a snatch team?" The idea of another potential abduction was alarming, because the only target they could have had in mind was Nancy. Was that to put more pressure on

Michael Hardman, picking up his wife as well as his daughter? It was a risky manoeuvre holding two hostages instead of one, especially the second being the mother. It would pile on the pressure of keeping them isolated. This group had to know what they were doing.

"I don't know. If it wasn't, the only thing I can think of is it might have been a local drugs intercept team and we happened to pitch across their line of travel." As he spoke he was on his cell phone calling up the pictures of the grey van and the tall man. He passed it to Ruth and she began flicking through the images.

She stopped, her mouth open.

"Who's this?" She pointed at the screen.

Vaslik took the phone and checked the image. It showed the van turning into the supermarket, after Gina and Nancy had walked into the car park. The tall man was in the background on the other side, walking away. "That's the tall guy. He cut away and disappeared. I'm pretty sure it was a hand-off." He meant that another follower had taken over, to avoid the same face coming up too often.

"Not him. Her." She was pointing at a female figure dodging the front bumper of a taxi turning into the car park. The woman was slim, wearing a coat and jeans and a colourful beanie hat jammed down over her head. But no glasses.

"What about her?"

"It's the woman called Clarisse—from the house that's supposed to be empty."

TWENTY

THE THREE OF THEM swung into action. The woman might have been the genuine article, going about her business of calling on a neighbour. A friendly gesture from one person to another, commonplace and harmless.

But their combined instincts and experience said otherwise. Even given the trauma of having her daughter kidnapped, Nancy wouldn't have made a mistake about knowing such an unusual name or the fact that a house just along the street was supposed to be empty.

Gina checked that the doors and windows were locked tight and all the camera monitors were in full working order, while Vaslik took a walk out to the rear gate and the lane outside. He came back and shook his head. All clear, with no obvious surveillance on the house. If they were there, they were being very cautious.

Ruth was standing at the front window, studying the building at No. 38 and hatching a plan of action. She was too far away to see much detail without binoculars, and without investigating closer, couldn't tell if they were currently under surveillance. But she had to gauge the effects of doing nothing against the risk of running into the mystery woman and her colleagues at the house in question.

"Do you think they know we're around?" Gina queried.

"They know somebody is. But not who. They've seen you with Nancy at the shops and seen me here in the house. That doesn't mean anything. Friends drop by all the time and people put on an act, even under stress. Hopefully they haven't seen Slik yet."

"I vote we go make a house call," said Vaslik calmly. "If they're gone they might have got careless and left a trace. It's better than sitting here wondering."

"What if they're in there?" said Gina.

Vaslik merely smiled. He looked as if he would enjoy finding out.

"I agree with Slik." Ruth looked at Gina. "We go take a look. Can you stay here in case the consultant comes round? We won't be long."

Gina nodded reluctantly. She wanted in on the action.

Ruth and Vaslik left through the rear gate and circled the block, scanning the area for parked cars with people inside. Nothing doing. Everything looked normal; houses, gardens, cars, voices, a loud burst of rock music from an open garage where a man had his head under the bonnet of a car.

They entered the road running past the Hardman house and approached No. 38 side by side, two people chatting casually, nothing out of the ordinary.

Just as they reached it, Vaslik took a deep breath and said softly, "Keep walking and don't look at it."

He'd just realised that this was the house where the real estate agent had been taking photographs.

"What's got you all fired up?" Ruth queried when they were fifty yards past the property. "Did you see something?"

"Maybe nothing." He explained about the photographer, and they debated abandoning their house call.

"It could have been a genuine agent," Ruth countered. "People do sell houses all the time—even empty ones."

"Sure," he agreed. "But why this one right now? It's spooky."

"So what do we do?"

He chewed it over for another few paces, then said, "Let's go for it. If they're in there, at least we'll know it. If it's empty, we can tick it off the list."

They turned round and walked back.

The paved area in front of the target house was bare, with dead leaf mould crushed into jagged gaps between the stones and a layer of gritty dust over the top. Twin pot plants held the remains of dead bushes, long dried out and abandoned, their branches decorated with bits of paper debris.

"No recent traffic," Vaslik murmured. He sounded very calm but Ruth could feel the tension radiating off him. He aimed for the side gate leading to the rear garden. "Won't be long."

Ruth let him go, eyeing the upper windows which had grey net curtains hanging limply behind dirty glass. The lower windows were impenetrable behind vertical blinds, the original royal blue colour of the fabric faded in places from sunlight and layered in dust. All the frames showed signs of peeling paint and gaps in the pointing.

Ruth stepped up to the front door and used the knocker. It echoed emptily back at her. She gave it a count of five and tried again. If anybody was in, they must have nerves of steel. If not, it might distract them long enough for Vaslik to take a good look and see what they might be up against. If anyone inside tried slipping out the back, they'd run slap into him. For some reason the thought encouraged her.

Nothing.

She followed the route Vaslik had taken down a paved path, past a small garden shed and a greenhouse grimy with moss and ancient cobwebs. Both structures were empty. The path opened out onto a patio surrounded by a foot-high brick wall topped with coping stones.

Vaslik was standing by a set of wood-framed French doors, peering through the glass at the inside. He was holding a lethal looking folding knife in his hand, the point inserted in the crack near the lock. He gave a sharp twist and the door sprang open.

Seconds later he was inside.

"Care to show me how you did that?" Ruth asked, following him in and closing the door behind her.

"Session three from the DHS Basic Investigation Techniques manual," he said, snapping the knife shut. "Somebody's been camping out in here. Smell it?"

She did. The air smelled musty and damp, of abandonment. And something else.

Takeaway food.

They checked the rooms quickly, not knowing how long they had got before Clarisse returned. The house had been emptied of all furnishings, and each sound echoed back at them. Slik ran upstairs while Ruth did the downstairs. Kitchen, utility, small breakfast room, toilet and living room. All empty.

She checked the sink. Water lay pooled in the bottom. She dipped her finger in it and sniffed. It smelled fresh. She gave the tap a shake. There was a gurgle and a spiral of residual water trickled out into her hand. She tasted it.

A faint chemical residue, but also fresh.

She went back to check the toilet. Whoever had used it last had forgotten to flush. She wasn't about to take the same taste test but she was willing to bet that the contents were not more than a few hours old.

She stepped through to the front window and teased open a slat in the blinds. From here she had a clear view of the Hardman's front door. She looked down at the floor, which was wood-block. Then she got down on her knees and checked closer. The blocks were covered in a layer of dust … except for the area right in front of the window. She felt a kick of excitement.

This had been an O.P.—an observation point.

She had no problem imagining the woman named Clarisse on her knees here; even though the house was empty, it would have been essential to remain still this close to the window, to avoid catching the eye of a casual observer or a neighbour with too much time on their hands.

Vaslik entered the room and saw what she was doing. "They watched from upstairs, too. There's a flattened area in the carpet. Great O.P."

"Did you check the bathroom?"

"Used but not flushed. The water's on but they wouldn't have wanted to alert the neighbours."

They left the empty house and walked back the way they had come. Neither spoke; the situation didn't need it. It was patently obvious that the Hardmans had been under observation before and after the kidnap, and the woman in the beanie hat had come over to check what was happening before they made a move on Nancy.

It meant the other side was getting impatient.

TWENTY-ONE

As they stepped back inside the Hardman house, Ruth's phone rang.

It was Richard Aston.

"I pulled in a couple of favours and had the management run a check on the CCTV at the leisure centre," he said. "We were lucky: it's kept on a secure system so nobody but the centre manager gets to handle it. I'm sending you a link to download the relevant footage. I think you'll find it interesting. The manager's name is Robert Curlow. If he plays up, tell him Godfrey Leander sent you."

"I'll do that," said Ruth. "Thank you."

"No problem. There's something else we need to discuss first: the bank account in Kensington. I've got Margie here with me. If you turn on your laptop we can talk over the possibilities. I'll wait for you to call."

Ruth agreed and disconnected, then took her laptop through to the study and switched it on.

"Where's Nancy?" she asked Gina.

"Upstairs in the bath. The doc came while you two were having all the fun. He prescribed some pills. I told her to have a soak before she took them. It might help her relax. He asked me to monitor her intake."

"Are you OK with that?"

"Sure. I've done it before." She rolled her eyes. "Some people just need protecting from themselves."

"Your call. What did he say about her?"

"Not much to me. But I think he's concerned about her mental state. He rattled off some jargon about secondary trauma and Post Traumatic Stress Disorder in the families of kidnap victims. To be honest I wasn't really listening; that's his job to sort out."

"But he's not going to hospitalise her?" She thought Gina was oddly cool about another person's suffering, and guessed the former protection officer was making subconscious comparisons to her own way of handling the trauma following her shooting.

"I don't think so. I got the impression he won't discount it, but he thinks the best place for her is here. It's familiar and all her daughter's stuff is here. It's all she knows."

"Makes sense. And she'll want to be here in case the kidnappers get in touch."

The three of them gathered in the study, Ruth and Vaslik by the laptop, Gina hovering by the door, one eye out in case Nancy finished her bath and came downstairs.

The conference link went through and showed Richard Aston, jacket off and relaxed in the Safeguard room with the researchers' story boards in the background. Margie the accounts supervisor was sitting alongside him, looking less comfortable out of her comfort zone.

"Let's keep this brief," said Aston. "Following your request, we approached the bank in Kensington for further details on the Hardman account. They declined to provide them." He glanced at Margie for corroboration.

"As expected," said Margie. "They're under no legal obligation to do anything unless there's suspected criminal activity. Even then we'd have to get a court order, which could take days."

"An order we will not get." Aston's tone was firm, the tone slightly acid. "We've had cause to try this before. Our industry background works against us. Because we're a security and investigative company, they think we're all tied in with News Corp and hacking."

"What will it prove, anyway—even if we could get it?" Margie asked. She clearly hadn't been fully briefed by Aston on why Ruth needed access to the account details.

"Go ahead, Ruth." Aston waved a hand at the screen.

"If the account has been closed since he took out the Safeguard contract," explained Ruth, who was thinking on her feet, "then that's it. We're no further forward. If it's still active, it proves Hardman has a separate account; one he's forgotten to tell his wife about. Through it we might be able to track his movements and maybe find out where he is now."

Margie looked cynical. "Lots of husbands have separate accounts, in my experience. Doesn't prove anything, though, unless you get to audit his spending. But I don't know how you'd go about that—" She stopped. "Forget I said that."

"I'm not saying there's anything wrong with having the account," Ruth said. "But it might lead us to a whole new set of details, addresses, telephone numbers. That would give us something to go at, to try and find this bozo and let him know his daughter's life is in danger."

"Quite." Aston sounded doubtful. "I'm not sure his wife would share your view but I see your thinking. However, it doesn't alter the fact that we don't have access, in which case I'm not sure where we go from here."

Ruth felt frustrated. She could feel this thing slipping away from her. There had to be a way of contacting the elusive and mysterious Michael Hardman, but the twin shadows of bureaucracy and the Data Protection Act were getting in the way.

"I'm bloody certain they'd give up my account details in a heart-beat if a government department asked them," she muttered. She looked at Vaslik for inspiration, but he shook his head, unable to help.

"Maybe there is a way," ventured Margie. She was staring above the screen camera, forehead creased in thought. "All you want to do is check that the account's still active, right?"

"Yes," said Ruth.

"Then what?"

"Then we might have reason to get a court order with Nancy's cooperation as a last resort. It might not work but it's worth a try. Anything's worth a try," she added heavily.

"Go on," urged Aston, looking at Margie. He sounded intrigued. "What's your idea and is it legal?"

"Perfectly. I'll have to make a phone call first. You'll have to promise not to laugh, though. There's a routine I have to go through to hook the fish."

Aston looked puzzled by what she meant, but picked up the phone in the centre of the table and handed it to her. "Do it."

144

Margie dialled a number, and seconds later asked to be put through to someone named George. "Hello, handsome," she trilled, with a sheepish look at Aston. "How's the best looking man in London?" She pressed a button and George's voice floated out into the room, gravelly and assured.

"Hi, beautiful," he replied. "What do you want and how much will it cost me?"

"Oh, you! It won't cost you a thing, I promise. But it might cost me a drinkie or two later this week, if you're around." She looked pointedly at Aston, who waved a hand in assent and smiled.

"Go on, then."

"Well, we need to make a refund to a client account in your Kensington branch, only we think it might be dormant. Is there any way you could … you know, give them a call and ask if it's worth sending the payment or not? I really don't want to go through a lot of hassle if it's dead; I'm on my own here and really, really busy. What do you think?"

"I think maybe I should come round and keep you company." George's voice was loaded with meaning, and they all witnessed Margie blushing. Even so, it didn't stop her winking at the camera.

"Oh, you," she said coyly. But the look said it all: fish hooked. She read out the account details.

"All right. Leave it with me, babe. I'll do it now." His voice dropped. "Stay by the phone, you—"

Margie's hand shot out and hit the mute button, cutting off whatever he was about to say. She replaced the handset and studied her fingernails, while beside her, Aston was having trouble keeping a straight face.

Two minutes later the phone rang and she listened to the call, then thanked him and cut the connection.

"It's live and active," she announced with a smug air.

"How active, did he say?" asked Vaslik.

"Nothing specific, but it sounded live enough to be recent."

"Good." Aston clapped his hands together. "Great work, Margie." He looked into the camera, a quizzical frown on his face. "Tell me, Ruth, what are you really looking for here?"

Ruth took a deep breath. She'd been afraid he might ask this question. This was bordering on something else altogether, and she was relieved Martyn Claas wasn't part of the conversation; as little as she knew of him, she was certain he would have closed it down by now. "If this works," she said slowly, "this payment might not be the only one made from that account. We can start digging further."

Aston said nothing, and she realised from his expression that it was deliberate. He'd doubtless been at the forefront of similar lines of investigation before, and was probably working out the ramifications for the company if things went too far. His silence meant that for now he was willing to let Ruth run with it.

"We have to do something," she said at last, aware that all eyes were on her. She lowered her voice. "So much about this makes no sense. An apparent child abduction seemingly focussed on the father—who's out in the wind and untraceable; his only legal footprint is a single bank account his wife is unaware of; a charity office that doesn't exist … and now a team of followers who might or might not be part of the kidnap team."

A thought flickered into her head about the CIA man following George Paperas, but she dismissed it. Paperas might have trodden on some toes in the past, or with his field work and UN contacts, he might have information the CIA considered useful in the war on terror. Unless it was proven otherwise, that was his business and no part of what they were here to discuss.

TWENTY-TWO

AFTER ASTON SIGNED OFF, Ruth checked her email and found the link from him with the CCTV footage from Fitness Plus. She clicked on it and waited while it downloaded.

The picture was grainy with a blue-ish tinge, but clear enough to make out details of faces and furnishings. It showed the main corridor leading from the corner near reception past the bank of lockers and vending machines. No doubt another camera showed the opposite end of the corridor leading to the pool, but that wasn't necessary right now.

A timer in the bottom right-hand corner showed a date, and the time at 09.05. About ten minutes before Nancy arrived, if the kidnap note was accurate. It was cutting it fine but she guessed Aston had vetted the footage first and sent her what was relevant.

Two women in gym gear walked by and went through the door into the fitness studio. The silence was slightly unnerving, Ruth thought, after the pounding beat of the music she knew was being played throughout the building. They were shortly followed by the young hunk Ruth had seen chatting to the receptionist. But instead of entering the studio he walked to the end of the corridor, checked a fire door then came back, bending to check out the slots in the vending machines before moving on to the lockers, where he ran his hand along the doors, pushing them shut. He seemed in no hurry to be busy.

When he stopped alongside the first bank of lockers and flicked a hand at the key in the middle, Ruth tensed.

"What's he doing?" asked Gina.

"That's the locker Nancy uses, where the note was left. It's got a large safety pin instead of an orange key fob."

The hunk opened the door and appeared to be checking the coin mechanism box on the inside. Then he closed it again and walked away, flexing his arms.

"Did you see anything?" Ruth murmured, and looked at the other two. "I didn't."

Vaslik shook his head. "If he dropped the card, he should be in Vegas—they'd pay top dollar for that kind of skill."

Two more customers came in separately; one an elderly man with a stick, the other a young woman wearing a hoodie and carrying a sports bag. She stopped halfway along the bank of lockers and opened one, then changed her mind and moved back towards the first row.

She opened the door to the middle one and pushed her bag inside using both hands. As she did so, they saw one hand was holding a flash of something white against the dark fabric.

Gina leaned in to look closer. "What's that?"

"Bingo," Ruth muttered. "It's the card. Now, who the hell are you, lady?"

The woman didn't lock the door, but turned as if to go into the studio, then appeared to change her mind before going back to the locker and pulling out her bag, this time one-handed. As she turned to leave, her hoodie fell back slightly, revealing one side of her face.

It was the woman Ruth knew as Clarisse.

As she walked out of shot towards the reception area, the three investigators looked at each other.

"She gets around," said Vaslik. "Can you freeze and copy a frame of that?"

Ruth was already reaching for the laptop's mouse pad. "I'm on it." She did so, then allowed the footage to run.

What was left was dynamite.

They saw Nancy enter the frame and go to the locker. She opened the door and stopped; went very still for a moment before reaching inside. When she withdrew her hand, she was holding the square of white card.

The shock was plain to see in the stiffness of her body and face.

Seconds later, she was running out of the frame, her sports bag forgotten on the floor. Moments after, the mystery woman appeared and looked inside the locker, then flicked the door closed and looked down at Nancy's bag for a second before looking along the corridor without moving.

She was smiling.

"What's she doing? Gina asked. "Why is she standing there?"

"She's waiting," said Vaslik, "to see if this fish took the bait."

———

Five minutes later they joined Nancy in the living room, where she was watching the BBC News Channel. A reporter in a hard hat and body armour was standing in front of a burning building in Mogadishu, Somalia's capital. In the background people were clawing at piles of rubble while emergency crews struggled to get victims into vehicles and away from the scene. Evidence of a bomb outrage, the reporter was saying, by a little-known extremist group that had, until now, been mostly vocal with attempting only limited attempts at disrupting everyday life in the capital.

Ruth turned off the television and showed Nancy the freeze-frame of the woman as she turned away from the locker.

"Do you know her?" she asked gently, hardly daring to breathe. She didn't want to pre-empt Nancy's answer in any way. This was the first break they'd had, and if it led anywhere they'd struck very lucky indeed. Sometimes that was all it needed: one moment of carelessness. Maybe this was such a case and would be the undoing of all the care Clarisse had taken not to be seen.

Nancy studied it, eyes flooding with recognition.

"Yes, I do—at least, to say hello to. Her name's Karen, or Helen—I forget which. Helen, I think. Sorry, but I'm terrible with some names. Why have you got this photo? What's going on?"

"How long have you known her?"

"A week, ten days … maybe a bit longer. She joined recently. We've hardly talked, really. She was there just after I found the card. She must have thought I was so rude—I ran off without stopping to talk."

"I wouldn't worry," Ruth commented. "I think she'll understand better than most. What do you think, Slik?"

When Vaslik nodded with a grim smile, Nancy looked at them both and asked, "What do you mean? Do you know her?"

"Not as well as we'd like to. We acquired footage of the CCTV taken just before you arrived at Fitness Plus yesterday morning. This is a freeze-frame taken just after she'd placed the card in your locker."

"What? But that's—" Nancy looked horrified. "*She* put it there?" Her voice was tiny, like a child's, and a pulse was beating at the side of her head.

"Yes. Your gym buddy, Helen. She also calls herself Clarisse and claims to live at No. 38. She doesn't, of course, but she—or somebody else—has definitely been there."

"Doing what?"

"Watching this house. Watching you. Sometimes from the ground floor window, sometimes upstairs."

"*What?*"

They waited while Nancy went through the stages of feeling angry, violated, resentful and frightened, offering reassurance. The last emotion was likely to be the most immediately worrying, but that was Gina's problem. Hand-holding was what she was trained for. The rest would, in time, diminish.

"It's OK," said Ruth. "She's gone now. We'll try and find her, don't worry." Find her, she thought, and lean on her with a big stick.

TWENTY-THREE

George Paperas called towards midday. Ruth took the call in the study, in case the conversation included something Nancy didn't need to know.

"Interesting person, your Michael Hardman," he began.

"You've found him?" She couldn't help it, she felt a tingle of electricity pass through her. But it didn't last.

"No. Nothing like that. In fact, that's the odd thing: he's actually proving very difficult to pin down. I rang a dozen names on that list of agencies you gave me. Fortunately, most of them were people I know. It seemed the quickest way to get some feel for him."

"What did you find?"

"In a way, more than I expected … and a lot less. Hardman's got something of a name for himself; he's a bit of a butterfly, is the general view. He first popped up as a field volunteer with Oxfam about four years ago, in Pakistan. He showed up one day at a transit camp near Peshawar and offered to pitch in. They were under pressure and grateful for any extra hands they could get. He quickly became a valued member of the team and even drove supply trucks close to the border when the local contract drivers got scared off by threats from the Taliban. Then a couple of weeks later, he disappeared, saying he had family stuff to resolve."

"Could be true," Ruth murmured. "His daughter's very young."

"Well, he never said anything about that. It was the same with five other agencies I spoke to. They're mostly small and don't have the resources to turn away offers of help, so when he turned up they took him on with open arms. But it was one-sided."

"How do you mean?"

"He'd be there as promised, work for a few days, maybe a week or two, then fade into the background. Not all the names ticked on the list had heard of him—and I know at least three of them who have excellent record keeping. For a committed aid worker, he doesn't seem to have left much of a footprint."

"Did anybody know anything about him?"

"That's the problem: nothing. He never volunteered information about his background or family, even in down-time, which is rare. Work in tough circumstances like field aid, and you talk about anything to take your mind off what you've seen, if only for a few hours. He didn't do that; didn't indulge in gossip and appeared to have no political leanings. Most aid workers are pretty open about where they're from; it's camp-fire stuff. Engaging with others is part of the job description if you're serious about it. But your Mr. Hardman doesn't appear to have been the type."

"Was he paid by them?"

"No. That was the thing they liked. He didn't ask for anything, so most of them figured he had private money and a conscience. He wouldn't be the first."

"What did they think of him?"

"Pleasant enough, organised and hard-working for the time they knew him … but not somebody they'd welcome back. Each time he left, he created a gap in the workforce that often couldn't be filled quickly enough. It happens, of course, when workers fall ill or suffer an injury of some kind; then they have to be evacuated out if it's serious enough and a replacement found. But this was different. He simply left with little or no notice."

Ruth felt a pulse beating in her throat. "And no ideas about where he'd gone?" She wasn't sure why that was important, but it was something she felt she had to ask.

"None. He simply left and disappeared."

She thanked him for his help and cut the connection, then went in search of Slik.

"He said he had something to do," said Gina, who was leaning against the kitchen sink working her way through a bacon sandwich. She pushed a plateful towards Ruth. "Here, get one of these down you. You look like you're thinking too much."

"Thanks." Ruth was hungry and took a bite, wondering where Slik had gone and why she had a bad feeling about Michael Hardman.

TWENTY-FOUR

ANDY VASLIK STEPPED INSIDE the rear of No. 38 and closed the French doors behind him. He stood quite still, listening for the slightest sound, the smallest shuffle of movement in the atmosphere that would signal the presence of another. He'd checked the outside of the building first, and only when he felt fairly sure nobody was in, he'd made his way down the side path and gained access the same way as before.

He waited, tuning in. This time he wanted to get a feel for the place. Last time had been quick and dirty, snatching a clutch of fleeting observations before anyone came back and found them. Now he was certain the place had been abandoned as an observation post, he wanted to take a closer look.

He started upstairs, going through every room, sniffing the air, absorbing the sense of the building, looking behind doors. Then he checked every inch of the carpets and fixtures. He was looking for any minute traces that might show who had been here, and what they had done. Every visitor leaves something, unless clothed in a forensics suit, and he was guessing the woman calling herself Clarisse would have been no different. She would have kept movement in the house to a minimum to avoid alerting the neighbours, but she would have been unable to remain totally still for hours at a time.

And when people move, they sometimes leave things behind.

He didn't want to jump the gun and call in Cruxys's own experts; instead he had confidence in his own abilities to tell him what he needed to know.

The two rear bedrooms gave him nothing. If Clarisse had been in here, she'd been careful to leave no obvious trace. Facing away from the focus of her attention—the Hardman House—would have been pointless and time-wasting, and he had a feeling Clarisse was too professional for that.

He checked the front rooms, giving a clear view each way along the road. This was where he figured Clarisse or her colleagues—and he was fairly sure there would have been others—would have spent most of their time. It gave a commanding view of their target, while avoiding the likelihood of anybody looking up from the road. People don't always look up at houses, but centre their attention on the ground floor where they expect to see movement. From here, the watchers could observe the Hardman's house in relative safety, while keeping an eye on the comings and goings of neighbours and alert to the possibility of random callers to this house itself.

He scoured the carpets, eyeing the flattened area he'd seen before, but finding nothing. He wasn't surprised; the empty room would have shown at a glance if they had left anything behind.

What he did see was three rounded indentations in the carpet. They had used a stool of some kind. He was willing to bet it was a folding camp stool, easy to conceal and carry, and putting the watcher at a comfortable level to see through the window with minimum exposure.

It pointed to expertise and planning; amateurs wouldn't think of comfort, and they would have left more in the way of traces.

He checked the bathroom again, noting the unflushed bowl, and stooped to look behind the seat, peering into the corners. Nothing.

The rest of the house was the same, devoid of debris, the way professionals leave a place because they know what the risks can be if they get careless.

He let himself out the back and walked down the side of the house, pausing to check the wheelie bins. You just never knew. But they were empty. As he passed through the side gate, he saw the neighbour's bin on the other side of the low fence, less than a foot away. On impulse, he made sure he wasn't being watched, then leaned over and took a look.

And smiled.

It was full with pre-filled white bin liners, knotted in the kind of neat, eco-friendly, responsible way people liked to live. But down the side was something that didn't match: it was a small paper carrier bag with a garish logo, the twin handles tied roughly together—the way people did after a picnic with their food waste and wrappers, when they were going to flip it into a garbage can on their way home.

He plucked it out and walked away, keen to see if his trash raid had been worthwhile.

————

Ruth was waiting for him by the back gate. She had a good idea where he'd been and eyed the bag in his hand. "Is that loot or did you stop for lunch on the way?"

He explained where he'd been and held up the bag he'd liberated, but refused to say anything until they were back in the kitchen. He spread an old newspaper on the working surface, then carefully tipped out the bag's contents and used a fork from the drawer to sort through the scraps.

It yielded the remnants of a working meal for one to go: a litter of orange peel, a paper coffee mug with a smear of dried foam around the rim, a plastic spoon, a scrunched-up paper napkin and an empty yogurt pot. A healthy eater, evidently.

They stood and stared at the evidence for what it was, each running the possibilities through their mind. This was either the neighbour's last lunch wrappings, casually tossed in the wheelie bin as they got home, or something else entirely.

"What do you think?" said Ruth.

Vaslik shook his head. "I don't think anything. It's nothing, is what it is." He excused himself and went to the bathroom, squeezing by in front of her. When she looked back at the debris on the work surface, something about it was different.

The paper napkin was gone.

She wondered why Vaslik had removed it, and was about to follow him to ask, when a shout echoed from upstairs. It was Gina.

"Ruth! Andy! Get an ambulance!"

TWENTY-FIVE

THE AMBULANCE WAS AT the house within eight minutes and the paramedics were wheeling Nancy out five minutes later, face covered in an oxygen mask. She looked sickly white, her hair plastered wetly against her skin from where Gina had dragged her out of the bath and deposited her on the bathroom floor to administer resuscitation.

"I heard a bump from the bathroom," Gina explained. "I went to check on her and she was under the water, staring up at the ceiling."

"You think she slipped?" asked Ruth. They were walking towards her car, ready to follow the ambulance as it pulled away from the kerb, lights flashing.

"Probably. I mean, it's the only explanation, isn't it?"

"Why do we all need to go?" Vaslik spoke from the back seat as they buckled up and Ruth took off after the emergency vehicle, referring to her insistence that they all follow close behind.

"She's going to an A&E unit. I didn't have time to get a private clinic sorted. We can do that once she's been assessed and treated. Until then we watch her closely."

"You think they'll try something there?"

"Maybe. She'll be wide open until we get her somewhere secure. If she's there any length of time, we'll need to operate a rota system to keep an eye on her." She looked at Gina. "You OK with that?"

"Suits me. If it's like most A&E departments, we'll have our work cut out." She flicked aside her jacket and produced a small semi-automatic pistol and checked the magazine. It fitted neatly into her hand without the bulk of a normal handgun, and she seemed quite at ease with the feel of the weapon.

"What the hell is that?" Vaslik queried. "A toy?"

"It's a Glock Twenty-Six." Ruth answered for her. "I didn't know the Met used them."

"They don't." Gina slipped the gun back into a polymer holster at her side. "It's a private thing. You really think the kidnappers might make a go for her?"

Ruth shrugged. "On what we've seen so far, I wouldn't bet against it. That business near the supermarket was too organised for merely keeping an eye on her; they were ready to pick her up. And Clarisse happening along was part of it. They knew Nancy had gone out and were scouting the terrain."

Nobody argued. There was no point.

The game was closing in.

TWENTY-SIX

WHILE RUTH PARKED THE car and called in a progress report to Aston, Gina and Vaslik made their way inside. She caught up with them at the emergency reception, where they were directed to a small waiting area close to where Nancy was being assessed. A nurse came and spoke briefly to Gina to ask how long Nancy had been underwater and what medications she was on, then disappeared after telling them that they would be kept informed.

Ruth called Aston again and asked for their consultant to be informed, so that he could find out what was going on.

"This is going to blow their minds," she told the others. "It's way too public for the board's liking." Unlike some crisis management companies, the Cruxys board of directors had always operated in the background, avoiding publicity and shunning any kind of limelight. The motivation was simple: if their staff and operatives became public material, they could no longer guarantee being able to work in secret. And for most of their clients, that would make them a danger, as known faces drew the media like moths to a flame.

When the consultant bustled in, resplendent in a grey suit and pocket handkerchief, he spoke briefly to Gina before disappearing in search of an authority figure he could bully. He returned a few minutes later with good news.

"She's responding to treatment," he assured them. "She has bruising to the back of her head where she hit the bath, but no obvious signs of concussion. She remembers feeling dizzy and was probably overcome by running the bath too hot."

"So she'll be all right?" Ruth pressed him. "Can we take her home?"

The look he gave her was larded with irritation. He lowered his voice as a nurse hurried by. "Miss Gonzales, I do have an idea of what Mrs. Hardman is going through. She's under immense stress and the continued pressure of not knowing what has happened to her daughter is weighing heavily on her mind. I gather there was some kind of incident earlier today—she mentioned something about a woman caller and a man following her in the street. She felt threatened. Is it true?"

"Yes, we think so." Ruth swore silently. In spite of her fragile condition, Nancy must have picked up on the possible snatch team near the supermarket and blabbed to the consultant. Coupled with the mysterious Clarisse turning up, it was no wonder she was freaking out. She wondered how many others had heard. "You know we can't talk about it," she said firmly. The doctor might be on a retainer with Cruxys, but that didn't mean he could be party to everything that was going on. "There are things happening in her life, yes; but she's also seeing shadows where there are none. We all are," she added for good measure.

He appeared somewhat mollified. "Very well. I'll take your word for it. I've asked for her to be kept in overnight so that more tests can be carried out in the morning. All being well, you can take her home then. But only if they pass her as fit enough."

"Can we see her?" asked Gina. When he looked doubtful, she added, "It might make her feel safer if she saw us all here."

His mouth gave a curl. "Of course. But only for a few minutes— and I suggest you don't allow the staff to know what's going on. These places are notoriously leaky with information; if there's a sniff of what she's going through the press and police will be around here in droves."

———

After speaking briefly to a drowsy Nancy and assuring her that she was safe and that they were watching over her, Ruth and Vaslik left Gina on watch and returned to the house to get her some fresh clothing for the morning. The journey gave Ruth a chance to ask Vaslik a question.

"Why are you armed, Slik? Bit early in the assignment, isn't it?"

"It's a habit I find tough to break," he answered briefly. "Aren't you?"

"No. Believe it or not, we don't all carry guns and nor are we routinely allowed to."

"But you could if you wanted."

"I suppose so. But we'd be on our own if we got caught." She looked at him. "They did explain that to you, didn't they—that the gun laws here are a tiny bit tougher than in the US?"

"Sure, they told me. I'll keep it under wraps, I promise."

"Good. Because if you shoot anybody, I won't be able to protect you—and nor will Cruxys." She was tempted to enquire where he'd

164

got the weapon but knew she'd probably receive the same vague answer Gina had given.

She pulled onto the kerb in front of the house and killed the engine. She wanted to ask about the missing napkin, but decided against it. Now was not the time. Instead, she stepped out of the car and led the way across the drive and opened the front door.

Once inside, they both froze.

Something was different.

———

Vaslik pushed past Ruth, drawing his gun and listening. He motioned for her to check the living room while he did the same upstairs. This was the most hazardous task in house clearance, as Ruth knew. Going up open stairs towards a potential threat left the upper body wide open and vulnerable; you had to move fast but quietly as you cleared the top steps, while checking both ways for a potential assailant. Along with all the doors to use as cover, it gave any intruder the advantage.

On the other hand, she reminded herself, Slik had a weapon and had probably done this kind of thing many times before.

She heard his footsteps moving lightly up the treads as she moved through to the living room. Empty. Next was the kitchen, also bare save for the flickering of the CCTV monitors covering the front, sides and rear. Nothing of interest there.

She moved across the hallway to the study. The door was wide open. She couldn't recall if that was how it had been left, but stepped inside and listened.

Nothing.

She stepped back into the hallway and heard movement above her. "Slik?"

He was coming down the stairs, tucking this gun away and shaking his head. "Nobody home but us bears."

"But there has been, right? Or am I imagining things?"

He shook his head. "If you are, so am I." They had both sensed it the moment they stepped through the front door: somebody had been inside the house while they had been at the hospital. It wasn't a specific smell, nor were there any visual signs; but they were experienced enough to have picked up the signals as surely as if the visitor had left a calling card on the hall table. Yet it didn't appear that anything had been disturbed or stolen.

So why?

Vaslik seemed to have one answer. He raised a hand to warn Ruth to stay still, then knelt by the study door and scrubbed at a minute trace of white powder on the carpet against the skirting board. He ran his fingers up the wall immediately above it, to a framed print of a desert scene. When he carefully pulled the frame away from the wall, Ruth saw a slim biscuit the size of a ten pence piece stuck to the back.

Vaslik turned to her and made a circular motion with his finger at the veiling and walls, then a zipping motion across his mouth and tapped his ear.

Ruth stared. She didn't want to believe it, but he was right.

He was talking about bugs.

Somebody had been inside and placed listening devices inside the house.

———

It took Vaslik an hour to scour the building, taking great care not to disturb anything until he was certain. One by one he discovered four similar devices. They were small, slim and easily concealed; one behind a photo frame in the living room, another in the kitchen above a cupboard, a third in the study close to the filing cabinet and one in Nancy's room.

He took them down and wrapped them carefully in a towel, and placed the bundle in the airing cupboard. Then he beckoned Ruth into the kitchen and turned on the kettle.

"It won't be all of them," he warned her quietly, once the kettle was making a satisfactory level of noise to mask conversation. "All I got was the ones they wanted us to find. There will be others but much better concealed."

"Won't they get suspicious when they don't hear us talking?"

"They'll hear plenty—but only what we want them to hear."

"Still, they'll know you found some of the bugs."

"Of course. But they'll keep listening because that's the way the game is played."

"Game?" She gave him a cynical look. "Is that what this is?"

"Sure. Spies spying on spies; it's the same the world over. You trick the opposition into thinking they know what you're doing, but you always have a plan B."

"And their plan B is to have more bugs that we don't know about."

"That's right—unless we bring in some electronic counter-measures and sweep the house. Then everybody's back to square one and it starts all over."

"Jesus, what a waste of time. Did you recognise the equipment?"

"You mean where it's from?"

"Yes."

"It's not really my scene. Electronic surveillance is a huge business; there are many different devices made and sold all over the world. I know the FBI and Secret Service use bugs from a variety of sources, as do your own intelligence agencies here, probably. And nobody uses bugs that can be traced back home, anyway; it's too big a giveaway."

Ruth didn't say anything. This whole affair was taking on a much bigger significance than a simple kidnapping—if a kidnapping could ever be referred to as simple. From the snatch of a small child, it seemed to have blossomed into something more and more complex, with ever more questions and fewer answers.

"I wish I knew what the hell was going on here," she muttered. "This thing's beginning to drive me nuts."

TWENTY-SEVEN

IT WAS HALFWAY THROUGH the next morning before Nancy was discharged from hospital after undergoing a battery of tests. They were all clear, but the duty doctor had recommended bed rest and no excitement, and agreed that she would be better at home in familiar surroundings rather than in a busy ward. If he had any questions about the presence of three people who were clearly not family members, he was discreet enough not to ask.

Gina shepherded Nancy upstairs into her bedroom and made sure she was settled, then closed the door and joined the others downstairs.

"She's groggy," she reported, entering the kitchen. The kettle was roaring, the button held down by Vaslik to prevent it switching off. "Thankfully she'll be out for a while and I can crash." She helped herself to coffee and checked the CCTV monitors, then gave a questioning look at Vaslik and Ruth. They had warned her about the bugs they'd found, and that others might be present. "So what do we do? Act like we didn't find them or go outside each time we need to talk?"

"Act normally," Vaslik suggested quietly. "They know we're here now, so there's no point pretending. They'll also know we've found some of the bugs. What we don't want to do is let them in on everything we know."

"Jesus, how much is that?"

"Not a lot, yet," said Ruth. "But Slik's right: they don't know what we've discovered yet. If we can keep them guessing, they might make a mistake."

"So we wait for them to make the next move?"

"Pretty much—at least, outwardly. It's all we can do."

"That sounds like you have a plan."

"Maybe I do." She had been thinking about what other avenues they could explore instead of sitting on their hands and letting the kidnappers dictate the game; any link they could follow up that might lead to the people behind the abduction. Since Michael Hardman seemed to be beyond anybody's immediate reach, it left few options to work on. But there was one they hadn't yet touched on.

Tiggi Sgornik. The nanny.

———

The house Tiggi had given as her address was in the middle of a Victorian terrace on a quiet street fronting a large cemetery. A low and rusted iron gate made a show of shielding two wheelie bins in a tight front yard with broken paving, and mismatched curtains and a peeling fascia showed the presence of renters, not residents.

Ruth drove past without stopping and hung a left at the end of the street and stopped. They were between two rows of houses at a point where the gardens at the back of each row butted up against each other. Some of the buildings had been extended into the gardens, giving a lot more room inside than a first look might indicate.

"How many residents, I wonder?" she pondered.

Vaslik assessed the size of the properties. "I'm not familiar with these places, but at a guess, could be anything up to a dozen."

She agreed. From what Nancy had said the house sounded like a base for a shifting population of visitors and transients from the homeland, ever changing, staying for a short while to fuel up and find another job before moving on. The same pattern could be found almost anywhere in London, the only difference being language and colour, each drawn to their own like magnets.

They left the car and walked round to the front door. The street was quiet, the row of houses silent and uniformly neat and uncommunicative. There was no sound coming from behind the door. Sleeping off late shifts, probably.

Vaslik leaned on the bell-push.

A movement behind coloured glass. The door swung back to reveal a dishevelled youth of about eighteen in tracksuit pants and a T-shirt, scratching his chest.

"Yeah, what?" Even in two words, his accent came out as if he were chewing on ground glass.

"Is Tiggi in?" Ruth tried to ignore the smell of over-heated and humid air drifting around the youth's shoulders like sour gas. With it came the smell of spices. A voice called out from the depths of the building but he didn't respond, busy trying to process the question and formulate a reply.

"Who wants her?" he said finally, eyes flicking coolly from Ruth to Vaslik. They stayed longer on the American, assessing the clothes and face, apparently not liking what they saw.

Wrong answer, thought Ruth. You're no great actor. Now we know we've got the right place. "She didn't turn up for work. We're worried about her."

The gears ground slowly for a few seconds, then the youth said, "She not here anymore." He began to close the door.

Vaslik's hand shot out and stopped it. The youth pushed harder but it was no contest.

"Hey—you can not do this—"

"Too late. We're in." Vaslik moved him aside without effort, pinning him against the wall with his forearm. The youth struggled but got nowhere.

Ruth checked the surroundings. They were in a narrow hallway running the length of the house, with a stairway to their left and two doors opening to the right. The atmosphere was close and dark, not helped by dark wallpaper and a scrubby brown carpet. A low hum of music was coming from the first door, which was either a living room or doubling as a spare bedroom, and voices rumbled from the end of the hallway, followed by a burst of laughter.

Vaslik said something to the youth. He spoke quietly and quickly, their faces no more than six inches apart. Ruth didn't understand a word but the threat was as clear as a bell.

Whatever he'd said had an immediate impact on the youth. He stopped struggling and went quite still. Only his eyes continued moving like marbles in a pinball machine.

Vaslik dropped his hand, allowing the youth to go free, and stepped back.

They followed the youth to the back of the house, and found three men in a large kitchen area. Two, dressed in jeans and tracksuit tops, were drinking coffee. They looked tired, their faces drawn and unshaven. The third, a large man with a bald head and hands like clamps, was stirring something in a large pot on the stove. It smelled of tomatoes and onions, and spices Ruth couldn't place. The place was surprisingly tidy and clean, and clearly somebody had control over what happened in this room at least.

The two coffee drinkers froze before putting down their mugs, while the cook stopped stirring and raised his chin in query at the newcomers.

"Who is this?" His voice was another surprise; it was soft, the accent obvious but the words precise, as if he had practiced his speech with great care.

The youth said something and all three men stared at Vaslik, who smiled without comment. Then the cook said something to the youth, who turned and left the room, throwing a quick sneer at Vaslik as he went.

"Care to fill me in?" Ruth murmured. She could feel the atmosphere in the room like a heavy fog, and wondered how long it would be before one of these men made a run for the door. He wouldn't get very far; the back door was blocked by a dustbin, which left the only way out down the hallway to the front. She figured they could already bid goodbye to the youth, who'd been given a head start.

"I explained who we are," Vaslik replied. "That we are from Immigration and need to speak to Miss Sgornik. Nobody else, just her." He nodded at the three men. "They're now trying to decide if it's worth telling us to go screw ourselves or whether we might bring down the ceiling on their status if they don't cooperate."

Ruth understood their reaction. It was very likely that there were some illegals in the house, and at least two of these three might be without papers. She could hear voices and footsteps coming down the stairs as the building woke up to the presence of newcomers, no doubt alerted by the youth, and somebody called out from the front room.

They didn't have much time before a crowd gathered, and she fixed her attention on the cook, who seemed to be top dog here.

"We've already had a long day," she said quietly. "All we want is to know where Miss Sgornik is." She gestured over her shoulder as somebody shouted from the stairs. "Tell your friends to go back to bed or whatever they were doing; we're not interested in them." She held her phone close to her mouth, like a radio. "Or we call in back-up and go to town on this place. Your call."

"Wait." The cook raised a hand and gave instructions to one of the coffee drinkers, who turned and disappeared back up the hall-way. He said something to the men gathered at the bottom of the stairs which had them retreating fast, two of them out the front door and the others back up the way they had come.

Great weeding-out process, Ruth thought, and turned back to baldy, the cook.

He was looking at Vaslik. "You're American?"

"Yes, I am. Problem?"

"Why are you here, dealing with this … stuff." He gestured at the house with his spoon, flicking a gob of tomato sauce onto the floor. He cursed under his breath and grabbed a cloth and bent to clean it up.

"I'm on an exchange program," Vaslik explained. "Not that it concerns you. What's your name, by the way? I'm Andrei."

"They call me Aron. This is my house."

"OK, Aron. Where's Miss Sgornik?"

The cook dropped his spoon in the pot and slid it off the heat. "OK. We don't want trouble, all right? If I help you, you'll go and leave everything as it is?"

"Yes."

"And you?" He looked at Ruth.

"Of course. Guides' promise."

He looked sceptical, but nodded. "Tiggi didn't come back. We don't know where she is. Probably on a yacht somewhere with her boyfriend."

"Does this boyfriend have a name?"

"Must do. But I don't know it. She never said. All I know is, she started talking about going away soon, when she had more money. Somewhere warm and nice, not like this place or home." His mouth took a sour twist. "I think she has ambition, our Tiggi. Trouble is, her brains don't match her looks, you know?" He snapped his fingers in thought. "She's like a fine racehorse but can't run for shit, you know what I mean?"

"You sound bitter," said Vaslik. "Did she leave you for this boyfriend?"

Aron gave a rueful smile. "No, not me. I am not in her class. I am too settled for her. I work in a restaurant and that's where I'm happy. Tiggi, though, she wants the world." He spread his arms wide. "Trouble is, she don't know the dangers out there."

"Why do you say that?" said Ruth.

"Because she's innocent—is that right—innocent?"

"Naïve."

"OK. Better. Naïve. She think money is everything, will bring happiness and a good life." He shrugged. "Maybe it will. But I don't think so. Last time she came home, it was very late and she had a mark here." He pointed at his face, just beneath one eye.

"What happened?"

"I ask her but she won't say. I tell her if it's her boyfriend, I'll go round and deal with him but she goes mad and tells me to mind my business. She looked real scared. I tell you, there's something not good going on there."

"You're worried about her."

"Yes, I guess so. She's a sweet girl, you know?" He blushed, the colour spreading across his crown as he revealed his true feelings. "But so damned naïve."

Love-struck, thought Ruth. She felt sorry for him. "We'd like to see her room."

Aron nodded. "Sure. I take you." He adjusted the heat on the cooker, then gave rapid instructions to the other man, pointing at the pot and making a stirring gesture. "But slow, understand?" he said in English, for the visitors' benefit. "Not like digging ditch. Slow. Or you don't eat."

He led the way upstairs to the top of the house at the rear, where a dormer window looked out over the back gardens. The room was small, neat and tidy, plainly decorated but with a few frilly items showing that the owner was a girl with a taste for colour.

"Nice," said Ruth. "Are all the rooms like this?"

He snorted. "You kidding, lady? The others, they live like rats, all together and lazy. Tiggi is the only woman and she pay more rent, so she get the best room."

"Doesn't that pose problems, all those men and one woman?"

He shook his head. "Never. They respect women or they have me to deal with." He ducked his head. "Anyway, Tiggi has this look, you know?"

"Look?" Vaslik.

"Yeah. She a girl but she has a look like everyone know not to mess with her. I don't know how she does that."

"It's called confidence," Ruth murmured, and moved over to check the wardrobe. "Trouble is, it shares room with being naïve, too. How long had she been here?"

"About two months. She got my name from someone in the community and call round. Lucky I had the room empty, so she moved right in. What you look for exactly?"

"Whatever will tell us," said Vaslik, "where she might be. That's all."

"Why is she in trouble with Immigration? She got papers, I know that. All legal."

"She's not in trouble," Ruth interjected. "But we think she's mixed up with some bad people." She dug out a card containing her number and handed it to him. "If you think of anything else or you hear from Tiggi, call me."

"Serious?"

"Very."

He seemed to deflate, the air going out of him in a long sigh. "I knew it. I could have done more. I should have." He said something at length in Polish, and looked sick.

"What you're already doing is plenty," Vaslik murmured, and moved into the room. "Believe me. We'll do our best to track her down."

It was Aron's signal to leave. He nodded and walked back downstairs.

TWENTY-EIGHT

NANCY CAME AWAKE SLOWLY, as if emerging from a sticky fog. Her mouth tasted stale and her head was spinning, bringing memories of long-ago hangovers at university, when restraint was simply a word in a dictionary. She struggled to move upright in the bed, for a moment unsure of her surroundings. Then she noted the familiar and the safe; the colours of home and the comforting silence. Even though mostly semi-conscious in the hospital, she had been all too aware of the constant rush of footsteps, of murmured voices and the clank and buzz of equipment.

The clock by the bed read 11:45 am. She'd been asleep only a short while but if felt longer. She sat forward, allowing her head to settle. Something had penetrated her sleep, tugging her out of the chasm she'd fallen into, but she couldn't pin it down. A sound. Something alien. Probably just a car outside.

She closed her eyes again, allowing the darkness to envelope her.

Beth.

The memories came rushing in, and with them a surge of guilt. She sat up, engulfed by a wave of nausea. How could she have not remembered the second she opened her eyes? What kind of mother was she? She threw back the covers in irritation. She had to speak to Gina or Ruth ... even the American, Vaslik. One of them might tell her if anything had happened. All she could remember was running a bath, then feeling overwhelmed by heat and humidity, and ... nothing.

She heard a low buzzing noise. Intermittent, it was coming in bursts from somewhere nearby. The sound was familiar; she remembered now. Like an angry bumble bee caught behind a net curtain. Softer, yet just as insistent.

It came again, three short bursts, then silence. Not a bee. Something electronic.

The dresser.

She slid out of bed, putting on her slippers and pulling her dressing gown around her shoulders, waiting while the room tilted, then righted itself. Don't move too fast. Take it easy.

She stood up and took the three steps towards the dresser, instinct making her tread softly, one ear cocked for movement outside her bedroom door, which was closed.

She pulled open the second drawer down. Her undies drawer as she called it. Her one indulgence whenever she could afford it, which wasn't often.

She burrowed down through the thin layers of silk and lace, and her fingers encountered something solid. She flicked aside a couple of folded bras and found the slim, glossy black shape of a cell phone.

What?

She took it out, the feel of the device strange, the balance lighter than her own phone, which was downstairs in the kitchen drawer.

The screen was on and the message icon was blinking. She pressed the View key.

It was from Michael.

Her fingers began trembling so much she almost dropped the phone. She wasn't sure if it was the journey from her bed to here or the excitement and relief of seeing his name, but she felt a rush of relief followed by a drumming in her head.

The text message was simple:

Text me at noon. Use a safe word that we both know to show you are alone and not under pressure. I need to know what is happening. I will explain everything. Delete all messages and hide this. M

She slumped against the dresser, her legs going weak, and managed to get back to the bed where she fell back against the pillows. Her face was wet with silent tears and her head bursting with questions, wondering why Michael was communicating with her this way, so cold and disconnected. If he could text, why didn't he call? *Why didn't he come home?* She felt a burst of anger at the remoteness of his words, but pushed them down somewhere deep inside. Anger was pointless, she knew that. Michael called it a wasted emotion, and that hard resolve was so much better. She had never got round to asking him what that meant, adding it to the various topics they had never discussed fully during their years together, like the Safeguard contract. But that was for another time. As always, she trusted him implicitly, and felt guilty at her brief surge of doubt. For now she had to continue trusting him, knowing that he would do the right thing, and that they would eventually be safe—and together.

She dried her eyes and face and checked the time. 11.55. Just five minutes to compose a text, but it wouldn't take long. Considering she had no-one else to communicate with in this way, other than the regular and uniform messages to Michael, it was something at which she was fairly adept.

She began pressing the keys, using alternate thumbs in a rapid-fire way to tell him what had happened so far, one ear cocked for Gina making one of her periodic checks. As she typed, she was thinking about a safe word to use; one that only she and Michael would know, and would fit into the text if an outsider saw it. Somehow she knew Michael would use one in return. She didn't question why he was doing this, only that it was necessary because he said so. She looked around her bedroom, hoping for inspiration.

Then she had it. Beth's favourite teddy; it was sitting on the end of her bed.

... *you must be Homesick,* she typed. The capital letter was deliberate, to catch the eye. Michael would see it and understand. She fastened on that thought, wiping away all other fears and doubts.

Michael was alive and safe. That was all she needed to know. Everything would be fine now.

———

The response from Michael came within twenty minutes, and Nancy felt elated by the simple words. Words of reassurance, of hope. Contact at last.

He texted, "*Don't worry. They won't harm her.*"

"*They? Who they?*" she responded.

"*Not sure. Best not trust anyone.*"

"*Not Cruxys?*"

"*No.*"

"*But you said call them.*"

181

"Yes. Things have changed."

"Why Beth? I don't understand."

"One day you will. For now you must stay strong. For Beth. For me. For us all. Delete this. M. x."

He was gone, the remoteness of his words burning into her brain. It hadn't sounded like Michael, and she wondered if it was the need to conserve words that made him come across that way. She deleted the texts as instructed and switched off the phone. As she returned it to the drawer, slipping it beneath her underwear where it would be safe from discovery, it occurred to her that she hadn't asked Michael how the device had got here. It hadn't been in the drawer yesterday—of that she was certain. The thought made her flesh creep.

Someone had been in their home.

In this room.

———

As Nancy slipped back beneath the covers and closed her eyes, a black 4WD entered the end of the street. It stopped at the kerb a hundred yards away, beyond the reach of the CCTV camera at the front, beyond Gina Fraser's watchful eyes. The driver was on the phone, listening to instructions. After a few minutes, he did a three-point turn and disappeared back the way he had come.

TWENTY-NINE

CAREFULLY NOTING WHERE EVERYTHING lay to ensure they missed nothing, Vaslik and Ruth took Tiggi Sgornik's room apart piece by piece. They lifted everything that could be moved, including the carpet, wardrobe and dresser; checked under the mattress, looking for slits in the fabric, signs that there had been repairs made, anything that might indicate a potential place of concealment. They emptied every drawer, checking the underneath, sides and backs, then moved on to the structure of the dresser and wardrobe, running their fingers across the wood for a trace of a raised or indented surface. They unscrewed the feet, looking for hollows or slots, the familiar hidey-holes for children, spies and those conducting illicit undertakings. Tiggi hadn't owned much clothing, but they scoured every item, pants, skirts and shoes, testing heels and hems, lapels and pockets, looking for signs that a line of stitching had been opened and re-done.

"She seems to have had money," Vaslik commented sourly. He was staring at the clothing, which was going to have to go back where they had found it. Among it was the empty packaging from a cell phone. He picked it up and examined the labelling. It was a cheap pay-as-you-go model with no retailer's marking. "Didn't extend to her cell phone, though. Maybe cute only goes so far."

"You're a cynic, Slik," murmured Ruth. "But you're right: I doubt it was her—not on a nanny's pay. She's a lucky girl." She dropped the pair of fluffy slippers she'd been checking and sat on the bed with a sigh. "Are we done here?"

He nodded, sure of himself. "I think so. If there's anything, it's in the fabric of the building and we're not going to find it without using a pickaxe—and I don't think we'd get that past the head chef downstairs."

Ruth was frustrated. She'd been certain they might find something here, even a sign that Michael Hardman *had* got something going with the nanny. At least it would have given them an avenue to explore. But this was nothing, leading nowhere. A big fat blank.

Her phone buzzed. It was George Paperas.

"I called a few more people," he announced, meaning aid agencies. "Two more knew of Hardman, another two had engaged him—one in Pakistan, the other in the Maghreb, in Tunisia. This guy gets around. I've got him popping up in Somalia, Kenya, and Algeria, and a couple of other places. The agencies who knew him or could remember him all reported the same story: he worked with them for a few days, two weeks at most, then disappeared. No explanations, just up and gone."

"How could he just move around like that? Don't aid workers have accreditation or visas?"

"It's complicated. Yes, all humanitarian aid organisations and their staff should have official permission to work in a region like, say, Pakistan. Sometimes they don't get it for local political reasons, sometimes safety. Each group would or should issue their staff with papers to identify them and their reasons for being there. But with the smaller ones, it's not always followed to the letter. To be honest, there are one or two I've come across who don't like the interference and simply want to get on with the job. I can sympathise with that; bureaucracy can get in the way of good deeds. But it's a dangerous thing to do. Like the Christian fundamentalists who got caught distributing bibles in Moscow."

"Proselytizing."

"Sure. It was deliberate or stupid, depending on your point of view. But with agency work, having no papers can get you suspected of being there for reasons other than humanitarian help. And in some of the remoter areas, no papers means you won't be missed if they decide they don't like your face."

Ruth felt her neck go cold. "They'd kill them?"

"Yes. It's happened, believe me."

On the wall across from the bed was an alpine scene showing a distant rock-face capped by snow and edged by cliffs of granite reaching into the sky. Ruth presumed it was somewhere that reminded Tiggi of home, but it prompted a thought about something Paperas had said in his last phone call about Hardman.

"You said that when Hardman was with Oxfam he'd been driving trucks close to the border near Peshawar. Is that right?"

"Yes."

"How close?" She didn't know what prompted the question, but the sight of mountain passes in the picture must have jogged her thought processes.

"Pretty close, if I remember the terrain. If he was delivering supplies, he'd have been pretty much on his own for long periods, and it's not as if he would have been monitored closely by security forces unless he hit a road block. Aid trucks are common, and they're more interested in looking for small groups or individuals travelling at odd hours of the day or night."

"What about the agency he was working for?"

"Drivers are expected to be independent and to get on with the job. The agencies don't have the time or resources to watch them closely. Why?"

Vaslik was staring at her with a fixed expression on his face, and she wondered what he was thinking. Whatever it was, it had him looking worried.

"No reason," she said. "Brainstorming, that's all."

THIRTY

On the way back to the Hardman house, Ruth called George Paperas. An idea had popped into her head while she was in Tiggi Sgornik's bedroom. It was bothering her and wouldn't let go, like a toothache. Even saying it out loud would sound ludicrous to almost anybody she could think of, which meant anybody in Cruxys. But Paperas was the first person she could think of on the outside who might have an answer.

Slik was going to be the first to hear it, too, unless she kicked him out of the car, but he'd have to suck it up. Maybe he'd learn something. She turned on the loudspeaker.

"Would any of the paperwork from the aid agencies in Pakistan," she asked Paperas when he answered, "have been enough to get Michael Hardman across the border?"

She had her eyes fixed on the road ahead, but felt Vaslik tense in the seat alongside her, his head turning to look at her in surprise.

"Into Afghanistan?" George sounded shocked, his voice booming in the car. "Why would he do that? He'd have to be crazy."

Or some kind of adrenalin freak who loved following disaster, she thought acidly. "Would it?"

There was a lengthy silence. Then he said, "Not by itself, no. I doubt he'd have got official permission anyway, even if he'd asked, not without the agreement of both governments, the coalition forces and God knows who else up to President Karzai himself."

"But he could still get across of he wanted to?"

"If getting into Afghanistan was that important to him, yes, I suppose so. And he wouldn't have needed any paperwork. The border is too long and porous to be tightly controlled along its full length."

"You mean he could simply have walked over?"

"If he knew where he was going, yes. It's not always easy to see. Anything's possible up there. It's wild country. All you need to do is find a guide who's probably halfway off his head on *Charas*—that's cannabis—or any of the opiates, and you can cross almost anywhere he's willing to take you. And you don't need paperwork to do it." He stopped speaking, and Ruth swore she heard the penny drop. "Christ, do you know what you're suggesting?"

"You tell me."

"Is he using the agencies to get into restricted areas?"

"No comment."

"I don't believe it. That's appalling."

Paperas was no idiot; he'd worked out what Ruth was thinking. But was she right and how could she confirm it? And what would it prove, beyond the fact that Michael Hardman was a certifiable lunatic? He was hardly likely to come out and admit it.

"I don't know for sure. I'm thinking out loud, that's all; trying to figure him out. If he's got background of any kind, the sort that would make his daughter worth kidnapping, I want to know what it is." If we don't, she was thinking, we may never get her back.

"By background, what do you mean?"

"Just that. I mean, what the hell do we know about him or his history? Nothing apart from what Nancy has told us—" She stopped dead and turned to stare at Vaslik. History. "Oh, my God."

"What?" George asked.

She answered but was now talking at Vaslik. "Something Nancy told me that Michael had said when they first got together. He said it gave him a sense of history."

"A nice sentiment. So?"

"What if that wasn't just a sentiment, but the absolute truth? What if it gave him a back story?"

Vaslik was staring straight ahead, but she could see the question in his face, and hoped it was giving way to a realisation that she was right.

"It makes sense," she insisted. "Something about Hardman brought him to the attention of kidnappers—whoever they are. And unless it's Oxfam trying a tougher line in recruiting procedures, it's something he's kept carefully hidden, even from his wife."

George sounded doubtful. "What are you going to do?"

"I'm not sure yet. Dig a little more, see what I come up with. Keep it to yourself, though, George," she finished. "There's a little girl out there still. And we never had this conversation."

"Of course."

She cut the connection and stopped in front of the Hardman house. What now?

"Interesting conclusion." Vaslik was looking at her with what appeared to be respect. And concern. "How the hell did you come by it?"

"It's a wild idea, that's all. Don't get your knickers in a twist." She wished now that she'd called Paperas when she was alone. In spite of Vaslik's reaction, she was still out on a limb with this one. "I'm simply trying to figure out things about this man. He's a puzzle … and I don't like puzzles."

"I agree. But there's still nothing to suggest Hardman's involved in anything suspicious. He's just not around … which is weird enough, I guess." He sounded as if he was talking it out, rather than criticising her, which she was pleased about. "He's got a few questions against him, that's for sure; but only because we don't know where he is. That doesn't make him a criminal."

"So what does it make him?" She turned to face him. "Let's get really wild and assume he used the agency in Peshawar to get across the border disguised as a field worker. Why would he do that? There has to be a reason—a really good one."

He pulled a face, but nodded slowly. "OK. But he'd also have to be certain of getting there. Nobody crosses that stretch of land without thinking carefully. It's wild, sure, but also under constant scrutiny. They've got drones up there day and night, looking for insurgents and arms shipments. It'd be like a turkey-shoot to anybody who didn't know their way around."

"Which knocks out George's idea of a junked-up guide; it would be too risky. Supposing Hardman had a sure-fire way across; a reliable guide who did the trip on a regular basis and who knew all the back trails and choke points, the observation posts and patrol routes?"

"Smuggling? Man, I don't know. I thought the Taliban and warlords had that region stitched up tight. There's no room for outsiders—especially Europeans."

He was right. Stupid idea. Any trip one individual could make across the no-man's land—even two men and a donkey—would find the rewards more than outweighed by the risks. If they weren't picked up by the security forces from Pakistan or the Coalition, or killed in a drone strike by mistake, there was every chance they'd be stopped and knocked off quietly by the local drugs gangs protecting their territory. What went on in those distant valleys usually stayed there.

And if he was a smuggler, why would he need to create a history for himself in the UK?

"On the other hand," Vaslik continued tentatively, working his way through the idea, "he wasn't only working in Peshawar, was he? Where else has he been?"

Ruth stared at him, her breathing rapid and her chest tight. Christ, why hadn't she thought of that? She called Paperas, again on loudspeaker.

"Sorry, George," she said. "Another question. I should have made notes. As a matter of interest, where else did Hardman volunteer his services apart from Peshawar? You said a number of organisations remembered him."

"Hang on. I've got a list here." They heard a rustle of paper, then Paperas came back on. "Definite sightings are ... good lord." He sounded surprised by what he was seeing.

"What?"

"Well, he was in Pakistan, as we know, near Peshawar. And Syria, Turkey, Kurdistan, Lebanon, all for definite. Then I've got Mali, Somalia and Nigeria as others places he was seen but not recorded for certain. But—"

"But what?"

"It's not really the kind of thing they'd mistake." He paused, his breathing loud. "Frankly I'm amazed he managed to operate in such a diverse area."

"How do you mean?"

"Well, languages for one. Work in this business long enough and most aid workers pick up a working knowledge of one or two. But this chap must have been something else."

"Wouldn't he have had local interpreters in some places?"

"Of course. But even so … he didn't let lack of familiarity hold him back. There's another thing that's just struck me. This list reads like—"

"I know what it reads like," Ruth cut him off short. They were all countries with or connected to highly active terrorist organisations. "Thank you for your help, George. Remember what I said."

She hung up and looked at Vaslik. "Aren't you going to say something? Like, am I out of my tree?"

"Well, fuck," was all he said, his voice soft. "I never saw that coming."

THIRTY-ONE

VASLIK FOLLOWED RUTH UP to the house, where Gina was waiting to let them in. He nodded at the former police bodyguard as Ruth went directly to the living room. He could see Nancy waiting for them, pacing up and down. Her movements seemed unnaturally jagged, and her eyes far too animated to be normal. When she smiled it was fleetingly bright but lacking depth, like a child trying to fool an adult that all was well when it really wasn't.

"What's with her?" he asked softly.

"Search me," Gina replied. "She's been like it since lunchtime; up and down like a hooker's drawers. It's like she's pissed. I'd have checked the booze stash but she doesn't have one."

He'd seen it before in relatives of kidnap cases in the US. The effect of the abduction of a loved one on the nerves was bad enough; the addition of prescription drugs plus whatever else the family had in their bathroom cabinets was generally enough to send them up and down like an express elevator, varying from dulled torpor to freaky bursts of activity and near manic anxiety levels.

He left them to it and ran a security check of the doors, windows and back gate, watched with amused detachment by Gina. He knew she would have been over this already, but it was something he had to do for his own peace of mind. In any case, she would have done the same had their roles been reversed. It was what made them pros in their business.

He ran another check for further listening devices but found nothing. They were there, though, he was certain of it; like woodworm in an ancient staircase. This worried him from two standpoints: the watchers, whoever they were, must know by now who was in the house and what they were—even who they worked for. But there was nothing he could do about that beyond being careful of what was said aloud. More worrying was that whoever had installed the bugs had access to technical facilities way beyond the norm. He had been allowed to find the easy ones, the decoys, but the rest, the ones he hadn't seen, would be undetectable without scanning equipment. And that took resources he could only guess at.

Back in the kitchen, he turned on the kettle and said, "I have to go out."

"Again?" Ruth was in the doorway. She gave him a quizzical look before waving him away. "Sorry. I'm being Mother Hen. Do what you have to. I'm going to make a report to Aston about what George Paperas told us. Then I'm going to talk to Nancy and see if there's anything else I can find out about our mysterious aid worker with the ability to cross borders."

"Good luck with that," Gina muttered. "Whatever she's high on, I wish I had some."

―――――

Vaslik exited through the back gate. He walked round to the supermarket where he had seen the near-confrontation the day before, and found a corner table in the cafeteria. It was quiet; a trio of utility workers in fluorescent jackets and boots, two mothers with small children and a waitress cleaning tables with a marked lack of enthusiasm. While deserted enough for him to have a corner table away from the others, there was just enough noise to cloak the conversation he was planning. He bought a mug of coffee and sat staring at his cell phone on the table, and chewing over what he knew so far and how that impacted on what he was about to do. He was concerned about the events of the past few hours, especially the topic of Ruth's conversation with George Paperas. That had taken an unexpected turn, and something he hadn't been ready for.

He was surprised by Ruth's doggedness, and the way she was able to stitch ideas together from very little. He'd seen it before in professional investigators, but usually those with vastly more experience and training. They'd take what seemed a slanted view of evidence or events, and out of nothing, formulate an idea that had been missed by others … and which usually turned out correct. Ruth didn't have the long experience, but she certainly had a natural talent for lateral thinking.

Which might be a problem.

For example the napkin he'd found at the house along the road; she had noticed it, he was sure, probably recognised it, too. Maybe not instantly, but that was why he'd removed it: out of sight, out of mind. But it would come to her sooner or later. And if it meant what he thought it did—and if she came to the same conclusion—then it would only be a matter of time before the questions began. And he could see no way of avoiding them save for playing dumb. And that would only work for so long.

He picked up the cell phone and wondered what the hell he was doing. Why was he even thinking about whether Ruth might be a problem or not? They were colleagues, for God's sake, tasked with working on the same assignment. What did he owe to anyone outside this immediate job, save a questionable loyalty?

He checked the contacts list. The number he selected was buried deep among home-based details, like his dentist and lawyer. The kind of stuff nobody would bother looking at. It was a number he'd been given shortly after arriving in London, with instructions that he should only call in if completely unavoidable.

The number had the Washington dial code 202.

Screw unavoidable, he thought sourly. This was a car wreck waiting to happen…

The number, which he figured would be a twenty-four-hour government switchboard, rang out ten times before it was picked up.

"It's Vaslik," he said simply, when a woman's voice answered. "I need to talk."

"Wait one." The woman sounded calm, almost casual. East coast, he guessed, possibly Virginia or round there. He had an ear for accents. "We'll get back to you."

"Hold on—" He wanted to explain, but the woman had gone. She hadn't asked for his number.

He dropped the phone on the table and sat waiting, feeling uneasy. His caller details would have shown up on the read-out display as a matter of course. But that wasn't how the woman would know where to call him back; they had the number on file and the moment he rang in, a data file was activated giving his name, background and every little detail down to the size of his shorts. Big government in action; it was high-tech and improbable to most ordinary citizens, but scary to those who really knew what went on in the name of national security.

Five minutes trickled by, then ten. He developed an itch in his back. That was a bad sign; it meant whatever instinctive antennae he'd been born with to warn against hunters had kicked in. It had served him well enough in the past, and he wasn't about to ignore it. The landscape here might be different from New York, but the predators and prey were the same the world over.

He finished his coffee and picked up his phone, and left the supermarket. He had no destination in mind but continued movement was better than being static. It would help pass the time and keep him off whatever radar might be tracking him. He wasn't familiar enough with the communications infrastructure in London to know if the locations of towers was sufficiently dense to triangulate his position quickly; but one thing he was sure of was that his call to Washington just now would have been pinged and added to an automatic trace log. At this moment a duty officer was probably checking out a map of London and trying to work out his precise location. To do that, they would need another connection with his phone.

It rang.

"Mr. Vaslik." The voice was male, heavy with authority, vaguely familiar, with a southern drawl. A voice accustomed to command. A voice he was surprised to realise he'd heard somewhere before. "You were told to watch and wait. To be ready to assist."

"I know." He took a deep breath, wondering why he knew that voice, then said, "Something's going on here … something I believe is potentially outside my control."

"How so?"

"I was told to stand by … to assist if called. It sounded like something specific might happen, maybe to do with national security. But I wasn't told what that was. I still don't know."

"Because you don't necessarily need to know." The man sounded impatient, as if talking to a child—or a junior officer pushing his head above his pay grade. "Are you mobile, Mr. Vaslik?"

"Yes, why?"

"No reason. Perhaps you could explain why you have called?"

"I need to know … there are plenty of specialists already here who could do whatever is necessary, without involving me. "I'm a private contractor now, and my scope of activities and experience is narrow. I'm no longer in DHS."

"So?"

"Is there a child involved in whatever's going to happen?"

There. It was out.

The line clicked and hissed, and the man on the other end said nothing. Vaslik became aware of a noise overhead. He looked up. Saw a shape in the distance. A helicopter, swinging towards him, too high to distinguish any markings, merely a dragon-fly shape against the clouds. A coincidence, he told himself. No way they could have locked onto him this fast *and* got a chopper in the air. But he started walking again as a precaution.

"Why do you ask?" the man said. He didn't question, Vaslik noted with a sinking feeling, what child.

"Because it's the only thing I've come across so far that could have a bearing on US security."

"What makes you say that?"

"There are certain … familiarities involved."

"Be specific."

"Methods. Language … and some hard evidence." He said the last word with a feeling of uncertainty. What he had was suspicions and nothing more. And he didn't like what he was coming up with. The problem was, he knew Ruth Gonzales had the same suspicions. She hadn't said anything, but he was beginning to know the way her mind worked. Armed with the same information as himself, she would soon arrive at the same conclusions. If she hadn't already.

"Evidence?"

"Trace material. The assignment I'm working on: somebody's got us and the house we're in under close surveillance. The technology involved is state of the art. But they got careless." The helicopter was moving away, and he kept his eye on it until it disappeared over the horizon. Then he changed direction and headed back towards the Hardman place. He'd been on too long already, but the call had been necessary.

"What do you expect from me?"

"I wish I knew. What I'm dealing with here is a missing child and a kidnap note. It's nothing new and I've seen this stuff before in my old job. But I have a gut feel that there's more to this than it seems. It's too complicated to be a simple kidnap; there's been no demands, no ransom figure … only that the father of the child be told. And that's proving a problem." He struggled to avoid saying too much. If he really voiced what he was thinking, it could all fold around his ears like a collapsing tent. "If this is what I've been expected to look out for and there's any information I can use to solve this, I'd like to find this little girl. But I have to know who else is involved."

"Else?"

"Government agencies … or others."

Another short silence, then, "Have you shared these thoughts?"

"No. Well, sort of. My problem is, somebody—my local partner here—saw the material and I think she'll eventually put two and two together. She's pretty smart."

"Her name?"

"Ruth Gonzales—" He stopped, wondering why he'd given up Ruth's name so easily. But it was too late; it was already out. Not that it would take this man more than a single phone call to know who he was working with here in London. He would have the kind of reach that could traverse borders with ease.

"Are you suggesting," the man queried, "the situation might be compromised?" His voice lingered almost affectionately on the last syllable, as if reluctant to let it go.

Vaslik stopped walking. The question was unexpected, and surprising. He'd been waiting for some direction, maybe to be told that he would not be required, or that he might be peripherally witness to something that he might be able to help stop, and therefore to continue working on it. That was what he'd been hoping for. Yet all he could think of was that the words "the situation" uttered by the man on the other end of the phone could so easily be interchanged with the word "we."

We might be compromised. Damn. Now he really was confused. This business had him questioning everything; every small nuance of conversation, every potential hidden meaning.

"I don't understand."

"No, you do not. Maintain your position, Mr. Vaslik and do nothing. We'll be in touch." There was a click and the man was gone.

THIRTY-TWO

RUTH'S CHAT WITH NANCY proved fruitless. In spite of approaching the topic of Michael with extra care, in view of her collapse, she got nothing from her other than an almost dreamy look of restrained excitement, followed by a volley of questions about why they weren't doing more to find Beth and how sitting around the house interrogating her was less than useless.

"You seem brighter," Ruth commented dryly at one point. "Those pills must be amazing." She didn't know if mentioning the prescription was a bad idea or not, but right now she didn't care. Nancy Hardman was going up and down the scale of emotions like Tigger on a moon rocket; one minute half-asleep and passive, the next like a kid who'd been told they were all going to Disney World.

She finally gave up and went in search of Gina. "Has she been taking anything other than the prescribed meds?"

"I don't know. She's been like this for a while. She was watching television earlier and laughing at a shopping channel. I mean, really laughing. I thought she was going to throw up. It's freaky, if you ask me."

It definitely wasn't good. "It means she's going to crash at some point. You'd better keep an eye out for it and hide all sharp objects."

"Will do."

Ruth checked her watch and decided not to wait for Vaslik to return. She needed to get out and do something positive. After checking Gina was OK by herself, she set off for the gym with a print of the mysterious Clarisse in her pocket.

She wondered what Vaslik was up to. He had every right to his privacy, she wasn't concerned with that. But this was the second time he'd gone off on some unspecified business, and although the first—going for a second look at the house at No. 38—had proved useful, if not exactly revealing, she was concerned that he might be getting bored with this job. So far he had shown no inclination for anything other than the task in hand, but that didn't mean he wasn't preoccupied by something outside the narrow world of Cruxys and its client base.

And there was a comment he'd made earlier that was bothering her. She couldn't remember the exact words or at what point he'd said them, but it wasn't long ago, possibly on the way back to the house after visiting Tiggi Sgornik's address. Something about it had pinged a bell in her mind at the time, then was gone again just as quickly. She should have paid more attention.

She pulled into the car park at the gym and cut the engine. Few of the spaces were occupied, and she guessed it was the afternoon lull in activity. She walked inside and saw the receptionist with the inflatable chest was on duty again. This time she was wearing a badge pinned to one breast that read "Laura."

"I'd like to speak to Robert Curlow," she said, dredging the manager's name from what Aston had told her.

"Is it a complaint?" The receptionist made no move to pick up the phone, but stood blinking in anticipation, eyelashes flapping like a dying bird's wings.

"Not yet." Ruth dropped the smile until the girl got the message and hustled away to fetch the manager. He turned out to be a poor advertisement for a fitness regime, carrying too much weight and the pasty look of a couch loafer.

"How can I help?" he greeted her.

"You've heard of Godfrey Leander?"

He blinked immediately and looked nervous. "Of course. He's a member of the management board." Then he got the connection. "Ah, right. He said somebody might call round."

"Good. Can we speak in private?" She didn't want the receptionist listening in, just in case the woman named Clarisse was still around.

"Sure. If you could go through the gate and down the corridor?" He pressed the gate button and disappeared, and Ruth met him down by the lockers. He led her into the interview room, which held two comfortable armchairs and a coffee table.

Ruth handed him the still photograph of the woman turning away from the locker.

"Do you know this woman?"

He studied it and nodded straightaway. "Yes. It's Helen Stephenson. She's a part-time admin worker here." He frowned. "Is something wrong? Has there been a complaint?"

She ignored the question. "How long has she worked here?"

"Not long. About four weeks. But she's been coming as a client a little longer. She stopped me one day and said she'd work in exchange for free sessions." He shrugged. "I wouldn't normally be allowed to do it, not with all the employment rules and regulations, but our usual admin lady is off having a baby so I agreed. It was win-win, really." He looked pleased with himself for a moment, then frowned. "What's the problem?"

"I'll get to that. As an admin worker, would she have had access to the CCTV system?" Ruth was puzzled as to why the woman's image was still on the hard drive. If she had really placed the card in the locker with such precision, ignoring the CCTV showed a degree of carelessness that didn't quite match up. Unless Stephenson knew she wasn't going to be around long enough for it to matter.

"No chance. It's in a secure cupboard and she wasn't authorised. I'm the only key holder—I already told Mr. Leander that. Why, what has she done?"

"Nothing to reflect on you."

"Will I get into trouble for taking her on?"

"I don't know. Do you have an address for her?"

He flushed and looked down at his feet. "I'm afraid not. I mean, I did have, but it's been mislaid. I can't recall what it was, I'm sorry."

"How do you know it's been mislaid?"

"Because she hasn't turned up for work or for any sessions and I wanted to find out why. I checked the file but it was empty. Has something happened to her?"

"That's what I'm trying to find out."

Curlow's face folded in on itself as he drew the obvious conclusion. "Oh, Jesus … did she steal from the lockers—is that what this is about? Is that why they wanted the CCTV footage? Only I swear I didn't know—"

"She didn't." Ruth stopped his rush of words with a raised hand. "The only thing she took was her address details from your files … although I think you'll find they were false, anyway. And you might need to get your story straight about how you took her on. This could get messy. Did she mix with anybody while she was here? Other staff or clients?"

"No. At least, I don't think so. She seemed friendly enough with everybody, but…"

"But what?"

"You can never tell, can you? About people."

She left him staring into the distance, no doubt contemplating how long his job was going to last, and walked back to reception. Laura was entering data on the computer, her fingernails clacking on the keys like a volley of brittle hammers.

Ruth asked her, "I don't suppose you know where Helen Stephenson lives, do you?"

The response was immediate and cold. "That nasty bitch? No. Good riddance, is all I can say."

"Why, what did she do?"

A shrug shifted the white uniform with a crackle of static. "I don't want to say."

"Please yourself. I'll ask Robert." She began to turn back and Laura's mouth dropped open in alarm. She held out a hand.

"No, wait. He doesn't know. You'll get him in trouble."

"Who, Robert?"

"No. Andrew—one of our instructors. Helen was strutting around like she was queen bee and getting all flirty with him, asking him to show her the ropes and going gaga at the equipment." Her face twisted. "Like she'd never seen the inside of a fitness studio before! God, it was sickening. Anyway, Andrew got the wrong message and thought he was in there."

"What happened?"

"She kicked his arse."

"What?"

"I mean, seriously. It was bad—he had to go to A&E. He told Curlow he'd fallen off one of the machines." Her face flushed. "He's a nice bloke, Andrew … he just likes to chat to the clients, that's all. Nothing wrong with that, is there?"

"Sounds like Helen Stephenson wouldn't agree with you. Did anybody witness the assault?"

"No. It was in an upstairs corridor—no CCTV coverage. Anyway, it was all over too quickly, he said."

"Did he report it?"

"You're kidding, aren't you? I think he was too embarrassed, her being a woman and all."

"What kind of work does this Andrew do?"

"General fitness and self defence … and karate. He's a black belt." She appeared not to see any irony in the fact.

"Yet she took him apart?"

"Yes. He reckoned she knew some awesome stuff. Psycho bitch."

Ruth was intrigued, although she fought back the temptation to waste time going down a blind alley. But what if that was the only one she had? "I'd like to have a word. Where can I get hold of him?"

Seconds later she was back outside with a phone number and address for the damaged karate instructor. He lived not more than five minutes' drive away, so she went straight round there, determined to strike while the idea was hot.

THIRTY-THREE

THE MAN WHO ANSWERED the door was in his mid-twenties, lean but muscular, with gelled hair. He wore tracksuit pants and a T-shirt, and was walking with difficulty. One of his hands was heavily taped with a splint across two of the fingers.

"Andrew?"

"Who wants him?" He gave Ruth a quick body scan, eyes hovering for a moment on her chest. If this was him, she decided, being beaten up by a woman hadn't exactly put a crease in his libido.

She introduced herself and explained why she was there.

He held the door open. "Great. So now the whole world knows. You'd better come in." He led her into a cluttered sitting room and said, "Sorry for the mess. I've got a mate crashing in here for a few days." He lowered himself into an armchair with a grunt. "Excuse me if I don't stand—my knee's killing me." He lifted one trouser leg to reveal a heavy bandage around his knee, then sat back with a groan.

"Just the knee?"

"I wish. I've got two busted fingers and a stack of bruising." He indicated his stomach. "Why do you want to know?"

"Let's say the woman who attacked you has form. I'd like to find her." She showed him the print of Clarisse. "Is this her?"

He gave it a quick look. "Yeah, that's Helen—mad bitch. Sorry … not PC, but I think I've got good reason, don't you?"

"You wouldn't know her address, I suppose?"

"No chance. I hear she's bunked off. If you do find her, give her a kick for me, would you? Only be careful, she's vicious."

Ruth sat down in another chair. "Your receptionist friend said something about her knowing some awesome stuff. What does that mean?"

He shifted in his chair and winced. "You talked to Laura."

"Yes. She's concerned about you."

He smiled. "She's a nice kid. Have you ever heard of Krav Maga?"

"Isn't that an Israeli army martial art?"

"Yeah. I started learning it a few years ago. It's a mix of styles but I recognised some of the moves. It's based on going in with maximum force and neutralising an attacker. She took me down with a kick to the side of my knee and some other strikes … I don't remember the rest." He sounded almost in awe. "Man, she was so fast. Like a tornado."

"Sounds like she was angry."

"Yes—but I never laid a finger on her. If she says different, she's lying." He looked resentful and defensive. "I tried a couple of cheesy lines on her, that's all. It was nothing to go all ballistic over."

"That's it? Are you sure? You didn't touch her at all?"

He hesitated, then confessed, "I might have touched her arm. To be honest, I don't remember much about it."

"*Only* touched her arm? And you teach self-defence?"

"OK, stroked her arm. Maybe. I don't remember. It was stupid, I know … but she seemed friendly, even a bit flirty, asking me to help find her way round the centre and point out who some of the clients were. I made a mistake." He scowled like a little boy robbed of his lunch money.

"Some mistake. Did she ask about anybody in particular?"

He frowned. "I don't think so. Women, mostly, like she might have been looking for gym buddies. But I honestly don't remember."

"And that was it? She didn't say anything before or after?" She felt frustrated; this was going nowhere fast.

He shrugged. "I guess. I mean, there was something she said just before she started in on me." Another frown, this time in concentration. "But I don't remember what it was. What exactly has this chick done?"

Ruth ignored the question and took out a card printed with her cell phone number. "If what she said comes back, give me a call. It might be important."

He studied the card and gave her a crooked smile, suddenly all buoyed up, his ego bouncing to the fore. "Sure will. It's Ruth, right? Ruth what?"

"Don't ask."

"Huh?"

"Don't let your libido carry you away or I'll come back and finish what she started. My advice is, stick closer to home—like Laura, for instance. She's much more your style."

He looked hurt. "Hey, touchy. I get the message."

Ruth stood up. "Good. And next time don't let them get in so close—especially women; we fight dirty."

He scowled. "You know martial arts, right?" This time his assessment was more professional, less lascivious. "Yeah, you look like |you do."

"You better believe it."

She let herself out.

As she got back to the car, her phone buzzed. She didn't recognise the number.

It was Aron, Tiggi's landlord. He sounded worried, even sad.

"You should come here now," he said. "I think maybe Tiggi is not coming back."

———

Aron was waiting for her at the front door, hopping from foot to foot. He smelled of onions and tomatoes. There was no sign of the men from their previous visit.

"What's happened?" Ruth asked.

"Come." He turned and led her up to Tiggi's room.

It was empty.

Ruth checked the wardrobe. A row of empty wire hangers clinked together in a sing-song. "She came back for her stuff?"

"No. Not her. Another woman. She say Tiggi is back home for family business and she is here to pay back rent and collect all her things. I didn't believe her but she pay me and show me a note from Tiggi to say is all right."

Ruth held her breath. This was too convenient. "Where is this note?"

He looked crestfallen. "I'm sorry. Too late after the woman is gone I realise she has taken it with her. But I know it is from Tiggi—

I recognise her writing. Also she say something that I know is her." He smiled sadly at the memory.

"What was it?"

"She say, "I will miss your meatballs, the best in London." Tiggi loved my meatballs—she would eat them every day if she could."

So, it sounded genuine. But it still didn't tell her where Tiggi was.

"I don't suppose you have a home address?"

He shook his head. "Sorry. She never say and I don't ask. Is private." He frowned. "Actually, I have to say something, but I hope it does not get her in trouble."

"Go on."

"In this house we speak English nearly all the time. Is my one rule because I don't want these people coming through here and never learning nothing, you understand?"

Ruth nodded. A man with community spirit. Pity there weren't more like him.

"Too many Polish kids come here and never learn the language properly," he explained. "Anyway, all the time we speak English and Tiggi is most happy. Trouble is, one time a new arrival speaks to her in Polish, and I overheard her reply."

"In Polish?"

"Sure. But it strange Polish, you know? It's good—I mean, perfect—but perfect like you learn from a professor. No lazy words, no short cuts."

"Too perfect—is that what you're saying?"

"Exact. Too perfect." He smiled a little sadly. "Is not a bad thing, speaking properly, don't get me wrong. But the way she talk, maybe she spend her life in a convent or something."

Ruth turned and walked downstairs. As she went to open the front door, she asked, "This woman who collected Tiggi's stuff—what did she look like?"

Aron pursed his lips. "Ordinary. But not very ... woman, you know? She like someone who is athletic, do too much exercise." He went on to detail her clothing, in particular her headgear, and Ruth felt a cold line trickle down her back as she recognised the description.

Just to be certain, she showed him the photo she had shown Andrew.

Aron looked surprised. "That is her, yes. You know this person?"

"Not yet," she told him. "But I will soon enough."

THIRTY-FOUR

"HELEN STEPHENSON," SAID RUTH. She was sitting opposite Nancy Hardman in the front room, with Vaslik and Gina close by. She hadn't yet told the other two about Tiggi's bedsit being cleared, only that they were to stick close and listen. She wanted them to hit the same conclusion running as she had done.

"Who?" Nancy looked slightly less spaced-out than earlier, but was still exhibiting signs of nervous energy, ringing a handkerchief through her fingers and plucking at her wedding ring. Ruth grabbed her hands to still them, forcing her to concentrate.

"The woman at the Fitness Plus: you thought her name might be Karen but you weren't sure. We now know it's Helen. Helen Stephenson."

"Oh. Yes. I remember." Nancy blinked rapidly and tried to pull her hands free, but Ruth held on tight. "I wasn't sure. What about her? Does she know where Beth is?"

"No. We're not sure. I want you to think back, Nancy—this could be important."

"All right. But you have to let go of my hands."

Ruth did so. "Sorry. Now, you said you didn't talk much to her, is that right?"

"Yes. She hadn't been using the gym very long, but she was always around. I . . . I think she had a sort of job there when she wasn't training."

"That's correct. She worked in the admin office. When you were with her in the gym, did you ever tell her anything about your family—about Beth and Michael? Anything at all."

A frown. "No. At least, I don't think so. I'm not sure. She may have asked, though."

"What did she ask?"

"I don't know—just stuff, the way women do. Why is it so important?" Her eyes flicked across to Gina and Vaslik. "What's going on? This is something to do with Beth's kidnapping, isn't it?" Her voice rose in pitch and she started to get to her feet until Ruth pulled her back down.

"No. It's all right. I'm just trying to find out about her, that's all. So we can discount her. Please don't be alarmed."

Nancy sank back down and Ruth gritted her teeth. Getting heavy with her would be counter-productive, but she was getting sick of the woman's lack of awareness. She was also convinced that there was something behind those freaky eye movements, a light deep down inside that meant she was hiding something, or hadn't told them something that could be important. If that were the case, how could she get to it without tipping her right over the edge?

"Let's start again. I want to ask you about Tiggi."

"All right."

"You told me the other day that she charged very reasonable rates. Now, I don't have kids, but I know childcare in London is expensive. How did you meet her? Did you advertise?"

"No. Michael didn't want any home help. He said we could manage. But one day I bumped into her outside Beth's pre-school group. I mean, literally—we collided. Anyway, we apologised to each other and got talking. She offered to buy me coffee." She gave a faint smile. "It had been a while since anyone had done that, so I said yes."

"And then she made a pitch." Gina looked scornful, recognising the set-up for what it was.

"Well, yes, I suppose. But the pre-school has lists of names, anyway, so I didn't think anything of it. People do what they can to make a living and everyone knows how hard-working the Poles are." She shrugged. "She told me she was trying to get a CV together but needed more experience and recommendations, and was willing to work for less money to get them. It seemed too good an opportunity to pass up, and I knew if I didn't take her on, somebody else would."

"Did you check her passport?"

"No, sorry. I never thought to look. I mean, why would I?"

Dumb, Ruth thought. But she wouldn't have been alone in that. Even government ministers got that wrong. "What did Michael think?"

Nancy gave a slight grimace. "He didn't like it when I first told him. He was quite angry—said I should have waited for him to get home before making this decision. But when he came back and met her, he said it was all right." She smiled at the memory. "Tiggi gets on with absolutely everybody, but with Beth most of all. I was relieved because I wanted Beth to have contact with another adult, to extend her learning. It's not good for a child to have too narrow a viewpoint. They need to be exposed to different people and cultures, don't you think?"

"I'm sure you're right. So Michael didn't approve?"

"He was doubtful at first. But when he saw how well they bonded, he let me keep her on. I was a bit jealous at first, because I thought he was … you know, smitten. But I know that wasn't true because he must come across attractive women all the time, don't you think?"

Nobody spoke, but had she looked at their faces Nancy would have seen scepticism written deep in their eyes. Tiggi had played them beautifully. It had all been too slick, too easy.

Too professional.

She changed the subject before Nancy could fasten on Tiggi as a focus for her anger. "Did you happen to mention to Helen about … I don't know—about your preference for the locker you use, for instance?" It was a fact that Stephenson must have known, but she needed to get Nancy talking about it and hoped it led onto other things.

"No. It wasn't that important—it was just a quirky thing of mine."

"You're sure you didn't mention it?"

"Yes. I don't talk about stuff like that. Never."

Ruth glanced at Vaslik, who lifted his eyebrows and tilted his head. He clearly thought the same: that the statement was too definite, too deliberate to be ignored.

"It was only a locker."

"I know. But Michael said." Nancy folded her handkerchief and sat quietly, suddenly composed, as if a switch had been thrown now she was on the safe topic of her husband. Vaslik and Gina noticed it, too. They stood perfectly still, unwilling to change the mood in the room.

Ruth leaned in and said gently, "What else did Michael say?"

A shrug as if the answer was obvious. "He said I should be careful about letting people in."

"In here?"

"No, silly." She gave a brief smile and patted Ruth's hand as if talking to a child. "He said to avoid letting people *in* in. He meant inside the circle." She made a twirl movement with her hand. "The circle of our private life."

"Well, that sounds like good advice. Go on." Ruth hardly dared breathe. This at last felt like it was going somewhere. But where?

"He said to avoid letting people know my routines. That when people know that, they know too much about you. And in a city like London it could be dangerous." She gestured towards the outside. "Don't you ever feel that everyone out there is looking at you, watching you? All those fucking curtained windows like eyes?" As she swore, her face went red with emotion, as sudden as it was fierce.

Ruth felt guilty at the thought that popped into her head. Jesus, this woman needs help. "I've never thought about it. But I suppose he's right."

"Of course he is. You see, most people never give their routines a thought, Michael says. They go about their business, and pretty soon everyone around them knows exactly what they do and when they do it. That's not right."

"Is that why you move so often—because Michael doesn't like people getting to know you too well?"

Nancy nodded. "I suppose so. I never really considered it. But that's Michael's way, don't you see? He has to be careful in his work, travelling to all those affected places." She smiled suddenly, lighting up her face like a child giving the answer a teacher wanted to hear.

Ruth resisted the temptation to slap her. Instead, after a second or two of thought, she remembered what George Paperas had said about the variety of places Michael Hardman had visited. She said, "Tell me about all those places he goes to."

"What about them? I told you I don't know much about them."

"Fair enough. But he must have an amazing grasp of languages to get around like he does. I mean, they're out in the middle of nowhere, some of them. I wish I had that kind of confidence."

Another shrug as she looked off into some distant place. "I don't know, either. He is amazing. I think he's merely got a retentive memory, that's all."

"So he doesn't speak any foreign languages?"

"No. Although …" She hesitated, this time accompanied by a faint crease of concern on her forehead.

"What?"

"We were in a restaurant near Oxford Street about two months ago. He'd taken me there as a special treat after being away for several weeks. It was wonderful—all these dishes I'd never seen before, and he seemed to know them all, telling me what to mix, what to be careful of because they were spicy. He even ordered them in the language of the menu. I told him not to show off, because I was sure he was just reading the words to impress me." Her face clouded. "Then he got into an argument with one of the waiters. It was horrible."

"What happened?" said Vaslik.

"I don't know—that's what was so strange. One second we were having this lovely meal, the next he called the waiter across and started shouting at him. I was embarrassed, but he said later he'd heard the man say something rude about me because I hadn't liked one particular dish. He said he was defending me."

Ruth glanced at Vaslik. She felt a tiny buzz of excitement. Was this significant or merely another dead lead? She saw Vaslik had reacted to it, too. "So he shouted at the waiter."

"Yes."

"In English."

"No. That was the surprise. I don't know what the language was, and frankly, I didn't ask Michael because I wanted to get home and forget all about it." She picked at her arm. "It was the first time I'd ever seen him really angry."

"Do you remember the name of the restaurant? Sounds like a place to avoid."

"God, how could I forget? It was called Mamoun. They specialise in Middle Eastern and Arabic food."

———

Ruth stood up. She had to get outside. Something told her this was worth following up. It might be nothing, only time would tell. But she couldn't simply walk out; she needed to use the situation to shake up Nancy's composure, taking her from friendly to hostile in the blink of an eye.

"Right, we're out of here."

THIRTY-FIVE

NANCY'S EYES WIDENED IN alarm. "What? Where are you going?"

Ruth winked at Vaslik, careful to not let Nancy see her, then turned back and said to her, "Listen, lady, I don't know what you think this is, but you called us in because your daughter has been kidnapped, right?"

"She has—I told you!" She looked at Gina and Vaslik. "You know it's true!"

"Maybe, maybe not," Ruth countered. "But if you want to get her back, you'd better stop hiding stuff from me. Somebody obviously thinks you have some kind of value, and if they've taken your daughter it's because they'll want to do a trade. Now, as we've said before, we have to know what that value is, and I can't start helping you until you level with me. That means about everything; you, your husband, your life—how many times a week you have sex and what you eat on Sundays. Have you got that or do we walk out of here?"

"*Wait*! Don't go —please. I'm sorry." Nancy scrambled out of the chair and gripped Ruth's arm, forgetting Michael's warning not to trust these people. "Please. I need your help. All of you."

Gina had stepped into the kitchen and Vaslik was by the door, poised to go. Ruth waited nervously, wondering if this sudden change of tactic was a move too far and likely to pitch the woman over the edge. She said nothing, allowing the silence to build its own tension.

Finally Nancy spoke, her voice tiny. "I'm sorry I don't … say a lot about us. Michael told me to start being careful of letting people know too much. That we might have to move again."

"When was this?"

"I don't remember for certain. He came back from a trip a few months ago and said we both needed to watch ourselves as there were some dangerous people out there. I thought he was talking about muggers and drunks, or that he'd been affected by the places he went to. I went along with it because I trust him."

"So this was a recent thing, this warning?"

"Sort of. But he's always been careful like that."

"Secretive?"

"I suppose so. But after that trip, he changed. Became more … cautious." She shook her head. "I wish I could speak to him. Then everything would be all right."

"Where was that trip to?"

"I don't remember. Somewhere in Africa, I think."

"*Have* you spoken to him?" Gina spoke from the kitchen doorway. The kettle was roaring in the background, muffling the talk.

"No. How could I? You won't let me use my phone, will you?" With that she turned and walked out of the room.

Nobody tried to stop her.

———

The three of them gathered in the kitchen with the radio on. They heard Nancy leave the bathroom and enter her bedroom, closing the door. The atmosphere felt leaden.

"That was interesting," Vaslik murmured.

"How?" said Gina.

"Well, I know a bit of Polish, but not enough to get in a fight with someone. It sounds like our guy speaks another language. Who knew?"

"More bloody secrets." Gina looked annoyed. "The woman's a head case. And so's her control freak of a good Samaritan husband. It's feudal, the way he is. Something's not right here."

"You're right," Ruth agreed. "And it gets worse." She told them about the women they knew as Clarisse clearing out Tiggi's possessions and paying the back rent. They said nothing. She looked at Vaslik. "What kind of woman do you know uses Krav Maga?"

He looked surprised at the switch in conversation. "Seriously?"

"Seriously." She explained what Andrew had told her about Clarisse's reaction to him coming onto her.

"She was probably feeling hormonal," Gina muttered dryly. "I feel like decking guys like that on a regular basis." She gave Vaslik a sideways look.

He ignored her. "Krav Maga. That's hard core. Could he have been saying that to make himself look good? One style overcoming another?"

"I don't think so. From what he and the receptionist said, Stephenson took him apart before he could blink. He admitted what set her off might have been something he said, but he couldn't remember what it was."

"A chat-up line that misfired?" Vaslik pulled a face. "Sounds a bit extreme, don't you think?"

"Exactly. And it doesn't answer the question: how come a part-time admin worker knows that kind of fighting style well enough to take down a bigger, experienced opponent in the flick of an eye?"

Just then her phone rang. She took it out and answered.

"Hi. Is that Ruth?" Talk of the devil. It was Andrew.

"What have you got?"

"I think I remember the line of the conversation we were talking about. But it's nothing, really."

"Let me be the judge of that. What did you say, word for word?" She signalled for the others to stay.

"Well, she wasn't English, but I have a lot of foreign students in the classes so it didn't stand out. But there was something about her accent ... I was making conversation, you know, trying to find common ground?"

"Smooth. Go on."

"One of my previous fitness students had the same way of talking. It sounded American at first, you know? Like West coast but with a throaty touch ... an accent. I thought it was really sexy."

Jesus, she thought, he was a sex-nut on legs. No wonder he'd taken a kicking. But he was spot on. Clarisse had talked with a slight American tone, too. It was a match.

"And?"

"It was a simple enough question, right? All I did was ask where she came from."

"Then what?"

"I remember now what she said, just before ... you know. She said I asked too many questions. Then the lights went out."

Ruth felt disappointed. It might be nothing after all. Simply a case of male hormones overtaking common sense and imagination. Out of a feeling of desperation, she asked, "So where did this former student of yours come from? Or did she kick your head in, too?"

Andrew chuckled. "No way. She was really friendly. She came from Haifa in Israel."

THIRTY-SIX

THE ATMOSPHERE IN THE Cruxys headquarters was sombre when Ruth and Vaslik arrived to give a report. It was late afternoon and news was coming in that one of the international response teams sent out to Nigeria had suffered gunshot wounds. The exact details were unclear, but the news had gone through the building like a virus. With most of the staff from military, security or police backgrounds, they felt it keenly when a colleague was taken down.

"They'd cleared the airport and got a small charter flight out to the oil installation that had been attacked," Aston told them, once they were seated in the briefing room, "but came under fire as the plane touched down. The Nigerians aren't saying much but the pilot says he saw men in army uniform around the perimeter. It could have been friendly fire." He flicked a hand towards the story boards where a single researcher was ready to take notes. "We've had to transfer one of the research teams to another assignment. Caroline, here, is fully up to date on the Hardman situation, although that doesn't seem to amount to much at the moment. That's not a criticism." He looked at the researcher. "I believe you have a query?"

Ruth had noticed that a number of photos from the frame at the Hardman house had been printed and stuck to the board, with names added in marker pen. The ones of Michael Hardman weren't particularly clear but those of Beth and Nancy, always smiling, served to highlight the tragedy of what had happened to split the family apart. There were two shots of Tiggi, showing a tall, leggy blonde with a devastating smile.

Caroline tapped a varnished fingernail against a blank square on the storyboard, next to the photos, and addressed Ruth. "There's a file you downloaded from the Hardman's digital photo frame which came up blank. At least, there's something there but it wouldn't open. Our technical guys are working on it, but doesn't look like a JPEG for a photo, like the others. Could you check it didn't get corrupted on transfer?"

"Of course."

"Better still, if you could get the smart card and bring it in, they might be able to open it. It might be a document file that got copied by mistake, but it's a small anomaly we need to tick off." She smiled at Aston. "That's all for now."

Ruth made a note to check. Any query, any such anomaly right now had to be looked at until it could be dismissed as irrelevant. She couldn't recall seeing the details of any such file, but she would go back and look at her laptop.

She turned to the question of what they had learned so far about Tiggi Sgornik and "Helen Stephenson." It firmed up their suspicions that this entire event had been carefully planned and coordinated.

"The timing's too neat to be a coincidence," she pointed out. "Stephenson's been around the gym for at least four weeks, probably longer. Tiggi turned up about eight weeks ago and got her flat not far away from the Hardmans at about the same time. Both seemed to have turned up out of the blue, both are foreign."

Aston looked puzzled. "You're suggesting they're working together?"

"I think they must be." She looked at Vaslik, who nodded in agreement.

"Interesting." Aston glanced at the storyboard, where the forensic team's report had been highlighted. "Jakers reports finding blood on the door jamb of the nanny's room. If you're right, then it might imply Sgornik changed her mind when they made the snatch, and there was a struggle."

"It's possible. But when she wrote the note to her landlord, Aron, it sounded upbeat."

Vaslik added, "She might have been acting under pressure. Nancy says she and Beth had bonded particularly well." He shifted in his seat. "I've seen examples where gang members in abduction cases have gone along with the plan, but once they actually get to see the kidnap in action and see what it does, they have a change of heart. It's traumatic stuff, seeing a child get taken." When they all looked at him, he explained, "I once had to assist taking a child away from a religious sect. They were brainwashing her but she couldn't see it. That stuff stays with you."

Aston pursed his lips. "I think we have to assume that she's one of them, pressured or not." He told Caroline to get working on tracing the names in Poland and Israel, although they all knew it was probably pointless. Stephenson was undoubtedly a cover name, and if Tiggi was still alive she wasn't likely to be easily found.

"There's something else you should all know," he continued. "We've received news of three men—one a westerner—killed by gunmen in Herat province, Afghanistan. One of them was carrying papers suggesting they were aid agency workers. After your talk with George Paperas I had several keywords added to our news watch list. This popped up as a result."

"What happened?" Ruth felt further dulled by the report. The killing of aid workers seemed so pointless. They were innocent people trying to help, yet presenting easy targets to extremists.

"That's the odd thing. The reports say they were killed in a fire-fight."

"They must have had an armed escort." Sometimes the local authorities provided escorts for aid workers in the region. It was usually down to local police chiefs to provide the personnel, but not all of them bothered.

Aston checked a sheet of paper in front of him. "According to at least two reliable observers who saw them earlier, they were well-armed and there were thought to be four men in the group. They were approaching a village ten miles from Gulran when they came under attack from unidentified gunmen, thought to be Taliban fighters. There was an exchange of gunfire lasting nearly an hour. When it ended three of the men were dead. There was no sign of a fourth. The local villagers brought the bodies to the nearest police post. The local chief thinks two were Afghani and one was European or American, but as they'd been stripped of personal effects apart from one with a card commonly carried by aid workers, they don't know anything more about them."

Vaslik said, "No indications of what they were doing there?"

"None. But they clearly weren't on a sight-seeing tour."

"How does this affects us?" Ruth asked quietly.

"By the time the bodies were at the police post, they'd been stripped of weapons and personal effects. Whether that was by the attackers or the villagers is a moot point. The European had been shot in the face, so identifying him is going to be a problem—or would be."

"What does that mean?"

"The police found a cell phone concealed in his boot. Under direction from us he took a look and reported several numbers. Two of them are here in London, one to a temporary charity base in Croydon. We're trying to establish contact with them but it's proving difficult."

"And the other?"

"The other we recognised through the report details." He jerked a thumb at the storyboard which included every aspect of the Hardmans' lives so far known. "It belongs to Nancy Hardman's cell phone."

THIRTY-SEVEN

THE SILENCE BECAME LEADEN as they digested the news. If this was true it changed everything. If there was no Michael Hardman, what would happen to Beth? Would she be returned unharmed, of no further use to the kidnappers? Or would the focus fall on Nancy?

Ruth felt sickened at the possibilities. She forced herself to concentrate on the next steps. Her head was buzzing with questions, but only one kept powering its way to the surface, demanding to be answered. She didn't expect a response, but she had to try.

"If we assume these men were *not* aid workers," she said slowly, wondering how to broach a ticklish subject, "and the fact that they were armed and fighting supports that supposition, then they must have been Special Forces."

"We don't know that," Aston was quick to point out. But he didn't sound convinced. "There have been several instances of fighters of European appearance joining the insurgents. This man could be one of them."

"True. But if we assume for a moment that they were members of Coalition Forces, it might answer a lot of questions for us."

"How?" One eyebrow lifted. If he was ahead of her, he was hiding it well.

"If Michael Hardman is the dead European ... was he one of ours?"

There was a long silence during which Aston blinked without comment. Eventually he said, "There's been no indication so far that he was ever in the military or the intelligence field, has there?"

"He might have been a sub-contractor," said Vaslik. "The US uses them; I'm guessing the UK does, too."

"It's possible," Ruth agreed, when Aston said nothing. "Think about it. There's been something odd about this whole set up from the start. Hardman's away a lot and keeps his family on the move from house to house; he's often out of touch, and phone numbers and at least one address are either fake or dead. He took out a Safeguard contract, when according to his wife they're always strapped for cash; he's supposed to be a low-level aid volunteer but doesn't seem to last more than a few days in any one place before he disappears; and he has no back story that we can find, save a bank account he keeps secret. To do all that he has to have money somewhere ... or access to resources."

"It doesn't mean he was working for the security industry or the military."

"Can we ask?" Vaslik suggested.

"No."

"Why not?" Ruth led with her jaw. This was going to go round in endless circles if they didn't pile on the pressure and get some answers. "If he is part of the military or the security forces, and his family's at risk, surely whoever's running him would want to know."

More silence while Aston digested the idea. Ruth didn't push further. He wasn't slow, but he was cautious. He would know that poking a finger into the dangerous world of spies, special operations and undercover warfare was a risky business. And companies like Cruxys and others in the field relied on keeping good relations with their secretive counterparts.

"I'll ask," he agreed. "Sir Philip might know." Sir Philip Cole-clough, Cruxys's chairman, was known to have close connections with the Intelligence and military community in the UK and overseas, and was even rumoured to have been an intelligence operative during the seventies. It would explain how the company never seemed to have problems recruiting good personnel with the right backgrounds.

"And fingerprint verification of the bodies," Vaslik suggested, "would be useful."

"Already on the way." Aston made notes on a pad. "Can you get some prints from the house?"

Ruth nodded. "There's bound to be something. I'm surprised we don't have them on file." It was meant as a dig, but Aston took it seriously.

"We do, normally. It's not acceptable to civil liberty lobbies, but if any clients do turn up dead, it helps to ID them." He gave a cool smile. "Some refuse, some prevaricate. Hardman must have done one or both, we don't know." He shrugged. "It happens; we can't exactly drag clients kicking and screaming into the building and take their prints by force, neither can we compel them to volunteer details they would rather keep secret. Anything else?"

Nobody could think of anything. As they stood up, there was a knock at the door. It was a painfully thin young man in his twenties, wearing heavy glasses, a crisp white shirt and pressed slacks. He looked like a young banking executive, but they knew he couldn't be.

"Sorry to intrude," he said, his accent American. "You asked for this as soon as we got anything." He handed Aston a sheet of paper.

"Thank you." Aston signalled him to stay and made introductions. "James here has joined us from places I'm not permitted to mention, but he has admirable skills in IT and all things electronic. He's been conducting some equipment tests for us." While Ruth and Vaslik nodded and sat down again, James took a seat alongside Aston, who excused himself and scanned the sheet of paper. When he'd finished, he dropped it on the table with a deep sigh and looked at the technician. "I think you'd better be the one to explain this; it's beyond my capabilities."

The American nodded and squinted at the other two. "We've been conducting some field tests into new equipment co-developed by MIT—the Massachusetts Institute of Technology—our National Security Agency and your own Electronics Security Group within GCHQ in Cheltenham." GCHQ was the British Government Communications Headquarters based in Gloucestershire, responsible for British signals intelligence and communications. "Not to go into technical detail, but the equipment is called Siege 2. It monitors telephony signals and works at isolating and identifying individual cell phones."

"What happened to Siege 1?" Ruth asked. She wasn't sure where this was going, only that it was taking up valuable time.

"It failed. They immediately began work on Siege 2."

"To what purpose?"

"Like a lot of other technological developments, it was an idea that came out of 9/11. The FBI were concerned that in hostage situations, or where suspects were concealed among innocent people in a particular location, like an office building or school, it was crucial to identify all users of cell phones in that location. Siege works at isolating each signal, tracing it to source—the provider or subscriber—and, ultimately, pinning down any unidentified users. The aim is to reduce the available targets dramatically and allow law enforcement to move in and … and neutralise the ones they can't identify." He looked uncomfortable at the final words, as if designing the technology was fine, but admitting to its ultimate purpose was something he preferred not to think about.

Aston said, "By 'unidentified' users, does that include pay-as-you-go phones?"

"Some, yes. The majority of extremist and criminal users rely on stolen, cloned, throwaways or pay-as-you-go cells. It's still at early stages yet, but the speed with which Siege 2 can narrow the list is increasing all the time." He thumbed the bridge of his glasses. "We conducted a test on this building a week ago and achieved an 88 percent ID rate within the first hour. That's pretty awesome." He smiled like the proud parent of a gifted child. "We're currently looking at other buildings in the area to see who we can spy on."

"Really?" Aston looked intrigued. "Will that include our neighbours in Grosvenor Square?" He meant the US Embassy.

Ellworthy lost the smile. "Uh … … no, sir, I don't think so. Unless you order it, of course. It might take some time to set that up, though." He sounded absolutely serious.

Aston gave a thin smile and shook his head. "Let's put that on hold, shall we?" He waved a hand for him to continue.

"Right. Well, the Hardman kidnap provided us with an ideal test situation. Because we couldn't rely on getting tracking equipment inside the house unobserved, we set up a Siege 2 monitoring unit nearby."

"You what?" Ruth stared at him. Ellworthy blinked and looked at Aston for support.

"It's OK—they had my approval." He looked directly at Ruth. "They didn't compromise your position in any way; we wanted to keep it to ourselves in case anybody listening in caught wind of it."

Ruth subsided, but still felt nettled at not being told. She glanced at Vaslik. His expression was blank, and she wondered what Aston would have done if the American had stumbled on their little "unit" while on one of his walks and gone in all guns blazing.

"Go on," she said. "But keep it non-technical; I have a headache."

Ellworthy nodded. "Sure. As I said, we placed a monitoring unit nearby, focussed on the Hardman property to detect and source-track any incoming and outgoing calls."

"Source-track?"

"See where they came from. Or went to. There was some interference from other devices, which we expected, but we managed to screen them out."

"Devices?" This from Vaslik.

"Listening devices. I believe you found some in the building. There are others."

"How many?"

"We detected three. Cute technology, too, going by the signals." He glanced at Ruth before continuing. "Siege also picked up signals indicating a cell phone user sending and receiving text messages. They were of short duration and spaced out, suggesting receiving and responding in turn."

"From a house nearby? The buildings aren't that far apart."

"I know. But Siege was able to pin it down to within ten feet."

"Somebody in the garden, then?"

Ellworthy looked at her as if she'd insulted him. He thumbed his glasses again with a vicious jab. "No, ma'am."

They all waited for the punch line.

"The signals were coming from inside the house. The northeast quadrant."

THIRTY-EIGHT

"But *how*?" Gina queried indignantly. "We've been with her 24/7. No way could she have got another phone in here." A radio was playing in the background to cover their voices. Nancy's phone lay on the kitchen work surface nearby, where Gina had left it after checking the call log. There were no calls or text messages in or out over the past forty-eight hours.

Vaslik and Ruth had returned to the house after the session with Aston and Ellworthy, by which time it was getting dark. They'd been turning over the latest events and wondering if Michael Hardman's unconventional and peripatetic life had finally taken him a step too far. They couldn't say anything to Nancy until the body of the dead European was identified, and this latest report of cell phone signals coming from inside the house merely added to the complexity of the problem.

"What about during the trip to the supermarket?" Vaslik suggested. "They sell disposables."

"They do, but no way. I didn't leave her side. And if you're suggesting somebody slipped one to her, not a chance." She looked absolutely certain of her facts and Ruth believed her. The first thing a pro body-guard looks out for is anybody approaching their charge. It was page one of the training manual.

"If she didn't get it on the outside, then whoever placed the bugs must have also left the phone for her to use."

Vaslik shook his head. "I don't buy it. Why would they? If they're spying on her—on us—they wouldn't need to give her a phone."

"Unless they wanted updates to conversations they couldn't hear," said Gina.

"No. They must know that we're being careful what we say around her. Anything they did get would be of low value."

"That leaves only one other explanation," Ruth said. "Somebody else got in here. Somebody who knows her husband." She shook her head at the implications. If it had been planted at about the same time as the listening devices, it had to have been in the house when she had come back from hospital to get some clean clothes for Nancy.

"Christ." Gina looked cross. "Right under our noses—it's like burglar central. What do we do?"

"Take her shopping again tomorrow," Vaslik suggested shortly, "and I'll take her room apart. If it's there I'll find it." The approximate location, narrowed down by Ellworthy to the northeast quadrant, took in Nancy's bedroom and the bathroom. Unless she had moved it since then, it left a narrow search zone on which to focus.

"We could always go and ask her right now," said Gina. "Why wait?"

"No," said Ruth. "We'll give Ellworthy and his little toy another chance to pick up the signals. If she is making contact with her husband, he might be able to figure out where he is."

"What about tonight? Do we watch her more closely?"

238

"I don't know." Vaslik glanced at Ruth for agreement. "We should let her think she's got us fooled." He hesitated. "How about we leave tonight with only Gina on guard. If Nancy makes any moves, she might just get careless."

"Good idea," Gina agreed. "I'm not sleeping much, anyway. If anything interesting kicks off I'll call you."

Ruth thought it over but was unable to see an alternative. She felt uneasy about leaving Gina here alone, but something had to break sooner or later. And having three people ready to answer a phone call was pointless if they were all exhausted.

"All right. But call if you have doubts."

She walked through to the living room, and picked up the digital photo frame. It had been turned off. She wasn't going to bother checking the failed file on her laptop. If it didn't open from there, it wasn't going to. Far better to get the smart card and take that in for Ellworthy's IT gnomes to work on. Nancy might kick up a flurry if she noticed it had gone, but she would leave copies on a spare data stick as insurance.

———

Andy Vaslik left the house and made his way to his rented flat in Edgware. He felt dog-tired and in need of food and space, his brain fired up with too many thoughts about what was going on behind the scenes. Trying to pull together the various strands of information when so much was unknown or new brought its own pressures, and he needed to kick back for a few hours and allow the facts to filter through his head from front to back. Front of head intake versus back of head analysis: it was something he'd learned from an experienced homicide detective in the NYPD. Let the two operate at their own speed; trying to force them together merely brought headaches and confusion.

He picked up a pizza on the way and settled down to catch up on CNN. Let the Hardman case flow out of his mind for a short while. Sometimes cases got you like that; you became so focussed on the detail that life outside—the normal, everyday *important* part of life— seemed to dip into the background. It was one of the reasons for the high number of divorce cases among law enforcement officers.

The rolling news covered the usual topics, including storms in the southwest, oil prices, a shooting at a high school in Tennessee and another failed Hollywood marriage. Par for the course.

He poured a beer and ate another slice of pizza. A number of terrorists attacks and bombings around the world over the previous six months had been summarised, with the usual talking heads from Washington think tanks and unspecified "experts" from the security and intelligence field. It all added up, was the conclusion, to a worrying rise in activity involving various insurgent groups, many of them previously little-known but all suspected of having links to the main players, al Qaeda being the biggest bogey of all.

He watched the usual parade of outrage from Iraq, Afghanistan and Pakistan, including a reminder of the Westgate Shopping Mall attack in Nairobi, Kenya, followed by the media circus around the establishment suits and uniforms all putting in their ten cents worth. Among the latter were a US Marine Corps general, buttoned up and sharp as a tack, jaw jutting as if about to go on the offensive, and a man introduced as a rear-admiral who sat on various committees and advised on security matters. This man stepped forward to announce in solemn tones that work was on-going to identify and deal with the perpetrators and those who gave them support and resources.

Vaslik sat up with a jerk, the food forgotten. The deep southern tones carried clearly with practiced authority, drawling out the reassurances the media wanted to hear and the people expected.

He knew that voice.

He knew the face, too.

THIRTY-NINE

THE MAN'S NAME WAS Drybeck. Rear Admiral Walter Drybeck, to give him his full title. Jesus, he'd met the guy once on a visit to some government facility run by the navy. He thought he'd disappeared into retirement years ago, put out to grass with a bunch of other senior warhorses to make way for the new fitter, younger generation.

He pushed the pizza to one side and turned up the volume.

"I can say to the American people that we are taking steps to deter and defeat these extremist organisations and those giving them funding. I can't say more than that as it might compromise the work of some very brave and resourceful people in the field. Thank you." He nodded and stepped away from the microphones, leaving behind a hubbub of clicking cameras, voices demanding more details, more reassurance, more drama.

Vaslik didn't move, stunned by the realisation of where he'd heard the voice before. The same voice with the long, drawn-out final syllable; the one he'd heard over the phone earlier that same day.

Compromise.

Drybeck? Was *he* the mystery man he'd been talking to?

———

Three miles away, Ruth Gonzales sat at a corner table in a deserted bar and sipped at a glass of red wine. She was also fired up—too much so to want to go home just yet. She didn't want to let go of this, but also recognised that some down-time was necessary otherwise she'd be no good to anyone, least of all Nancy and Beth.

But now some other things were occupying her thoughts. The first was nothing to do with work; it was a private text message from somebody she hadn't expected to hear from again. She read it through again and felt oddly unsettled. Someone had once said you should never take a backward step. She couldn't recall who it was—probably her father, who was always good for a wise word or two in moments of crisis.

The second matter came from listening to Ellworthy, the techno-geek, explaining the operation of Siege 2. Something he'd said had popped into her head. Now she was struggling to think back, because at the time, she'd known it was important but hadn't been able to grasp it before it dropped off the edge.

And that feeling hadn't gone away.

She closed her eyes, trying to claw back what he'd been saying. It had been in the final few minutes of his talk, she was certain. He'd been drawing to a dramatic close, talking about the wonders of Siege 2 and how it could isolate mobile phone signals inside a house from any other telecomms traffic.

No, wait. He was American; he hadn't said "mobile," which was common in the UK. He'd said "cell." She opened her eyes with a snap, nearly spilling her drink. Ellworthy had also been talking about the listening devices located inside the house; the ones Vaslik hadn't been able to find. He'd said "Cute technology."

Damn, that was it! She'd heard Slik say: *"Didn't extend to her cell phone … cute only goes so far."* It was no more than a throwaway comment, but the three distinct words had echoed in her brain for a split second before fading. Now she remembered them—and where they had first appeared.

It was in the note left for Nancy at the gym: *Your cell phone is dead, your home phone won't answer and your daughter, Beth, is alone with Tiggi, her cute Polish nanny.*

The note had been written by an American … or somebody schooled in the American system. Brits didn't use the words "cell phone," and "cute" usually referred to kids, kittens, and baby ducks.

Helen Stephenson aka Clarisse. She had sounded American but with something deeper, more foreign. And she was highly trained in an aggressive Israeli martial art.

And there was Tiggi, the too-perfect sounding Polish nanny. Not by itself an anomaly; she knew one or two English people who talked as if they were in the nineteen-forties. But it was yet something else that stood out.

What the hell did it all mean? Her thoughts began to rush with detail, drawing in snippets from the path of the investigation. The napkin in the lunch remains Slik had picked up from the bin next door to No. 38. In spite of only a glimpse, she had instantly recognised the stylish lettering of the logo. The Mount Street Deli was one she knew well, and not more than a spit away from the Cruxys office in Mayfair. And the US Embassy in Grosvenor Square.

And now the third thing that was bugging her: it was the Mamoun Restaurant across the street from where she was sitting. Before coming to this bar she'd called in and spoken to the manager, Mr. Khouri. He was a plump, sharply-dressed man with a voluminous moustache and soulful, dark-rimmed eyes.

"Yes, I recall the incident," he'd said immediately, when she asked about the argument. Perhaps with the inbred caution of a man wary of a scene, he'd drawn her discreetly away from nearby diners. "May I ask what is your interest in this, please?"

"I'm working with the police. The man is missing and we're trying to find him. His wife says he is depressed and unwell. You can probably guess what we're thinking." The fabrication came easily, with the awareness that anything approaching the truth in the form of a kidnap enquiry, might scare him into silence.

Understanding touched his face. "Ah, that is sad. He was very angry, I remember, and it was very quick—like a man on the very edge of his temper. Before, he was very pleasant, a nice man and valued customer. Then suddenly, very different."

"Before? So this wasn't his first visit?"

"Not at all. He had been here a few times, always I assumed with business colleagues. But this was the first time with a lady."

"Do you recall if he paid cash or card?"

He smiled regretfully. "I am sorry—I cannot. Also, that is beyond my authority. I have to respect customers' privacy, even the difficult ones."

"I understand." She felt the manager beginning to close up as he turned to eye the restaurant, which was busy. "Just one thing more."

"Of course."

"What language did he speak to your waiter?"

"Language? Why, Arabic, of course."

———

She jumped as her phone buzzed, bringing her back to the present. It was her father.

"Dad? What's wrong?" He almost never called her. "Is mum all right?

"When did you last speak to George Paperas?" He sounded short of breath, with none of his usual attempts at humour, as if trying to get something difficult out.

"Umm, I don't know … it was—hang on." Her brain wouldn't function; it was too full of detail, of questions—and now concern about why her father was asking about George Paperas. "Yes—it was this morning. We spoke on the phone. Why?" Even as she uttered the last word, she had an awful premonition. "Dad?"

"George is dead. He was knocked down, hit by a car on his way home."

"Oh, God." It was all she could think of to say. So inadequate.

"A witness claims it was deliberate. The car was waiting in a side street, engine running." He paused, then, "I got that through a mate in the Met. It's not public knowledge yet so don't tell anyone. What kind of dirty business did you get him involved in, Ruth?"

He sounded too upset to continue and ended the call abruptly. She mumbled a goodbye, flinching at the accusation in his voice.

Deliberate? But why? Paperas was just a charity expert. He'd been helping her out and … she felt a cold prickle travel up the back of her neck as she recalled something.

The two men Vaslik had seen following Paperas from the pub.

According to Vaslik, one of them was CIA.

She dialled Vaslik's number.

"Slik? Are you at home?"

He sounded distracted. A television was blaring in the background; a news presenter with a nasal American accent. Slik was getting a taste of home courtesy of CNN. She envied him being able to switch off like that.

"Yes. What's up?"

"Stay where you are. I'm on my way round. I'm going to blow your mind." She checked his address in her contacts page and left the pub, aware that she probably shouldn't be driving; she was over-tired and had consumed the best part of a glass of wine. But this was too important to leave until morning.

FORTY

"George Paperas is dead." She let Vaslik have the worst news first. It would prepare him best for what came next; after that anything might seem possible.

"You'd better sit down." He pointed to a chair and handed her a coffee. She thought she noticed a tiny tremor on the surface of the drink. "Tell me what happened."

She relayed what her father had told her, certain that Slik would check the details for himself. He listened carefully, a frown clouding his face when she mentioned the two men he'd seen following Paperas from the pub.

"I know the CIA doesn't get great press," he murmured, "but it doesn't make them responsible for every unexplained death."

"Maybe not. But there are other pointers."

"Really? Like what?"

She hesitated, using the coffee to gain time, organise her thoughts. Now she was here, facing him, nothing seemed as certain or as compelling as it had back at the pub. What if Vaslik laughed her back out onto the street? As an experienced investigator he'd have every right, because from his viewpoint the few scrappy bits of "evidence" she'd assembled were at best lame, at worst, pathetic.

She put down the coffee and started talking, laying out everything she knew or suspected. She began with Helen Stephenson's appearance, her possible nationality and her part in making Tiggi Sgornik's effects disappear; the obvious professionalism of the bugging exercise carried out on the Hardman house; the surveillance and failed snatch on Nancy near the supermarket—both involving Stephenson; the interest in George Paperas which had probably begun with her own meeting with the charity consultant. That brought her to Aron's comments about Tiggi, her thoughts about the language of the kidnap note and the napkin from the Mount Street Deli.

All through her talk, Vaslik had remained expressionless, letting her speak. Even the American-sounding connection hadn't raised a glimmer of movement. But the last one brought a look of incredulity to his face. "You're serious? You think a napkin points to this being… what—a CIA plot?" He gave a bark of laughter. "Jesus, Ruth—can you hear yourself? Next you'll be saying they're running this out of Grosvenor Square and Tiggi is actually a Polish graduate and CIA officer! That's a hell of a stretch."

She stared at him, surprised by the passion in his voice. Slik the obelisk, the unemotional, reserved former cop, who took a slap in the face from a furious Nancy without a flinch, suddenly transformed.

"Hey—I know it's shaky, OK?" she countered with just as much passion, but feeling the colour rise in her cheeks at the possibility that he might be right, that she had slipped into the realm of fantasy. "If you have anything better, let me have it."

It was a weak gambit, but it was all she had left. If Slik didn't go with her on this, at least enough to consider it as a possibility, she was lost. She might as well shut up shop and go home.

To her surprise he sighed and shook his head. "No. I don't." It seemed to deflate him, and she recognised how difficult it must have been for him to admit it. It gave her the confidence to tell him about the results of her talk with Mr. Khouri at the Mamoun restaurant.

"Christ," he ventured, when she finished. "That's something else she never told us."

"I know. But I'm wondering if she even knew, like so much else in this case. It explains how Hardman managed to move around such a wide region. Arabic's not the only language, but coupled with English it would certainly help in a lot of the areas he visited."

"I guess."

"So where do we go from here?"

He leaned forward, elbows on his knees. "About the Arabic thing, I don't know. It's not my field. But about the CIA connection, I guess I can make a phone call … ask a couple of questions. It might not get me anywhere, though."

"Ask who—the CIA?"

"No, not them. I don't know anybody at Langley and I doubt they'd even talk to me. But I can ask around, see if anybody has heard anything."

"Won't that be risky?"

"Not if I'm careful."

She waited, but he said nothing else. She stood up suddenly feeling the length of the day. Or maybe it was the wine earlier. "Thanks for the coffee. I'll see you in the morning."

Vaslik saw Ruth out, then turned and thought about the theory she had laid out. It was wild, he knew that; it was a scenario off the silver screen, full of imagination and colour, with exotic women and shadowy followers and a kidnapped child.

And a voice on the phone that he couldn't get out of his head. A voice that shouldn't have been there.

He took a short walk to clear his mind, one eye on his back-trail to check if he was being followed. Ingrained habits didn't die out that easy. If anything, you made damned sure that you didn't get careless even if you had a lot on your mind.

Half an hour later he was back inside.

And that worried him.

Because if Ruth was right and George Paperas *had* been targeted for surveillance, whether by the CIA or an outside organisation, it followed that Ruth would be on the watch list, too. He knew the way these things worked, probably better than she did. Just because she hadn't seen anybody didn't mean they weren't there. The old paranoia joke was closer to the truth than people knew.

He worked it through, knocking aside his own objections with cool logic. Surveillance and monitoring of activities was all about discovering connections; find a person of interest, and that person would lead to another and another, like links in a long chain. You checked each link to see where the next connection lay, because that was the way these things worked out. Degrees of separation wasn't simply a wild notion first proposed by a twentieth century Hungarian author, or later given colour by a Hollywood actor; it was real and it worked.

All you had to do was find the links. Simple.

The trouble was, pros in the intelligence and security world knew the theory of old; they had polished it, improved on it and made it their life's work to isolate themselves from such connections wherever they could. It was their key to survival. And they were very good at it.

He just had to hope he could be better.

FORTY-ONE

HE PICKED UP HIS cell phone and ran through the list of contacts until he found the one he wanted. This was quite possibly the stupidest thing he'd ever considered doing. But there was no way round it. If he did nothing, he'd spend the rest of his days wondering what he had become part of. He would also, by inaction, be allowing Ruth Gonzales to stumble into something she would be unable to identify or handle. As adept as she had proved herself at unwrapping puzzles, if she was correct in her theorising she was about to walk into a big, black hole.

He checked the time and made a quick calculation of the time difference, then dialled a number. The man he was calling was a senior analyst with the Federal Law Enforcement Training Center (FLETC) headquarters in Washington. Eric LaGuardo was responsible for advising on analytics to a range of agencies, but specifically Homeland Security. He also held a training position with FLETC, which was where Vaslik had met him.

The two men had struck up a strong friendship, in spite of Eric being a self-confessed alpha-geek, whereas Vaslik was anything but. But Vaslik had taught Eric to shoot on the training range, which had cemented the bond in a way nothing else would have, and allowed the geek to feel he had a touch of the Action Man about him.

He checked the time. Eric worked unpredictable hours, but when he wasn't at his desk he had a call divert to his cell phone in case he had to go in urgently. Part of his brief was to sift the constant flow of information, rumour and data that flowed across his desk, and providing reports to his superiors.

"Eric LaGuardo is at his desk. Wassup?" The response was flip, a sign that Eric knew the call was not from anyone on the VIP list.

Vaslik identified himself, and the two spent a few moments catching up. Then Eric said, "I'm guessing this isn't a call to suggest a fishing weekend, right?"

Vaslik immediately felt guilty. He was bringing an element of risk to his friend, which he didn't want to do. But he could see no way round it. "Yeah … that's right. I need some information. But you don't have to if you don't want."

"Are you kidding?" A shuffle noise and the creak of a chair being relieved of its burden. His voice went soft. "I'm going quietly nuts here. If I see another analysis request, I might just shoot somebody. It's not like they ever take notice of what I say, except when it suits them. Right, keep talking, man, I'm heading for the ground floor where I can talk."

Vaslik waited while Eric continued talking about nothing in particular, occasionally breaking off to mumble a "hiya" to somebody in passing. Then his voice took on an echo and he explained, "OK, I'm in a conference room which I happen to know is not bugged, because this is where my boss comes when she wants to talk dirty with her old man. What's on your mind?"

Vaslik told him nothing about the Hardmans, even by name. The less Eric knew about that the better. All he said was that he was involved in an operation involving a possible kidnap attempt in Europe, and that the CIA might have a peripheral interest. Eric had once applied to Langley for a position, but had been turned down on grounds of "unsuitability for post." They had never specified what this amounted to precisely, only that it probably meant he mixed with the wrong people.

His response to mention of the ultra-secretive agency was predictably terse.

"That bunch of limp dicks? It can only be something nasty, then. How can I help, buddy—does it involve guns? I've been putting in some heavy hours on the range, you know? My grouping's getting pretty darned tight, I have to say."

Vaslik smiled. Eric was keen. He had to give him that. "Glad to hear it. This is just a rumour, nothing else. But I'm looking to see if there's any truth in it. It could have ripples. It's important, Eric—you'd be doing me a big favour. But be careful, right?"

"You know me. Give me a few minutes and I'll get back to you."

"That quick?"

"Sure. I've got a bunch of data and a new program to filter out key words super-fast. It can crunch stuff in nanoseconds that would have taken hours just a few months ago. Later." He rang off without waiting for a goodbye.

Vaslik waited, the tension chewing at his patience as he pictured Eric flicking away at the keyboard and sending out electronic ripples into the vast system that was US intelligence. Pray God he didn't get cocky and trip an internal alarm; otherwise he'd have a heavy squad knocking down his door in seconds.

Eventually his phone rang. This time Eric sounded serious.

"Uh, Andy? There's nothing about planned abductions; I mean, none of the groups we're currently monitoring are into that stuff unless it's random or spur-of-the-moment, like somebody goofs and goes somewhere they shouldn't. Journalists, for example— they're always getting picked up."

"Aid workers?"

"Them, too, sure. But they mostly get turned loose after some posturing. There's no mileage or money in aid, and the backlash can be counter-productive. However ... hell, I'm not sure I should be telling you this."

"What? Eric?"

"OK, but you never heard this from me, right?"

"You have my word."

"Right. I don't know if this is your thing, but the only abduction—although they wouldn't call it that—is some talk on the wires about a team being put together to execute a lift on a major terrorist cheese. There's no name attached, nor a time-frame. But it's got the feel of something big, like there was with Bin Laden, you know what I mean?"

Vaslik knew. Targeting a terrorist leader carried its own energy and excitement, no matter how secret it was supposed to be nor how restricted they had made the need-to-know list. But those in the right places invariably picked up on the vibrations surrounding a planned major target-and-acquisition operation, like there had been with the al Qaeda leader, and waited eagerly to see whose name emerged from the hat—or in his case, some remote building—usually courtesy of CNN with dramatic camera footage and screaming headlines.

He felt a surge of disappointment. This wasn't what he was looking for. Such an op wouldn't be in Europe, but in some dusty backwater location hundreds of miles to the southeast, with Predator drones high in the sky looking down on the unsuspecting target, and the special ops snatch squad nearby waiting for the green light.

"Nothing about a child?"

"Wha—a child? No. No. It's an anti-terror thing. There's even a code name for the intended target. They're calling him 'Boxer.'" He gave a bark of derision. "Christ, who thinks of these names, huh? Anyway, it's a guy, that's all I can tell you. Probably some skinny dude in a turban and a dress, right? You'll have to watch the news—if they catch him."

"OK, forget it. Thanks, Eric. I owe you."

"You do that. Don't forget me if you hear of any juicy employment opportunities, right? I could do with a change of direction. Oh, hang on, wait. There's more coming in." There was a rustle of a keyboard in the background. "Wow. God-damn!"

"What?" Vaslik felt Eric's excitement level all the way down the phone, the geek learning first-hand something that nobody else would yet know. "Eric?"

"Forget what I said about the news. There won't be any. Hang on, lemme read—" Eric sounded awestruck. "Fuuuuuck!"

"What?"

"This just came in. The team I was just talking about? There's a question on jurisdiction been kicked up by a senate committee who got wind of the op. They're thought to be black ops. Nothing to do with us ... but they're already operational and in the field, ready to go.

Sorry, man—this sounds ultra high-spec with a five-star and above rating. Not what you were looking for at all."

Vaslik was intrigued in spite of himself. Any pro would be. Five stars was very high level indeed. "So who are they?"

A furious tapping of keys. "According to this, from a stringer who watches stuff in that part of the world, they're ... wow again. How about that? They're never too far from the crazy stuff, are they? You gotta hand it to them."

"Eric, *who*?"

"Oh, sorry. According to this source, they're a mixed contract black ops team ... but mostly Israeli."

———

Seconds after putting down his phone, it rang. Probably Eric with second thoughts about using agency resources on his behalf. He didn't blame him.

"Mr. Vaslik. Are you safe to talk?"

He stared at the screen. It wasn't Eric. Number withheld. But he knew exactly who it was from the extended pronunciation of his name.

Rear Admiral Drybeck.

"Yes, sir."

FORTY-TWO

"You've been busy. You and your lady colleague." The dry tone indicated that it wasn't meant as a compliment.

"It's what we do. Can I help you?" He suddenly felt an acute dislike for this man. Retired rear admirals should stay retired, not pop up years later in some spook desk job pulling strings halfway around the world.

Especially not his strings.

"You don't sound pleased to hear from me. Have I done something to upset you?"

"Not yet. But I'm sure you're considering it." Vaslik was surprised by his own courage. Retired or not, you didn't cross swords with a man in Drybeck's position. If he was calling the shots on terrorist activity, as his media appearance seemed to indicate, he would have the ears and eyes of everyone who could make irritants like Vaslik disappear overnight with nary a ripple.

"A man who speaks his mind. I like that. No doubt you picked that up from your days in the rough-and-tumble of the NYPD, Mr.

Vaslik. How would you like to go back there?" The threat was right there, out in the open.

He swallowed, tasting for a split second the bitter tang of fear. Then he steeled himself. "What do you want?"

"That's better. You were correct in your earlier assumption: the 'event' you spoke of concerns a child."

"Beth Hardman."

"Yes."

"Why? What's the point? It's not about money, I know that."

"Really?" Drybeck sounded amused for a second. "That shows how little you do know." His voice changed to one of hard authority tinged with impatience. The verbal sword-play was over. "I suggest you listen carefully to me, Mr. Vaslik. What I have to say is of the utmost importance to the safety and security of this great nation of ours. You do not have to like what you hear; you do not even have to respect it. But you will accept it."

Vaslik said nothing. He was numbed by the sheer wave of power in Drybeck's voice; a man who had commanded warships and thousands of men and women, now focussing that authority of command down the phone. At him.

"It seems matters may have gone beyond what we originally foresaw."

"I don't understand. What has a child got to do with anything?"

A puff of air. "The event, as we call it, was expected, but we had little intel to go on. We knew the location and the names, but not the execution timetable. All we knew for sure was, it was in the planning stages. Then it accelerated, faster than was anticipated and before we could react."

"You got side-stepped."

"If you wish."

"So why involve me?"

"Because of your expertise in these situations … and because you were there on the ground. It was a logical use of resources in a difficult situation."

"You still haven't told me anything *about* the situation or who's responsible."

"We were aware that a target had been selected for abduction. The group involved is not important for this discussion, suffice to say they are experienced and adept at hiding their tracks."

"Why are they doing it?"

"That is not your concern. Unfortunately, the situation has gone beyond our control, partly due, I have to say, to your interference."

"How? I haven't done anything. I don't *know* anything."

"The kidnap was planned to ensure a reaction by certain parties. I don't need to explain what that was—"

"You don't have to," Vaslik cut in. "It was intended to get Michael Hardman's attention. Why? What does he have that's so valuable? The guy's an aid worker, for Chrissake, not some high-tech billionaire!"

"Calm yourself, Mr. Vaslik; you're getting emotional." The reprimand was soft but contained a core of steel. "It doesn't matter what Hardman has or doesn't have. All you need to know is that this … operation has signally failed in its intended outcome, and the group responsible has now gone underground."

"With the girl."

"It would seem that way." His voice was lacking all emotion, as if he didn't care, and Vaslik had to bite back an impulsive retort.

"What will they do?" He was guessing they would have orders in the event of a fail; that could be anything from leaving the little girl at a safe place to … He didn't like to think of the alternative.

"I have no idea."

"So how do I find them?"

"Find them? Why on earth should you do that?"

"Wh— you want me to stop them, don't you? Isn't that why we're having this conversation? You give me directions and I'll run them down. It's my expertise, as you put it."

"Actually, quite the opposite. Forget any heroics, Mr. Vaslik. What I want you to do is run interference while we get this mess cleaned up. It's time to close the door on this thing."

"What?"

"You know what the term means, to run interference?"

"Of course I do."

"Fine. Then your task is simple enough. You will proceed to divert attention away from this situation. Your focus is on stopping further investigations into this group by your colleague while we pull a cloak over it. That means keeping her and Cruxys away from any further attempts to locate the child or the team involved."

Vaslik couldn't believe what he was hearing. Drybeck was talking about Beth as if she were a lump of metal or plastic. He exploded. "You want me to help in covering up the kidnap of a little girl? Are you off your freaking head?"

The blast of anger seemed to have no impact on Drybeck's armour. "Hardly. Since that has already taken place, it's too late to stop it. In any case, we doubt she will come to any real harm. What we want you to do is to make sure this investigation goes away."

"How do I do that?" Christ, the thought of trying to deflect Ruth away from this was unthinkable. Even if he wanted to, she had the bit too firmly between her teeth for that and would smell a rat.

"Derail it, deflect it, use any means at your disposal to put Cruxys s—and more importantly, your relentless lady colleague—off the case. This matter has serious ramifications, Mr. Vaslik. If it goes any further and becomes public knowledge ... well, we don't even want to think about that."

We. It wasn't the first time Drybeck had said it. "Who do you mean by 'we'?"

"Again, not your concern."

"What if they—she—won't stop?" He threw it in as an instinctive response—a delaying tactic. He was trying frantically to read beyond this conversation and get a glimpse of what was really going on here, what this man Drybeck was *not* saying. He'd agreed to help out his old employers in an unspecified situation; but not this. Not a cover-up.

And there was Ruth: with her solid, bulldog approach to a problem that had surprised him. She had already uncovered much that he and others like him would have missed, and had knitted the facts together in a way that, no matter how "shaky," as she had described it herself, would be enough to catch the attention of people paid to look into these things. And he had seen the way Richard Aston had acted around her to know that if she shouted, he would take notice. Aston trusted and respected her, it was easy to see.

"Are you saying," Drybeck said softly, interrupting his thoughts, "that you can't do this? Or won't?"

"I'm saying—"

"You should think very carefully about your response, Mr. Vaslik. It *will* affect your entire future, I promise you."

Vaslik nearly choked on his reply. The threat was unambiguous. The fact that it came from this man made it all the more real. Drybeck had the power to carry it through and Vaslik was sure it was no bluff. It wouldn't matter what his own defence was, it would be goodbye to his job with Cruxys, and almost certainly a block on any other work he tried to get in this industry, here or anywhere else.

He'd be finished.

Was it worth it? After all, what did he know of all the minutiae behind what Drybeck was working on? He wasn't part of that world anymore, so why should he concern himself by what went on behind the screen of US intelligence and security?

But what about the little girl, Beth? She was a total innocent in all this. Hadn't he got a duty to try to find her?

"I can't. It's not as simple as you think."

"I see." There was a lengthy silence. "Very well. You leave me no choice."

The connection went dead.

FORTY-THREE

A FINE DRIZZLE WAS coating the windscreen by the time Ruth arrived at the Hardman house next morning. It was just after seven, and she had called Gina earlier to check in. Nothing happening.

She felt exhausted. A restless night's sleep after talking to Vaslik had left her wide awake and unable to clear her mind of the facts sloshing around inside like so much flotsam.

She stepped out of the car and walked to the front door, glancing along the road and noting instinctively the detail of the road. Cars glistening with rain, groups of wheelie bins at the kerb ready for collection, and a woman pedestrian with her shoulders hunched beneath an umbrella as she hurried along the pavement.

Suburban London, the start of a new day. Innocent for some, not for others. She wondered what those other residents of this quiet street would say if they knew what was happ—

She slowed and looked again. Something about the everyday scene was different, a part of the uniformity she'd become accustomed to now out of place.

Her eyes were drawn back along the line of dark vehicles.

Then it hit her. A hundred yards away, parked by a short run of brick wall: a dark-coloured 4WD. Slick with wet, but with one detail out of kilter with the rest of the vehicles: the windows.

They were coated with condensation on the inside, save for a small arced area of the windscreen, where a hand had swept away the moisture.

As soon as Gina opened the door Ruth stepped inside and took out her phone. Swore silently when she saw the battery was dead. Careless. After talking to Slik last night, she'd forgotten to put it on charge.

Gina noted her body language. "Problem?"

"My phone's dead, and there's a car along the road with misted windows which shouldn't be there." She asked to borrow Gina's phone and dialled Vaslik's number. As soon as he answered she told him what she'd seen and to come in the back way.

He didn't sound surprised. She heard the sound of traffic in the background, which meant he was already on his way. "Thanks for the warning. I'm five minutes out. How many inside?"

"I couldn't see."

"Let them be; don't go near them. I'll take a look."

Ruth shut off the phone and wondered what taking a look meant in Vaslik's lexicon.

"What are you doing here, anyway?" Gina was watching from the kitchen doorway. She seemed tense, her arms folded tight across her body.

"Why not? Where else would I be?"

"Aston called. He's been trying to get hold of you. He wants you in the office right away. He sounded pissed."

Ruth felt a prickle of concern. That didn't sound like Aston's normal manner. "Did he say why?"

"No. Have you done something to annoy him?" Gina walked across and retrieved her phone.

"Why do you say that?"

"He didn't sound happy. Thought I'd warn you." She gave Ruth a look of concern and turned back to the kitchen to keep an eye on the monitors.

Ruth decided not to wait for Vaslik. If Aston wanted to chew her out for something, she might as well get to it. She went back to her car, ignoring the 4WD, and plugged her phone into the charger and headed for Marble Arch and Mayfair.

———

Andy Vaslik was worried. He was remembering Drybeck's threat the night before, and what it might mean for Ruth. After the call from her using Gina's phone, he'd called her back only for Gina to answer and say that Aston wanted her in to the office double quick.

"Any reason?" he asked, although he knew one reason that might outweigh any other.

"He didn't say. But he didn't sound a happy camper. I thought you might know ... you and Ruth working together." There was a clear tone of query to her words, and he wondered if she was jumping to the wrong conclusion. It happened all the time with a male-female team; everybody assumed that sharing a car for hours on end meant they had to be sharing other stuff, too. Sadly, as he knew from his days in the NYPD, the conclusion wasn't always wide of the mark.

"No idea," he said shortly. It wouldn't convince her but that was her problem. He shut off the phone. He was just three minutes away from the Hardman house and formulating what he was going to do about the watchers in the car. If it was a surveillance team—and he had no reason to doubt Ruth's instincts —he wanted to know who or what they were. To do that he had to get a look at their faces.

He turned into the road and threaded his way through a gaggle of wheelie bins left out ready for collection. Others were placed at the kerb further along, wherever there were gaps between the cars. Among the bins were refuse bags and cardboard boxes. He scooped up one of the bags without stopping and studied the cars ahead of him, most of them facing towards the Hardman house. He located the 4WD immediately, the windows covered in condensation, sitting there like a duck among chickens, out of place but unaware.

Not clever, he thought. Not clever at all. Who do they think they're dealing with—a bunch of boy scouts?

As he got near the car, he clamped his cell phone to his cheek and began a one-sided argument about missing spreadsheets and how anyone with a brain could open an email attachment. The cars were on his right and he had the bin bag in his left hand, with his right clutching the cell phone shielding his face. He checked the 4WD, noting the number and make, then scanned the windows. The condensation was heavy, making it impossible to discern much detail through the rear windows save that there were two figures in the front, neither of them moving. The wing mirror on his side, however, was smeared clear where the passenger had stuck out a hand at some point and wiped it with his fingers.

At least one of them was awake.

He slowed his pace, nodding vigorously as the one-sided argument continued, aware that the passenger was watching him through the wing mirror. All he could make out was a blur of face; youngish, male, well-fed. Didn't mean a thing; it could be a couple of local authority public health inspectors on an early shift to watch the garbage trucks at work.

As he drew abreast of the rear doors, he caught a glimpse across the dash. Two take-out coffees were balanced on top, steam rising from each one. It explained the level of condensation, and that they hadn't been here very long.

He passed the passenger door and in his peripheral vision saw movement as the man turned his head to watch. Vaslik thumbed the screen on his cell and heard the clicks as it recorded a burst of images.

Ten yards ahead stood a group of wheelie bins. He paused long enough to drop the bin bag alongside them and flick some moisture off his hand, before continuing along the road and out the far end, circling the block to the rear access lane to the Hardman house.

Gina was waiting to admit him. He nodded his thanks and made for the radio, flicking it on. There was no sign of Nancy.

"How many?" Gina asked.

"Two guys with coffees to go. Been there five, maybe ten minutes, max." Not an all-nighter, he meant, and she nodded. The difference between a round-the-clock surveillance and a short–term watch wasn't simply about budget or manpower; it more often than not showed the degree of official concern. And he had no doubts whatsoever that the two men outside were official in some way.

"Who do you think they are?"

Vaslik shook his head. He didn't want to speculate aloud on it. "I don't know. Is Ruth back?"

Gina said no, and he felt his gut sink at the implications. It could mean only one thing: *Drybeck*.

The rear-admiral must have already flexed his muscles to put a stick in the spokes of the investigation. And Ruth was the sacrificial goat. With Vaslik refusing to help, he'd used his position in Washington and called in a favour. The result was Ruth being dropped from the assignment. He swore silently, knowing he was responsible; he'd told Drybeck exactly what he'd wanted to know: that Ruth Gonzales wouldn't give up, no matter what.

He shook it off. He'd deal with the fallout later. For now he had something to check. He took out his cell phone and called up the image file. The photos he'd taken along the road looked similar, as he expected, but with slight differences. The first showed the passenger of the 4WD, face slightly blurred by the condensation on the side window. He had dark hair, almost Latino looks, clean shaven and roughly about thirty, with a hint of bulk in the shoulders. The driver was just a shadow beyond him, face half-turned to watch as the passenger said something. The last two images had been taken just as Vaslik had drawn level with the windscreen, and showed the driver leaning forward from the shoulders to get a better view. It brought his face into better relief. The results weren't brilliant, but better than nothing.

He dialled Eric LaGuardo's number and attached two of the best images. It was a long shot, but Eric had once bragged of having access to the latest in FRS—facial recognition software—on the market, and was dying to use it.

Maybe this would be the excuse he needed.

He added the text *Who these?* and hit SEND.

FORTY-FOUR

"I'm sorry, Ruth. We're taking you off the Hardman case."

Richard Aston sounded matter-of-fact in his apology, but his hands clenched in front of him showed a visible sign of tension. Martyn Claas, sitting alongside him, looked completely calm, even pleased.

The three of them were alone in the Hardman briefing room, with Ruth facing the two senior Cruxys men. The building was still quiet save for the usual skeleton staff manning the operations desks, and only the vague hum of traffic outside signalled the activity of a normal day. She had been summoned up here the moment she had arrived, but hadn't expected this.

She felt a genuine sense of shock on hearing the words, and wondered what had happened. "Why? What's changed?"

"Lack of progress," Claas muttered, "if you really need an explanation." He waved away Aston's attempt to cut him off and continued forcefully, "You haven't even scratched the surface of this business, and that's not good enough. You may not be aware, Ms. Gonzales, but every day spent on these cases is a dent in our bottom line. We need a swift conclusion, not a lengthy investigation that goes nowhere. There is not an unlimited budget at your disposal to take a leisurely view of a missing person or their private circumstances. Nor do we have the resources of the authorities. For that reason I am closing this down."

"It's been just three days and there's fuck-all leisure about it," she protested fiercely, and wanted to slap the smug smile off Claas's face. "What are you going to do—leave Nancy Hardman hanging while her daughter's being held captive God knows where?"

"I'm sure the police will be happy to take over. They are accustomed to dealing with cranks. What is your problem?"

"It's immoral!" She stopped. "What do you mean, the police? You can't."

"We have to take a pragmatic view. For all we know the girl had been taken by her father—a domestic dispute. It happens all the time. We must hand this matter over to the proper agency to deal with it. It will ensure the best outcome all round."

"That's precisely what the kidnap note said *not* to do. You have no idea what will happen when the cops show up." She looked at Aston for support, but he shook his head, his lips set in anger. She guessed he had been outvoted and the signal was telling her not to push back. But she was beyond caring. "Have you any idea of the dimensions of this case? Have you even considered what's behind this kidnap?"

"The whys and wherefores are not my concern," Claas replied and made to stand up with a glance at Aston. "I think this discussion has gone far enough. I do not intend trading words with an employee in this way."

"Wait!" Ruth stood up too and walked round to the storyboard. It carried nothing of what she had discussed with Vaslik last night, nor of her suspicions about who might be behind Beth's kidnap. But now maybe it should do, because if this Dutchman had his way, this was the last throw of the coin she had left. Good or bad, it had to count.

She stabbed the board with her finger, standing in a way that blocked Claas's progress to the door. "See this? It's all bullshit. It's detail, but none of it counts because there's something going on here that's a million miles away from Nancy and Beth Hardman. That kid's been taken for reasons we can't even begin to know about—and there are people not far from here who know why."

"People?" Claas looked at her with an expression of pity. "What on earth—I don't have to listen to this hysteria. Please get out of my way." He made to push past her but Ruth wasn't moving. She was too angry.

"I haven't finished yet. You really want to treat this like a domestic? See this?" She pointed at the copy of the kidnap note, which had been enlarged for emphasis. "The language: American. It's also intelligently constructed, so not the work of some crank. This woman?" A stab at the photo of Clarisse taken from the CCTV footage at the gym. "She sounded American but we believe she's Israeli and possibly a former member of the Israel Defense Forces. Tiggi Sgornik?" Another stab at the board, where Tiggi was smiling out at the room like a catwalk model. "Also *probably* Israeli, born of Polish immigrants, because the one thing she isn't is a first-generation Pole." Claas made to interrupt, going redder in the face, but she waded on, determined not to allow him to close her down without a fight. "The listening devices in the house? Installed by experts so that we were meant to find some, but not all. The visual surveillance on the house? Also expert. An approach by a team that included Clarisse was clearly a run-up to a kidnap attempt on Nancy Hardman, possibly because they saw lifting Beth wasn't producing the result they wanted quickly enough."

She saw George Paperas' name had been added to the board and grabbed a red marker pen, slashing through the name with a vicious cross. "George was a UN aid expert who was helping me with background information that might have found Michael Hardman. He was followed from a meeting with me by two men, one identified as a CIA agent."

"I don't see the relevance—"

"You should. Two days later he was dead, murdered by a hit-and-run driver that a witness claimed appeared to be waiting for him." She paused for breath, aware that somebody else had entered the room. But she wasn't willing to stop now. "And this morning, there's continued close surveillance on the Hardman house, only they're not even bothering to hide anymore." She tossed the pen onto the table, where it clattered across the surface and pinged loudly off a water carafe before landing on the floor.

Claas looked ready to burst. "What is your point?"

"My point is, this kidnap was conceived and carried out to get the attention of a man we know absolutely nothing about; a man with a secret bank account, who keeps disappearing into countries where he can't be contacted; who manages to support his family with no visible income. I don't know about your home life, Mr. Claas, but that's not a domestic where I come from. And if you leave Nancy Hardman and her daughter hanging like this, word will get out and our reputation will be in ruins within twenty-four hours."

She walked out of the room, brushing past a vaguely familiar figure with short-cropped grey hair and steel spectacles. Another new board member, she recalled, although she couldn't remember his name. She carried on down to the basement where she found James Ellworthy crouched over a monitor, humming to himself over a screen full of data. She dropped the smart card from Nancy's photo frame on the desk in front of him. She wasn't sure why she was bothering, but it was better than inactivity or kicking the furniture. And another confrontation with Claas would not end well for either of them.

"Hi," he said, pushing his spectacles back on the bridge of his nose.

"Can you run this through whatever machinery you have and see if you can rescue a file? It shows up blank. It might be something that got caught up and loaded in error, but I'd like to check it out."

He smiled and nodded as if thrown a challenge. "Sure thing, uh…"

"Ruth. Ruth Gonzales. Thank you."

"Sure. Are you OK? You look pissed—and I don't mean drunk."

"Actually, I wish I was drunk. I'd feel a hell of a lot calmer than I do right now." She pointed at the smart card. "As quick as you can, please?" She handed him a card with her phone number.

He nodded. "I'll call you."

She turned and went back up to the ground floor. She had to get out of this place. The atmosphere was suddenly cloying and she wanted to throw something—especially at Claas the Arse.

Aston was waiting for her. He looked faintly amused and said, "Got that out of your system?"

She said nothing at first, not trusting herself to be discreet enough to remain professional. Finally she asked, "Am I fired?"

"No. I confess he tried, but there are areas where I still hold some authority. Bob Zitterman backed me up, but I wouldn't count on that lasting long. They're much too close and Claas has powerful connections. He's also a big-money man in the investment community. But your comment about the damage to our reputation was right on the button; it won't be just Cruxys affected—any fall-out will include Greenville as well, and they wouldn't like that."

"So where does that leave me?"

"Until the police step in you're still working this case."

"Thank you. Zitterman's the new American board member?"

"Yes. He arrived yesterday from Washington. He has friends, as they say, along the Beltway and he's taken an active interest in the Hardman case—I suspect prompted by Claas." His expression remained blank. "I'm not sure why, but they form a formidable front if they want this to go away. Never underestimate the powers of accountants, Ruth."

"If that's all it is."

"I don't follow."

"Well, it's obvious Claas wants this assignment stopped in its tracks. But why? I don't buy his argument about bottom lines; I may be a simple employee but I know we have enough paying clients on the books who never make a claim to make this division profitable."

He looked worried. "I know. There's been a sudden change of atmosphere in our connections with Greenville, that's all I can tell you. Almost as if somebody threw a switch. I don't know where it stems from, but I'm trying to find out."

Greenville was the American half of the Dutch-US parent company that now owned Cruxys, Ruth remembered. "You mean they'd be happy to see us lose our reputation and go to the wall?" The security and crisis management sector had already been hit by several scandals; walking away from a kidnapping and being seen to be lambasted by the police and press would surely finish Cruxys overnight. What would make Claas and Greenville take that lying down?

"I wouldn't overestimate our financial value to them," he cautioned her sombrely. "We're probably little more than loose change on their balance sheet. But in PR terms, even a hint of bad news in the current climate means they'd let us go like a snake shedding skin."

"Thanks for the warning. So what do I do now?"

"I spoke with Sir Philip Coleclough about Hardman after you left yesterday. He made a few phone calls, called in some favours. He got back to me with an answer just before you arrived this morning."

Ruth waited.

"Michael Hardman is not, and never has been in the employ of Her Majesty's armed forces, the Security Service or Secret Intelligence Service. Sir Philip ran the name and photo you supplied through all the agencies. They've never heard of him. In fact they came up blank."

Blank. It was an odd word. At the level of checking to which Coleclough was rumoured to have access, there would surely have been *something*—even a parking fine. "Blank as in—?"

"There's nothing. He's a ghost."

"How can he be? He has a bank account in Kensington."

"It shouldn't be possible, I agree. But that's not all: the passport office has no record of him, either."

"*What?*"

"All I can say is that Michael Hardman has now become a person of some interest."

"And the dead European in Herat?"

"An import—a Chechen fighter in his mid-twenties. He has a tattoo on his back linking him with a hard-line Islamist group with its roots in Grozny. There's been a steady flow of young men from the area into Afghanistan and now Syria, and he appears to be one of the latest casualties."

"But he had a phone on him with Nancy Hardman's number."

Aston gave a cool smile. "There were reports of a fourth man, although he's rather conveniently vanished. Think about it: what would you do if you wanted to disappear, believed dead? You have an item identifying you … and a dead body with no face." He shrugged. "Classic misdirection."

FORTY-FIVE

Ruth was halfway back to the Hardman house when James Ellworthy called.

"The smart card you left me?" he said. "There's definitely a file on there, but the data's corrupted. Could be it got hit by a virus in the original system, but I don't have enough to work with."

"You didn't get anything at all?"

"I didn't say that." He chuckled. "I managed to lift off maybe five lines of text, but it didn't make a lot of sense. I need some kind of context. It looks to me like it could be a list, but it's mostly numbers and like, file references. If you could get the original source data, I'd have more of a chance of building a pattern."

Ruth thanked him for his efforts and disconnected. It was probably nothing—a wild goose chase and a waste of time. But it left her feeling dissatisfied. For reasons she couldn't explain, it was simply another oddity about this whole business. Why would a document file find its way onto a smart card for photos? Whoever had transposed the photos onto the card must have lifted it along with the

JPEG files; yet wouldn't they have noticed the difference in icons? Then she recalled that the Hardmans didn't have a computer. That pre-supposed that they weren't too computer-savvy. And if Nancy had done it at work, where she did accounts, it might explain the list aspect of the data that Ellworthy had come up with.

She pulled up in front of the Hardman house and walked up to the front door. The 4WD from earlier was gone. It was pointless being discreet now; she wasn't supposed to be here, but if Claas got his way, the place would soon be swamped by police. Better to get in and out again before they turned up. They would undoubtedly want to interview her along with Gina and Vaslik, but she wanted to warn Nancy about what was going to happen first.

Vaslik opened the front door. He looked worried and she wondered if he'd heard the news.

"We need to talk," she said. It felt better to take control of this; no way was she going to play the loser who'd been dumped.

He nodded and jerked a thumb towards the ceiling to indicate that Nancy was upstairs, then turned and led the way to the kitchen, Gina was watching the monitors with the radio playing music.

"I'm officially off the case," Ruth said shortly. It was no good delaying the news, and they'd soon find out if they hadn't already heard.

"Shit," Gina swore. "Why?"

Ruth recounted what had been said in the briefing room, including what Aston had told her afterwards about the dead Chechen, and Ellworthy's call about the corrupted file on the smart card. If she was off the case and the cops came in and took over, then it was only right these two should know everything, even if it was a blind lead.

Vaslik said nothing all the time she was talking, and he hadn't lost the worried look.

"I'm surprised you're here," he said finally. "In your shoes I'd be taking time out, working my way down a bottle or two."

"I will. But first I need answers to a couple of questions. Whatever Claas might think, there's a little girl still out there."

"What questions?"

"If Hardman was one of the men in the gun battle, what was he doing with a bunch of Islamist fighters? Or did the four men happen on him earlier and steal his phone and charity documents?"

"If they did," Vaslik commented, "he's dead and buried in a deep gulley or ravine somewhere."

"Agreed. But what if Aston's right? What if Hardman was the fourth man and left his phone on the body to blur the trail?"

"What would that accomplish?" Gina queried.

"That's the big question. If Aston hadn't told me what Cole-clough had found, I'd have said Michael Hardman was Special Forces, and he's been working undercover all these years. But they've never heard of him and neither have the passport authorities."

"Oh, boy," Gina murmured, reaching the obvious conclusions. "So what is he?"

Ruth looked deliberately at Vaslik. "Search me. But if he's not one of ours … maybe he's one of yours. How about it?"

Vaslik pursed his lips. "I can run it by a guy I know … but I don't expect any answers. If he's with one of the really elite black ops units, there's no way his name will come to light; they bury those guys so deep not even their old colleagues can find them."

———

Vaslik stood in a patch of shadow under the front porch overhang, staring along the road and checking everything while barely moving a muscle. After Ruth's news, he needed some fresh air. She was being treated like dirt and he didn't like it. But short of putting himself back on a plane to the US in protest, there was nothing he could do about it other than continue until the police stepped in and took over. At that point his assignment would be over, too.

The road looked pretty normal; a few cars, a couple of pedestrians, an old lady wrapped in a raincoat pottering in her front garden. No more signs of cars with steamy windows or houses with the blinds pulled 24/7, but then, he hadn't expected them to hang around.

It was probably a waste of time worrying about it. If the watchers were still in the area, they'd have already chosen another location and settled in, their neighbours none-the-wiser. In fact, if they had the means they could have paid off a neighbour to get lost for a few days, leaving their house as an OP with no fears of anybody stumbling on them. It was a tactic used by Homeland Security agents when a suspect turned up in some quiet neighbourhood and had to be checked out through careful surveillance. *Su casa es mi casa*, Jimmy Marriot, a fellow DHS agent used to say when persuading a householder to go on a few days' vacation so he could take over the place as a base. Your house is my house. Most were only too pleased to comply, especially knowing they could talk about it in the neighborhood afterwards and gain kudos for helping out in the fight against terrorism.

His survey flowed across Nancy's car parked on the driveway where she had left it after rushing in from the gym. It probably needed a run sometime soon to keep things ticking over. Cars were like dogs; they needed exercise and a chance to blow off some dust.

This one was a Nissan and looked about ten years old, with a couple of rust spots over the fenders and a small star-shaped crack in one corner of the windshield. Plenty of life left in it yet, though. Not that he knew much about cars; live in New York and you got used to public transport.

A flicker of light caught his eye on the driver's side, just inside the glass. He stepped across and peered at it. Shiny, like gold, and rectangular. He leaned closer and knew instantly what it was: it was a smart card, like they use in digital cameras, and stuck on the windshield side of the sun visor.

He remembered what Ruth had told them a few minutes ago about the corrupted file from the photo frame, and wondered. Could there be two of them? He turned and went back inside, and came out moments later with the car keys.

He opened the car and slid behind the wheel, then pulled the flap out and up against the car roof. The smart card blinked back at him, the gold colour slightly dulled in the reduced light. He took out his visa card and fed it behind the card until the adhesive used to hold it in place gave way.

The card looked innocuous in the palm of his hand; a tiny piece of chip technology most people never saw, never realised was even there. They clicked away with their cameras and only downloaded what they needed direct to their PC or Mac without realising that given the correct piece of kit, you could store stuff other than photos on the memory card inside.

He sat watching the street for a few moments, his chest thumping as he thought about what he might be holding. If what Ruth had suggested was right, this might hold the key to the corrupted file she'd handed Ellworthy.

But what if it held more than that? What if it gave a clue to the whereabouts of Michael Hardman? Of Beth?

He took out his cell phone and stared at the smart card. It might be nothing, of course, in which case he was barking at the moon. This should go to the techs in Langley; they would have the machinery and software to open the card up like soft butter and prise out its secrets. Corrupted file or not, it was what they were good at. If they said it was a dud, then so bit it. But he had to find out and duty was leaning on him to go the correct route.

He touched the button that would connect him with Drybeck in Washington. Hand him this and the rear-admiral would forget all about his rebellious refusal earlier. It wasn't that Vaslik wanted his old job back, but he could do without the kind of trouble a heavy hitter like Drybeck could bring down on him. Common sense said it was better to play safe and stay on the side of the angels.

But.

There was always a but. What if he said go fuck the angels? They'd had their turn, and he had a more powerful instinct driving him.

He pocketed the cell phone and walked back inside.

———

He handed the card to Ruth and told her where he'd found it. "Hidden in plain sight. It could be a copy of the other one, could be nothing. Weird place to stick it, though, if it means nothing. Kind of place someone with a secret to hide would leave it."

Ruth took it and smiled gratefully. "Thanks, Andy. I'll get Ellworthy to open it."

Vaslik lifted an eyebrow. "Andy? Just as I was getting used to Slik, too."

Ruth's phone rang, cutting off her reply. It was Ellworthy. He sounded breathless, as if he was on the move.

"I just got a call from our Siege 2 operator. I'm on my way to your location right now."

"Why—what's up?"

"Are any of you guys using your cell phones?"

Ruth looked at Gina and Vaslik, both with hands in plain sight. "No. Why?"

"We got low-level signals less than two minutes ago from inside the house. Somebody there is sending and receiving text messages."

"When?"

"Right now."

FORTY-SIX

RUTH CHARGED UP THE stairs with Vaslik and Gina close on her heels. This had gone far enough; she'd had it with all the twists and turns and—what was it some politician had once said about being economic with the truth? How about plain bloody lies and evasions? As far as she could tell, that was all Nancy had done so far. She had no solid proof yet, but somehow the shocked mother act was looking just a little shy of the genuine article.

Now this.

She twisted the handle and pushed at Nancy's door. It didn't give. Damn, she hadn't given a thought to a lock before; there had been no need.

"Slik." She stood aside. There was no time for niceties; this needed a fast entry.

Vaslik pushed the door with his hand to test it, then threw his shoulder against the centre of the panel close to the lock. It burst open with a shriek of wood, and a long splinter came away from the jamb, carrying the metal strike plate with it.

There was a sharp cry of alarm inside the room and Ruth saw Nancy on her bed. She was dressed in a T-shirt top, her legs bare. A dressing gown lay across her feet.

She was thrusting her hand beneath the pillow.

"*What are you doing?*" she protested. "You have no right!"

"Tough," said Ruth. "Give me the phone." She held out her hand, although she guessed it was too late. "Now."

But Nancy shook her head like a child caught with her hand in the cookie jar, denying all responsibility.

"I don't know what you're talking about," she muttered, unnaturally calm and leaning back against the pillow. "I don't have a phone—you kept mine downstairs, remember?" Her eyes were wide and she was almost smiling, as if innocent denial would be enough. She eyed Vaslik, standing by the door, watching silently. "Has he come to watch the fun or are you two dykes going to gang up on me?" She gave Vaslik a coy look and deliberately parted her legs, the cotton T-shirt shifting up her thighs. "What do you think, Andy? The charity widow needs a bit of action, is that it?"

"*Stop that!*" Gina stepped forward, eyes blazing with anger. "What the hell are you doing?" She grabbed the end of the pillow and ripped it from under Nancy and hurled it across the room, then dragged the dressing gown over her bare legs.

As she did do, a slim, black cell phone slid off the bed and bounced to the floor.

Ruth picked it up. She checked the log, listing calls missed, received and dialled. Empty. She checked the messages log. The same.

Nancy had beaten them to it.

When she looked up, Nancy was staring at her defiantly. She looked angry, but there was something else lurking in her eyes, too.

Was it an expression of *triumph*? Christ, how could she?

"Who are you in contact with, Nancy? Is it Michael?" Ruth tossed the phone to Vaslik, who caught it and dropped it into his pocket. "Never mind, we'll have our techs look at it and they'll know exactly who you've been talking to. Trust me."

Nancy remained silent. She tucked the dressing gown around her in a belated show of modesty and stared at the floor.

Ruth sat on the bed. "Nancy, I don't know what you're doing—or what you think you're doing. But this isn't going to help us find Beth. You do want her back, don't you?"

"Of course." The answer was a whisper. If she had any fight or resistance left, she had pushed it down deep inside where they couldn't get at it.

"So what's the thing with the secret messaging? Did Michael arrange for the phone? How did he get it inside? Was it hidden here in your room?"

Nancy's head jerked up in surprise.

Ruth continued, "What—you think we couldn't tell when you began communicating with him? You really think we haven't had this place locked down ever since we arrived?" She pointed towards the window, hoping the fabrication didn't show in her voice. "There's a unit out there can tell when you call or send a text message … and when you receive one. It also has the capability of back-tracking on Michael's texts and pinning down his location each time. Sooner or later, we'll know where he is to within a few metres. Is that how you want this to end? Because we're not the only ones who can do this, you know. There are others—and they're not so forgiving."

A double blink of the eyes. Nancy whispered, "I don't believe you."

"Tell her, Slik." She reckoned it would sound scarier coming from Vaslik, and hoped he would pick up the baton and run with it. They had to do something to shake her composure otherwise this could go on forever.

"Cell phones use microwaves," he said easily. "When you talk, your voice is encoded into signals which are transmitted to the nearest tower, which bounces them on to the destination device in what's called a pathway or control channel. The nearest tower then tells the device to ring and that's how you get contact. When you send or receive a text message, it's pretty much the same; the signal goes over the pathway in a small packet of data. Darned thing is, Nancy, people think text messaging is easier to hide because it's smaller and faster … the signal doesn't last long enough for anybody to fasten on to it." He smiled coolly. "Fact is, your cell phone is constantly active, exchanging data with the nearest tower, or if you're moving, checking to find the next tower and so on. Cell phones are like little lost dogs—they hate being out of contact. Didn't Michael tell you that?"

She said nothing, eyes dulled by the shock of what she was hearing.

Vaslik gave a snort of disgust and said, "Over to you two. I'm done here." He turned and left the room and went downstairs, his footsteps soft on the carpet.

"Where is he, Nancy?" Ruth asked softly. Hard soft, hard soft; it was a common enough technique to wear away at a person withholding information. Hit them with something that would frighten them, then soften them up to coax them into talking. It was a variation on the good cop, bad cop approach. But like many such techniques, it wasn't guaranteed to work every time.

And bad cop had just walked out.

FORTY-SEVEN

"I DON'T KNOW WHAT you mean," Nancy muttered, and stared out of the window. "Why don't you all leave if you distrust me so much?"

"What did he say in his message just now?" Gina asked. "The one you just deleted." She ducked her head, forcing Nancy to look at her. "Michael told you to do that, didn't he—right at the beginning? He told you to wipe every message and hide the phone. Why would he do that? What is he hiding? What are *you* hiding?"

"That's rubbish." But Nancy sounded uncertain and was looking at Gina with a new sense of awareness, as if her confidence had been dented by how much they knew.

"Does he know about Beth?" Ruth asked, piling on the pressure. "He must. He must be worried for her."

No response.

"What have you told him, Nancy? What did he tell you? He knows we're here, right—from Cruxys?"

Not a flicker. It was like talking to the wall. She decided to go for broke instead, to push her emotional buttons.

"The thing I don't get, Nancy, is what kind of father won't come back for his daughter? It's not the action of a reasonable man, is it—leaving you to handle everything? Why is he hiding? What's so important that he'll risk Beth's life—and yours—to keep it safe?"

Nancy said nothing, but slid down on the bed and lay down on her side, cutting them off.

Ruth shrugged and left the room, with Gina close behind.

As the door closed, Nancy could not prevent a tear rolling down her cheek. But she refused to cry. Whatever happened next, she had to believe in Michael … and fate.

———

Vaslik was waiting for them in the kitchen. He'd put the kettle on to boil but it wasn't to hide anything they might say. It had gone too far for that. He felt irritated with the reaction of the woman upstairs and her unseen husband, and wanted to explode at her. But that wouldn't help.

He'd encountered a variety of responses in the families of kidnap victims over the years, ranging from the helpless to the outright hostile, as if the police were actively seeking the worst possible outcome. Some were ashamed by whatever had brought about the kidnap—even if it was simply the wealth sought by the kidnappers; some were defensive, closing in on themselves as if that might offer some protection; others were noisily and emotionally fearful of what might happen to the kidnapped person; others still were clearly hiding something—a very few concealing something so awful that they were willing to risk the death of the victim to keep hidden.

He watched Gina and Ruth enter the room. They were clearly as puzzled by events as he, filled by equal parts frustration and anger at the lack of progress.

"She's talking to him, isn't she?" Ruth said. "She's in touch with her husband. Tell me I'm wrong."

He nodded. There really wasn't much more to say, no other conclusion to reach. She'd fooled them and got round their precautions, even though they were trying to protect her. Short of beating the information out of her with a big stick, they were up against a brick wall.

"What do we do now?" asked Gina. "This isn't a crisis, is it? Why are we even still here?"

"Because there's an innocent child out there," Ruth murmured. "What's going on is not her fault. And we don't know for sure if Hardman's got any control over what's happening. He must have told Nancy everything's all right but he's hardly proven himself Father of the Year material so far, has he?"

"Right." Vaslik nodded in agreement. "Whatever's keeping him from coming in, it must be serious. Which means he must know the people who snatched Beth and that they want him bad."

"If so, what won't they do to get him? And what's he got that's so damned important?"

Vaslik was about to reply when his cell phone rang. He took it out, checked the screen. No caller ID. Probably Drybeck with more threats. "Vaslik."

"Hey, Andy." It was Eric LaGuardo. He sounded excited. A buzz of background traffic told Vaslik he was outside, away from the office. The geek must have found something good.

"What's up?"

"Uh ... those faces? You sure about them being in London? I mean, absolutely certain?"

"I'm sure. I saw them myself in a vehicle not a hundred yards from where I'm standing." He turned on the loudspeaker and told Eric to keep talking, that the other people in the room were trustworthy.

"Uh, right. Hi, folks." Eric sounded guarded.

"Why do you ask, Eric?"

"Because," Eric's voice echoed around the kitchen, "if you're right, they both used to work for you-know-who."

"Langley?"

"Jeez, don't say that! Haven't you heard of keyword analysis?"

"I have, but come on—a single word in the ether? They'd need more than that."

"They wouldn't, believe me." He didn't sound mollified.

"Okay, no more keywords. What have you got?"

"Well, these two subjects are listed as ex-employees, but that's all I can tell you, except that ... hell, how do I put this?" He breathed heavily, the noise coming out of the speaker like a snorting bull.

"Just say it, Eric," Vaslik told him coolly. "Spit it out and you can go home."

"OK. The work these ... two used to do—they were in a specialist unit overseas. Then they ran into some trouble over their treatment of detainees."

"Abu Ghraib?" The Baghdad prison where systematic abuse had been discovered being meted out against detainees, including water-boarding and mental abuse. It had created a storm of international protest and sullied the US military for a long time.

"No, not that. Field prisoners."

"Fighters."

"Yes. Some disappeared after being taken. Others had accidents."

"They probably deserved it." Gina's voice was flat. She shrugged at looks from the other two and a signal from Ruth to zip it .

"Pardon me."

"What happened to these two?"

"They disappeared. Shipped out fast on a military transport . . . then gone like smoke. Google their names and you get zilch. Believe me, it takes muscle to disappear a person just like that."

Vaslik grunted. It certainly did. But for some the muscle was there. If you wanted things to vanish off the radar, they could. All you had to do was know who to call.

"How come they're still around?" said Ruth.

"Simple: they never left. It's smoke and mirrors. You'd be amazed at how much of that shit goes on around here. These guys went private sector and their records disappeared into a big, black hole. It happens all the time. Nobody's admitting it but there's talk, you know? You get a feel for the subtext when you work in this business long enough."

"And what are they doing now?" Vaslik asked. He was guessing Eric knew; this was way too juicy a subject for the geek to have ignored, and he'd have done a lot more digging to find out more.

He was right.

"What I hear is they do contract work for some shadow organisations with connections in you-know-where."

Washington. The centre for all things shadowy, where the very air was heavy with intrigue. Vaslik exchanged a look with Ruth but said nothing. He was suddenly wishing he'd taken this call in private. Too late now, though.

"Doing what?"

"I don't know. But it can only be one thing, right? Heavy stuff. What else is there for their kind?"

Anti-terrorism. The biggest game in town and for people like Eric was describing, the only game they knew how to play. For seasoned pros who had seen it and done it all, there was always a call for their skills, always a budget for their deadly commitment.

Vaslik found himself holding his breath, trying to entertain just a healthy glimmer of doubt. But there was none. Either Eric had been drinking or what he'd stumbled on was absolutely genuine and buried in a file deep in the archives.

But Eric wasn't interested in booze; his kicks came from a different source. Eric had a wild imagination and an enquiring mind. It was what made him so good at his job. Put the two traits together with the kind of computer skills he possessed and he couldn't fail to go hunting bugs. Or, in this case, spooks. And because he was trusted and had undoubtedly been vetted down to his grandfather's socks and back, he had access to some seriously scary information. All it would have needed was a start, like the photos Vaslik had given him, and a couple of lines of data that hadn't been correctly expunged by the keepers of the records, and it would have been enough to set him off.

For that reason, the glimmer of doubt faded and vanished.

"Should I be worried?"

"Hell, yes. If I was you, I'd get out of that place right now and find a deep hole to hide in. From what I've heard, if they've got you under surveillance it's for a reason—and they're not trained to take prisoners."

FORTY-EIGHT

JAMES ELLWORTHY LOOKED NERVOUS. Maybe it was being out of the office, as if he were afraid the great outdoors was waiting to ambush him now he was away from his electronic toys and subdued lighting. He followed instructions and came in via the back garden like a ghost, and unfolded a neat laptop on the work surface. He eyed Gina with awe when he saw the butt of her semi-automatic showing under her jacket, and she smiled coyly and asked if he wanted coffee. He shook his head and focussed on the smart card, slipping it into a plug-in reader and waiting while it loaded.

"How much do you guys know about encrypted data?" he asked, generally.

"Me? Nothing," said Gina.

"I'm a dunce," Ruth told him. "Speak slowly and in simple words, otherwise I'll get Gina to shoot you in the kneecaps."

He blushed again and eyed Gina with a glint of respect. "Right. That's good to know. Uh … how can I put this? I've got a high-spec decryption program on here; it unravels codes and looks for passwords

296

and back doors into protected programmes or documents, like I think this might be."

"Does it work quickly?"

"Pretty much, yes. If I can get the smart card to download without crashing, I'll run it through the program and see what it comes up with. Shouldn't take more than a few minutes." He smiled "How's that?"

"Awesome," Gina murmured throatily. "No guns for you today." She smiled when he went bright red and walked out of the kitchen, deliberately twitching her hips on the way.

"Wow," he croaked, looking at Ruth. "Is she for real?"

"She is, but not for you," Ruth warned him. "You've got work to do."

Ellworthy hummed vaguely while waiting for the decryption software to do its tricks, then gestured for Ruth to take a look.

"It's some kind of spreadsheet," he explained. "Like Excel. Only this is something tailor-made. Some of the cells are individually encrypted—see the hashtags? I'm not sure I can punch through them without losing the data."

Ruth studied the screen and scrolled down through line after line of numbers and letters, each in their own cells. Some were filled with hashtags, but enlarging the cell didn't automatically reveal the contents as she knew the Excel programme would do. Neither did hovering the cursor over the cell. She tried to make sense of the blocks of letters, hoping they would form a pattern, but they were a meaningless jumble. "OK. What do you think this is?"

He shrugged. "I've seen this kind of thing before, so I'm only guessing. But you won't like it."

"Try me."

"I did an exchange program a while back with the DEA—that's our Drug Enforcement Administration. They'd liberated a ton of DVDs, flash drives and paper from a Mexican cartel. The stuff on the drives looked like this, only much bigger. It was transactional data used by the drugs gang listing sales by volume, product and market. It was huge—those guys deal in millions, maybe billions." He flicked a hand towards one side of the screen, where some of the cells contained a series of abbreviations, like words in text messages. "The one thing they didn't encode is this column here."

He was pointing at a cell containing the alphanumeric HNDA650L, and another with HNDACG125.

"OK, thrill me," said Ruth. "What are they?"

"Honda motorcycles. Small, fast, and Chinese-built."

She stared at him. "How the hell do you know that? It could mean anything."

He grinned. "My kid brother's a bike freak. He races these things in indie meetings. Every time I see him he bores me to death with the numbers. It's like he wants to race every two-wheeler on the planet."

She scowled. "So this spreadsheet comes from a *bike* dealer? I don't get it."

"Me neither, but that's what it says." He pointed further down to where other cells contained the letters DUND606 and CONTTKC80. "And see these? They're tyre makes. Tyres for motorcycles. I'm pretty sure they're off-road models." He indicated other cells. "And these look like parts numbers for spares."

"If they are," said Andy Vaslik, entering the kitchen and leaning over to take a look, "somebody's been buying bikes and replacement parts. Big deal."

Ruth took a turn round the kitchen, eyeing the laptop as if she wanted to hurl something heavy through the screen. What on earth was a bike dealer's transaction record doing on a digital photo-frame? Was it simply a random error, picked up by mistake from another computer? Or something less innocent?

"Damn." Vaslik murmured softly. He tapped a fingernail against the screen, watched by an anxious James Ellworthy, protective of his high-tech toy. "What if these aren't bike parts?"

"Say again," said Ruth.

"What if they're code for something else? I mean, if the rest is encrypted like Boy Wonder, here, says, then why leave this column in clear?"

"It's only in clear," Ruth countered, "if you know about motorbikes."

"Exactly. Which would be enough to put most people off the scent. But what if the transactions in this column *are* for bikes and parts … but others are for something else entirely?"

Ruth scowled. She was getting a glimmer of an idea and she didn't like it. "Go on."

"Well, we don't know where this data comes from; it could be anywhere in the world where bikes get traded in large numbers."

"Funny you should say that." Ellworthy moved the mouse and placed the cursor on a cell adjacent to one of the parts numbers. A grey box appeared with the letters PESH in black type.

"Pesh?"

"Peshawar," Vaslik said immediately. "In Pakistan." He looked intense, as if they'd found a locked secret. "The Pakistanis use motorbikes. Lots and lots of them."

"That's right." Ellworthy was nodding excitedly. "I've been there and they're everywhere. You get whole families on one bike. It's like, nuts. But why not? In cities the traffic's a nightmare and in the countryside the roads are dirt tracks. The only way to get around is on two wheels. Jesus, I should tell my bro—he'd freak out." He scowled at the thought, then turned and got ready to switch off the laptop. "Well, guys, it's been fun but I have to get back. What do you want me to do with this stuff?"

Ruth looked at Vaslik, who shook his head. "It's your call. But don't quote me on any of this. It still might not mean anything."

"Fine," said Ruth, and looked at Ellworthy. "Send it on up the ladder. Talk to Aston—nobody else, you hear?"

"I got it."

"Good. He'll know what to do." Something told her it was too important to hold onto. She didn't know for sure what it meant, but there was too much going on for this to be overlooked. And right now, any lead was worth exploring.

"Anything else?"

"Yes. Great work. Forget you saw it and you were never here." She was taking a risk on him keeping quiet, but it was all she could think of. She hadn't got the resources to take this further, and for all she knew it could be a glorious waste of time. Aston, at least, would know who to consult. She just hoped he stayed well away from Martyn Claas, who would kill the thing stone dead on cost grounds alone.

Ellworthy looked uncertain. "What if I'm asked about it?"

"You lie." It was Gina, speaking from the doorway. "If you don't, I'll track you down like a dog." For added emphasis, she flicked back her jacket revealing the butt of the pistol. "You get me?"

Ellworthy nodded and swallowed, as if unsure whether to laugh or cry. He scooped up his laptop. "I get you. I won't tell anyone." He gave a weak smile and Gina turned and led him to the back gate.

Ruth watched them go before turning to Vaslik. "If those records are what you think they are, and this house is being watched by former US special forces, what does that say about Michael Hardman?"

Vaslik shrugged. "I don't know. Seriously. There could be any number of explanations."

"But if the spreadsheet is anything to do with him, why leave it on the photo card?"

"What better place? Who would look there?" He smiled wryly. "Apart from us, of course. But we're security geeks."

"Thanks. It still doesn't explain what his connection is."

"No. But I'm willing to bet one thing: Hardman ain't no charity worker."

———

An hour later Ruth had a call from Aston. He'd been briefed on the spreadsheet records by Ellworthy, but he wasn't calling about mystery motorcycle parts or missing husbands.

"I'm coming over," he told her. "You and Vaslik stay there; and keep Mrs. Hardman isolated. What I have to say is not for her ears."

FORTY-NINE

"Tiggi Sgornik's dead," Aston announced quietly. He loosened his tie and collar, a gesture that was as surprising as if he had suddenly announced a profound belief in aliens. It was accompanied by a pull of the mouth as if the words tasted bitter.

They were in the living room, with Gina keeping Nancy occupied upstairs. They had taken seriously Aston's warning that the news he had was not something she would want to hear.

Ruth and Vaslik were on the sofa, with Aston slumped in an armchair opposite. He looked beat, as if he had run a marathon, his usually neat, sharp edges slightly rumpled. Before speaking, he'd placed a small plastic box on the coffee table and flicked a switch, explaining that it was one of James Ellworthy's toys—a jammer to counter the listening devices in the house.

"I had to tell you in person," he continued, "and I'll have to ask you to keep this from Mrs. Hardman for a while until more is known."

"Will do," Ruth agreed. "What happened?"

"Miss Sgornik's body was found late last night just below Putney Bridge. Early indications are she was beaten to death. The Serious Organised Crime Unit is involved and the Foreign Office wants answers."

"What now?" Ruth felt numbed. Was this a precursor to Beth also being found dead, a grisly sign that the kidnappers had finally given up waiting for Michael Hardman and cut their losses?

"I'll come to that. We'd put out her name earlier as a person of interest and got the heads-up of her death from a contact in the Met. That gave us some leeway."

"To do what?" This from Vaslik.

"Initially we're handing over everything to them." At their looks of surprise, he explained, "If we don't and they find the link later on, they'll slaughter us. There are already questions being asked in the House about the involvement of private security contractors in criminal investigations. And since our guards went missing in Nigeria, we're under even closer scrutiny." He winced. "It seems that along with the military nowadays, we're not supposed to lose people; as if it had never occurred to anyone before that fighting or protecting others in openly hostile areas is an inherently dangerous occupation. If we're accused on top of that of withholding evidence about a child abduction here in London, I doubt we'll survive the fall-out."

"Not even with our new friends in Washington and Amsterdam to back us up?"

Aston gave a bleak smile at Ruth's acid tone. She was referring to Martyn Claas and Bob Zitterman.

"They won't protect us." His voice was blunt. "If their investment is threatened in any way they'll drop us like hot coals. We're hardly in the same territory as Blackwater, but neither are we big enough to fight off a government enquiry unscathed. The publicity would rip us to shreds."

Blackwater was a powerful American private security company, some of whose men had been accused of brutality and excesses in Iraq. With the suspected help of influential friends, the company had weathered the media and political storm, but had since changed hands and name. Aston was correct: Cruxys wasn't in the same league.

"How was the body identified?" Ruth queried. It seemed pointless to pursue it but she was curious to know what role Tiggi had played in Beth's abduction. Had she been an innocent caught up in the kidnap … or something darker?

"A label was found stitched inside the pocket of her jacket, believe it or not. It led to her father, a clothing manufacturer named Czcibor Sgornik. She was allegedly in the UK on an extended visit to improve her English, although there are doubts about that. However, she had a habit of calling her father once a week—his instructions, I gather. He was worried about her. When he hadn't heard from her for a few days he rang his embassy and got them involved. It seems he carries a lot of weight with the government, courtesy of making, among other things, uniforms for the Israeli police and army."

Vaslik's eyebrows shot up and he exchanged a glance with Ruth. He hadn't missed the significance. "Israel? Is that where's she's from?"

"Yes. Czcibor's parents arrived in Israel from Poland sixty years ago. Tiggi was educated in Haifa. This is another reason we're having to step back from this: with the involvement of another country it's simply too messy. Let the police and security service sort it out."

Ruth leaned forward. "Why MI5? Is there a spying connection?"

"Not as far as I know. They're playing safe, that's all. Hardman works in some very questionable, even threatening places; place that in connection with almost anything Israeli and the warning flags go up as a matter of course."

There was a "but" in there somewhere; Ruth could hear it. Aston hadn't given up that easily, surely. "What about Beth? She's still out there."

"I'm aware of that." Aston met her glare with absolute calm. He tapped his knees and looked at them both in turn. "We probably have twenty-four hours to get this cleaned up. Find the kidnappers and bring Beth home. But," he paused, "I'm giving you both an opt-out. If you want nothing more to do with it, I will understand. You can transfer to other assignments and we'll let the authorities do what they can. In fact, Claas is demanding it; he wants the publicity of being seen to be a responsible company. If that means you two disappearing into the background with a gagging order, all the better." His expression was wintry, clear enough evidence of his feelings about the Dutchman's tactics.

"Everything goes to the police?"

"Yes. Briefings, data, the listening devices—even your reports and the briefing boards. Full disclosure." He lifted his hands, wrists close together. "I have no choice."

"What about the smart card?" said Ruth.

"No. Not that. At least, not yet."

"Why?" asked Vaslik.

"It's a question of jurisdiction. This is a fair bit of supposition on our part, but the moment Ellworthy brought it back I sent it to a friend at Vauxhall Cross." He was referring to MI6, the Secret Intelligence service. "It took them about ten minutes to crack enough of it to get excited. As far as I know they haven't yet shared that excitement with their friends along the embankment." This meant MI5.

"But they will have to sooner or later. I can put Claas off until to-morrow, but that's it." He looked at them. "Are you in or out?"

"I'm in," Vaslik muttered.

"Me, too," said Ruth. She was damned if she was going to allow Claas to kick her off the job and leave Beth to God knew whatever fate awaited her without at least trying to find her. And if that meant risking bumping up against the police and the security services, so be it.

Aston smiled. "I was hoping you'd say that." He reached in his top pocket and took out a slip of paper which he passed to Ruth. "Because of the information on the smart card there's somebody you need to talk to. I don't know if it will help find the Hardman girl, but it might explain why she was taken."

"Do you know why?"

"I can only go by what I've been told, which is limited informa-tion only. All I can say is, talking with this man will answer a lot of questions, but it won't necessarily mean you'll find her. She may be beyond our reach. You'll have to judge that for yourselves. It might, however, influence what you do next. Be at this location in Hyde Park at six this evening. Sorry about the cloak and dagger, but he's flying out from Northolt immediately afterwards and it can't wait."

"How will I know him?"

"You won't—but he will know you."

The knowledge didn't reassure her. "Why are you letting me do this? It could be messy for Cruxys if it all goes wrong."

"Because I trust you. Because you care. And I want to see an out-come for this, not for it to be swept under the carpet like a minor dust problem. But take great care, Ruth. Claas is watching you and we're dealing with some very ruthless people."

"I will. Do I get any help?"

"Vaslik here, if he's willing."

The American nodded. "Damn right."

"You can also have Fraser if you think she's up to it. If I can get one of the specialists, I will, but don't count on it. We're a little stretched right now."

"What if we tread on any toes?"

Aston's mouth curled. "What can I say—just make sure they're the right ones. And in that respect, I advise you to take precautions."

Ruth blinked in surprise. Aston was talking weapons. It wasn't like him.

"Serious?"

"Just to be safe. Fraser will kit you out." He studied the pair of them. "I don't like sending people out into the field unprepared; I never have and never will. But you know the rules."

Ruth nodded. He meant no comeback. If they got caught carrying weapons, they were on their own. "I know."

———

When Aston had gone, Ruth looked at Andy Vaslik. He'd been quiet throughout Aston's talk, content to stay in the background. But his demeanour worried her; something was going on that seemed to be distracting him but she couldn't put her finger on it. She didn't know him well enough to guess his mood swings, but she sensed a tension in him that she hadn't witnessed before.

"You're very quiet."

"I'm just wondering where this is going." He laid his hand out flat and waggled it from side to side. "The way he was talking, it could get heavy. Are you sure you want to continue?"

Ruth felt a tremor run through her, like a tiny charge of electricity. *Was he warning her off?* If so, what did he know? Or should that be what *else* did he know?

"Why do I get the feeling you aren't as blind here as you pretend?"

"I don't know what you're talking about."

She waited for him to say more but he didn't. The silence in the room was intense.

"Does the American connection worry you?"

"Why should it?" His face was still, and that concerned her.

She waited to see if he would unload, but he remained silent. In the end she said, "No reason." She checked her watch. It was going to be tight and she didn't want to be late. "Come on, let's go talk to a spook."

"You think that's what Aston's friend is?"

"Of course. Didn't you know, London's full of them."

FIFTY

HYDE PARK HELD ITS customary evening mix of tourists and com-
muters, the first enjoying the open space, while the muted roar of
traffic from Park Lane showed the concentration of cars and buses
deploying the latter out of the capital heading to the west and north.

The note from Aston had specified the area on the northern edge
of the park, along the road known as North Carriage Drive. It was a
pleasant mix of trees, road and pathways across a large expanse of
grass, much favoured by horse-riders and others, and a convenient
step for residents on the other side of the Bayswater Road to get out
from the narrow streets and buildings.

Ruth entered the park from the north side opposite Albion Street
and paused briefly to check her surroundings. She was deliberately
early. She would have preferred being here an hour ago to give
the place a thorough inspection, but suspected that was something
the man meeting her had avoided intentionally by suggesting the
rendezvous at such short notice.

Unable to see anything noteworthy, she walked as far as the inner road and turned right along the pavement. It put her in full view so that the man would see her, but its very openness gave her a tiny edge; she might be able to spot anyone taking an undue interest in her, too. And in clandestine meetings like this, you took whatever advantages you were offered with both hands.

She used the pretence of checking her phone to scrutinise the people nearby. Some were jogging, others walking dogs or children, others more purposeful and focussed, on their way to work or home. But no obvious lone spooks lurking beneath the trees.

She couldn't see Vaslik, although she knew he was there. It was a basic precaution having him watching her back, although she had no reason to be wary of meeting Aston's mysterious contact. But if there was anybody to see, the American might be able to get a snap-shot for future reference.

A movement showed up ahead where there had previously been none. A man with a briefcase had stepped out from behind a group of obvious tourists fifty yards ahead, and stood waiting for her. He gave a nod. Middle-aged, dressed in a charcoal grey suit and shiny shoes, unremarkable, a typical Mr. Nobody, an office worker taking time out to smell the grass.

As she drew level with him he turned and walked with her, grad-ually leading her off towards the open green of the main park.

"Don't worry, Miss Gonzales," he said easily. "I'm not a stalker."

"It's your lucky day, then," she replied. "You'd have got yourself drop-kicked into the bushes. You've got some information for me."

Up close he was older than she'd first thought, with the weath-ered stringiness of a man who spent a lot of time outside. Early six-ties, she guessed; smart, well-dressed, a mid-level civil servant but no regular pen-pusher. There was something too undeniably hard about him for a desk jockey. Maybe they'd pulled him out of retirement for this.

"I don't have long," he said without preamble or introduction, "so please listen. This is a once-only meeting."

"Do you have a name?"

"I do, but you don't need it. I'm merely delivering information."

He was a messenger. A courier with no back-trail. "Suits me. Go ahead."

"Like you, my colleagues and I are trying to find a missing person. We think you might be able to help us."

"Really?" She was puzzled, and wondered if they had been working unknowingly in tandem. "If you are what I think you are, why would you be looking for Beth Hardman?"

"If you keep interrupting, this meeting is over."

"Sorry."

"Thank you. The person we're trying to locate is a man, and is known in criminal quarters as a bag man. He moves money from one place to another. Lots of it. He travels light, avoiding customs hot spots and using back-door entry and exit routes known to very few people."

"A smuggler?" She stopped and stared at him, bringing him to a halt. "Are you Revenue and Customs?" Maybe a drop-kick would be in order. Why the hell was he talking to her? This was a waste of time.

He gave a dry chuckle and turned to walk on, waiting for her to catch up before continuing. "Hardly. Bank transfers, as you know, leave electronic trails. The bigger the sum moved the more it stands out and risks coming under official scrutiny—especially with recent crack-downs on money-laundering … and the movement of terrorist-related funds around the globe."

Ruth felt her mouth go dry. The pause had been intentional, she was certain. But where was this leading?

"I still don't see how this involves me; I'm looking for a kidnapped child."

"I'm aware of that. Have you ever heard of Hawala?"

"Yes, It's a banking system in Islamic countries."

"More or less. It's centuries old, a form of honour system using a chain of brokers, often outside traditional banking. It's especially efficient for making payments across continents. Experts refer to it as money movement without moving money. I don't see the distinction from normal banking and credit, myself, but that's me."

"Go on."

"We've known for some time that a number of fringe extremist groups have been working together to amass and move funds, basically in the manner of co-operative banks. It's nothing new, of course; it spreads the costs, gives access to a wider source of fund-holders, and as long as everyone plays their part and they stay lucky, it reduces the risks. This way they've been moving money without the risk of being recorded."

"And it works?"

"Yes. We occasionally get lucky and hit on supply-line or a block of currency, but in spite of closing down more than a dozen such lines, there's been a steady flow continuing across borders all through the middle east and Europe. Somali pirates, for example, are using it to finance their trade."

"Go on."

"We crash one route and a few days later it's business as usual. Even with some of the known money men behind bars with their accounts blocked or closed down, still the organisations have all the cash they need. Or valuables."

"Is that significant?" She was fast getting used to this man's obliquely direct way of dropping information. If he'd used the word "valuables," it had been for a reason.

"Very. We've noticed a growing pattern over the past eighteen months, especially with some of the smaller freelance groups. Whereas before they were struggling to find support or cash, mostly relying on local sources, they now shop on the world's market like all the bigger names."

"How do you know that? You can't be following them all."

"We don't have to. We follow the money. We've noticed a sharp rise in the trade of jewellery and gold—even blood diamonds. Much of it turns up miles from where it would normally be found. But it doesn't stop long before moving on, traded just like electronic money but with no trail unless somebody gets careless … or we get lucky."

"They use mules?"

"That's one way. But there's another—and not some witless uni student on a gap year hoping to make a quick few bucks on the side by hiding diamonds in their knickers. There's been a lot of chatter picked up on phones and emails about something called *khazenat al wada'aa* or *khezanha*. At least, that's as near as we can make out."

"What does it mean?"

"There are many variations used by different sources and dialects, but we've pinned it down under a generic word meaning "locker" or safe deposit box. Frankly, it makes little difference when you know what it refers to. All we knew was that it was constantly on the move."

Ruth said nothing, surprised by the irony of the word. A locker was where this had all begun.

"We thought we were following an actual item to begin with," the man said. "Something tangible like a strong box of some kind. It would certainly make sense bearing in mind the topic. But we soon realised that wasn't it; the word had been coined, if you'll excuse the pun, to divert attention if anybody picked up on it, which we eventually did. Talk of a box and that's what everyone looks for. We spent too long checking left luggage areas, storage facilities, even trucks and cars, looking for travellers or small groups of men with heavy bags they didn't like leaving alone. It was a simple distraction technique to put us off." He sighed. "It worked, too, until we realised it was moving too easily to be anything so specific."

"So you're saying this 'locker' is a person?"

"Precisely. And whoever it is seems able to move through borders without hindrance, carrying money and valuables from place to place, from deal to deal. He's effectively using what he carries to sign off against weapons, equipment—even manpower. He's trusted implicitly and each group knows that anything he agrees to carries more weight than any bank, more reliability than any authority they can name save one." He pointed a meaningful finger at the sky. "But down here, this mule is almost as powerful. The deal is the deal and the mule is the teller—the broker or *Hawaladar* to use the correct term."

"Clever."

"Very. But risky for him in the long term."

"What are we talking about—hundreds of thousands of pounds or what?"

"More like millions. We know the current market price of weapons, so we can work out a reasonably accurate estimate of what's he's carrying by the stuff being financed."

"One man." It didn't seem possible, although nothing she'd heard so far seemed too far-fetched, given the twisted but inventive nature of extremist organisations.

"Certainly—why not? He's carrying high value items and he is adept at not standing out or drawing attention to himself. He seems to have the skill to blend in wherever he goes and the credentials for being in places Europeans don't normally go. He undoubtedly has back-up funds with local brokers too, if the deal to finance requires more." He shrugged. "We don't know where he keeps it and probably never will, but that's for somebody else to worry about."

He stopped and looked at her, head cocked to one side, and she realised he was waiting for her to make the necessary connection.

And then it clicked. He'd mentioned a European.

God, she'd been so bound up in thoughts of Beth that she'd ignored the blindingly obvious. "You're talking about Michael Hardman."

"Yes."

FIFTY-ONE

SHE STRUGGLED WITH THE idea of Nancy's husband being a bag man for anybody, let alone terrorists—even though she had never met the man. If what Nancy had said about their finances was true, clearly none of the money stuck to his fingers. Or given the people he worked for, maybe he was aware of the consequences if it did. Still, from charity worker to funding extremist groups was a hell of a jump. And yet, maybe not. Humanitarian convictions came in many guises. "It's a hell of a job to have on your CV." She couldn't think of anything else to say.

He gave her a patient look. "Hardman doesn't do this as a job; neither does he work for a criminal organisation—at least, not in the normal sense. He does it because he wants to. Think about it: he's a natural fit."

He was right. In a weird way the job fitted Hardman like a second skin. The charity worker, the westerner, the man on a mission—well, several missions—with a background of working for various aid agencies, using one as cover to gain access or acquire the necessary passes, a seasoned traveller, good at hiding his tracks, even from his wife. And with no apparent connections to anyone else.

"How did he get himself involved with terrorism?"

"He didn't get 'involved'—at least, not by accident. There have been previous cases of aid workers doing a bit of smuggling on the side, some even forced into it by unscrupulous criminals. It's hardly new. But this one's taken the job to new heights. In fact, you might say he's made it his life's work."

"If you know who he is, how come you haven't picked him up?"

"We've tried. And that was before we knew or suspected his name. The French got very close once in Lahore, but lost him. We had intel on his location three times, but it led nowhere. He's unbelievably skilled at staying below the radar. In fact," he almost smiled, "if he ever changes sides, there'll be a six-way auction to sign him up—including us."

"But if it is Hardman, he lives right here."

"We know that now. We didn't until very recently, so we couldn't exactly knock on his door. And, as you know, he hasn't been around for a while."

"How did you find out?"

"Let's say an ally let it slip."

"Ally?"

"A person of interest."

Ruth let that go; it wasn't her business how the information had come to light, nor how it had been acquired, whether by luck or circumstance. "How did Hardman get the job in the first place. And why would they trust a European in such a role?"

"Why do you ask?"

"I was wondering how he became a money man for al Qaeda."
She was trying to picture Michael Hardman, husband and father,
with a wife and daughter in suburban London and photos in a neat
electronic frame to prove it, having this double life of extremes.
Until now it might have been laughable. But apparently not—if this
man was telling the truth.

The man shook his head and stopped walking. Turned to face
her. There was nobody within a hundred yards, but he spoke softly.
"It would be bad enough if he were simply a fellow traveller, a naïve
sympathiser who'd fallen under the spell of human injustice and
wanted to do his bit to help. We might have been able to cope with
that; naivety is often coupled with impatience and a lack of awareness in the real world. That leads to risk-taking and simple mistakes.
It would have saved us a lot of time and countless lives."

It was something she hadn't yet had time to consider: that whoever the terrorist money man was, he was ultimately responsible for
the provision of weapons, explosives and the paraphernalia of death.
The fact that it was being done under the guise of a charity worker
seemed to make it so much worse.

"A convert, then?" The idea seemed wild, but Hardman wouldn't
be the first westerner to have changed faiths so dramatically. And
converts were usually the most intense and fiery of all extremists.

"Not even that. Michael Hardman never actually existed; he's an
invention. The man we know as Hardman has a variety of aliases
but his real name is almost certainly Wesam Bahdari. He hails from
Palestine."

"Are you sure?"

"He's been reliably identified by a childhood friend. They
bumped into each other in Paris one day. The friend was working at

a hotel desk where Hardman was booking in. Hardman has a small scar above the thumb of his right hand—his writing hand. His friend recognised it when he signed in."

"And he reported it?"

"Yes. It took a while. The young man he'd known as Bahdari was supposed to have died carrying out a bus bombing in Haifa twenty years ago. Yet here he was walking the streets of Paris using a British name. Bahdari was always paler than many Palestinians, he said, which explains how he was able to pass as European. Bahdari's reaction to the meeting was apparently quite unpleasant. At first he denied any knowledge of anyone named Bahdari. Then he began making threats. The friend was so terrified by the encounter he went into hiding before deciding to call French Intelligence, who passed on the information."

"That was good of them."

He gave a wintry smile. "We work much closer than many people think. But for once the information landed on the right desk at the right time."

Ruth recalled the images from the photo frame. She'd thought Hardman appeared vaguely Mediterranean, but could see how difficult it would be to pinpoint his true origins.

"So all the trips abroad, the extended periods away?"

"Nothing to do with charity. He's a mobile banker, using the charity organisations as cover to move around. It made him virtually untouchable."

"No wonder he didn't show up for long in the aid agencies' records." She was remembering what George Paperas had found.

"He couldn't afford to. There was always another group to talk to, another cover to assume."

They walked on a little further. The man was beginning to angle their path back towards the road. Ruth looked back and saw a dark saloon car drifting at walking pace towards them on an intercept course. She sensed the meeting was coming to a point.

"So what's the kidnap about? We haven't heard a peep from them yet. What do they want? Is it money, a rival organisation trying to horn in?"

"Nothing like that. Hardman's a wanted man, pure and simple. He possesses the kind of information that some people would give their grandmothers to acquire. Details of accounts, contacts, acquisitions, deliveries, codes … and people who mean us great harm. I doubt there has been anyone recently on the planet with quite the value this man has."

"Like the spreadsheet."

"Yes, but that's just the tip of the iceberg. He knows names we couldn't even begin to find. Not even Bin Laden knew the kind of stuff Hardman has in his head. So much so that our sources tell us the kidnappers have orders to do whatever they have to in order to get him."

"So they're official?"

"As far as we know," he said carefully, "they're a freelance team."

"Same thing these days. That's appalling … they're using his daughter as bait!"

"They're doing what they have to. I'm not saying I endorse it, but it's a reality." He appeared unruffled by the idea, as if it were an academic exercise in logic.

"Then what? What will they do to him if he does turn up?"

"He'll be moved on somewhere else."

"Where?"

"That's not relevant to this discussion."

"You're talking about extraordinary rendition."

"Of course not. That's been abandoned."

"Can't you do something to stop it—to get Beth back home?"

"I wish we could. The operation has gone too far. The team looking for Hardman is believed to be a former CIA sub-group aided by a covert Israeli cell, all private contractors with no governmental ties—at least, none that are traceable. We don't know who the individual members are or where they're based, nor do we know who controls them ... although we have our suspicions. The group itself is small, very mobile and completely off the grid. The members could be in the next street or fifty miles away."

Ruth remembered the paper napkin from the deli near Grosvenor Square and said, "Have you tried the US Embassy?"

FIFTY-TWO

"THAT'S NOT EVEN FUNNY," the man countered mildly. "We asked them, but the Americans say they have no connection with the operation."

"And you believe them?"

"Of course. There are some individuals in the various agencies that I will never get to, but there's nothing I can do about that. Whoever they are, agency or private, American or Israeli, they won't stop now they've started; they're operating in isolation for security reasons and have a simple objective: to draw Hardman out of cover. They're counting on him coming back to London once he hears about his daughter."

"He knows by now—his wife's been texting him."

He looked sceptical. "Yes, we heard about that. For good measure we also spread the word among some back channels his wife wouldn't have been able to reach. It was worth a try; anything to get him to come in."

"Do you believe he will?"

"No, I don't. If he's as committed as he seems—as others are—his family is part of his cover. In fact, given what Nancy Hardman told you about their first encounter in Paris, it's possible even then that he was looking for a European woman to get close to—to groom as cover and provide him with a legend. Nancy happened along at the right moment."

Andy had suggested something similar—that Nancy and Michael being together had seemed almost deliberate. "So," she said, "they're a means to an end, nothing more."

"Correct. She's collateral damage in the greater cause, I'm afraid. Threatening her and Beth will have no effect other than to harden him in his aims."

If this was true, Ruth had to face an awful thought: she'd been taken in by Nancy all along and that it had all been part of an act. "Is it possible she knows what Michael does?"

"We simply don't know. Nothing's certain in this business, but I wouldn't bet either way. We don't have anything worth a mention to hold against her. Anyway, I thought you might have a better take on that than I." He looked at her for a response, and she was surprised he actually seemed interested in her answer.

"I don't know, either. I don't want to believe that she does, but it's possible." Ruth couldn't imagine any mother being capable of living with the knowledge that she was part of a situation that had led to her daughter being kidnapped. It defied belief. And yet she knew there were women, mothers, sisters, who had done just that in various parts of the world, in the belief that almost any loss was worth the cause. "She loves Beth, I know that."

"I'm sure she does. I just don't think Hardman feels the same; he'd be here otherwise."

"So you think Beth's expendable in his eyes."

"It doesn't matter what I think. All I can judge is the reality of the situation." His tone was almost indifferent. "I wouldn't concern yourself about the daughter. I understand she's perfectly safe, being looked after by the nanny."

"*What*?" Ruth wanted to slug him, to jolt him into her vision of what was real. Then she realised the awful truth: he didn't know. He obviously hadn't yet heard about Tiggi Sgornik's murder. She wondered what he did know and gritted her teeth to hide her anger. She decided to test him. "Is she American, too?"

"I have no idea. I doubt it. Probably Israeli. Their female operatives are particularly adept at this kind of assignment." He glanced at his watch. "I have to be going."

"Wait." She grabbed his arm to stop him. It was stringy and lean, all sinew and bone. "Why are you telling me all this? Why this ..." She swept her other arm out, indicating the park and the two of them. " ... this charade?"

He shrugged her hand away. "Because I don't believe they will get him—at least, not today or tomorrow. But they will soon. It's inevitable. Somebody close to Mrs. Hardman should know. I'm hoping you can prepare her for what she will undoubtedly hear one day."

"What—so I get to break the bad news: that her loving, albeit distant husband is not a charity worker after all, but a slush-fund pal of al Qaeda? Is that going to be on top of telling her that her daughter's nanny, Tiggi Sgornik, in whose care she was, in your words, perfectly safe, was found beaten to death near Putney Bridge last night?"

He said nothing, but she was rewarded with noticing a slight tic in his cheek as the news hit home. Perhaps it would serve as a reminder to him that he and whoever he worked for were not as all-knowing as they might think.

When he finally spoke, it was with an air of sadness. "I'm sorry to hear that, truly. But it changes nothing. In fact it should serve as an additional warning. Don't make the mistake of starting a crusade and don't ask questions when this is all over; any over-interest could be detrimental to your future."

"Are you threatening me?"

"Of course I am." His voice had gone flat. "Never forget, Miss Gonzales, that terrorist money has a two-way movement. It buys weapons and resources to build IEDs in far-off places, to blow up buildings and tear the limbs from soldiers and innocent civilians alike. Syria is a recent case in point, where we believe Hardman's been assisting in arming various factions. These things happen in the main away from this green and pleasant land, but some of the cash and valuables that pay for it originate right here. There's also a risk—a substantial risk—that some part of the arsenal Hardman is helping finance by his activities may be used to train and equip terrorists who might one day end up here in London. On your doorstep. So don't waste your emotions or energy feeling too discomfited by what might happen to Michael Hardman. Rest assured in the coming days he won't be thinking about you … or his family."

Ruth watched as he walked away and climbed into the car waiting at the side of the road. Then she reached inside her blouse and took out the cell phone nestling just inside her bra.

She held it to her ear. "Did you get all that?"

FIFTY-THREE

ANDY VASLIK WATCHED FROM under cover of a tree as the car left the park and turned towards Marble Arch. He wasn't yet familiar with London or the logistical trappings of the British establishment, but he recognised an official car when he saw one. They all moved with the same steady yet deceptively smooth turn of speed that took extensive training and practice on the part of the drivers. Serenity and a polished bodywork hiding God only knew what secrets.

And what he'd just heard pretty much beat any secrets he'd come across just lately. Well, almost. It left him breathless. He had to do something.

"Got it," he confirmed shortly, thinking fast. "I'll be in touch later."

"Wait—"

He shut off the cellphone and watched as Ruth stared at the screen of her phone, then looked around for him. But it was in vain. He was already on the move and nowhere near where she would have thought of seeing him. And right now he needed absolute privacy.

He turned and hailed a cab. Time to get clear of the area in case the mystery man had posted a few friends to watch over who else came and went in the wake of his chat with Ruth. They wouldn't be interested in her now; they had seen her face-to-face. But they might not yet have his details on record and he wanted to keep it that way for as long as possible. He certainly didn't want anyone following him.

He got the cab to drop him off in Piccadilly near Green Park, and walked into the park until he was alone.

He dialled the Washington number and waited for it to be picked up, as he knew it would be. Drybeck might not work conventional hours every day, but he would have people who did. And they'd be just a call away, especially now.

He had begun rehearsing this call while listening to what the mystery man—he had to be a member of one of Britain's security or intelligence agencies, it didn't matter which—had told Ruth about Hardman. And nearly everything he had said chimed too closely with what Drybeck had told him to be fiction.

"Drybeck." The man was in.

"I have some information," Vaslik said, adopting a suitable chastened tone of voice; the humbled subordinate recognising his place. Senior officers like Drybeck always liked a little humility in lesser beings.

"I'm pleased to hear it. Wait one." He heard a mumble of conversation in the background followed by a door closing. Drybeck was getting rid of a visitor. Then he was back on. "Go ahead."

"The British security services are aware of the group you mentioned."

"I'd be very surprised if they weren't; they're hardly amateurs. So what?"

He gave Drybeck the bare guts of what the mystery man had told Ruth, skimming over some details for brevity. He doubted it was giving away confidences at this stage, and in any case there was no way Drybeck would be able to identify the source of the information.

"Really? Is that all you've got? It's hardly news."

"But the methods they're using?" He wanted to test the water, to see if Drybeck would let anything out. He was shocked to find it worked.

"You're very naïve, Mr. Vaslik, if you think normal methods are practical in the fight against terrorism. Some of us do what we have to ... even if the establishment seems disinclined to approve openly. This is a war we're engaged in, and I intend to see we do not lose it."

The arrogance behind the words was sickening. The admission that Drybeck was connected with the kidnap could not have been more open, Vaslik was certain of it. Unintended, perhaps, although what did a man like Drybeck have to fear from him? He probably even got a kick out of letting it be known to a subordinate that he had such knowledge, such power.

"You said you had information," Drybeck reminded him. "Was that it? Please don't waste my time."

Vaslik took a deep breath. This was going to fly or it was going to crash and burn. There was no halfway house. "I've got more. About Michael Hardman. Or, should I say, Wesam Bahdari." He'd kept the name back in case he needed a trigger. Now the time had come to try it out. He would soon find out if it worked or not.

The silence went on so long, Vaslik thought Drybeck had given up and cut him off.

"Hello?"

"I heard you. Where did you get that name?" Drybeck's voice was ice-cold. And in spite of himself and the dangerous situations he'd been in over the years, Vaslik felt a chill touch the back of his neck. This really was a man not to mess with.

"It doesn't matter, does it? You obviously know it, too. Thing is, I know where he's going to be tomorrow. He wants to see his daughter."

"Where?"

Vaslik was thinking on the hoof. He hadn't planned on doing this; all he'd wanted was confirmation that Drybeck had connections to the kidnap of Beth Hardman. Now he had that confirmation he was formulating a plan off the top of his head. Quite where it would lead was impossible to predict but Beth's safety was paramount. And he now had no doubts at all that given the chance, Drybeck was going to brush this entire incident under the carpet... and the Hardmans along with it.

If there was going to be a hand-over or an exchange, which is what Drybeck would expect, it needed to be somewhere busy, somewhere difficult to police. Somewhere Vaslik could exert some degree of control. He was sure Ruth would blow a fuse when he told her, but that was too bad. From what they had learned so far, with Tiggi Sgornik's death and the way Drybeck was reacting, time was fast running out for Beth Hardman. He had to think fast.

"Central London," he said. "He wants to see her first, to know she's safe."

"Really?" Drybeck was suspicious. "That doesn't gel with what we know of him. He's shown no concern for her so far, so why now?"

Vaslik heard a noise in the background, a door opening and closing and a muted mumble of voices. Suddenly he knew: the trigger had worked. Drybeck was starting the ball rolling.

"I don't know the man so I can't tell. But he seems serious."

"Our intel says he's nowhere near London." Still a seed of doubt.

"Why do you think nobody's found him? He's been on his way here all along. It's taken time."

"How? By what route? We've been watching for him."

"The same way he moves everywhere else. Back roads; paths nobody else uses. He's an expert at this stuff. The guy's good at what he does, but he's paranoid, too."

There was a puff of contempt from Drybeck, an indication that he didn't share Vaslik's views. "Very well. What time and where?"

Vaslik breathed easier, and felt a deep loathing for this man. The final decider: the only reason for Drybeck to be interested in the time of the meeting was if he had direct contact with the group holding Beth hostage. It meant he was in a position to direct their movements and do so at short notice.

Their controller.

He could hardly believe it. Drybeck probably had them on speed-dial.

"I said, what time and where? Don't mess with me, Vaslik. This is too important."

Vaslik hesitated, but not because of the threat in Drybeck's words. The moment he gave the man time and place, events would be set in motion over which he had no direct control. There would be no going back. Drybeck's people would be waiting, all on the lookout for himself, Ruth and Michael Hardman. And he knew the kind of assets they would be; they would be ready to do anything to snatch Hardman and get him away and out of the country. He didn't like to think about the possibility of the collateral damage involved.

He wavered for an instant, suddenly fearful of what might happen. One option was to simply not take the next step, to allow Drybeck's people to run around central London in vain, chasing their tails. They'd be seriously pissed off and there would undoubtedly be an outcome he didn't like to think about.

But it wasn't an option he could control. At least following through with his plan would provide proof of who was running this business and allow him the chance to stop Drybeck in his tracks.

"Noon. He'll be there at noon. Trafalgar Square. But he wants to see the girl. Agreed?"

There was no answer. The line was dead.

FIFTY-FOUR

WHEN RUTH ARRIVED NEXT morning, the Hardman house was being systematically taken apart by a team of security people. Furniture was being searched and scanned with hand-held scanners, the floorboards were being taken up and the walls were being tested and scanned for recent re-painting or plastering work. The woman in charge answered to the name of Mitchell; no rank, no details. She was standing in the kitchen when Ruth was allowed inside by a constable on duty at the front door.

There was no sign of Nancy, Gina, or Vaslik.

"What's going on?" Ruth demanded, although in the wake of the meeting in Hyde Park yesterday evening, she could guess the answer. That man then had merely been a front-runner. His task had been to lay out the reasoning the security agencies were following. What was happening now was the hard reality of security work. They had a suspect and this was to see what, if anything, lay beneath the fabric of the building; what secrets lay behind the façade of the Hardmans' seemingly everyday suburban existence.

"I've got the necessary paperwork if you want to see it," Mitchell replied, although she made no move to produce it. A tough-looking woman in her forties, with hair cut short and the businesslike attitude of a professional, she gave a ghost of a smile. "Not that you have the authority to ask. But I like to be polite. Ruth Gonzales, isn't it?"

Ruth nodded, nettled by Mitchell's superior tone. "That's correct. We searched the place already. What are you looking for?"

Grey eyes settled on her. "You know what the householder is suspected of doing?"

"Yes."

"Then you'll know what we're looking for. Anything and everything." She gave a puff of air and a wry smile. "Not that it's looking too promising right now. Interesting set of listening devices, though." She nodded at the kitchen worktop where a scattering of tiny electronic components had been dropped. "I'd love to find out where they originated from. Somebody else is interested in the Hardmans, I take it?"

"Yes. We're just not sure who, though. Where's Mrs. Hardman?"

"Upstairs with Fraser. Now there's an odd choice for this work. I thought she was classified unfit for service. Or does the private sector not worry too much about the fine detail, like if someone's still traumatised and a danger to herself and everyone around her?"

It was a long speech but Ruth was determined not to rise to the bait. Mitchell was merely setting out their respective turfs: Ruth's in the private sector, her own in the official one where the firepower was infinitely greater. "Gina's fine. She's solid, in fact. Are you going to put any of this back?" She was referring to a thick layer of plaster on the floor and worktops where a man in overalls was digging into the wall with a hammer and cold chisel. Some of the cabinet base-boards had been kicked in to search the cavities underneath, and the sink was hanging by the water pipes while another man lay on his belly checking the furthermost corners of the kitchen with a flashlight.

"Of course. It'll be back in top condition by close of play today. The owner won't even know it's been touched."

An exchange of voices came from the front door. Moments later Andy Vaslik appeared, barely restrained by the constable, who was looking red in the face.

"Sorry, ma'am," the officer muttered. "He insisted."

"That's fine," Mitchell nodded. "Let him in. You must be Vaslik."

"That's me." He waved a hand. "Don't worry—I can see you're having fun." He looked at Ruth. "You got a minute?"

Ruth didn't, after his vanishing act the previous evening, but it was better than staying here listening to the sounds of destruction going on around them.

She excused herself and followed him outside.

"I'm sorry about last night," he said immediately, and sounded genuine. He nodded towards the end of the street. "I don't trust this place enough to talk freely. Let's walk."

He led the way a half pace ahead of her, his shoulders set, and Ruth followed, intrigued by his manner. He looked shaken, his lips tight, as if he hadn't slept well. Eventually he began talking.

"After hearing what the spook said yesterday, I had to talk to somebody. It turns out we have what some would call a situation."

"No shit," she muttered. "I knew that much last night. Why the secrecy?"

"Because I had something I wanted to check and I could have been wrong. I like to get my facts straight."

"And?"

"I wasn't wrong. I now know who's behind the kidnap."

FIFTY-FIVE

Ruth stopped walking. They were out on an open street, with nobody within earshot. She wondered what she was about to hear.

"Go on. Yours or ours?"

He explained, relating the phone conversations with Drybeck, the threats and the call to Washington yesterday evening that had told him what he had begun to suspect. He admitted that a tiny part of him still wasn't sure he believed it.

She listened carefully, wondering how much he was leaving out. She still didn't know him well enough to trust him completely, but she had a feeling he wasn't being entirely open.

"I'm guessing this Drybeck is higher up the pole than your pal Eric. How come you know him?"

"I don't, not really. He's a Washington power player and sits on at least one security committee." He hesitated. "That's all I know for now. I'll tell you more later."

She leaned towards him, sensing he was being evasive. "Bullshit. You've been acting strange right from the start of this job, Slik. Actually, forget that—*Andrei*. Is Vaslik even your real name or is that a load of bullshit, too? The Russian family background and the balalaika crap—real or not?"

"It's real."

"Great. Pity I'm not sure if I believe you or not. You've had me fooled, you know that? But then, it's not too hard to pull the wool over my eyes, is it? I'm just an ex-cop, whereas you're—what are you really—CIA? FBI? One of those black ops departments run out of a Washington brownstone with a budget the size of our national debt?"

"I'm what I said, which is freelance. It was after I got the job with Cruxys that I was contacted by Homeland Security. I was asked to be on standby while I was here in London. There was no threat to you, Cruxys or your country; I was told it was purely a watching brief and to be ready to give whatever assistance I could if requested. I was misled. I didn't know Drybeck had gone rogue."

Ruth said nothing, so he continued.

"The DHS is now one of the biggest departments of the federal system. They work with other agencies and sometimes wires get crossed—which is kind of what happened here."

"Well, that's OK, then." Her tone was brutally cutting and made him wince. "Did somebody not get the memo?"

"Something like that. Nobody will admit to it publicly, but there's a lot of competition and rivalry between departments and agencies. Sometimes bad choices get made trying to do the right thing."

"Oh, boo-hoo," Ruth muttered savagely. "So the right hand doesn't know when the left hand is stabbing itself up the arse. That's no excuse. How long have you been in on this?"

"Not as long as you think." He raised a hand to stop her and continued quickly, "Let me go right back to the beginning. A few days after arriving here I got a call from the DHS. I knew the woman who rang me; she told me they might need my help if anything came up."

"Just like that?"

"Yes. It was a stand-by call, that's all."

"And you, of course, told her to get lost. You already have a job in the private sector; you're no longer on the US government payroll."

"No, I didn't do that. Would you?" When Ruth didn't say anything he carried on. "I thought she was talking about a terrorist attack, something big aimed at a major target." He took a deep breath. "I asked and was told it might be a kidnap attempt on an important American. I thought they'd jumped on my credentials as a specialist." He gave a bitter smile. "I didn't think we'd be the ones actually running the kidnap."

"It was a rogue group—Grant said so."

"Same thing; it was done on our behalf."

"And the rendition of Michael Hardman? Did you know about that, too?"

"Of course not. How could I?"

"But you said nothing, even when you knew Beth had been taken—even when we were running all over the place looking for her and her mother was going mad."

"I wanted to, Ruthie—"

"Don't call me that! You don't get to call me that."

He blinked at the forcefulness in her voice, and looked for a moment as if he might turn and walk away. But he said, "I couldn't tell you. As soon as we began working together I could see how it was going to end, but I was in a bind." He looked up at the sky. "You're relentless, you know that. You don't fucking stop. Nobody counted on that."

It was the first time she'd heard him swear. "What do you mean?"

"You're on the case and you dig and dig; you rip things open and never stop thinking things through." He turned away then back again. "Christ, I was told I'd have a partner who hadn't done this kind of stuff before, so I could lead the investigation, control the flow of events. But that didn't happen because you didn't allow it. You took this thing by the balls and ran with it."

"You thought we were a bunch of hicks, is that it? Is that how we're seen by you and your *people*?"

"No. Not at all. There are guys I've worked with who would have obeyed orders; taken whatever intel they could get on this and closed it down, stuck it in a file and passed it to a higher pay grade for action. In other words, they'd have done the minimum, the obvious. But you didn't. You continued digging because it's what you do. You got too close."

"I'm sorry for being such a disappointment."

He blew out air. "All I could do was follow and hope you didn't run into the others."

"Others?"

"The kidnap team; the ones waiting to take down Hardman when he came in."

"What would they have done if he had come in?"

"I think you saw what they were capable of. I don't even want to think about it. They were out of control, that's all I know."

Ruth breathed deeply, not willing to let it go. "I may be a former cop but I can read body language like anyone else. I knew there was something deeper going on."

"I don't know what you mean."

"Crap. That napkin you picked up from the O.P. across from the Hardman place: I know that deli—it's just round the corner from the Embassy in Grosvenor Square. You took it away as if you wanted to hide something. Want to tell me why?"

He breathed deeply, then said, "As soon as I saw it I knew what you'd think. What are the chances? We already knew there was some kind of American angle, and a napkin from a deli right near the embassy? It was too much. I admit I jumped to the same conclusion and wanted time to look into it. I shouldn't have done it but I did. I'm sorry."

"And?"

"And in the end it was meaningless. I had no way of checking. What if the neighbour next to the observation house worked near the deli? We'd be chasing our tails for nothing. It was a dead end."

"Now you're talking like a cop."

"Just like you. And know there's a point where evidence fails to become proof. That's where I got to. Then this came up."

"You still haven't told me where your chat went. Or is that a big fat secret?"

Vaslik nodded and pulled a wry face. "I told him Hardman's here in London."

"You did what?" She stared at him. "What the hell for?"

"Because it's the only chance we have of getting Beth back. They will bring her, I'm certain of it. It was the one condition I threw in and an easy one for Drybeck's people to deal with."

"And what if it goes wrong?"

"It could do that anyway. They could lose patience and simply kill Beth like they did the nanny."

"We don't know that for sure. It could have been a mugging gone wrong." But even as she said it, she knew in her heart that Tiggi Sgornik would never have been walking the streets by herself and fallen prey to a random mugger. She would have stayed with Beth. The fact was, she had undoubtedly been an asset who'd become unreliable, even threatening. The fact that she had a label stitched inside her clothing pointed to her amateur status compared to the others in the group.

And amateurs were never fully trusted.

He sensed her doubts. "They're getting desperate. They'll get to a point where they will cut their losses and get out of town. We'd never know what happened. This way we have a slim chance of getting Beth back."

"Us and whose army?"

"Just us. The guys running this are ex-military pros; they'll spot other pros in seconds."

"But they know our faces—Clarisse saw to that."

"True enough," he conceded. "And Drybeck will have fed them our backgrounds. But that's where we might have an edge."

"How?"

"Drybeck's an arrogant prick and former military. He'll have told them we're simply ex-cops, so no contest. They'll see us as easy meat."

She chewed it over, trying to decide whether to believe him or not. He had a point, though, about the way seasoned pros looked down on ordinary cops. But it was mention of Beth that was the decider. "OK. You're on. But don't bullshit me again, Slik. I need you to trust me, too."

Her phone buzzed, interrupting further discussion. It was Richard Aston.

"Can you come in?" he asked. "We need to talk—urgently."

"On our way." She cut the connection and said to Vaslik, "Something's up. I'm wanted back at base. And don't think about bunking off—you're coming with me."

FIFTY-SIX

She drove fast towards Marble Arch, wondering what could have happened to make Aston sound so tense. And why so urgent that it couldn't be discussed by phone? Vaslik was saying nothing, staring out at the other traffic, which suited her just fine.

Aston was waiting for them in the boardroom. He was looking up at the ceiling, deep in thought, an empty coffee cup in front of him.

Standing by the window was the man in the grey suit from Hyde Park.

Aston gestured for them to sit. "You've met Neville Grant, of course."

So he had a name. Ruth nodded. "Last I heard, you were flying off somewhere in a hurry."

"I was. I came back. There has been a development."

"Like what?"

He tapped a folder on the table in front of him. "I've received news from a source in Washington. The man you know as Michael Hardman is dead."

There was a stunned silence. Grant said nothing, apparently content to wait for a reaction.

"What happened?" Ruth asked finally.

"Left hand, right hand, I'm afraid. Not ours, I'm relieved to say." He opened the folder in front of him and extracted a large photograph, which he pushed across the table. The subject was black and white, grainy and none too clear, showing what appeared to be a road or track running past a collection of buildings with an outer wall. It was a farm or compound of some sort.

It was the centre of the photo that instantly drew the eye.

Ruth felt her chest go cold. She was familiar enough with the subject matter to know exactly what it represented. She was close enough to Andy Vaslik to feel him going through the same reaction.

They were looking at what looked like a large, ugly flower blossoming in the middle of the photo, obscuring a section of the road and spreading out on either side to touch the compound wall.

"Was this a drone strike?" Vaslik asked.

"Yes. It's a farm not far from the border with Afghanistan. Hardman was spotted in Pakistan, travelling with a group of armed men thought to be a subset of *Lashkar-e-Toiba*. They're an extremist Islamic group responsible for a number of attacks in India and elsewhere, with strong links stretching from Pakistan to Saudi Arabia and Europe."

"He certainly gets around," said Ruth. The last potential sighting had been in Herat Province in western Afghanistan, with the dead group of Chechen fighters.

"He does. We suspect Hardman—or Wesam Bahdari as we should call him—might have been on his way to Kabul to fund an operation by this group. They want to draw attention to their fight for an extended Islamist state across the region." He smiled thinly. "It seems they were somewhat lax in their selection processes. One of their newer members was on a watch list held by Indian Intelligence; they let it be known where he was going and why. He'd told a cousin that they were with a man who had lots of money and were going to perform what he called "an outrage." A photograph taken at a police post along the way shows that one of the passengers in the car was Michael Hardman. "A rare moment of instant co-operation between agencies in those two countries."

"Are you saying Hardman was part of the operation?" Vaslik asked.

"I doubt it. But we can't be certain. The Indians had nothing on Hardman, but they had more than enough on the men with him. They passed on the information to the Americans and gave them the coordinates for where they were crossing into Afghanistan. According to my source, the risk was considered serious enough to take immediate action."

"Without checking with other interested persons?" Ruth queried. "Such as?"

Vaslik said, "A man called Drybeck."

Grant blinked. "How do you know that name?"

"I picked it up. I forget where."

"Really? Then I suggest you drop it again quickly."

"Why?" Ruth enquired. "Is he so untouchable?"

"Nobody's untouchable. Let it go."

There was another lengthy silence, finally broken by Aston. 'Where does that leave us with Beth and Nancy Hardman? Will the kidnappers let Beth go?"

344

"It's thought not." Grant looked conflicted and stared at the back of his hands. "They probably don't know about Hardman yet, as the news is on a restricted issue list. But they'll find out sooner or later."

"Drybeck," Vaslik murmured.

"Yes."

"And when they do?" Ruth knew what the answer was going to be.

"It's likely they won't react well. My source believes these people will seek to clear the decks of everybody who knows about this operation. That means you two, as I believe you've seen some of them. And Beth Hardman."

"That's crazy," said Ruth. "Why would they harm her? She's just a kid."

"They're specialists. They've conducted a number of extreme operations over many years."

"Assassinations?" Vaslik again.

Yes. Killing a child probably won't cause them to lose much sleep; I hear they've done worse. I would strongly advise you two to keep a very low profile until this group is caught."

"We can't do that," said Andy Vaslik, and told the two men why.

———

A few miles away, Nancy Hardman felt a deep, abiding anger as she stared at the ruined interior of her home. Broken plaster covered the floor, ripped furniture was piled up in every room and the carpets had been taken up and dumped in the garden. Even electrical appliances had been taken apart down to the plugs, their guts opened like dissected metal laboratory rats.

The neighbours were having a field day, she noted, and pulled the curtains to block out their stares.

"Why have they done this?" she screamed, turning on Gina, who was watching from the hallway. "What were they looking for? I don't understand it!"

"I told you why," Gina said bluntly. "Do I need to go through it again?" Her expression was ice cold, a clear indication that she considered this wreckage all in a day's work, and something Hardman had brought on them himself. "Are you sure you didn't know what Michael was really doing?"

"No! I told you. This is all *wrong*!" Nancy swung away from her, kicking at a lump of plaster on the floor. "It's lies … all of it. Michael wouldn't do any of those things!" She ran back upstairs and into her bedroom, slamming the door behind her. The anger subsided quickly, its energy unreal, and was replaced by an overwhelming flood of panic as she thought of Beth, still out there somewhere. What would become of her now—of them both? The bitch downstairs clearly didn't believe her, any more than the Gonzales woman or the American.

Would they be coming for her next?

She sat on the bed, fighting to compose her thoughts. She mustn't let this development take over. If Michael was here he would tell her what to do; Michael always knew what to do. It was one of the things that had drawn her to him, the steady confidence he exuded, the confidence that allowed her to trust and believe in him absolutely, even when things looked at their bleakest.

But he wasn't here. Until he was, it was up to her to handle the situation.

In the meantime, she had to hope and pray that Beth was safe.

And that Michael stayed away.

That thought prompted another; something she'd been meaning to do since Michael's first text message. She went to her dressing table and opened the drawer where she kept her diary, some spare cash and her passport.

The passport was gone.

FIFTY-SEVEN

RUTH CHECKED HER WATCH and felt a tremor go through her. Trafalgar Square at eleven forty-five and barely a minute since the last time she'd checked. She'd arrived early hoping to make a thorough survey of the area and get some idea of the opposition's numbers and locations. There was a danger in being too long on a static watch, but moving around too much when she knew the other side was out there waiting for her was a bigger one.

It was tough on the nerves waiting to see what developed; the instructors on the surveillance refresher courses run by Cruxys hadn't gone into the psychological detail, lingering instead on how to deal with toilet breaks and the physical discomfort of holding static positions for long periods.

She scanned the square again, filtering out tourists and passers-by, the innocent and the official. Andy Vaslik was roaming loose somewhere in the centre, confident that he would recognise any professionals from their body language and training, while Gina

Fraser was sitting on a section of wall close by the upper steps, sucking on an ice cream.

Persuading Aston and Grant that they were capable of handling this had been a tough argument. Grant in particular had opposed the idea, preferring instead to bring in a Special Forces team to cover the area and take out the opposition in what he referred to as a surgical strike. Even Aston, the ex-military man, had baulked at that.

"There'd be carnage," he countered. "You can't control a situation surrounded by hundreds of tourists. They'd be hostage meat the moment your team showed up."

Vaslik had agreed, pointing out that the kidnap group would recognise instantly the presence of other professionals, no matter how cautious they were.

"If they're the kind of people I think they are," he'd said, "they'll have nothing to lose."

In the end their words had prevailed, and both men had promised to keep the police and military out of it, on the proviso that if anything did kick off, they would have no option but to send in a team hard and fast to protect the many civilians in the area.

"There is a minor problem, remember," Aston reminded them. "If they hear about Hardman's death, they won't be there to show Beth Hardman alive and well."

With that caution ringing in her ears, and hoping they hadn't overstepped themselves, Ruth was now using the cover of a book store window in the southeastern corner of the square, holding a magazine while looking across a steady stream of traffic running from Trafalgar Square into the Strand to her right. It wasn't the best observation point but safe enough; most observers would be drawn to scan the northern and higher part of the square above the fountains, where they would expect Hardman to be waiting, and for Ruth or Vaslik to be stationed in order to make contact with him.

If they found either of them they would quickly expect to find Hardman. The cold, hard logic of hunters.

She was looking for vehicles; or more accurately, a particular vehicle. It would have to be a model that would blend in easily, and big enough to carry a party of at least four plus one, maybe more.

The plus one had to be Beth.

She watched a Renault Scenic people-carrier edging its way along the kerb, attracting a few angry hoots from other vehicles. It looked full, with faces inside turning to scan the square. She saw a little girl at one window moving around on her seat, and her heart flipped.

They were early.

The driver signalled and pulled to a stop. Nobody got out.

Ruth felt a jab of apprehension and reached up to her right ear, tapping the small ear-piece. She checked nobody in the store was close enough to hear and said, "Green Renault Scenic on the east side. Stationary. At least four up with a small girl at right rear."

"Got it. On my way." Vaslik's voice sounded unnaturally calm over the phone. She looked away from the Renault and tried to find him in the crowd, but couldn't. She saw Gina hadn't moved from her position, which was what they had agreed. Gina was the back-up.

When she looked back the Renault was moving away, the long lens of a camera poking from the passenger window in the hands of a middle-aged woman. With a flick of an indicator, it joined the main stream of traffic and was gone, heading north.

"Hold that," she said quickly. "False alarm."

"Right."

She checked her watch and was surprised to find it was nearly on midday. Several minutes had gone by in a flash. She forced herself to remain calm. Impatience now could ruin everything.

There would have to be some give and take if Vaslik's plan was to have any meaning. If Drybeck did what Vaslik suspected, the other side would be here and itching to get Hardman without fuss. But they would expect him to be utterly cautious in making his approach, knowing that a man in his position would not want to give himself up without getting the one thing he had demanded; sight of his daughter.

A BMW estate with ambulance chevrons and a light array on the roof nosed into the stream of traffic from the west and cruised along the lower edge of the square. The windows were slightly tinted, with the corner of one chevron plate missing, Ruth noted. The vehicle looked full, no doubt on its way to a hospital or a private clinic.

The BMW didn't stop but continued north at a steady pace and was soon swallowed up by other traffic.

Ruth felt a rush of frustration at the thought that they were wasting their time, that the kidnappers weren't going to show and Vaslik had been wrong in his suspicions about Drybeck. She breathed deeply, forcing herself to remain calm in spite of the situation here. She was accustomed to surveillance work, but not where something so important was riding on the timing and circumstances.

Ten minutes later the BMW ambulance was back.

It was the same one; she recognised the torn chevron. This time it stopped against the kerb and allowed two men to climb out before moving away. They were carrying camera bags and bottles of water, and dressed in sports shirts and jeans. Tourists.

Then she recognised one of the men and felt a tension in her chest.

Tall and bulky, packing a lot of muscle; it was one of the men Vaslik had snapped near the supermarket, following Nancy and Gina. As the man closed the car door, a little girl's face appeared in the opening.

Beth.

"Slik. You there?"

"Where else?"

"Lower square. Two men, cameras, sports shirts and jeans, just decamped from a BMW ambulance estate making its second run. It's a fake. Beth Hardman's inside. Recognise the tall guy?"

A slight pause, then, "Got him. Looks like we're on. Have you seen any others?"

"Not yet. They might be keeping this operation tight."

Ruth left the book store and headed across the road at the lights. She was lucky and was able to attach herself to five large women with shopping bags, one of them struggling to hold onto her load. She helped her cross, then skipped free of them and dodged across the road into the square proper, stopping alongside a party of school kids being handed their lunch in paper bags by a stressed-out teacher.

"Stay together!" the woman was calling, eyeing up three boys who were already making a move to scuttle away. "And don't leave Trafalgar Square, you hear me?"

The ambulance had disappeared. Making another tour, Ruth guessed, while the two men did a close recce. They probably had others already in place and ready to move.

She saw Vaslik. He was close by one of the fountains, chatting to a couple of girls and offering to take a picture with their phone. They were blushing and laughing but nodding enthusiastically.

The BMW appeared again. It was ghosting along the kerb on the east side, this time slowing to a halt. The move was a disaster for Ruth; as it stopped, the group of school kids moved away, leaving her exposed with no time to find alternative cover.

She froze. A woman's face was at the rear passenger window, staring right at her.

Clarisse. She looked surprised, then turned away and said something to the driver, who responded by shaking his head vigorously in disagreement.

But she waved a hand, dismissive and angry, before opening the door and stepping out. A sharp exchange of voices echoed from inside the car before she turned and walked away.

The driver shouted, then dipped his head and clamped a phone to his ear. He listened for a moment, his head snapping up in shock before leaning over, clearly seeking out Clarisse. He shouted again but she either didn't hear over the noise of the traffic or wasn't listening. He looked agitated and hit the wheel with his hand, and the look on his face told Ruth everything she had feared.

He'd just been given the news about Michael Hardman.

She experienced a feeling of unusual calm. She knew all she needed to know: from the two men prowling loose in the square, to the group using a vehicle capable of moving fast if necessary without being questioned, to Clarisse's over-aggressive manner.

Beth being in the car was for show; they weren't going to let her to go and had probably never intended to.

FIFTY-EIGHT

RUTH EXPERIENCED WHAT IT felt like to be under the gaze of a hunter. Clarisse was coming straight at her, eyes focussed and shoulders squared, unwavering. She was walking quickly, brushing aside anyone who got in her way and making it look simple, almost graceful.

She was wearing a light anorak with patch pockets over a short T-shirt that gave a glimpse of bare stomach, and had one hand out of sight under her clothing.

A gun or a knife, Ruth guessed. She'd come ready for action.

She glanced past Clarisse and saw movement in the BMW. A small face topped by blonde hair was staring through the rear side window, which was down, eyeing the crowds.

Beth.

"Slik," Ruth snapped. "The ambulance. Beth's in the back."

"I'm on it. Watch the woman—she's deadly. Gina's on her way in."

"Good to know." She unclipped the tiny earpiece and stuffed it into her pocket, and moved into a clear space. As she did so she took a slim object from her pocket and held it concealed behind her leg.

Whatever this woman was going to do, it would be fast and furious with no holds barred. She was undoubtedly disobeying orders by coming out after Ruth instead of staying with the vehicle and Beth, but maybe she'd got stir-crazy on this assignment and wanted to take it out on somebody the way she had with Andrew the luckless fitness instructor.

A woman of extremes. Normally ideal for this kind of mission, where orders had to be followed even at the risk to self, she was now making a mistake. Hopefully it would be to her detriment, not Ruth's.

Clarisse was six steps away when she drew her hand out from under her anorak and dropped it by her side. There was a brief flash of silver and Ruth's stomach flinched involuntarily. It was a blade of some kind—small and probably razor sharp, it would be ideal for close-up covert work. She would aim at inflicting the maximum damage on the way past before walking on as if nothing had happened, and be gone before the first cry of alarm.

Before the first drop of blood hit the ground.

Ruth took a deep breath, then settled, feet square, eyes fixed on the attacker. She was only vaguely aware of sightseers around her, all busy enjoying their day, most looking up at the various statues around the square, enjoying the play of light through the fountains or taking photos. They wouldn't see a thing.

Lucky them, she thought.

Four more steps and Clarisse would be on her. She already had her hand drawn back behind her leg, ready to strike. Ruth shook off the instinctive desire to turn and run. Running wouldn't work; she'd never been that fast and this woman looked like she could outrun Usain Bolt.

She took another deep breath and steeled herself, knowing she had just one chance. This had to be timed to the very last second.

"*Clarisse!*" She shrieked instead, and rushed to meet the woman, waving the magazine in the air to attract her attention. A few tourists turned and smiled, one or two glancing instinctively towards the object of Ruth's cry. If they noticed anything unusual in the greeting, they didn't react.

But Clarisse did.

She faltered, a frown touching her face at this sudden change of tactics; Ruth should have been frozen to the spot or running away, not coming to greet her like a long-lost friend. Her eyes flicked to the magazine, seeking the obvious threat as her training would have taught her. A rolled magazine can inflict painful damage or conceal another weapon.

But she recovered quickly and evidently dismissed the threat as minimal. She came on again, the distance between them closing faster.

Two more steps.

Ruth waited until the last moment, then side-stepped, turning her body to present the slimmest possible target. Hurling the magazine into Clarisse's face, she swept her right hand from behind her into the woman's stomach and squeezed.

Clarisse batted the magazine away with her free hand, a look of contempt on her face. Then she stopped dead, eyes wide in shock.

A low fizzing sound was coming from her unprotected middle, and she staggered sideways, her legs giving way. For a split second she remained upright, glancing down to see what had stopped her, before dropping to the ground like a dead weight.

"Someone get help!" Ruth shouted wildly. "This woman's having a heart attack!" She dropped the stun stick she'd used into her pocket then knelt and scooped up the fallen knife. It was four inches long and razor sharp, with a moulded rubberised handle that fitted snugly into the palm of the hand.

A killer's weapon.

She stared down into Clarisse's eyes, which were fluttering faintly as she tried to hold on to consciousness. She couldn't tell if the woman could see her through the pain, but allowed herself a brief smile just in case.

She hoped it would really piss her off.

Then she stood up and let others crowd around her before stepping back.

Two of the newcomers claimed to be doctors and began checking Clarisse for vital signs and telling others to stay clear and give them some room. Another was calling the emergency services and rattling off instructions about location and apparent symptoms.

Ruth glanced towards the ambulance. The driver was staring at her, shocked by the outcome. He began shouting into his phone, gesturing furiously at her position in the square. He was rallying his troops.

Ruth looked round. The two men in sports shirts must be close. And by the animation on the driver's face, their orders were simple: end it now.

When she looked back at the ambulance there was more movement. This time it was Vaslik framed in the window, standing behind the driver. The door opened and Vaslik moved fast.

The driver slumped over the wheel.

Ruth caught a flash of rapid movement off to one side. It was the tall, bulky man. He had made his way along the pavement up the side of the square, no doubt acting as a lookout and back-up. He must have spotted what was happening but had been unable to intervene before Clarisse went down. Now he was responding to the driver's call and closing in on the ambulance and Vaslik.

She began running. She left the square and ran along the pavement, pushing through the groups of sightseers. Beth. She had to get to Beth and get her out of that car.

But she'd forgotten about the second man. Just as she was closing in on the ambulance she was hit broadside and nearly knocked off her feet. She bounced off a lamppost, feeling her left shoulder give way with a horrible crunch followed by a vicious stab of pain. Something had gone, she was certain, but she didn't have time to react to the shock or worry about what had happened.

Survival. That was all.

She looked round and saw the man who'd hit her picking himself up. He'd sized up the situation and moved to take out the threat, and was feigning an accidental collision. But now he was moving towards her, his hand out towards her as if to apologise. But his other hand was clutching the strap of his camera bag, swinging it like a slingshot.

Ruth thrust her hand into her pocket, grabbing the stun stick. She had no idea if the stick had enough charge left to inflict more than a sting, but it was all she'd got and the camera bag looked heavy and dangerous. The knife against this man would be worse than useless.

She held the stick out in front of her. It was no more than six inches long and in spite of its colour, unobtrusive. She could hardly breathe with the pain in her shoulder; her left arm was useless but her right was still functioning. She had to give Vaslik a chance to get Beth out of the vehicle.

The man looked solid and had the confident stance of a professional. He almost smiled until he saw the stun stick, then appeared to have second thoughts and stepped back a pace. She felt a surge of relief. He'd recognised the stick for what it was and it was enough to put him off.

With a shrug, he turned and walked away, clearly deciding it was a no-win situation, and disappeared into the crowd.

Ruth hobbled along the pavement towards the ambulance, where Vaslik was talking to a traffic warden, trying to warn him off approaching. As she moved she pocketed the stun stick and took out her phone and hit speed-dial for a number Grant had given her.

"I see you." It was Grant, sounding tense. He was clearly nearby and had got an eyeball on the situation.

"Situation critical," she breathed. "One down, one gone, the ambulance is a fake and I'm just going for Beth."

"We're on the way. Be careful." The connection was cut.

Ruth looked around, wondering what had happened to the bulky man. Then she saw Gina. She'd intercepted him and was standing very close, dwarfed by his bulk but not the slightest bit intimidated. She saw why: Gina had her jacket wrapped round her hand which was pushed into the man's belly.

She was holding her gun on him, daring him to make a move.

Ruth shook her head. The woman was a danger to herself, but just what they needed right now.

She focussed on getting to the ambulance, reached the rear door and pulled it open. Leaned in and unclipped the buckle of the child's seat. Beth stared at her for a second, her face blank, and Ruth wondered if she'd been sedated to keep her quiet now Tiggi was gone.

She smiled. "Come on sweetie," she whispered. "Let's get you back to mummy and Homesick, shall we?"

The child came willingly enough, sliding to the ground and grasping tight onto Ruth's hand. She seemed curiously innocent and trusting among strangers even after everything that had happened to her, and Ruth wondered at the resilience in one so young, and how it would hold up in the days and weeks ahead.

"Homesick," Beth echoed. "I dropped him."

Ruth said, "I know you did, Beth, but don't worry. He's fine— your mummy's looking after him and they're both waiting to see you."

She led Beth away and seconds later Vaslik was on one side, holding her by the waist, with Gina close behind, watching their backs.

"Hi, Beth," Vaslik said easily. "I'm Andy."

"Hello, Andy," Beth replied. "Are you taking me home now?"

"You bet."

Vaslik looked at Ruth and said softly so the little girl couldn't hear, "Was that a stun stick you used? Aren't they illegal here?"

She nodded. "Only if you get caught. But I don't think Clarisse will be telling the cops, do you?" She was feeling nauseous but exultant, the pain in her shoulder dulled by the relief of getting Beth away safely. She was holding tight onto the little girl's hand and wouldn't let go until she was able to hand her over to Nancy.

"Sure. But it was pink. *Pink.* What were you thinking?"

She didn't really care for guns; they got people killed. So she'd asked for something else instead.

"Blame her," she said, nodding towards Gina, who was grinning. "She got it for me." She turned her head just enough to give the former bodyguard a silent thank you before the pain made her stop. "Anyway, it worked, didn't it? What are you complaining about?"

FIFTY-NINE

THE REUNION PROVED BITTER-SWEET. It was an emotional and tear-laden relief for mother and daughter, who went upstairs the moment Beth was carried across the doorstep. But having to explain later to Nancy about her husband was something Ruth wished she hadn't taken on. She felt dizzy with the pain of her injured shoulder, but she had to finish this. She swallowed a couple of painkillers and got on with it.

It didn't go well.

"I don't believe you." Nancy said it again and again, a mantra helping her close in on herself at every attempt by Ruth to explain the unexplainable; that her daughter had been kidnapped by an unknown group seeking to capture her husband. She was talking quietly but with cold fury, with Beth fast asleep upstairs. The Cruxys doctor had examined her and found her well, other than suffering the lingering effects of a mild sedative.

"It's true, I promise you."

"Is that why you wrecked the house? Took my passport? Show me the proof! You can't, can you?"

Ruth had no idea what Mitchell had told Nancy about why they were taking the house apart, and it wasn't her place to do so. Neither could she comment on the passport being confiscated, which might have been Mitchell's doing on instructions from her bosses. She had no authority to mention the kidnap group or who they were thought to work for, either, nor how the authorities had come by the information about Michael, since that was a matter of the highest secrecy. All she could say was that his activities had put them all in danger … and he still hadn't shown up, even though he must know by now what had happened to his daughter.

She dropped a copy of the spreadsheet for motorcycle parts on the table in front of Nancy, along with a decoded version which showed that the components were less likely to be used in any kind of transport but in a far more deadly array of equipment. It would probably do little to convince the woman, but it was all she had.

Nancy brushed it away without looking at it. "You've made this up—you've made it all up! And you're the ones who put my daughter's life in danger. Do you think I'm stupid—that I don't know this was a government operation? Who was it—the British MI6? The American White House? The Israeli Mossad?" She picked up the papers and flung them in Ruth's face, hitting her on the cheek, before subsiding on the settee, her face white with anger.

Ruth looked at Vaslik, who shrugged. He had said earlier that it was a no-hoper; that there was no way she would believe any of it. It seemed he was right.

Gina appeared in the doorway and gestured towards the stairs, where she had been watching over Beth. "She's awake. She wants her mum."

Nancy jumped to her feet and glared at them all. "Yes, leave me with my daughter," she hissed. "All of you. And don't come back. *Get out!*"

―――

Ruth led the way outside and drove home. Gina and Vaslik went their separate ways. They had been told to take time off and kick back. A full debrief would come later.

Ruth felt bad for Nancy; whether she believed them or not, her husband had not shown up when he was most needed. It was the end of her world and she would have to pick up the pieces knowing that something in the story must be right; that her husband was not what he had pretended to be.

Unable to settle, she went to see how her father was coping with the death of George Paperas. He was tight-lipped but unwound sufficiently to wrap her in his arms. It was a welcome surprise after their last brief conversation.

"Not your fault, Ruthie," he said softly. "No way you could have foreseen it. Don't dwell on it."

―――

Two days later, her shoulder heavily bandaged, Ruth entered the Cruxys building and was surprised to see Grant along the corridor in conversation with Aston. Aston beckoned them into his office and closed the door.

"Miss Gonzales," Grant said. "I'm not obliged to tell you this, but I think you have a right to know, in view of your involvement with the Hardmans. Just over two hours ago, Nancy Hardman and her daughter were taken to Northolt airfield on their way to Washington, accompanied by three special agents from the FBI. She has agreed to accompany them to answer some questions in return for a safe location."

"Questions?"

He seemed to be debating what to say, then took a deep breath. "This is for your ears only, although I suspect it might come out sooner or later, the news channels being what they are. There are strong indications that Nancy Hardman was—is—not quite the innocent she seems to have pretended."

"What does that mean?"

"From evidence just uncovered, she not only knew what her husband was doing but might recently have become actively involved."

"*What*?" Ruth felt her stomach flip. She couldn't believe it. Nancy Hardman, the apparently naive yet outwardly normal suburban housewife and mother?

"It's true. Her fingerprints are all over it. We checked the computer at her place of work. There are traces of deleted documents and emails going back several weeks, all connected to Hardman's activities in the Middle East. The trail leads to known money men with terrorist connections, and sources in Europe linking donations and collections within the Muslim community being channelled to banks overseas. Those same banks were listed on the Excel file you discovered, concealed in an encrypted sub-folder. We suspect she was processing and harbouring the information for him, but she probably knew what it was for."

"Can you prove that?" Ruth recalled Nancy's reaction to the spreadsheet: she hadn't even given it a look. Was that genuine ignorance, or because she was frightened she might give herself away—that she didn't have to look because she knew exactly what it was?

"Not conclusively. She has already intimated that she was acting in innocence, merely providing a back-up storage facility at her husband's insistence. But that won't fly for long."

She didn't know what to say. It turned everything on its head. "It was pretty careless, leaving that information lying around."

"You'd be surprised. Most of the people we catch are delivered by their own hand. They firmly believe they'll never make a simple mistake … until they do. Hers was thinking we'd never have cause to check her work computer." He shrugged. "We probably wouldn't, either … but then her daughter was kidnapped."

She stared at the man. "And knowing this about her you let her go. Why?"

"Because the Americans have the resources and manpower to throw at her and unravel the network of accounts. Here in the UK we wouldn't even get to first base; she'd be in court and protected by Human Rights legislation and a gallery of lawyers. It would be months, possibly years before we got anywhere, by which time it would be too late. From the files on her work PC we found the name and details of a firebrand legal representative. She knew what was coming and was prepared for it. You shouldn't feel sorry for her."

"I don't. It's Beth, poor kid."

"She'll be looked after, don't worry. There's more, too, on the nanny. Tiggi Sgornik wasn't quite the innocent she seemed, either. She was recruited a couple of years ago as a potential operative by Mossad, Israeli Intelligence. They needed young, good-looking girls to work in the field. She dropped out during training and disappeared off the scene. Next thing she's here in London and getting friendly with Nancy Hardman. It was clearly part of the set-up: get close to the mother and daughter, then wait for the signal to go."

"But she ended up dead."

"Maybe she decided that when it came to the crunch she didn't want to go through with it. If so it was a threat to the others; they retired her to protect themselves."

"How do you know all this? Were you involved?"

"No. The Americans discovered what was going on and sought to regain control of the situation. When it was obvious it was too late, they allowed the information to come out to see if we could help."

"Were Greenville and Claas in any way connected?"

"No comment."

"So what will happen to Beth and Nancy?"

"Nancy will be watched wherever she goes. She will know that, of course, and won't put a foot wrong—at first. But she's not a pro. When she slips up, they'll be waiting."

"Playing the long game."

"Yes. She has an added complication to deal with: we suspect her husband won't have revealed to anyone else where he kept the bulk of the money he used as his bank. A lot of the funds will have belonged to other money men or owed as collateral against deliveries of weapons. Sooner or later they'll start asking questions . . . and they're not a forgiving crowd."

"So she'll be used as bait again."

He frowned. "That's not my call—or yours. I think you should worry about yourself instead of her."

"What do you mean?"

"You'll be pleased to hear we recovered three members of the kidnap team, and they are now in police custody."

"Three? What happened to the fourth?" She remembered the man she'd threatened with the stun stick after knocking her off course. He must have got clear and left the others to their fate. Some colleague.

"She got away."

SIXTY

RUTH DID A DOUBLE take. "*She?*"

Grant looked pained. "I'm sorry, but the woman you knew variously as Helen or Clarisse escaped from a police van following her release from A&E." If he had any thoughts about Ruth's use of an illegal weapon, he didn't voice them. "During the escape she seriously injured the escort. We believe she will leave the country with assistance and we're keeping an eye out for that. You might be wise, however, to take some time out and keep your head down for a while. We consider her extremely dangerous." He glanced at Aston, who was nodding. "Richard concurs and has agreed to an immediate leave of absence."

"Thank you, but there's no need. I'll spend time with my physio instead." She spoke calmly enough but a small voice of caution wondered how serious the threat was. Professional operators didn't normally carry grudges; setbacks were inevitable at times and were part of the rough and tumble of their chosen trade. But she recalled the vindictive expression on Clarisse's face as she'd come at her with the knife.

Using a weapon like that in public took a particular mind set. The woman was clearly not normal so those rules didn't apply. It was enough to make her reconsider her decision. "OK, maybe not. Thanks."

"Very wise." He stood up and nodded to them both, and left the room.

———

Outside, Ruth found Andy Vaslik leaning against a car, with Gina Fraser standing nearby, eyeballing the traffic moving along the street.

"What do you two want?" she asked. Vaslik seemed relaxed but she knew him well enough now to judge that he was more on the alert than he looked. Gina was as ready for trouble as ever, with one hand under her jacket, probably clutching the butt of a semi-automatic and hoping she'd be given a chance to use it.

"We're taking you home to pack," said Vaslik. "Your orders are to go somewhere quiet and remote for a couple of weeks. Any ideas?"

"None that I'd share with you," she muttered, glancing involuntarily along the street. She doubted Clarisse would be insane enough to pop up here, but Grant's warning had been serious. "I don't need babysitting, thank you."

"Not your call, sister," Gina said easily. "Our orders include tying you up if we have to and putting you on the first available flight out of Heathrow, courtesy of Cruxys. So you'd better come up with a destination, otherwise it could get messy." She smiled the sting out of the comment, and for once her face looked almost serene.

Ruth let it go. They were right; looking over her shoulder until Clarisse was caught or went back to wherever she called home was pointless. She thought about where she might go. To her parents first, to reassure them, to salve their hurt. But that wouldn't last long. Then … where?

"Anywhere?"

"Anywhere," said Vaslik. "We can even bump another passenger to get you on board if we have to. As long as you agree to come back, of course."

"That's not your say."

"I know. But we get on so well." He snapped a quick grin at her, and she felt her resolve crumble.

"OK. But what about you two?"

"We're on vacation, too, as soon as you're away. I have a meeting in Washington, which won't be fun but it will be interesting. I think the suddenly retired Rear Admiral Drybeck and his dirty hands will be the main topic. Then I'm coming back."

"Are you sure you're safe going back there?"

"Absolutely. I have some big hitters on my side, including Grant and his people."

Gina stepped up and patted the car roof. "Come on, guys. I've got a hotel room in Barbados with my name on it, so let's get moving. Where to?"

Ruth nodded. There was only one place. It was a long flight but far enough away from all the craziness to be ideal. And she'd received that text message. It held a promise of something, but she couldn't yet tell. Maybe taking a step back would be a good way to find out.

"Sydney," she said. "Australia. I hear the beaches are good this time of year."

THE END

ABOUT THE AUTHOR

Adrian Magson (UK) is the author of the Harry Tate novels, the Lucas Rocco novels, and the Marc Portman novels. He is a member of the International Thriller Writers and the Crime Writers Association, and has been short-listed for the CWA Debut Dagger and the East Midlands Book Awards. Adrian writes two regular columns for *Writing Magazine*. Visit him online at www.adrianmagson.com.

BEAUTIFUL LOSERS

EVE SEYMOUR

Beautiful Losers
A Kim Slade Novel
EVE SEYMOUR

Kim Slade has many admirers, but only one wants her dead.

Kim Slade is a clinical psychologist specializing in young women with eating disorders. She also has someone who specializes in her: an anonymous stalker.

When Kyle Stannard, a former male model with a facial disfigurement steps suddenly into her life, Kim assumes he's her stalker. Partially scarred after a childhood accident, Kim believes this the reason for Stannard's obsession and reports him to the police. But smartmouthed Stannard denies the accusation and has a plausible explanation for every twisted move he makes.

Can Kim nail him?

Or is the person who wants to destroy her closer to home…

978-0-7387-4643-2, 480pp., 5¼ x 8   **$15.99**